"HAVE YOU EVER HUNGERED FOR THE WAYS OF THE WHITE MAN?"

Runner yanked her against his hard body. "No, I haven't," he said huskily. His steel arms enfolded her. "Not until I saw you."

Everything happened so quickly then, Stephanie's head began to spin. His mouth closed hard upon hers. She clung to him as he kissed her deeply and passionately, with a fierce, possessive heat.

Runner for the moment cast aside his dislike of her being a photographer for the white man's railroad. All he saw when he looked at her was a woman.

A lovely, alluring woman. One he could no longer resist.

Licking flames built into dangerous fires within Runner. He ground his mouth onto Stephanie's. His hands made a slow, sensuous descent along her spine, molding her slender, sweet body against him. He had never felt so alive.

He had never wanted anything as fiercely as he wanted her.

CASSIE EDWARDS

Savage STORM

LEISURE BOOKS NEW YORK CITY

A LEISURE BOOK®

June 2007

Published by

Dorchester Publishing Co., Inc.
200 Madison Avenue
New York, NY 10016

ISBN-10: 0-8439-5885-5
ISBN-13: 978-0-8439-5885-0

The name "Leisure Books" and the stylized "L" with design are trademarks of Dorchester Publishing Co., Inc.

Printed in the United States of America.

Visit us on the web at www.dorchesterpub.com.

Savage
STORM

1

The breeze is whispering in the bush,
And the dews fall from the tree.
All sighing on, and will not hush
Some pleasant tales of thee.

—JOHN CLARE

1881—The Arizona Territory

The sun was just rising behind the distant mountains.
Billows of smoke were pouring from the smokestack of
a train, rolling upward into the sky as the locomotive
rumbled onward on new gleaming rails.

Stephanie Helton sat at the window of the train, gazing at the extravaganza of a varied and wonderfully
beautiful land. Brightly colored rocks jutted up from
flat valleys, which were covered with soft, gray-green
sagebrush.

Deep canyons gashed the high plateaus and steep gul-
lies wound snakelike through the flat bottomlands. The
sky was the roof of this world, and every mesa was
duplicated by a cloud mesa, like a reflection.

Stephanie was a photographer for the Santa Fe Railroad and had traveled by rail many times, but never
before had she felt such an anxiousness to arrive at her
destination. She had developed a passionate interest in
Indian culture after her step-brother had spoken of his
childhood friend so often.

"Adam?" she said. She turned her eyes from the window to look at her step-brother, who sat across the aisle from her in their private car. "How can you remember Runner so vividly? You were only five when you last saw him. Surely your recollections are not as accurate as you make them to be."

Adam took a cigar from between his lips and smiled over at Stephanie. "I remember quite well all about my friend, who is now sometimes called the White Indian," he said. His smile faded into a frown. "Trevor was his real name. He was my best friend when we lived at Fort Defiance. Our friendship became even closer when we were taken captive by the Navaho. I'm sure we would still be loyal friends had his mother not died. When she did, everything changed."

Eager to know more, Stephanie moved closer, into the seat closest to the aisle. "Tell me more, Adam," she said, running her fingers through her hair, drawing it back from her face. "I know you must tire of telling me about your experiences with the Navaho, but I don't. I'll be among them soon, myself. The more I know, the better it will be for me. I'm determined to photograph them, but I must draw them into accepting me first. So tell me, Adam, how your friend's name was changed from Trevor to Runner, and how it was that he adapted to the changes so quickly."

Tall and long-legged, Adam shifted in the small seat. He drew a gold watch from his pocket, studied the time, then slipped it back inside his pocket.

"We should be arriving soon," he said somberly, "where the work gang is laying the rails closer and closer to Fort Defiance. My dream come true: my new spur. I'm glad Father and the rest of the Santa Fe shareholders allowed me to have my private spur to Fort Defiance, but I've got to go farther into Navaho territory. I want a town all my own. I want it to have my name."

He paused, then feeling impatient eyes on him, turned his gaze to Stephanie. "All right," he said with a grumble, "I'll tell you more about my experience while I was held captive in the Navaho stronghold with the others from the stagecoach attack, even though you must have heard this all before."

He paused again and looked at his step-sister. "It was because of someone like you that everything changed for Trevor," he said thickly. "As I recall, Leonida was as beautiful and alluring." He kneaded his chin thoughtfully. "But that was as far as the resemblance went. She was tall and willowy; you are petite. Her hair was golden; your hair shines like copper wire in the sun."

"Oh, Adam," Stephanie said with a deep sigh. "Will you go on with the story instead of comparing me with another woman? What on earth does that have to do with anything?"

"It's because of Leonida's loveliness that Sage, the Navaho chief, took captives from the stagecoach, and Trevor became involved with the Navaho," Adam said, closing his eyes, recalling it now as though it was being reenacted before him. "Leonida was also one of the captives. The day that Trevor's mother died, Leonida took him under her wing. From that point on, everything for Trevor changed, for soon after, he also became a part of Sage's life. When Leonida and Sage fell in love and were married in a Navaho ceremony, Trevor became their adopted son."

"It was then that his name was changed?"

"No, it was a short time later. Sage named Trevor Runner because of his ability to run so fast, after Trevor outran all of the Navaho and white children in foot races."

"You do remember it well, don't you, Adam?" Stephanie said, gently placing a hand on his arm. "Is it painful to recall? Were the Navaho cruel to you?"

"They were never cruel," he said, patting her hand. "In fact, I believe it's because of their kindness that I'm able to remember everything as though it happened only yesterday. It was an interesting experience. I shall never forget it. And Runner? Hopefully soon our friendship can be rekindled."

"If Sage was so kind, why did he take white captives?"

"He was fighting for his people's survival," Adam said, a frown furrowing his brow. "Like now. I'm sure the Navaho hate like hell that the railroad keeps inching farther and farther into their homeland."

"Yet, even knowing that, you are still determined to move your spur further into Navaho land, for your own selfish ideals?" Stephanie said, feeling somewhat guilty for her own reasons for being on the train today.

When Adam did not answer her, Stephanie returned to her seat by the window and became lost in thought as she watched the land flitting past outside. Not only was she anxious to meet this white man who now lived as though he were an Indian, she was in quest of the marvelous photographic opportunities this land offered. Scenes of grandeur were luring her to the Arizona Territory made accessible by the opening of the railroads. The quality of native life with its bond to the earth and elemental primitiveness was a palpable force she found hard to resist.

The Santa Fe Railroad had also employed her. She was to get the most intriguing photographs of the land and people to be used on calendars and postcards, to lure tourists to the Arizona Territory on the Santa Fe.

Her father was a major shareholder of the Santa Fe. She knew that because of him the railroad had been over-generous to her. She was traveling lavishly in a specially equipped car, which included a front parlor, a fully-serviced darkroom, and living quarters. She would be paid five dollars a photograph.

Stephanie understood why the railroad was so eager for the photographs. The men in sole charge of the Santa Fe had discovered a new culture in the wilderness, and recognizing its potential, had taken up at once the task of exploiting it. America was promise. The West was a jumping off point, a fable waiting to be told. It was still a new frontier in the minds of many who sought new vistas and quick fortunes.

The West was unfolding with the Santa Fe. It fulfilled a longing for adventure and discovery. The Santa Fe was already advertising promises of holiday excursions. It proffered a new world, simple and exotic, in the wilderness of the American West.

Stephanie felt lucky that the golden era of railroading had overlapped with the golden era of photography. Both were setting the stage, paving the way for tourists. The Santa Fe was extending its campaign for a monopoly of the tourist market by circulating grand and enchanting images of Indian life and the scenery of the Southwest.

A sudden shiver rose along her spine at her realization that she was ignorant of the Indians. And since she didn't know them, except for what she had read in books, and what Adam had told her about the Navaho, she feared them somewhat. Yet she was determined to know how they lived and what they did. She had traveled to a distant place, not only to photograph the people and the land, but also to learn.

She was recalling how fondly Adam spoke of the

Navaho, again feeling guilty for what she had planned for them. The railroad was, in truth, planning to exploit the Indians. Adam, who seemed hell-bent on furthering his private spur past Fort Defiance, was going to be exploiting his childhood *friend*. Stephanie could not imagine the Navaho wanting to have another town spring up, especially one which would bring more white people into their land, gambling, drinking, and raising hell.

"Do you actually believe you can talk the Navaho into agreeing with you about having more tracks run along their land?" Stephanie blurted out as she looked quickly over at Adam.

"I don't have to have their permission," Adam said, shrugging. "Out of politeness and old friendships, I'm only meeting with them to seek some sort of acceptance of my plans."

"My father has spoiled you rotten, Adam," Stephanie said, flashing angry eyes at him. "Don't expect the Indians to give in to you as easily."

"Look who's spoiled!" Adam retorted. "Who's got a private darkroom all their own on this train? And God, Stephanie, your private car is far more lavishly furnished than mine."

She said nothing in return, realizing that what he said was true; but her reason for being on the train was much more important than Adam's. Having his very own private spur was a folly granted by a step-father who was going far beyond what a true father would allow.

Stephanie knew that her father did everything to please Adam, in order to please his wife, Sally. She had been widowed twice. He wanted her life to be sweet and comfortable, even if that included having to do more than tolerate her greedy, spoiled son.

In truth, Stephanie knew that her father had agreed to the private spur to get Adam out of his hair. If it meant going on past Fort Defiance, so be it.

"The farther the better," her father had voiced aloud to a railroad associate one night, when he had not known that Stephanie had overheard.

That had been the night of the board meeting of all of the shareholders of the Santa Fe, when her father had introduced the idea of Adam's private spur to them. He had explained that it would be a spur that would run from Ferry Station, New Mexico, to Fort Defiance, and even then somewhat farther, on land occupied solely by the Navaho.

She knew that her father had only gotten the men to agree to his son's folly, knowing that they were afraid that if they didn't agree, and her father would withdraw his shares in the Santa Fe, the railroad might come close to bankruptcy.

Stephanie glanced over at Adam, who was smoking another cigar and thumbing through a magazine as the train continued rumbling along. He was now twenty-three, five years her senior, yet in many ways he was less mature than herself.

It was this immaturity that she feared when he became acquainted with the Navaho again. If they didn't bend to his wishes, he would take what he wanted anyhow, ignoring the danger in which he might be placing himself *and* Stephanie. When he went into council with them, flashing his diamond rings and sporting the most fashionable suits that could be purchased, revealing his arrogant nature to them, who knew what to expect?

Stephanie's thoughts were brought to an abrupt halt when the train blew its whistle in three long blasts. Wondering why the engineer had the need to make such a racket, she lifted the window and leaned out to take a look outside.

Up ahead, hundreds of sheep were slowly crossing the tracks. The locomotive shuddered, slowed, and shuddered again, its whistle shrieking.

But to no avail. The sheep walked no more quickly, nor did the sheepherder, who had now stepped into view, hurry his pace as the train came finally to a screeching halt.

Adam moved over and crowded in next to Stephanie, peering out the window with her. "Damn sheep," he grumbled. "But I guess I'd better get used to them. They are the Navaho's bread and butter. There'll be plenty roaming the land."

He lifted a frustrated hand into the air. "Just look at 'em," he stormed. "The dumb animals. They don't even know to be afraid. And look at the Indian. He's not paying the train any heed, either."

Stephanie was hardly hearing anything that Adam was saying. Her full attention was on the sheepherder. She had imagined she would see the Navaho in poor clothing. Instead, this man was dressed in brightly colored pants and shirt, and the sun was reflecting onto his turquoise necklace. His long raven-black hair was held back by a red velveteen band, and his knee-high moccasins were intricately decorated with silver buttons.

"Adam," Stephanie said, giving her step-brother a quick glance, "do you expect these Navaho to be poor? It doesn't appear to me that—"

Adam interrupted her. "The Navaho do not measure their wealth by material things," he said, moving back to his seat. "As for Sage, he said often that he measured his wealth in the respect his people gave him."

The train lurched, shuddered, and slowly began picking up speed as the tracks were cleared. Stephanie settled back down onto her seat and started to lower the window, but she had waited too long. Billows of smoke wafted inside, bringing with it sprinklings of stinging soot as it settled onto her face.

Coughing and spewing, Stephanie finally got the window down. A low, teasing laugh drew her eyes around. She glared at Adam while he chuckled at her appearance.

Taking a mirror from her purse, she gazed at herself and moaned. Muttering beneath her breath as the train continued huffing and puffing along, she began wiping her face clean with a handkerchief. She was glad that she was dressed in a charcoal-gray suit: the soot blended in well enough with the fabric.

Adam turned his thoughts from his step-sister and gazed from the window at the rugged, lovely landscape. He wanted like hell to be a part of this setting and would fight fire with fire if he was forced to, to achieve his final dream. The chore of convincing the Navaho that what he wanted to do would not cause them any harm would not be easy. He would be asking to take more reservation land from them, for his own private purposes. There was already more than one white ranch on land allotted to the Navaho.

Adam knew one rancher in particular—Damon Stout. Adam had wired Damon that he was coming. If Runner refused to help him, Damon Stout was known for his skills with ropes, horses, and guns.

Adam lacked in all three.

He looked over at Stephanie, who was still fussing with her face. "Ah, leave the soot on," he teased. "You'll blend in with the Navaho."

He laughed raucously as Stephanie glared over at him.

2

I love thee freely, as men strive for Right;
I love thee purely, as they turn from Praise.
I love thee with the passion put to use
In my old griefs, and with my childhood faith.
—ELIZABETH BARRETT BROWNING

Leonida stepped out of her hogan. Stretching about her in all directions was shadowy grassland. Above her, the sky was filled with fading, glimmering stars.

She walked a few steps toward the pole corral at the back of her house and sprinkled an arc of cornmeal in the air. This was an offering to the gods, who she believed would rise with the sun and pass over her hogan and her family.

She silently prayed for a blessing, then went back inside and joined her family.

"Now I walk with Talking God. With goodness and beauty in all things around me I go. With goodness and beauty I follow immortality. Thus being I, I go, *ka-bike-hozhoni-li,* happy evermore," Sage said, repeating the Navaho prayer that he sometimes used before the morning meal.

He shoved another piece of wood in the fireplace of his hogan. He then settled down again beside the fire on a white sheepskin, along with his loved ones, his precious family. There was only one of them missing—his daughter, Pure Blossom.

Sage understood that she enjoyed weaving in the earlier hours of the day. And most mornings she awakened with inspirations for new designs for her blankets. She had recently moved into her own hogan so that she could have more room for her looms and other various instruments used for making her breathtaking woven, woolen coverings.

Leonida gave Sage a soft smile as she poured coffee in an earthenware mug. She inhaled deeply as the aroma of the coffee wafted upward, smelling as good as it tasted. She was glad that the Navaho, as a whole, had adopted this drink as their preferred nonalcoholic beverage. She had always loved it and had missed it when she had first joined the Navaho to become as one with them, as Sage's wife.

"That prayer is always such a lovely way to start the day," she murmured, handing Sage the steaming cup. She gazed lovingly at her husband. He was still a powerful leader, revered by the *Dine*, the Navaho people. He was as handsome as the day she had met him. His eyes were intense and dark, his shoulders broad, his hips lean, handsome with his bronzed, sculpted features.

She looked past him at Runner. It was hard to tell by looking at him that he was not Navaho by birth. He dressed in the Navaho tradition, sometimes in fringed buckskin, other times in bright velveteen breeches and shirts, his moccasins fancied up with shining, silver buttons.

He had spent so much time in the sun that his skin was bronzed almost as dark as his adopted Navaho father and brother. His black hair had been allowed to grow to waist length. He took much care in grooming it, brushing it until it glistened like a raven's wing.

Handsome was the only word that anyone could use to describe Runner.

And his eyes.

Leonida did not know how it was possible, but Runner's eyes were even more intense and dark than his adopted father's.

She looked over at Thunder Hawk. He was her youngest son, and her most defiant. He was the image of his father in all ways, but he had weaknesses that troubled Leonida. He disobeyed his parents far too often.

She poured another cup of coffee, shifting her gaze to Runner. "Son, it's wonderful that you've joined us this morning for breakfast," she said, handing him the cup. "Since you've built your own hogan and live away from us, I've missed you."

"Runner has more on his mind than eating with family," Thunder Hawk interjected, giving Runner a teasing smile. "What girl are your eyes following now, my brother? There are many who have made special blankets for you. Do you not know that they do this to give you a hint that they wish to share their gift with you? Of all the blankets that you have been given, which do you like the most? That will tell this brother which girl you prefer."

When Runner didn't answer and only responded to his brother by glaring at him, Leonida shoved a cup of coffee into Thunder Hawk's hand. "Hush now, Thunder Hawk," she said firmly. "Quit teasing your brother. You should be concerning yourself about things other than women. Your brother and father are escorting you to school today. Now do I have your promise that you will stay? It gets so tiring to discover that you've skipped another full day of schooling. When will it end?"

"Sitting at desks is *bogay-gahn*, bad. It is always strange to me," he complained. "It is too confining. It has few windows from which to see the loveliness of the land."

He paused, then said, "This Navaho wants to ride horses alongside his father and brother. It was not meant for a Navaho to sit on a bench in a white man's school every single day, when his hands might be used to help his parents in hard work."

Thunder Hawk paused, then glowered from his mother to his father. "And this Navaho is too old to be in school," he said, curving his lower lip into a pout.

"My son, had you not slipped away from school so often, you would have been finished with the teachings long ago," Sage said firmly. "With the white men pushing against the boundaries of Navaho land, some even already living inside the reservation, it is necessary that the Navaho children learn as much as the whites who, themselves, attend schools."

Sage paused for a moment. Everything in the hogan was silent except for the sounds of grease spattering and popping as white flour dough fried in deep fat in a skillet over the fire.

"When treaties were signed long ago, the Navaho promised the United States Government that their children would 'learn paper,' " Sage finally said. "And, Thunder Hawk, so shall it be for this family. Your sister went to school until she learned enough to return to her weaving skills. Your brother has much knowledge learned at the schools on our reservation."

He nodded over at Runner. "He went," he said proudly. "He learned. And now he is finished. He has his father's permission now to even live alone, in his own hogan. You go. You learn. One day you will also build your own hogan and run free on your horses whenever *you* like."

"But, Father, I am now seventeen winters of age," Thunder Hawk dared to argue.

"And so we might still be discussing this same issue when you are thirty winters of age if you do not busy yourself and get the book learning behind you," Sage said, setting his empty cup aside. He folded his arms over his bare chest. "Thunder Hawk, this discussion is closed. Your father and brother will escort you to school today. I would not hope to think that we would have to go into the schoolroom with you and stand over you to make sure you stay."

Thunder Hawk lowered his eyes. "*E-do-tano*, no," he said, barely audible. "That is not required of you."

Sage heaved a deep sigh. "*Han-e-ga*, good," he said, smiling at Leonida as she handed him a platter of fried bread. "Now we can talk of other things. Runner? Have you recently gone and watched the tracks being laid closer and closer to Fort Defiance?"

Runner nodded a silent thank you to his mother as she handed him his breakfast. "Yesterday and the day before I watched," he said, his dark eyes narrowing at the thought of the railroad inching farther and farther into Navaho land. "I questioned some of the laborers. They said this portion of the railroad is called a private spur. It is not planned to go far, yet it will pass Fort Defiance by several miles."

"They plan even further expansion for that black iron fiend they call a train?" Sage said, enraged at the thought. "It was enough to know that it was being brought to Fort Defiance. I was anxious to see the last tie laid. And now you tell me that it comes closer now to our village?" His eyes flashed angrily. "That would mean more saloons and fire water ruining our young Navaho braves."

"That is so, Father," Runner said somberly.

"Is it not enough that the Navaho have already suffered at the hands of white people?" Sage said, glumly shaking his head slowly. "We have been cut off, lost, as many of our people were, years ago, during the 'Long Walk' to Fort Sumner."

"Father, I am sorry that people of my past continue to cause the *Dine* so much heartache," Runner said, sighing. "I have been a part of both worlds, but never torn about where I belong. It is with a proud heart that I live as Navaho, shamed often by those of my own kind."

Leonida smiled weakly at Sage, her own feelings mirroring those of Runner. Like Runner, she was glad to be a part of this culture, where the only greed within the People's hearts was for the constant struggle and desire for peace.

"And what is the purpose of this added private spur?" Sage asked. He took a bite of his bread, smiling his approval over at Leonida, then focused his attention on Runner again, frowning.

"I did not get such answers from the men laying the tracks," Runner said. "I did find out that a train arrives today as far as the tracks are already laid. Let us go and meet this train. Perhaps then we can find answers from those who are troubling us."

"We know already why this is being done," Sage said, his eyes narrowing. "The Navaho will be further exploited by the white people." He slumped his shoulders and laid his plate aside. "How can the spirit of the earth tolerate the white man? Everywhere the white man has touched it, it is sore. As our people increase in number and flocks of sheep expand and press outward in every direction from our treaty reservation, will this black demon train cut our people in half?"

"Father, long ago, when Kit Carson came with the

white pony soldiers and took a good portion of our people away on the 'Long Walk,' did you not despair as much then as now? Did not the Navaho return to their land even stronger? Nothing will ever stand in the way of our progress. Nothing. In fact, Father, if you will allow it, the coming of the train might benefit *us*."

"How can you say that?" Sage said, giving Runner a disappointed look. "Do not speak so only because you were once a part of their lives. Always think Navaho. Never white."

"I will never walk in the path of the white people again," Runner quickly defended. "My very heart and soul are Navaho. My thoughts are only on the welfare of the *Dine*. That is why I am thinking about *who* might be exploiting *whom* if the white man bring their black demon engines farther into our land. With the engine comes people. What is wrong with having more people for *our* people to sell our wares to?"

He paused, as though measuring his thoughts before putting them into words, then said, "Think of the blankets that Pure Blossom could sell. Selling only to those who come to Fort Defiance and the trading posts nearby is only a small portion compared to how many will come with the railroads. It will give Pure Blossom great joy, and perhaps ease some of the pain from her illness."

"What he says sounds reasonable," Leonida said, sitting down beside Sage. She placed a gentle hand on his arm. "Darling, you have seen Pure Blossom lately. Have you not noticed how her back is becoming more hunched?" She cringed at the thought of her daughter's obvious pain. "I have seen her kneading her fingers, as though they are paining her," she murmured. "She has to realize now, as we do, that she has the same affliction as her namesake, your dear sister, Pure Blossom, who is at peace now in the Hereafter. How it would thrill our daughter to be able to sell her beautiful blankets to many people, instead of only just a few. Perhaps we could look to the arrival of the train as a blessing. Could we, darling? It would make it much easier to accept what is going to happen. It will, anyhow, no matter what we say or do."

Sage gave Leonida a lingering look, seeing her as no less lovely than the day they had met. It had been during one of the times, those many years ago, when he had accompanied his sister, Pure Blossom, to Fort Defiance. He had stood watch as his sister had sold her fancy blankets and jewelry in a tent alongside many other Navaho who were there for the same purpose. When Leonida had come along, so sweet and gentle in manner, and so beautiful with her long golden hair, she had stolen his heart.

With her hair swept back from her face in a bun today, her cheeks flushed from having prepared the morning meal, anything she said would not be easily ignored. She was a woman of much intelligence. He always listened to her suggestions, usually agreeing with her.

But today he was not sure if he should see the worth in his son's suggestion and his wife's agreement. He had to think it over. He had to weigh the good and bad inside his heart before he came to any decisions.

"We shall see. I will give it much serious thought," he said, cupping Leonida's chin in his hand. He drew her lips to his and brushed them with his. Then he rose to his feet. "Runner, if we are to get your brother to school on time, we'd best be on our way."

Thunder Hawk rose to his feet only half-heartedly. Runner reached for his arm and teasingly yanked him to his side. "Come now, brother," he said, fondly placing an arm around Thunder Hawk's broad shoulders.

"Let's look at it this way. This time next year, *if* you behave, schooling will be behind you. *Then* what will you find to grumble about?"

"If I never have to step inside a schoolroom again, I will never again have cause to be unhappy," Thunder Hawk said determinedly. "I wish only to be a sheepherder. More respect is given to families who have large herds of sheep that are well cared for."

"That is so, son," Sage said dryly. "But *much* respect is given a man who has a school education."

All was quiet for a moment, then Leonida went to Thunder Hawk and Runner and gave them each a quick kiss on their cheeks, giggling when Sage whipped an arm around her waist and drew her around, against his hard body.

"My woman," he whispered, giving her a lingering kiss now that he knew that his sons had left the hogan.

Then he eased her from his arms and walked on away from her. "Ready the blankets for us while I am gone," he tossed absently over his shoulder. "Tonight we will warm them again with our bodies."

Leonida wanted to allow herself to be lost in thoughts of passion, but knowing how Sage was so troubled by the Santa Fe train closing in on the Navaho land, she could only worry as he walked away from the hogan.

She hurried outside just as her three men rode off on their horses, silver ornaments on their stamped leather saddles flashing in the sun.

"Be careful," she shouted, waving as one by one her three loved ones turned and gave her a smile over their shoulders.

Then she looked at Pure Blossom's hogan. She sighed with relief when she saw smoke spiraling from the chimney. Her daughter was surely busy at work, eating her own breakfast.

"I shan't bother her," Leonida whispered to herself. "When she's ready to take a break from her beloved weaving, she'll come to me."

She tried to shake the remembrance of another Pure Blossom of so many years ago from her mind, and how she had slowly faded away. Perhaps if it had not been for the prairie fever that had taken its final toll on her, Pure Blossom would have lived many more years, happy and content with her own special skills at weaving.

Turning, gathering the hem of her skirt into her arms, Leonida went back inside her own hogan. She glanced around, seeing the changes that had been brought to the far reaches of Navaho land by the white settlers. For days Sage and Runner had gone and watched ox teams draw up to various spots near springs and unload axes, saws, and nails. They had seen straight-walled houses being built of logs, with glass windows and iron hardware.

Sage and Runner had returned to the reservation and encouraged their people to begin making houses of thick, sawed logs, instead of poles covered with bark and earth. When they did, they had not kept to the four-sided style. They had laid their logs in six or eight sided shapes, so that the inside of the houses would still be circular and fit for Navaho ceremonies.

Leonida's house was filled with many more comforts of the white settlers, making life easier for her. She was proudest of her huge iron stove that she now used for cooking.

"Oh, Lord, please let Sage make the right decision," she whispered. "What Runner said made so much sense. He's such a brilliant young man."

Every day she thanked the Lord for having been blessed with the opportunity to have seen Runner grow from a young boy of five into a young man of twenty-three. She had to believe that his mother, Carole, was up there in the heavens somewhere, looking down at her son and smiling.

Runner rode his feisty black stallion beside his father's strawberry roan and gave Sage a quick glance. "I have to think that Damon Stout has some involvement in this railroad spur going on past Fort Defiance," he said, his long, black hair fluttering in the breeze. "That rancher has been nothing but trouble since he settled on land that is part of the reservation. What are treaties for if the government hands out land as though it is candy to ranchers like Damon Stout?"

"The government has watched *us* cross the treaty boundaries as our sheep need more grazing land, so they see no harm in allowing white men to come onto land that by treaty is *ours*," Sage said, frowning at Runner. "Yet what does the government do when our horses are stolen by the likes of this man called Damon? They look past the truth, ignoring it."

"What are you going to do if our horses continue to be stolen?" Runner asked, his eyes filled with fire at the thought of someone coming under the cover of darkness to steal from the Navaho.

"In time, my son, the one responsible for the stealing will make a wrong move," Sage said, nodding. "Then he will never steal from anyone again." He tightened his hold on his reins. "Damon. Damon Stout. *He* will be caught redhanded one day. Pity him then."

The small adobe schoolhouse came into view, the sun beating down upon its flat roof. Thunder Hawk emitted a groan, then broke away from Runner and Sage and rode in a hard gallop away from them, toward the school.

They drew a tight rein and stopped their horses.

They watched Thunder Hawk tie his horse with the others at the hitching rail, then walk with slumped shoulders into the schoolhouse.

"He does not walk like a man," Sage complained.

"That will come to him when his education is completed," Runner said, reaching to clasp his father's shoulder. "Learning *is* best for him."

Sage nodded, covered Runner's hand with his own, then drew his hand away and gripped the reins again. "*Ei-yei!* Let us ride, my son," he shouted, sinking his moccasined heels into the flanks of his horse.

Before they had ridden far, they heard the shriek of a train whistle in the far distance. Great billows of black smoke rising into the sky drew their attention.

"The iron fiend," Sage said, then urged his horse into an even harder gallop, Runner keeping steadfastly at his side.

Runner could not help but feel a strange, building excitement every time he watched a train traveling along on the gleaming tracks. Like something magical, on and on it would go, rumbling and flashing in the sun.

3

Love sent me thither, sweet,
And brought me to your feet,
He willed that we should meet,
And so it was.
—JOHN NICHOLS

The sun was pouring its heat from the sky, reflecting on the steel rails of the railroad tracks like white lightning. Runner rode at a gentle canter beside his father, squinting his eyes as he studied the new rails being laid, even now, by the work gangs. Although he felt a deep hatred for this invasion on the land of the Navaho, he was undeniably in awe of the power of the trains that rode these sorts of tracks. Distances were joined like magic.

"Do you see how the land is being destroyed by those men?" Sage said, as he edged his strawberry roan closer to Sage's stallion. "The earth is Mother and is to be revered. Not to be made ugly by steel rails."

Runner nodded, his eyes shifting to the men who had stopped their labors and were now leaning on their pick axes staring at him and his father. These men, who performed the labor for the Santa Fe Railroad Line, were quiet, self-effacing men. They worked by day, and drank and played by night in the saloons and bawdy houses in Gallup. It was this sort of men who were not welcomed in these parts. The threat of them corrupting the young of the Navaho was too severe.

Runner rode onward with his father. They left the work gang behind and inched their way alongside the rails that had already been installed. Runner looked over his shoulder. "There are but a few rails left to be laid before it reaches Fort Defiance," he said, mentally counting those that lay strewn along the ground. "Then perhaps the laborers will leave."

"But today, even now, the iron fiend and its carloads of white people come to invade our land, freedom, and privacy," Sage said, his dark eyes angry. "This Navaho has always searched for ways to keep peace with the whites. But now? Now I feel that I was wrong to have given in so easily to their demands. See where it has taken us? To a time and place of more invasions of the whites."

"It is not something that can be changed, Father," Runner said somberly. "Unless—"

"Unless we rip these tracks up, and all of the others as they are being laid from day to day," Sage said, casting Runner a heated glance.

"That would bring the white pony soldiers to our village," Runner said, his eyes locking with his father's. "I have known you long, Father, and I know that you do not want this."

"Nor do I want to flee again, as I did when Kit Carson brought heartache to our people," Sage said, in his mind's eye remembering the day that he had been forced from his stronghold by flames lit by the white man.

"Then let us wait and see how all this truly affects our people," Runner said, reining in his horse beside Sage's. He reached a comforting hand to his father's shoulder. "This son means no disrespect by saying his mind."

A smile quavered on Sage's lips. He reached up and

patted Runner's hand. "It is always good to hear you call yourself my son," he said. "You are not of my blood, but you are even more my son than if you had been. Your thoughts often match my own, so do not despair when occasionally we disagree on how things should be."

"It is not that I disagree," Runner corrected. "It is . . ."

His words were stolen away and he dropped his hand from his father's shoulder when the long screaming whistle from a train drew his quick attention. He turned from Sage. His spine stiffened and his gaze was drawn to the sky, where again he watched billows of black trailing along in the wake of the approaching train's belches.

His jaw tightened when another loud, long shriek came from the train. He was now able to see the black engine coming into sight, black smoke pouring from its smokestack that was shaped like a great kettle.

"Is it not an ugly monster?" Sage said in a grumble. "And listen to it. Hear how it snorts, puffs, and screams?"

"That is so, Father," Runner said, yet the white side of him could not stop the fluttering of his heart as he watched the train's approach. When he was a child, he had heard rumors of trains. The thought mystified him no less now than then.

And here he was, a grown man, coming face-to-face with such an invention.

If he could but only see that it was true progress for his Navaho people, as he knew that it was for his white heritage.

But everything pointed to it being *hogay-gah*, bad, for the Navaho. Bad, ugly, and a disgraceful thing to happen to the land of his Navaho loved ones.

He fought off feelings that were wrong and accepted

that he must hate this train as much as his Navaho father. Yet their hate seemed as bad as the train itself.

Hating anything meant trouble.

They rode on until they met the train, then began riding alongside it as it approached the end of the private spur that had been laid thus far.

"There is only one cattle car and there are no cattle, but instead only a few horses," Runner said, forking an eyebrow. "And there are only two passenger cars."

"I can see enough through the windows to see that there are only two passengers," Runner said, exchanging quick glances with his father when they both saw two people staring intently at them from one of the passenger cars. "Have we been wrong to think that the trains on these tracks will bring scores of white people to our land?"

"Do you think they would spend so many white man's dollars to lay such tracks for only two people?" Sage scoffed. "Son, they are only the beginning of our people's total ruin and unhappiness. There will be others. Many, many others will follow."

"I am sure you are right," Runner said, tightening his hold on the reins and holding his knees tightly to the sides of his steed when the train shrieked again.

Runner and Sage rode away from the train, stopping a few feet from the end of the line. Ignoring the glares from the work gang, they sat quietly and sternly, waiting to see more clearly these two invaders of their land.

Adam leaned closer to the window of the train. "Come and see, Stephanie," he said, motioning to her with a hand. "Our welcoming party has arrived."

"Welcoming party? I didn't know we were going to be met by anyone," Stephanie said, scampering to her feet. She lifted the hem of her skirt and scooted onto the seat opposite Adam. "Why, it's Indians, Adam. Two Indians. Are they Navaho?"

Adam's past was coming back to him in flashes. "Yes, they are Navaho," he said, his heart beating anxiously. "And by God, Stephanie, one of them is Sage. You know, the chief that I've so often talked about."

"Truly?" Stephanie said, her eyes widening. "Which one? The older one, no doubt."

"Yes, the older one," Adam said, grabbing for the seat back when the train came to a sudden, rumbling halt. "The one who has his hair clubbed and wrapped with strands of white wool."

"And the younger Indian?" Stephanie said, her gaze taking in the handsome man, realizing that he was not altogether Navaho. It was only in his attire, and how he wore his hair, that she saw him as Navaho. His clothes were colorful. He was dressed in a shirt of handwoven, woolen cloth with a vee-neck, and dyed buckskin trousers that had silver buttons down the sides and tied with woven garters. The bandana knotted about his head was of red crimson silk, holding back his long, flowing black hair. Otherwise, she saw his white skin, burned dark by the desert sun and wind, not by heritage.

"Good Lord, Stephanie," Adam said, staring even more intensely at Runner. "You wanted to know about the White Indian? I believe you're looking at him."

"Runner?" Stephanie gasped, still staring at him. His features were sculpted. His eyes flashed with dark intensity. "Is that truly Runner?"

"There's only one way to find out," Adam said, rising from his seat.

Stephanie turned quickly to Adam, who was already at the door. "Where are you going?" she blurted.

Adam ignored Stephanie. He stepped out into the

heat of the day and ran to the cattle car. He slammed open the door and placed a plank from the car to the ground, leading his horse down it.

Stephanie bunched the hem of her skirt into her hands and ran after Adam. "Wait for me," she shouted. "Adam, I want to go with you."

Adam still ignored her. He was too anxious to resume ties with his old friend, and not only for friendship's sake, but hoping to find an ally in this friend who was, by birth, white. He mounted his brown mare bareback and rode hard toward the two waiting Navaho.

As hell-bent on meeting the Navaho as Adam, Stephanie also bridled her horse in the cattle car, then led the chestnut stallion out and mounted him bareback. Gripping the reins with sure hands, she rode after Adam.

When she finally reached her step-brother, he had already drawn up beside Runner.

Runner raised an eyebrow as Adam sidled his horse closer to his stallion, seeing something familiar about the man, but could not place him. His gaze shifted when Stephanie came and drew rein beside the white man.

Memories rushed over him of white women of his past: his true mother and her friends. He had been young when he had been living among the white community, but he could recall seeing such lovely women as this, with their ivory skin, supple and slender figures, glowing cheeks, sparkling eyes, and full, ripe mouths.

Even this far from the woman he could smell a sweet perfume wafting toward him, reminding him of the perfumes his mother had worn.

But even though he could recall those women long ago, and seeing Leonida every day now, and thinking them all so beautiful, this woman was even more than his wildest dreams could conjure up. She was more lovely than any that he had ever seen before.

She had an entrancingly curved mouth. Her eyes were as smoky gray as the spring sage on the mountain slopes. Her feathery dark lashes flared widely so that they cast shadows on the pale skin beneath, and her hair was a magnificent torch of copper.

She was a picture of feminine daintiness, the snug fit of the bodice of her traveling suit emphasizing a tiny waist and high bosom.

The more he looked at her, the more she caused him to realize that he had been without someone to share his nights with him for far too long. Her mere presence was setting little fires throughout his body. And he could not allow such feelings.

In a sense, this woman was an enemy, an enemy of the Navaho.

"Trevor?"

Hearing the name of his youth being spoken by the white man made Runner jerk his eyes back to the man. Only people of his past knew the name that he had been given on the day of his birth.

He looked at the white man more closely and began seeing something familiar about him. This close, he could see the features of his boyhood friend—Adam.

"Adam?" Runner said, his voice low and measured.

"Runner, it *is* you," Adam said, reaching over to give Runner a fierce, manly hug. "It's really you."

Runner returned the embrace, feeling awkward. He saw the woman as an enemy; he could feel no less for Adam. It was obvious that Adam was involved with the expansion of the railroad, or he would not have been there.

Across Adam's shoulder, Runner looked at Stephanie again, finding it hard to continue labeling her as the enemy. He silently studied the gentle loveliness of her face and the breath-taking color of her hair and eyes.

Remembering again the differences in their beliefs where the railroad was concerned, he quickly shifted his eyes away from her and eased away from Adam.

"And Sage?" Adam said, leaning so that he could look around Runner. "It's so good to see you again."

Sage's lips were pursed tightly. He refused to give this man of his past a greeting that would be the same as speaking with a forked tongue. Although he was happy to see the boy of his past now turned into a young man, he would not allow his happiness to show. Adam was bringing trouble to the Navaho. His presence on the train made that fact evident.

Adam's eyes wavered. He looked clumsily over at Runner, then at Stephanie. "I would like to introduce my step-sister to you," he said, motioning for Stephanie to move into view.

When she did, Adam took her hand. "This is Stephanie. Stephanie, you have heard me mention Runner and Sage to you often." He motioned with his free hand first to Runner and then to Sage. "I am sure they are pleased to meet you."

Runner nodded in acquiescence.

Sage sat stolidly quiet, offering no comment.

"I'm pleased to meet you both," Stephanie murmured, blushing somewhat beneath Runner's steady stare.

Sage moved his horse forward, then stopped. He looked over at Adam. "Your mother Sally," he said. "She is well?"

Relieved that Sage was finally speaking, Adam's eyes took on a lively sparkle. "My mother is quite well, thank you," he said, relaxing somewhat. "Mother has been widowed twice but is now happy with her third husband, Stephanie's father."

"It is *han-e-ga*, good that she is well," Sage said. "She was a good woman."

"And your wife?" Adam said smoothly. "How is Leonida faring?"

"She is happy among the Navaho," Sage said, his eyes taking on a dark glittering. "She *is* Navaho now. As is our son, Runner."

"I can see that Runner has changed," Adam said, raising an eyebrow as he roved his eyes over Runner. "A *lot*."

Sage turned his gaze from Adam, shifting it to his son. He could see the instant attraction between Runner and the white woman. He was reminded of how quickly he had become enamored with a white woman, himself, all those years ago. Although Sage's marriage had been blessed with happiness, he would much rather his son choose a Navaho bride.

If Runner married a white woman, his children would most certainly be white. If he married a Navaho, there was always a chance that the children would be at least part Navaho, which would be preferable since Runner would one day be the leader of the People.

He could not allow his son to fall in love with a woman who was aligned with a man who had returned to Arizona for all of the wrong reasons. It was most certainly not to renew acquaintances—there was no logic in why he would.

His gaze swept over the richness of Adam's attire, stopping at the two diamond rings on his hands. This man was not guided by the heart. It was evident that he put too much faith in what money could buy. Sage could not help but feel that Adam was there only because of the railroad, and if so, he could not be made to feel welcome.

"Adam, what has brought you to Arizona?" Runner asked, guardedly watching Adam's reaction. He knew the foolishness of asking the question that he already knew the answer to. As each moment passed, Runner suspected that his old friend had strong ties with the Santa Fe Railroad and was there for all of the wrong reasons.

Adam looked over his shoulder at the train, then slowly looked from Runner to Sage. He felt that it was important to talk to Runner alone, to explain about being responsible for this new Santa Fe spur and his ideas behind it. Sage had already shown his resentment by his cold behavior. He could instantly reject the idea. Adam wanted the chance to slowly persuade Runner into accepting everything. And then he could spring it on his father.

He turned glittering eyes back to Runner. "I've come to see my old friends," Adam said, placing a hand on Runner's shoulder. "And to escort my step-sister to this great land so that she can photograph it. She's a photographer for the Santa Fe Railroad."

Runner's and Sage's expressions became instantly cold and distant as they glowered at Adam and then Stephanie. Their thoughts were the same on people taking photographs of their People: it was exploitation of the worst variety.

Stephanie smiled awkwardly at Runner and Sage. Their reaction to the mention of her being a photographer made her realize that nothing she had planned in the weeks ahead would come easy. She was already meeting resentment she had never expected.

Her gaze stopped on Runner. Having him resent her for any reason was going to be hard for her to accept.

She was attracted to him as never before to any other man. She could not allow anything to stand in the way of their knowing one another.

She would fight for her rights, not only to take her photographs, but also to be free to become closer to Runner. She had to find a way to tear down this barrier that he had just placed between them.

And she would.

She scarcely ever lost at anything she fought for.

4

I never saw so sweet a face
As that I stood before
My heart has left its dwelling place
And can return no more.
—JOHN CLARE

Stephanie had read somewhere that Indians distrusted cameras and wouldn't allow their pictures to be taken for fear that their images on paper might capture their soul. Realizing that photographing the Navaho might be even less accepted among their people than the new spur line, Stephanie decided it was best to put aside further talk of it.

"Adam and I have been invited to supper at Damon Stout's ranch tonight," she said in an effort to break the silence. "Sage, would you and your family like to join us? Perhaps we can become better acquainted. We can talk things over that . . . that . . . obviously displease you."

Adam's eyes lit up. He saw that he had been clever in bringing her with him. She could have more control of these Indians than he could. She was a beautiful young woman, hard to resist. It had been hard, but he had resisted loving her long ago; their feelings toward one another had always been those of brother and sister.

His eyes wavered when he saw that her suggestion

had brought no change in Sage and Runner. Instead, he saw an even deeper anger in Sage's narrowing, dark eyes.

"And how do you know Damon Stout?" Runner finally said.

"I have not made his acquaintance, personally," Stephanie said, wishing now that she had not mentioned Damon. She could tell that both Runner and Sage did not take well to the man's name, which had to mean they had no good feelings toward the man.

She nodded over at Adam. "He's Adam's friend," she murmured. "I believe they made an acquaintance when Adam was last here, while surveying the land for his private spur. Isn't that so, Adam?"

Adam gave a quick, steely glance upon her mention of the private spur. He had not wanted to spring that on the Navaho until later.

"*Your* private spur?" Sage said. "These tracks belong to you?"

"That is something I would like to discuss with you later," Adam said nervously. "Tonight? At Damon's ranch? I'm sure he would not mind if I'm extending this invitation to your family, Sage. Would you please bring them? I would love to see Leonida."

"Yes, please bring Leonida," Stephanie said. "I've heard so much about your family. I'm very anxious to make Leonida's acquaintance."

"And isn't there a daughter?" Adam said, taking this opportunity to focus more on family than on reasons for him and Stephanie being in Arizona. He knew of this daughter and that she had been named Pure Blossom, after Sage's late sister. It was best to show innocence now, to make room for more light conversation between himself and the Navaho.

"Yes, a daughter has been born into our family," Sage

said, nodding. "Pure Blossom. She is called Pure Blossom." He cast his eyes on Stephanie. "She is perhaps the same winters of age as you. And there is also a son: Thunder Hawk."

"I am most anxious to meet both your daughter and your other son," Stephanie said, smiling over at Sage.

"You will come, then, to Damon's ranch?" Adam asked quickly, while there was some rapport being reached, thanks to Stephanie's sweet, vibrant personality and her way of drawing people into not only liking but loving her. "You will bring your entire family?"

"*E-do-tano*, no," Sage said, his voice stern. "Never."

"This Navaho son accepts the invitation," Runner quickly interjected.

Runner's spine stiffened when he felt the scalding look from his father, but ignored it. Once his father heard his reason for deciding to go to Damon's ranch, he would understand. This was a perfect opportunity, not only for the obvious reason, but for another that he would not share with his father. Although he was fighting his feelings about Stephanie, he could not deny himself the chance to get to know her better.

He also wanted to question her further about being a photographer. This, as well as the woman, intrigued him, although, for the sake of the Navaho People, he should be hating the thought of both.

"That's magnificent, Runner," Adam said, seeing his plan slowly falling into place. He clasped an eager hand on Runner's muscle-tight shoulder. "It is good to be with you again, my friend. I never thought it possible."

"Times change," Runner said, his voice drawn. "But most of all, people change."

He reached up and eased Adam's hand from his shoulder. "Tonight, Adam," he said, purposely not using the term "friend." He saw Adam as anything but that. He could see that the boy of his youth was now a scheming man.

Runner turned to Stephanie as her eyes locked with his. "Tonight, Stephanie," he said, then swung his horse around and rode off beside his father.

After Runner and Sage were some distance from Stephanie and Adam, who were now riding in the opposite direction from them, Sage turned angrily to Runner. "You are going to Damon's ranch?" he said, glowering at Runner. "Do you not see this as foolish? There is much bad blood between the Navaho and Damon. You know that he is suspected of stealing Navaho horses."

"That is exactly why I am going to his ranch," Runner said, smiling at his father. "Do you not see? I can sneak out to Damon's corral and check the horses. I know all of our People's steeds as well as one knows his best friend."

A slow smile moved on Sage's lips. "I have raised a clever, intelligent son," he said, his smile erupting into a pleased laugh. A wizened man, his movements were spry with vigor and his eyes were shrewd and twinkling.

"Then you agree to my going?" Runner asked, riding tall in his saddle, the wind lifting his long hair from his shoulders. "I never wish to disobey, Father."

"Go, but be warned, my son, against having feelings for the white woman," Sage growled out. "Always remember the importance of looking forward to a future of raising Navaho children in your hogan, not white."

"Father, I am white, am I not?" Runner said guardedly. "Do not I represent our People of Navaho, even though by birthright I am white?"

"By saying this, are you telling your father that you do have eyes for the woman called Stephanie?" Sage said, his jaw tightening.

"It is too early to know or to say," Runner said, turning his eyes from Sage, fearing they would betray what he was trying to hide from his beloved, adoptive father.

"Be careful with your heart and to whom you give it," Sage warned. "I see much treachery in Adam. Who is to say that his sister is not the same?"

Runner turned to Sage. "She is not of his blood kin," he said, in defense.

"That is so," Sage said, nodding. "One other thing, Runner. See if Adam is solely responsible for this thing he calls a private spur."

"It is as good as done," Runner said, smiling over at his father, realizing that his father had not pursued the question of ownership of the private spur with Adam on purpose. He knew that his son would get him enough of the answers.

They rode onward in silence, their horses urged into a hard canter.

Runner's thoughts were on his father's warnings and remembering his own reservations about the white woman. Thus far, no woman, white or Indian, had caused him to take a lingering, second look.

Not until now.

Not until Stephanie.

In this one case, he might have to go against the wishes of his Navaho father and follow the rulings of his heart, yet he would proceed with much caution.

He frowned when he recalled again why she was there: to bring a camera into the land of the Navaho. This could be why he felt that he should not allow his feelings for her to become stronger.

He hoped that he would not be forced to make the choice between this woman and his people.

* * *

The sun was streaming through the window of the private railroad car, splashing golden light on the plush furniture and reflecting like sparkling diamonds in the long-stemmed wineglass that Adam was turning in his fingers. The train's engine had been abandoned by the engineer and workers. They had taken their horses from the cattle car and had ridden off to seek their own amusements back at Gallup, at a place called the "Big Tent."

"Stephanie, you were magnificent," Adam said, laughing. He stretched his long, lean legs out and crossed them at the ankles. "Absolutely stupendous. If not for you, Runner would have gone with his father and would not have accepted the invitation to Damon's ranch."

Stephanie was at the window, illumined by a beam of sunlight. She gazed out at the mountains in the distance, only half hearing Adam, still under the spell of Runner's midnight dark eyes and the mystery of this man called the "White Indian."

"Stephanie?" Adam said, turning to look at her. "Did you hear what I said? You're one clever sister. If not for you, Runner wouldn't have agreed to go and meet with us at Damon's ranch. Don't you see the value in that? If I can sway Runner over to our side, he'll persuade the Navaho to accept my private spur. It's apparent there is a mutual trust and respect between Sage and Runner. Sage will do as his son suggests."

Adam's mention of Runner drew Stephanie's thoughts back to the present and her brother. She turned and looked at Adam. "What was that you said about Runner?" she murmured.

"Aw, nothing," Adam said, shrugging. He set his wineglass aside on a table. "It seems you'd not hear me, anyhow." He smiled wryly. "He's in your blood, isn't he? You're falling for Runner, aren't you?"

A heated blush rose to Stephanie's cheeks. She avoided Adam's knowing stare and walked smoothly across thick carpeting, past grand, overstuffed chairs. She hurried into the smaller adjoining rooms that served as her bedroom and darkroom.

Fumbling through the darkness, she found a lamp and match. She almost dropped the match when Adam came quickly to her side.

"Let me light the lamp for you," Adam said, striking the match and placing it to the wide, kerosene-soaked wick.

"Be careful, Adam," Stephanie said, holding the lamp steady. "Always remember the danger of my photographic chemicals."

"Always," Adam said, chuckling. "Do you think I want to go up in smoke just as I'm about to see my dreams come true?"

Stephanie saw the need for another warning to her brother. "Don't count your chickens before they hatch," she said, setting her lamp on a counter, far from the trays of chemicals that she used for developing her negatives. "Didn't you see Sage's reaction? It's obvious that he's not only against the railroad but also my being a photographer."

She turned to Adam and reached a hand to his lapel, smoothing it out with a soft touch of her fingers. "My dear brother, I do believe you have a battle on your hands," she said, smiling up at him. "Now, be on your way. I want to develop the photographs that I took while we had our stopover in Gallup. That town is quite colorful, don't you think?"

"No less than what I propose for mine," Adam said, bending to kiss her brow. "I see it as a magnificent place, sis. Absolutely magnificent."

"Magnificent," Stephanie said, laughing softly. "To

you everything is magnificent." She reached her arms around him and gave him a hug. "Sweetie, I hope you get your dreams."

Adam returned her hug. "With your help, I believe it's within reach," he said, then was jolted with alarm when she swung quickly away from him.

"My help?" she said, raising an eyebrow. "What do you mean?"

"You didn't hear anything that I was saying a few minutes ago, did you?" Adam said, sighing. "Oh, well. I'm not going to go into it again. You'll see soon enough what I mean without me spelling it out for you now."

Stephanie started to say something else, but Adam was already gone, leaving her alone with her thoughts.

"I wonder what he meant?" she whispered, then began stirring fresh chemicals into water. All around her hung the proof of her love of photography.

Stephanie's heart was not on her work as she began to unload her case of plates. All that she could think about was Runner, anxious now to begin taking photographs of the Navaho and their lovely land. She had met the man of her dreams; she had to find a way to get him to understand why her photographs could be used for the good of his people, not the bad.

"I must find a way," she whispered, stopping to slip her suit jacket off. She rolled the sleeves of her white blouse up to her elbows and unbuttoned the two top buttons. She swept her hair back from her shoulders.

Then she proceeded to develop her plates, her heart pounding at the thought of seeing Runner again, under *any* circumstances.

5

I ne'er was struck before that hour
With love so sudden and so sweet
Her face it bloomed like a sweet flower
And stole my heart away complete.
—JOHN CLARE

Sheep were scampering downhill in a cloud of white and dissolved into the swelling herd, bawling their complaint as a sheepherder began driving them into a pole corral behind his hogan.

Sage and Runner nodded a silent hello to the man and rode on into their village, where Leonida stood waiting for them outside her hogan.

She wrung her hands nervously as she waited for Sage and Runner to dismount and tether their horses to a hitching rail at the side of the dwelling, then met Sage and flew into his arms.

"*Yaa-eh-t-eeh*," Leonida said in a Navaho greeting. "Darling, I'm so glad you've returned home." She gave him one last hug, then stepped away from him.

"Mother, what is it?" Runner asked. He went to her and took one of her hands. "You are upset. Why?"

"It's Thunder Hawk," Leonida said, sighing heavily. "He sneaked away from school again. This is his last year. Why can't he see how important it is to have a full education? All dealings now are with schooled people. To compete, one must have the same schooling. Runner, you completed your studies. You have prepared yourself well for standing up against those who would cheat you. But what of Thunder Hawk? His stubbornness could be the ruin of him."

Knowing the truth of his mother's words, Runner's thoughts turned back to Adam. He could tell that his boyhood friend was quite educated and could be a challenge to Runner's *own* intelligence.

Also, the white woman proved to be a woman of much intellect. Anyone who knew the secrets of the device called a camera had to be very schooled in the subject. She would also be a challenge, yet one that he looked forward to.

"Where *is* our younger son?" Sage asked dryly.

"He has gone to help bring our sheep in," Leonida said, entering the hogan with Sage and Runner. "He says that he wants to feel useful now, as well as in the future."

"He is finding it hard to break with the traditions of our past," Sage said, settling down on a chair before the fireplace. He accepted a cup of coffee from Leonida with a nod of thanks.

"In part that is good," Sage continued between sips of coffee. "*Edo-tano*, no. It is not good ever to forget the ways of our past. But one must always prepare one's self for the future, and I fear that herding sheep is not for our son. He must learn how to fight logic with logic when he comes face-to-face with the white people. Schooling is the only way to survive. The only way."

"I feel as though I am ready to face any difficulty that may be laid in my path," Runner said, sitting down beside his father.

"Even Adam?" Sage said, frowning over at Runner. "You are putting yourself in such a position tonight, my son, by promising to have council with Adam and Damon."

"It will not be a normal council, by any means," Runner said, laughing softly. "But, yes. I believe that I am ready for anything that Adam says or does."

"And the white woman as well?" Sage said, reaching to add another log to the fire.

"We shall see about her when the time comes," Runner said. He took a plate of food as Leonida handed it to him.

"Surely I was mistaken, but did I hear you speak a name of our past?" Leonida said. She reached to the table for Sage's plate of food, then handed it to him. "Adam. Did you say something about an Adam?"

She had already eaten. She slipped her apron off and settled down on a chair opposite Sage and Runner. She waited for a reply, raising an eyebrow when she realized that neither son or husband was offering it to her.

"Sage? Runner?" she persisted. "What did you say about Adam? Could it be our little Adam? Our Sally's Adam?"

Runner lay his plate aside. He reached for his mother's hands and squeezed them affectionately. "Mother, it *is* our Adam," he said softly.

Leonida's face glowed with joy. "Truly?" she gasped. "You ... have ... seen him? Where, Runner? Where?"

Runner cast Sage a troubled glance, then knelt by his mother. "Mother, Adam has arrived on a train," he explained softly. "Do you know the tracks that have been laid farther than Gallup? Adam came in a train on those tracks."

Leonida's eyes became shadowed with worry. "He came to see us? That is why he was on the train?"

"Not entirely," Runner said stiffly. "I believe he has

come because of some connection with the railroad, *and* because of his sister."

"What sister?" Leonida asked, her eyes widening.

"Her name is Stephanie," Runner explained. "She is a photographer. She has come to Arizona to practice her skills."

"Truly?" Leonida said. "She is truly skilled in photography?"

"Yes, and it *is* intriguing, mother," Runner said solemnly. "But it is also something the Navaho would not want to be involved with. They would be exploited. That cannot be allowed to happen."

Leonida did not reply. She understood about the Navaho being exploited. But she could not help but want to know this woman who knew the skills of taking pictures. She admired any woman who knew the ways of a man's world.

Yet, as far as the Navaho were concerned, she did see a danger in this.

Pure Blossom entered the hogan, interrupting the silence.

"See my newest finished blanket," Pure Blossom said. Spread across her outstretched arms was a blanket of many designs and colors.

Leonida went and took the blanket and shook it out to its full length, sighing as she was taken in by its sheer loveliness. "I do not know how, but your skills improve with each of your blankets," she said.

Then her attention was drawn from the blanket. She watched how Pure Blossom kneaded her fingers, her eyes revealing the pain she was in.

Leonida lay the blanket aside and drew her frail daughter into her arms. "Now, now," she murmured. "Do your fingers hurt so terribly today, Pure Blossom? Perhaps you should not weave for a few days now that your latest project is finished. Why not just rest beside the fire? I have recently brought you some books from the trading post. You could read. That could take your mind off the pain."

"Using my fingers keeps them limber," Pure Blossom said. She eased from her mother's arms and looked at Runner. "Big brother, you seem so serious. What were you discussing?"

Runner rose to his feet and went to Pure Blossom. He took her hand and led her to a seat on a cushion of sheepskins before the fire. He gazed at her, again noticing how frail and small she was, yet so beautiful. She had coal-black, thick hair that almost hung to the floor when she stood. He scarcely looked at her back; the knot forming at the base of her neck was hidden beneath her hair.

He knew that her future was bleak, and that one day she would be stooped and bent, but to *him* she would never be ugly. He feared that she might never find a man who could look past her frailties. His heart bled to think that she would probably never be given the chance to bear children.

This frailty of hers was a curse that no one could take away, not even the Navaho singers who were used to cure ailments of many kinds.

"We were talking of someone that we knew many years ago," Runner softly explained. He lifted her hair from her shoulders and let it sift through his fingers like soft earth.

"Who?" Pure Blossom asked anxiously.

"You do not know him," Runner said, his mind drifting. He wished that time would go faster, so that it would be evening, and he could once again see the white woman. He hoped that somehow they could get past their differences. Their eyes had spoken as they had gazed at one another. To touch her surely would be heaven.

"His name?" Pure Blossom persisted, seeing that Runner's thoughts had drifted elsewhere.

"Adam," Runner said, dropping his hand to his side. "He was my friend long ago. I lost touch with him over the years."

"And he is here?" Pure Blossom said. She rose anxiously to her feet. "He has come to see you? Where is he? I enjoy visitors."

Leonida went to Pure Blossom and placed an arm around her waist. "No, he isn't here," she murmured. She looked over at Runner. "Is he coming soon? I can hardly wait to meet him." She paused and smiled. "And also his sister."

"I am sure they will be here one day soon," Runner said, gazing into the fire. "But first, I must meet with them tonight, by myself. Perhaps it can be arranged that they can come to our village."

"No, son," Sage said in a grumble. "Do not bring trouble to us that easily."

Leonida paled. "Trouble?" She placed a hand to her throat. "You truly believe Adam has come to stir up trouble for our people?"

When neither Sage or Runner responded, Leonida knew that it was best not to pursue the subject of visitors when it was obvious her husband did not want them. "And Sally?" she could not help but ask. "How is she?"

"Married a third time," Runner offered. "The white woman with Adam is the daughter of Sally's latest husband."

"Her step-daughter," Leonida said. "Adam's stepsister?"

"Yes, that is their relationship," Runner said. He

watched his father saunter from the hogan, obviously tired of hearing any more mention of Adam and his sister, making Runner again feel uneasy about tonight.

Yet still nothing would dissuade him from going. *Someone* of the Navaho had to see what could be done to protect their interests. He was trying to convince himself that this was the reason for going, when his every heartbeat told him that it was because of a woman, a very entrancing woman.

Leonida was watching her son with much interest and how his eyes always lit up when he spoke of Adam's sister. She could not help but think that something had transpired between her son and this woman photographer. She wondered what.

And how far had it gone?

It was obvious that Sage did not share his son's enthusiasm for the woman or Adam. She expected that there were some interesting times ahead for this family, especially for her son Runner.

6

Take all that's mine "beneath the moon,"
If I with her but half a noon.
—WILLIAM WORDSWORTH

Evening had finally arrived. For the most part, Stephanie had been silent while riding on her chestnut stallion on the way to Damon Stout's ranch. Her thoughts had been on meeting the handsome Navaho brave again. She could hardly wait, yet she feared how he might react when Adam told him the truth about his plans for building a new town within the boundaries of the Navaho reservation.

If Runner's reaction was what Stephanie expected, she doubted ever having a chance to get to truly know the man who was called the "White Indian." And that bothered her. It bothered her so deeply that it caused an ache to circle her heart.

But no matter how hard she tried to stop thinking about Runner, she found it impossible.

Adam's thoughts were also on Runner, but for a much different reason. As he rode his gentle mare through the twilight toward Damon's ranch, he was worrying about revealing everything to Runner this soon. Perhaps he should wait until friends became friends again, who might then become allies.

And then again, perhaps Adam held the trump card:

Stephanie. She could make it all happen for Adam tonight, and every night after this as far as Runner was concerned. Adam had seen the attraction between them.

And what if Runner fell in love with Stephanie? Yes, that was the secret to Adam's success. He had to see to it that it happened.

Wearing only fringed buckskins, his hair loose and flowing across his shoulders, Runner rode toward Damon's ranch, his thoughts straying from Adam to Stephanie. He could not allow Adam to stand in the way of his feelings for the white woman. He was determined to see if she was the sort of woman that he could feel free to love. As far as her being a photographer was concerned, he had ways of handling that.

First, to get the business with Adam behind him. Then he would take time for the woman. Just looking at her made his heart melt.

Everyone had arrived at Damon's ranch at almost the same time. Chatting only briefly, they had gone into the dining room for a large Mexican meal of spicy, tongue-tantalizing dishes. Only a few polite words had been exchanged, the atmosphere tight, as though something might explode at any moment.

Stephanie was glad when they retreated to the parlor to have coffee and sweets in front of the fireplace. Sitting comfortably in a plush overstuffed chair, she sipped on her coffee while Adam and Runner talked of old times, Damon's concentration centered more on Stephanie than the discussion at hand.

Stephanie was nervous with Damon's attention. She inwardly shivered, finding him repulsive. He was a squat, slovenly figure of a man, with short, bandy legs and a bulging potbelly. He was a hard-bitten, trail-driving Texan, tough and defiant with a "don't crowd me" attitude.

Beneath an open vest bulged the seams of a dark calico shirt. His legs were encased in leather chaps, greasy and dark from long wear. The butt of a Colt pistol protruded from a holster on his right flank, and a bright red bandanna was knotted at his throat.

His expression was wooden as his dark eyes examined Stephanie from above a bristling mustache. She was glad that she had her small, pearl-handled derringer holstered at her waist. Her father had warned her that the potential for violence along the railroad was palpable. He had given her the gun for protection whenever she was away from her private railroad car.

He had teased her, saying that with the Derringer slung around her waist, she could protect her charms even though she flaunted them.

Still uneasy, she turned her eyes away from him. The walls were decorated with exquisite Navaho rugs, buffalo hides, and mounted heads of buffalo. Bright paintings enlivened the Spanish house, its tiled hip roof spreading like an umbrella over a wide porch around the entire house.

In this room, the puncheon floors were filthy, chairs were thrown around in disarray, and a whiskey barrel complete with spigot and dipper sat in one corner.

Stephanie turned her gaze back to the large, stone fireplace. A tremendous fire was ablaze, logs five feet long resting across andirons.

"Stephanie, did you know that Runner and I played Indians and cowboy at Fort Defiance when we were youngsters?" Adam said, finally drawing Stephanie into the conversation.

Stephanie looked quickly over at him, now aware of another pair of eyes on her, making her pulse race. Runner. He had glanced over at her from time to time, while talking with Adam about their childhood.

But now he was looking openly at her.

Beneath Runner's steady, warm gaze, Stephanie's knees were suddenly weak and her heart was pounding within her chest. She could feel her face heating with a blush. She smoothed her hands down the front of her riding skirt and then up again, grazing the leather holster at her waist.

"Sis?" Adam said, leaning to look at Stephanie. "Did you hear me? I was talking about the times when Runner and I played cowboy and Indian. I was always the cowboy, Runner the Indian. Don't you think it's somewhat amusing Runner is still playing the role of an Indian?"

Runner turned a sharp look at Adam. "Playing?" he said. His eyes filled with a sudden fire. "You call my relationship with the Navaho a game?"

Stephanie scarcely breathed as she looked over at Adam, whose face had grown suddenly ashen.

She turned toward Runner. She could tell that he was livid with rage. His face had lost all expression and had settled into a cold neutral look. Only his midnight dark eyes were quick and alive as he awaited Adam's reply and, most certainly, an apology.

"Don't be so quick to jump to conclusions over a mere slip of the tongue," Adam said, nervously fidgeting with his stiff, white shirt collar. "I didn't mean anything by what I said. Of course, I see how seriously you have taken your life with the Navaho. And ... I ... see that as commendable on your part, Runner. Quite commendable."

"I apologize, Runner," he added after an awkward pause. He reached a hand over to Runner. "Shake on it?"

Stephanie inhaled deeply as Runner reached over and clasped Adam's hand, obviously forgiving Adam this time. She doubted that he would be so quick to accept a handshake from Adam once he knew the full story. She was wondering when Adam was going to get the nerve to tell Runner the truth. After this small confrontation, she doubted it would be tonight.

She was stunned when Runner then rose quickly to his feet. She stared up at him, her eyes wide, her lips slightly parted.

"I must go," Runner said, giving Adam a nod.

Because Runner had wanted to get answers out of Adam, and because of his fascination with Stephanie, he had ignored the taunts Adam had been throwing all evening, but it was obvious now that Adam was eluding all talk of the private spur, instead lingering on the subject of their boyhood. Runner would not sit by any longer and be humiliated by first Damon and then Adam. The cost was too high. He would get his answers later about the railroad *and* the white woman.

When he turned to Stephanie, his gaze reached out and clung to her for a moment, then he turned on a moccasined heel and walked toward the door.

Damon and Adam rose quickly from their chairs and followed Runner to the door. Disappointed that the evening had ended so quickly, Stephanie sat numbly in her chair.

She still felt the warmth of Runner's gaze, but because of Adam's bumblings, Runner was leaving too soon. Because of Adam, Stephanie felt that she might never get the chance to get to know Runner better.

And now that she had spent an evening with him, she knew that she wanted more than a mere acquaintance. She wanted to feel the wonders of his arms around her. She wanted to know the bliss of his kiss.

Runner gave Adam another handshake at the door, only offering Damon an icy stare. When he departed, he left a strange, quiet void behind him.

Stephanie rose quickly from her chair. She could not let Runner leave her all that easily. She would follow him. She would stop him before he mounted his horse. She would draw him into conversation with her. Somehow she must, or she would not get a wink of sleep tonight, nor would she be able to go about her business of taking photographs tomorrow without a heavy heart.

"Damn it," Adam said, thrusting his hands deeply into his trouser pockets. "As a child, he wasn't so temperamental. How am I going to be able to talk to him about anything ever again, much less tell him that the private spur is being built solely for me?"

"I warned you, Adam," Damon said. "I've never been able to communicate with the Navaho. They're a damn nuisance. I don't know why you're wastin' time on them. Take what you want, and to hell with anything else."

Damon watched Stephanie's approach. His gaze raked over her. He had bedded many women in his lifetime, but none as pretty as her.

He glanced down at her firearm. Only women with spirit carried derringers. He could envision how feisty she would be in bed. She probably knew all the ways to make a man's head spin.

Stephanie brushed past Damon and Adam and rushed outside. A half moon spilled its silver light over the sky as she hurried toward the hitching rail, where she hoped to find Runner before he had the chance to ride away. Runner's horse was still there, but he was nowhere in sight.

Stephanie turned and took a slow look around her. "Runner?" she said, her voice echoing back to her in the silence of the night. Her breathing slowed as she peered more intensely through the dark shadows of the night. The only sounds that she heard were the crickets in the grass, the soft neighing of the horses in the corral, and a distant coyote baying at the sliver of the moon in the sky.

As she became more acquainted with the cloak of night, she could make out several outbuildings on all sides of her, a barn, the ranch hand's bunk house, and a pole corral filled with horses.

Stephanie's heart leapt when she saw a movement among the horses. She watched guardedly, then jumped with a start. A man was moving from horse to horse, checking them over.

She did not think that he was any of Damon's ranch hands. This man was moving too stealthily and was obviously trying to keep his movements hidden in the darkness.

Her hand moved instinctively to her Derringer. She rested her fingers on the leather holster, feeling safety in the feel of the shape of the firearm against the palm of her hand.

Her pulse racing, her throat dry, Stephanie began moving slowly toward the corral. Although she knew that it was none of her business who came and went from Damon's corral, and disliking the rancher so much, she could not help but go see who might be stalking about in the night.

Her first thought was of Runner. He had not gone directly to his horse when he had left the house. Where else could he be then, except possibly in the corral?

Stephanie was curious to see why he found such an intent interest in Damon's horses. If, indeed, it was Runner who was with them.

When she reached the pole corral, Stephanie crouched low and watched for another movement.

Beneath the spill of the moonlight, she was suddenly able to make out Runner's features. His face was revealed to her as he stepped into view for only a moment, and then, just as quickly, was hidden among the horses again.

Stephanie's heart pounded with the discovery. "It *is* Runner," she whispered to herself. She knew that it was best not to reveal herself to him. Adam had come close to making enemies with him tonight.

She waited for awhile longer. She still caught an occasional glimpse of Runner, then decided it was best to return to the house. Turning, she started to walk away, then her footsteps froze when she heard someone coming up behind her. Eyes wide, her knees feeling weak, she spun around and found herself eye to eye with Runner.

"What are you doing here?" he growled, his eyes lit with fire.

Stephanie found herself speechless at first, then listened with surprise as she found herself saying, "What were you finding so interesting in someone else's corral?"

7

Her loving yielding form I pressed,
Sweet maddening kisses stole,
And soon her swimming eyes confessed
The wishes of her soul.
—ROBERT DODSLEY

Realizing that she had placed Runner in an awkward position, Stephanie instantly regretted having spoken. She was just getting ready to apologize for her rudeness, when he suddenly answered her.

"I admire all horses," Runner said, having found a way to answer her without incriminating himself. "Horses are a great love of the Navaho. We admire and own many. Mine are a part of me, my best friends, my companions."

"You speak of yourself as though you are, indeed, Navaho, yet by birthright, you are not," Stephanie said, again speaking without first thinking. When she saw his frown, she just as quickly regretted what she had said.

"In every way I am Navaho," Runner answered. He tried not to allow her innocent questions to anger him, when what he truly wanted was to take her into his arms. "Since I was six winters of age, I have been raised in the tradition of the Navaho. I am proud to be called Navaho."

Stephanie recoiled when she realized the bitterness

in his last statement. "I'm sorry for being so thought-less," she said, swallowing hard. "Of course I can see how proud you are of your adopted heritage. It's wonderful to see someone who stands so firmly behind his beliefs."

"And your beliefs are?" Runner said, tempted to reach his hands to her hair, to feel its softness. He fought off the temptation, as he still did not know enough about her to allow his heart to rule his actions.

"My beliefs?" Stephanie said, feeling uneasy. She had seen how quickly Runner had reacted to things Adam had said that had annoyed him, and only moments ago, to what she had so absently said. She had to guard her words much more carefully until there was some trust built between them. Yet, when she looked into his eyes she felt as though she were drowning beneath his dark, penetrating gaze. Her pulse was racing. Her knees felt strangely weak again.

Certainly, she wanted no hard feelings between them, instead, something wonderful and sweet, where they could share everything, even their deepest hopes and desires. Even her desire to be a successful photographer. She feared that Runner's desire might be to make sure that this did not happen in Navaho land.

"Yes, your beliefs," Runner said, trying not to speak so stiffly. He did not want these moments to be this awkward, yet he wanted answers, the same as she. "You have brought a camera to Arizona. Is it for making yourself a great profit? Or do you do it for enjoyment?"

While the silence grew, his gaze slowly moved over her as the moon spilled onto her lovely features. Her lips were ripe. Her eyes were innocently wide, and although she was petite, he could see her breasts pressed sensuously against the inside of her white, cotton blouse, the shape of her nipples defined as she held herself stiffly.

"You say that you like horses," Stephanie said, her voice drawn. "Do they not give you a sense of being, of fulfillment while being with them?"

"Yes, that is so," Runner said, now gazing into her fascinating gray eyes.

"That is how I feel while with my camera," Stephanie said, sighing to herself. "While taking photographs I truly feel fulfilled."

She paused, then added, "I would not venture to deny you the pleasure of your horses, the same as I would hope you would not take it upon yourself to deny me the pleasure of my camera."

"It is easy to see that you are an intelligent woman," Runner said, clasping his hands behind him. "So you must know that no Indian, whether it is Navaho, Shoshone, or Ojibway, wants to be exploited by anyone's cameras. Do you see how impossible it is for me to tell you that I see how your pleasure of a camera compares with mine for horses? Horses are loved by all Indians. Cameras are hated."

"Are you saying that I will not be able to take photographs in Navaho land?" Stephanie said in a low gasp.

"At this moment, I would prefer not to say," Runner said, his jaw tightening.

"And when can I expect for you to make up your mind?" Stephanie said, anger welling up inside her.

"In due time," Runner said. His eyes danced into hers. He found her even more beautiful while she was on the edge of anger. "The Navaho as a whole should decide."

"I plan to start taking photographs tomorrow," Stephanie said, stubbornly lifting her chin. "I will not wait for any Navaho's permission. I have traveled too far not to use my camera."

"This Navaho will not stop you," Runner said, admiring her independence. Like his adopted mother, Leonida, this woman was the sort of person who would fight for her rights.

"Why, thank you," Stephanie said, surprised that he would give in so easily, yet doubting that he truly was. Tomorrow might be a different matter.

It seemed that the moonlight was affecting them both. She could see it in his eyes. She could feel the vibrations of some unseen power moving between them.

She shuffled her feet nervously, her heart pounding as he took one step closer to her, his dark eyes almost hypnotic in their steady stare.

"Do you mind being called the 'White Indian'?" she blurted, trying to find something to say that could fill the sudden, strained silence between them.

"I pay no heed to the ignorance of those who feel they are ostracizing me by labeling me a 'White Indian,'" he said thickly. "In truth, I am always quite proud of any reference to my being Indian."

"You lived in the white community for enough years to become attached to their ways," Stephanie said softly. "Do you ever hunger for the ways of the white man?"

Runner thought for a moment. Then he placed his hands at her waist and yanked her against his hard body. "*E-do-tano*, no, I haven't," he said huskily. His steely arms quickly enfolded her. "Not until I saw you."

Everything happened so quickly then, Stephanie's head began to spin. His mouth closed hard upon hers. She clung to him as he kissed her deeply and passionately, with a fierce, possessive heat.

For the moment, Runner cast aside his dislike of her being a photographer. All that he saw when he looked at Stephanie was a woman. A lovely, alluring woman, who he could no longer resist.

Sweet currents of warmth swept through Stephanie, leaving her weak. She had not been prepared for the intense passion his kiss was arousing within her. The euphoria that was filling her was almost more than she could bear. She felt his hunger in the seeking pressure of his lips. Without thought, she began to answer his kiss with a need that rose up inside her. It was so deliciously sweet, she clung even harder to him.

Licking flames were building dangerous fires within Runner. He ground his mouth into Stephanie's lips. His hands made a slow, sensuous descent along her spine. His hands clasped her rounded bottom through her skirt and molded her slender, sweet body against him. His breath quickened with a yearning. He wanted her fiercely.

Then his heart made a wild jump and he drew quickly away from her as someone nearby cleared his throat to reveal their presence.

Trembling, left shaken with desire, Stephanie tried to control her breathing as she stared wild-eyed at Damon standing close by in the darkness with a mocking smile on his lips.

Her face flamed with embarrassment, and then an intense anger swept through her. She wanted to slap him, but stood her ground, for her knees were still too weak to move, even in defense of herself.

She looked over at Runner, expecting him to say or do something. When she saw the utter hate in his eyes as he stared at Damon, she realized just how much Runner detested the rancher.

She gasped and took a step backward as Runner brushed suddenly past her, loosened his stallion's reins from the hitching rail and swung himself into his saddle.

She wanted to cry out for him not to leave, but her words seemed frozen in her throat while he rode off in a hard gallop.

"He ain't fit for the likes of you," Damon said, drawing Stephanie's gaze quickly back to him. "Now, for example, take me. I'm more your kind. I live by the rules of the white people. When I take you to bed, you won't have to worry about what Injun wench I may have been with the night before. I don't like the savages, so's I don't touch 'em."

"Don't fool yourself into thinking you are ever going to take me to your bed," Stephanie said, inching away from him. "I don't know why Adam has made your acquaintance. I see you as nothing but vile."

Damon took a quick step toward her and grabbed her by a slim wrist. He yanked her against him and glowered down at her. "I don't like being talked to like that, especially by a woman," he said between clenched teeth. "I think you need to be taught a lesson or two, and I'm just the gent to do it."

Damon crushed his mouth to Stephanie's, in a wet, slobbering kiss, and her insides grew cold with disgust. She tried to wrench herself free, but he tightened his grip.

Panic seized her when he started lowering her to the ground.

She pushed at his chest. She kicked at him. But none of this stopped his attack.

He threw her to the ground and then loomed over her, leering.

She struggled to get back to her feet, but he was too quick, spreading himself atop her, his mouth again assaulting hers with hard, bruising kisses, one of his hands groping beneath her skirt.

Her one wrist left free, Stephanie saw no other choice

than to draw her derringer from its small holster and hold its barrel against Damon's chest.

"What the—?" Damon gasped, recoiling at the feel of the gun. He moved to his knees and stared blankly at the derringer, stunned that Stephanie had the nerve to pull it on him.

"Put that thing away," Damon said guardedly, moving slowly to his feet.

"Get out of here and leave me alone," Stephanie said, slowly standing, though wobbly.

When Damon did not venture to make a move away from her, Stephanie leveled the derringer at him. "*Now*, Damon, or by God I *will* pull the trigger," she said, her voice a low hiss.

"I think you would," Damon said. He took slow steps away from her. He held his arms out away from himself, as a way to show her that she had gotten her message across. "Just lower that thing, Stephanie. I meant you no harm. I was just havin' a little fun."

"You call that fun?" Stephanie said tersely. She motioned with the firearm. "Go on. I'll take my leave only once I know you are back inside your house. I can see now why Runner shows such little trust in you. You have surely given him and the Navaho many reasons not to."

"What I do ain't none of your business," Damon said, stopping to leer at her. "And don't you go tellin' Adam what happened here. We're partners. We've got things to do."

"What the hell's going on?" Adam said as he ran toward Stephanie. "Is this why you asked me to stay in your house while you had something to get done in the corral?" He gasped as he discovered the derringer being held at Stephanie's side. He gave it a lingering look, then gazed at his sister and saw the fear and anger in her eyes as she stared over at Damon, then he turned toward Damon himself. "Is my sister that business you spoke about? She'd not have her gun drawn on you if you hadn't caused her trouble."

"Like I told her," Damon said, shrugging, "I was just havin' a little fun. I see now that she ain't got no sense of humor."

"Sense of humor?" Stephanie said, her voice breaking. "Adam, he would have raped me if I hadn't drawn the gun on him. His . . . his . . . filthy hand was already up my skirt. He . . . forced . . . me to kiss him. He even forced me to the ground."

"It's only because I found her kissin' the Injun," Damon said, again shrugging. "I just thought she might share some of that lovin' with me after Runner left."

Adam looked quickly over at Stephanie. "You were kissing Runner?" he asked, slowly smiling.

Stephanie lowered her eyes, her cheeks hot with a blush. "Well, yes," she murmured. Then she raised angry eyes at Damon again. "Runner and I were kissing because I allowed it. As for Damon . . ."

Adam's heart was hammering inside his chest, but not because of being repelled over Damon having taken advantage of his sister. Adam saw that his plan to see Stephanie and Runner together had begun to happen. He wanted to shout hallelujah, but instead had to pull himself together and give Damon the scolding that was expected of him.

"Damon, I'd think twice before doing a crazy stunt like that again," Adam said sternly. "If not, you'll have me to answer to."

Adam smiled slyly as he looked over his shoulder at Stephanie, then back at Damon. "But I think my sister can take care of herself, don't you?" he drawled. "You see, Damon, there's something I forgot to tell you about my sister. She might be petite and pretty, but she's been taught not to let any man mess with her if she doesn't want him to."

Adam looked over his shoulder at Stephanie. "Ain't that right, sis?" he said, laughing softly.

Stephanie smiled sweetly as she slipped her derringer back into its holster at her waist.

8

Shall I love you like the fire, love,
With furious heat and noise,
To waken in you all love's fears,
And little of love's joys?
—R. W. RAYMOND

As the heat of the day diminished with the setting of the flaming sun, a breeze moved across the land, stirring the cloudy branches of smoke trees into a whispering. The ocotillo made a faint rattling with its wand-like, thorny bushes. There was a deep breathing sound as the desert was released from the harsh heat of day.

A shadowy figure was riding through the twilight. He lay low over his horse, his raven-black hair blowing in the wind. His eyes were intent on a stray buckskin horse that he was pursuing, its hooves scattering dirt, grass, and sand as it thundered across the land ahead of him.

Thunder Hawk made no sound as he sank his moccasined heels into the flanks of his steed, a tall dappled gray with a black mane and tail and four black stockings. His horse stretched into a swifter run, its stride long, beautiful, and even.

Thunder Hawk swayed easily in the saddle. His one hand held the reins firmly, his other held a rope.

It was hard to resist roping just any horse Thunder Hawk found that strayed onto Navaho land, no matter whose it might be. He needed many to take to his secret corral in a hidden canyon, where he kept those that he was saving to use as a bride price.

A man's importance was judged by the number of horses he owned, and by the number he gave away to win the hand of the woman he loved and wished to marry. Although neither his parents nor his brother knew it just yet, he had plans to take a bride, and soon.

Thunder Hawk sank his knees into the sides of his horse and slapped the reins, realizing that the buckskin was wearing out. He could see how it nervously shook its head back and forth. He could hear its snorts. And he could see the white ghostly breath coming from its nostrils, blowing steam into the air, gathering around the steed in the accumulating frosty shadows of night.

Thunder Hawk plunged his horse into a hard gallop, its thrashing hoofs plowing up a boiling cloud of dust. Gaining ground, he lifted his rope, readied into a lasso. He began swinging the rope overhead, breathless now as he came closer and closer to the gelding.

In one throw, he had the lasso around the gelding's head. Straining all of his youthful muscles, he yanked back. When he finally managed to get the horse to stop, he reined in his own steed to a quavering halt.

Dismounting, Thunder Hawk moved cautiously to the captured gelding. When he reached it, he realized that it was definitely not one of the horses that ran in wild herds. This horse belonged to someone. It had already been tamed for riding. It even nuzzled Thunder Hawk's hand as he offered it to him.

"And so whose *are* you?" Thunder Hawk whispered.

As the gelding pawed and stamped nervously, Thunder Hawk moved moving slowly around the animal, noting its black mane and tail, checking it for a brand.

When he found the brand, a capital D overlapping a capital S, he smiled.

"Damon Stout's," he said. "Did you find the loosened poles?"

He patted the gelding's neck and admired it. He smiled, for he knew the worth of the horse. It was short-coupled and deep-chested with a heavy-muscled sturdiness.

Only last night had he been brave enough to get so close to Damon's pole corral that he could loosen the fence posts. He had hoped that some of Damon's horses would escape for Thunder Hawk to eventually find, to claim as his own.

"I had hoped for more than one horse to take to my corral," Thunder Hawk said, running his hands across the horse's sleek, thick mane. "But for tonight, you will have to do. As it is, I have been gone from home far too long."

After securing the gelding to his horse for its journey to the corral, Thunder Hawk swung himself into his saddle and once again rode across the land. He kept a look out over his shoulder, as he did not want to be caught with another man's horse. At least, not until he obscured the brand that would condemn him as a horse thief.

He especially did not want his brother or father to discover what his nightly hobby had become. He did not yet want to explain about his desire to take a wife. He knew what their reaction would be. He was only seventeen. Their argument would be that he was too young to take on the responsibilities of a wife.

But he had his life and they had theirs. He wanted a wife. He would have one.

After riding for many more miles, Thunder Hawk toiled up a steep slope, the trail swerving cautiously

between pale spears of mescal and green bursts of man-
zanita. Cedars rustled through frayed ribbons of bark
in the dry wind, aromatic from lilac-berried junipers.
The night shadows were dark between the hills.

Thunder Hawk worked his way into a canyon and
proceeded with care up the rocky bed of a dry stream.
On both sides, sandstone boulders rose up into immense split-rock cliffs.

Hoofs clicked over rocks as Thunder Hawk guided
the horses carefully between the rocks. It was now dark.
The way was hazardous in the murky black of night.

Finally the floor of the canyon lifted and widened.
Thunder Hawk came to his private corral on the grassy
floor of the canyon. Happy over his latest catch, he led
the gelding in with the others, then secured the pole
corral and stood and proudly watched his small herd
for awhile.

Thunder Hawk silently counted the number of horses
that were now his. He smiled when he discovered that
he had enough to win the hand of Sky Dancer, the
lovely maiden of his heart who lived in a neighboring
Navaho camp. She was beautiful and petite, and knew
well the art of weaving. She would make an excellent
wife.

His smile widened and his eyes took on a slow gleam.
Marrying Sky Dancer would be convenient to him in
many ways. One major convenience was that once he
was married, surely schooling would no longer be
forced on him. His parents would see that he was a
man who was ready to take on the chores of caring for
a wife.

"They will have no choice but to accept my new
status in life," Thunder Hawk whispered to himself as
he swung up into the saddle and began riding back in

the direction of his village. "What will be done, will be done."

He and Sky Dancer would be married before anyone of his village knew or could stop them. Surely no one would try and make him and Sky Dancer take their vows away from each other once they were spoken.

His shoulders squared, feeling important with his ownership of many horses and his plans to take a wife, Thunder Hawk scarcely realized that there was someone else riding in the path of the light of the half moon. His thoughts dwelled on Sky Dancer.

Soon. He would have her soon.

Suddenly Thunder Hawk was aware of the approaching horseman. He swallowed hard, always fearing being caught while on his nocturnal outings. Although tonight's catch was safely in his secret corral, he could not shake off the feeling of fear that came with running across a stranger in the night. His hand went instinctively to his sheathed knife, then his hand relaxed and his eyes widened when he recognized the horseman.

"Big brother?" he whispered, then rode on ahead and made a wheeling stop beside Runner's stallion.

"Thunder Hawk, what are you doing so far from home?" Runner asked, raising an eyebrow. "Do you know that you give both Mother and Father cause to worry when you disappear for so long?"

Thunder Hawk had always prepared himself for such a surprise confrontation. He lifted his chin and squared his shoulders with confidence. "Thunder Hawk rides alone at night, the only time I feel the true freedom that my ancestors once knew," he said solemnly. "Do you not feel it, also, my brother? The feel of the wind? The quiet of the night? And the touch of something invisible all around you in the night? It is these things that bring me out on my horse, alone. And you? Why are you here? What has taken you away from *your* hogan?"

"There was a council held at Damon Stout's ranch," Runner said stiffly. "I was in attendance."

"You were at Damon's ranch tonight?" Thunder Hawk said, his eyes widening. Then an icy fear crept over him. Should this have been last night, his very own brother might have caught him sneaking around Damon's corral, weakening the poles.

"Why were you at Damon's, Runner?" he said. "What would you have to say to Damon Stout? He is not a friend to sit and smoke with."

"Hardly," Runner said, chuckling low. He reached over and gave his brother a pat on his shoulder. "And if not for one thing that happened at the Stout Ranch, I would have seen this, for the most part, as a waste of your brother's time."

"What could happen there that was good?" Thunder Hawk scoffed. "Anything to do with that man has to be deceitful."

Runner's smile faded, not wanting to think on any possible deceits that might be attached to Stephanie. He wanted her to be separate from any dealings with Adam and Damon. Yet he knew why she was in Arizona Territory, and that, in itself, was a deceit to the Navaho.

Not wanting to think about it anymore this evening, much less talk about it, Runner again gave his brother a pat on the shoulder. "Enough talk tonight," he said. "You need to have some rest. You have to think about having a clear mind when you attend school."

"School," Thunder Hawk said in a hiss. "I hate school."

"If you would allow yourself, you could find your studies interesting," Runner said. He sank his heels into the flanks of his horse, urging it into a gentle lope. He looked over at Thunder Hawk, riding alongside him.

"Little brother, do you not enjoy learning about geography, and how it is in other countries?" he said. "I found it fascinating. Imagine being on a huge ship in a wide body of water headed for the place called England. Do you not think that it would be interesting to see how they treat their Indians? To see if they steal their land and kill their buffalo? In my studies, the teacher did not reveal these things to me."

"You are a dreamer," Thunder Hawk scolded. "Mother placed too many 'dream catchers' on your bed when you were a child."

Runner gave Thunder Hawk a frustrated, annoyed look, then galloped hard away from him.

Dreams. What did his younger brother know about dreams? He did not even know yet how to accept the reality of life!

As the moon spilled in through the open window beside her bed in the private car, Stephanie tossed and turned, pulling the satin sheet one way, and then the other. First she would lie in one position, and then another.

His kiss. His *arms*. How on earth was she expected to go to sleep while remembering being with Runner so vividly?

Shaking her hair back from her shoulders, Stephanie sat up in her bed and sighed. "I just can't go to sleep," she groaned.

Stepping lightly from the bed onto a plushly thick carpet, she slid her feet into slippers and slipped into a silk robe. Tying it at the waist, she moved sleepily toward her darkroom. She would busy her hands by putting her photographic equipment into various satchels. She would tire herself out so much that she would have to go to sleep. It was important to get her needed rest. She and Adam would be on their horses for many hours tomorrow. She wanted to get as many photographs of the scenery as possible before someone attempted to stop her.

It did seem, though, that she would not get the chance to photograph the Navaho, unless she was deceptive. And she did not like the thought of sneaking around doing anything that might displease not only the Navaho as a whole but Runner. After being held by him, and melting in his arms as he kissed her, she did not want anything to stand in the way of their loving one another.

"Yes, love," she whispered, feeling as though she were floating on air at the thought of being with Runner again. "I am truly in love. For the first time in my life I am—"

"Sis?"

Adam's voice outside her car door made Stephanie stop with a start and lose her train of thought. She tightened the sash at her waist and drew her long, lean fingers through her hair to straighten it, then went out to the door and opened it.

"I'm having a hell of a time sleeping," Adam growled, brushing past her. "There's so much to do. I just can't turn my brain off." He turned to her as she closed the door behind them, the moon's soft glow the only light in the room. He smiled mischievously over at Stephanie. "And you? I don't think I have to ask what has kept you awake."

Stephanie struck a match and lit a kerosene lamp, turning the wick up high enough to spray its faint light around her private car. She shook the match out and dropped it in an ashtray, then sank down into a soft, cushioned chair.

"Taking photographs tomorrow, Adam," she said, pulling her feet up beneath her. "That's why I couldn't sleep." She ignored his obvious reference to what he knew had transpired between her and Runner only a few hours ago. "It's the first time I've tried to take my camera among Indians. It worries me."

"Aw, you're worrying about nothing," Adam said, slouching into a chair opposite her. "Leave it up to Runner. Because of his attraction to you, he'll make sure you can do as you damn please."

"I would rather you didn't discuss Runner's feelings toward me with me, or anyone else for that matter," Stephanie said stiffly. "But I do thank you for coming to my defense tonight. Damon Stout is a rogue. How can you associate yourself with him for any reason? I bet if you would look long enough you would find that he has had scrapes with the law. Adam, I see it in his eyes. He is a man with no feelings. He is surely a criminal of some sort."

"You asked me not to discuss Runner with you," Adam said, glowering over at her. "Well, then, sis, I ask the same of you as far as Damon Stout is concerned. My association with him is purely one of business. Once I'm done here, I'll not bother with him anymore."

Stephanie leaned forward. She questioned Adam with her eyes, then leaned back again, knowing that he would not say any more about business affairs with Damon were she to pursue the matter.

Perhaps she was better off not knowing. She feared that whatever Adam's association with Damon might be, they would not be in the best interests of the Navaho. She would never forget how coldly Runner and Damon had treated one another.

Perhaps it best to stay out of those situations. She had enough to worry about, herself, with her own problems at hand.

"Sis, even though you told me not to discuss Runner with you, I've got to ask," Adam said, giving her a guarded look. "Is there a strong attraction between the two of you?"

"Adam, please," Stephanie said, standing quickly. She went into her darkroom and lit a lamp. She stiffened when Adam came after her and held a satchel open, so that she could place plates inside it.

"Stephanie, since there is obviously already something going on between you and Runner, play up to him," Adam said, his jaw tight as he watched for her reaction. "Get him on my side. I need Runner, Stephanie. If I'm to expect no trouble from the Navaho, I need Runner's alliance."

Stephanie turned angry eyes to Adam. She placed her hands on her hips and spoke up into his face. "Now, you listen here, Adam," she warned. "Just keep your suggestions to yourself. Especially those concerning Runner. You know I'm not the sort to play those types of games with men."

"Aw, sis, this is different," Adam said, setting the satchel of plates aside. "Come on. For me? For your brother? You know how important this project is to me. I want to have this town worse than anything else I've wanted in my entire life. With your help, it could happen much more easily and quickly."

"I'll have no part in your schemes," Stephanie said, brusquely brushing past him. She left the darkroom and stepped to a window. She looked at the shadowed mountains in the distance, wondering where Runner was and if he was also having trouble sleeping. She had felt the need and hunger in his kiss. She knew without a doubt that he was falling in love with her. She would not take any risks that might turn his feelings into loathing.

Adam placed his hands on her waist and turned her around to face him. "Stephanie, I've never asked for much from you," he said thickly. "But this time, I've got to. You've got to do whatever you can to get Runner on my side. Do you hear? Anything."

Stephanie's lips quavered as she stared up at her stepbrother. "You would even have me seduce him if it comes to that, Adam, to draw him into your schemes?" she said, her voice breaking. "You truly want me to do even that?"

"Well, yes, if you believe that is what it would take to achieve my goals," Adam said. He jumped and gasped when Stephanie slapped him across the face.

"How could you, Adam?" Stephanie said. She glared up at him, her fists doubled at her sides. "Now listen well to what I have to say, for it is the last time I shall say it. If you see me with Runner, and should I be showing affection for him in *any* way, it will only be because I want to be with him because I have true feelings for him. I won't be with him because of a brother who is blinded by greed."

Adam's eyes narrowed as he gingerly stroked his stinging cheek. "Dear, sweet sister," he ground out between clenched teeth, "you are as blinded by greed as much as I. You have come a long way to make money by taking photographs, haven't you? You knew that the Indians would not want you here, yet you came anyway. Because of money, Stephanie. That's why you're here. Nothing else."

Stephanie paled and took a step away from him. She was shaken by what he had just said, knowing that, in part, it was true.

"Touché, brother," she said flatly, then walked away, her chin held high.

The money that she had expected to make *had* sounded good to her. But now, after meeting Runner . . . ?

Money was no longer the entire fascination of being in Arizona Territory. She had to find a way of balancing her love of photography with the love and passion of the handsome "White Indian."

Money came last, now, in her list of priorities.

9

Guard her, by your truthful words,
Pure from courtship's flatteries.
   —ELIZABETH BARRETT BROWNING

Adam at her side, Stephanie stood on a sandstone ledge, gazing out onto a land fed by roistering small streams of delicious, cold water. The vast, empty sky was a cornflower blue directly above, which darkened gradually to a deep, rich turquoise before it finally met the distant mountain peaks.

The morning had been long, but the length of time had been scarcely noticed by Stephanie as she had so excitedly taken photographs. She had become enamored by everything about this lovely land. She could see why the Navaho did not want to lose their rights to the land. Wanting to be as one with the land could become an addiction. She felt the bond already, and she had only been there a very short time.

"Don't you think we'd better call it a day if you want to stop by the Navaho village?" Adam said, tipping his wide-brimmed hat back from his brow. He smiled and wiped a smudge of dirt from his sister's face. "Or do you think we should first take a bath in that stream?"

"No, no bath required." Stephanie laughed, handing her camera to Adam. She folded up her tripod. "A hair brushing and a spray of perfume is all I need and I'll feel refreshed enough."

She went to the pack mule that was being used to transport her equipment. "I'm anxious to get to the Navaho village," she tossed over her shoulder. She cast a look at the canopy of blue above, then at the sun, which had drifted from its midpoint. "I'd like to get back to the train before dark," she added.

"Whatever you say, sis," Adam said. He took quick steps toward the pack mule. He secured the camera case in a saddlebag, then took the tripod and tied it to the side of the mule and covered it with a leather drop cloth.

He folded his arms across his chest and gave Stephanie a soft smile as she took a bottle of perfume from the saddlebag on the other side of the mule and gave her shirt a spray. He then watched as she brushed her hair in long strokes, making it glisten in the sunlight.

He was glad that he and Stephanie had made up their differences today, while traveling together. And it would be no problem keeping their relationship this pleasant. He had already said enough about Runner to her. She needed no more reminding about his old friend who was now Navaho in Adam's eyes, instead of white.

When she had suggested that they swing by the Navaho village, to meet Sage's family, Adam realized that she mainly wanted to go there to get a chance to see Runner again. It took no damn crystal ball to figure *that* out. Making herself smell especially good, and taking such effort with her hair, was proof of that.

Adam had quickly agreed to her suggestion. He would play up to the whole Navaho nation, if that became necessary, to sway opinion his way so that the town bearing his name could be built without interference. Somehow, he would soon have the whole damn Navaho tribe eating out of his hands.

"I'm ready to go now," Stephanie said, mounting her horse.

Adam gave her a mock salute and swung himself into his own saddle. They turned their steeds in the direction of the Navaho village. Their bridles jangled. Their horses pranced in a light canter, heads high, obedient to the reins.

When silence fell between Stephanie and Adam, he was keenly aware of it and did not attempt talking to her. One glance told him that she was deep in thought, and he felt confident with whom her thoughts lay: Runner.

He looked at her carefully, as if for the first time. She wore a faded calico shirt tucked into her divided riding skirt. The dark riding shirt was snug about her lithe hips and swung above her ankles, which were covered by undecorated high-heeled riding boots. The sleeves of her shirt were rolled above her elbows and the neck was unbuttoned, the cleavage of her breasts just barely visible.

But she looked no less lovely than if she wore a low-swept, satin ball gown. It did not take fancy clothes to bring out her loveliness. It was all natural, from her pretty nose and rosy lips to her slim and shapely legs. He admired her as all men did, but without passion. Although no blood kin to him, she was his sister, in every way.

Should he have had a true sister, surely their bond could not have been as true as the bond felt between Stephanie and himself.

"Adam," Stephanie said, suddenly looking over at him. "Please try and behave yourself at the Navaho village. Will you please watch what you say?"

Adam was taken aback. His contented feelings of only moments ago were as quickly shattered. "Sis, if you're going to monitor my every word while I am with the Navaho, I think it best that we return to the train instead of going to their village," he said, his eyes cold as he glared at her. "Lord, Stephanie, sometimes I think you don't want my dreams to come true."

"It's not that, Adam," she said, her eyes wavering when she saw how quickly she had angered him. "I just wish there were other ways to make them happen."

"Other than making friends with the Navaho?" he snapped back. "That's what I'm going to do today, Stephanie: make friends. Is that wrong?"

"Not if that was your only motive," Stephanie said. She looked ahead and got her first glimpse of hogans a short distance away.

She cast Adam another quick glance. "For me, Adam?" she softly pleaded. "Please don't say or do anything we both might regret."

Adam wiped a sweaty palm on his dark trousers. "I wouldn't ever purposely do anything to hurt you," he said. "That's all I can promise you. I would think that would be enough."

He scowled at her for a moment longer, then jerked around and stared ahead, silent. He wished now that he had said a flat no to her when she had begged to come with him to Arizona Territory. She could prove to be more of a nuisance than a companion. Yet if she had not been there, he felt that he would have already been at a deadlock with the Navaho.

Adam felt unnerved when they rode into the outskirts of the village, dogs yapping at their heels and people turning to watch. He ignored these people. He was looking straight ahead. His spine stiffened when he saw Sage and Runner step from one of the larger hogans of the village. A lovely woman came quickly to Sage's side, who Adam recognized as Leonida.

Her appearance gave him cause to relax somewhat. He could still feel the warmth of her smile those many years ago, and the sincere hugs that she had given him. Especially when the day came for him to leave the Navaho's stronghold, to return to life as he had known it before being taken captive by Sage and his warriors.

He looked over at Sage. Adam had forgiven him long ago for having taken captives from the stagecoach. While living among the Navaho that short time, with Sage as their leader, he admired the man and the reason behind his decision to take captives. Sage's life had been filled with many injustices.

Adam had to confess to himself that it made him a bit nervous to try and swindle Sage into more injustices, yet he would not, for the world, change what he had started, and would fight for it to the end.

Even if that fight was with Sage.

Tense from the audience of Navaho, Stephanie glued her hands to the reins and sat straight and unmoving in the saddle. Out of the corner of her eye, she could see Navaho women sitting outside in the shade of their hogans. They had momentarily stopped carding and spinning their wool to stare at her and Adam.

Her gaze also took in the flocks of sheep and goats that were corraled behind each Navaho dwelling. A garden of corn and other vegetables was squared off on a small plot of ground a short distance from the corral. From her studies of the Navaho, before coming to Arizona Territory, she had learned that their four sacred plants were corn, squash, beans, and tobacco.

She shifted her gaze and saw that the doors of all of the hogans opened to the east side. She remembered reading that the Navaho constructed their dwellings in this fashion so that they could welcome the morning sun and receive good blessings. An old Navaho house-blessing hymn that she had read came to mind: "Beauty extends from the fireside of my hogan. Beauty radiates from it in every direction."

Stephanie looked ahead. Her heart leapt and her knees grew weak with desire as her eyes met and held with Runner's, where he stood with his parents outside a large hogan.

Self-conscious, she turned her eyes away from him and looked over at Sage. She recoiled somewhat when she saw his sour expression. She knew then that she and Adam were not welcome.

Swallowing hard, she turned her gaze only a short ways, finding the tall and stately woman beside Sage smiling at her. Her eyes were warm, which proved that she indeed welcomed those who were coming today to pay a short visit.

Leonida, Stephanie thought to herself. *That must be Leonida.*

Stephanie's gaze swept over Leonida. She was a beautiful woman of an imposing presence, her wealth of golden hair flowing across her shoulders. She wore a lovely velveteen skirt and blouse, and a lacy apron over the skirt. The apron proved that Leonida had not entirely let go of her white past just because she was married to Sage.

Stephanie looked slowly over at Runner again. She had hoped that by now he would have come to her to welcome her, instead he remained with his parents even after Stephanie and Adam drew rein close by, the pack mule behind them.

Leonida was the first to step forward. She went to Adam, and when he dismounted, she swept him quickly into her arms. "Adam," she said, hugging him tightly. "I need no introductions. You have not changed all that much."

He returned the hug, hope rising within him that *she* might be more willing to help him than anyone.

Leonida stepped away from him and held his hands. "Yes, there is some change," she said, laughing softly. "You are no longer an adorable little boy. You are grown now, and very handsome."

"Mature is more like it," Adam said, chuckling.

"Come inside and tell me about yourself and your mother," Leonida said, ignoring her husband's unpleasant glance. She looked over at Stephanie, then went to her. "You must be Adam's sister. Runner told me all about you."

Stephanie blushed as she cast Runner a soft smile, then moved into Leonida's embrace. She found it comforting, especially now that she could tell that Adam had a fight on his hands as far as Sage was concerned. Sage had yet to smile, or make any effort to welcome her and Adam to his village.

Nor had Runner.

Yet it was in Runner's eyes how he felt. Stephanie knew that she would be welcome anywhere as long as he was there.

Leonida swung away from Stephanie. "Come inside and sit by the fire," she said, lifting the hem of her skirt. "The air is cool today."

She went to Sage and took his hand, their eyes meeting. When she smiled up at him, he was, as always, unable to resist her and went with her inside the hogan with everyone else.

Adam walked beside Stephanie. His heart did a strange sort of flip-flop when he discovered someone sitting beside the fireplace on a Navaho blanket, her sewing resting on her lap.

Adam smiled awkwardly when Pure Blossom turned

her face up to him and gazed raptly at him. A magical connection linked them at first glance.

He swept his eyes over her in silent admiration. She was slight and fragile and ever so beautiful with wide, dark eyes. Her luxurious black hair flowed smoothly over her shoulders, the ends resting on the floor of the hogan.

She wore a blue velveteen blouse and a skirt of bright calico. A beautiful thick string of coral hung around her neck. Just scarcely exposed beneath the long hem of her skirt were moccasins adorned with silver buttons.

Stephanie smiled a thank you as Leonida took her arm and led her over to the fireplace, offering her a comfortable, cushioned hand-hewn chair. She eased into the chair and, as she looked around her, found the interior of the hogan hardly any different from the cabins of other settlers.

The log walls were mellow with flickering light from the great rock and clay fireplace. A stew pot hung over the coals on an iron arm in the fireplace. More food simmered on a huge, black cook stove. The aroma of cabbage and beans wafted through the air from the pots. A pot of coffee sat on the edge of the hearth.

Stephanie could see that at least two more rooms led from the main living quarters and surmised those were bedrooms. She had to wonder if one of those bedrooms belonged to Runner but doubted it. He seemed too independent to sleep under the same roof as his parents.

She smiled at Runner as he eased into a chair not that far from her. She melted when he returned her smile, even though somewhat guardedly.

Her gaze was quickly drawn to Sage.

"You have come without proper invitation to my hogan?" he said, breaking the strained silence as he sat down in a leather chair on the far side of the fireplace.

Adam had sat on the same blanket on the floor with Pure Blossom.

"You know how badly I wanted to see Leonida," Adam said. He accepted a cup of coffee Leonida handed to him. "And I was anxious to meet the rest of your family." He looked over at Pure Blossom. "And this is your daughter?"

"Yes, this is Pure Blossom," Leonida said, placing a hand on her daughter's thin shoulder. "Pure Blossom, you've heard me speak of Adam. Darling, this is he."

Pure Blossom extended a slender hand to Adam. "*Yaa-eh-t-eeh*, hello and welcome. It is good to meet you," she said, her voice so soft it sounded hardly more than a breath of wind.

Adam's hands tremored as he circled his fingers around hers. "It is nice to make your acquaintance, also," he said.

So quickly taken with her, he felt awkward in her presence. He held her hand for only a moment, then slid it away and gripped the saucer and took another sip of coffee from the cup. Yet his eyes were still on Pure Blossom.

Hers were drawn away when her mother spoke to her.

"And, Pure Blossom, this is Stephanie," Leonida said, nodding and smiling over to Stephanie.

Pure Blossom and Stephanie smiled cordially at one another.

"Our son, Thunder Hawk, attends school each day," Stephanie said. She settled down at the foot of Sage's chair and rested an elbow on one of his knees. "I'm sorry he wasn't here to meet you. But in time, you will make his acquaintance."

"Leonida, they have not come solely to make acquaintances," Sage said dryly. "Adam, Runner did not get the opportunity to question you yet about this private spur that is planned to reach Fort Defiance. You tell us now. What are your connections with this new railroad line? Why is it being laid except for purposes of exploiting my people?"

Adam was momentarily at a loss for words. He had not expected to be thrown into such troubled waters so soon. In fact, he had not planned to get into this discussion at all today with Sage. He had yet to get Runner alone first, to encourage him to be his ally. He cursed the very idea now of having come to the village today.

Yet would it be any different tomorrow, or the day after? he despaired to himself.

He now realized that it wouldn't be. He had to face the music today, and perhaps it *was* best to get it over with, after all.

Runner eased to his feet and loomed over Adam, his eyes narrowing at him. At this moment, Stephanie was the farthest thing from his mind. Her brother, Runner's boyhood friend, was the main concern now. Runner doubted that Adam had any answers that would please him, or his father. Too much pointed to Adam being guilty of having come to Arizona Territory for all of the wrong reasons.

"I truly came today only out of friendship," Adam said. He set his cup and saucer aside and slowly rose to his feet. He edged away from Runner and went and stood behind Stephanie. "But if you insist, I do have things that need to be said."

"Continue," Sage said, nodding.

Runner folded his arms across his chest. "But be warned that you best carefully guard what you say," he said. "The private spur. It *is* yours, is it not?" He ignored Stephanie's steady gaze and that his sister was showing too much interest in Adam. He gave Adam a steady, unnerving stare, as though daring him to continue.

"In part, yes," Adam stammered.

"Either it is, or it isn't," Runner said stiffly. "Which is it?"

"If you put it that way, it belongs entirely to the Santa Fe Railroad," Adam said, his jaw tightening.

"Then explain your connections to the railroad," Runner said, taking a step closer to Adam. "Stephanie once referred to the private spur being yours. Explain how it can be yours one day, and it is not the next?"

"It's too complicated to explain in detail," Adam said. He shuffled his feet nervously when all eyes became intent on him. "To make it short, the spur is being built at my request, but at the expense of the Santa Fe Railroad."

"And why would they agree to such an exorbitant, wasteful expense?" Runner prodded.

Sage allowed his son to continue with the questions, since he was succeeding at putting Adam at a disadvantage. He smiled smugly as Adam noticeably became more uneasy.

"If you must know," Adam said tightly, "the private spur will go past Fort Defiance and further still into Navaho land, for the development of a town for tourists. This town would be run by me. It would bear my name."

"That cannot be allowed to happen," Sage said, unable to keep quiet. He stood to his full height, towering over Adam. "The Santa Fe Railroad right-of-way closes off further Navaho advance."

"Sage, you know that a series of presidential executive orders have added expanse after expanse of land to the Navaho Treaty Reservation," Adam defended. "I will go farther to say that it seems to me that you are too greedy with this land."

Sage was fighting to control his anger. He glared at Adam. "The reservation is not all good pasture land," he grumbled. "There are great barren stretches far from water."

"Yes, I am sure that is true," Adam said. He purposely softened his tone, afraid to anger Sage too much. He did not want to have to watch his back every time he rode away from the safe confines of his train. "But there are countless new horizons that still exist for not only the Navaho but the white man. Surely you can feel it. Whenever you hear the whistle of a train you should be proud. There is room for everyone's expansion."

"The black iron fiend has already brought a new evil to this land," Sage grumbled. "The Navaho never had much to do with liquor before the train brought drunken white men to our land. The new railroad towns have saloons. The men who frequent them are tough, hard-drinkers. These men offer alcohol to our innocent youth. They become shameful in the eyes of their people when they come staggering into town, stinking and drunk."

"In moderation, alcohol doesn't hurt anyone," Adam defended.

"It is a new, cheap way to happiness and security," Sage said somberly. "Those Navaho who have become discouraged in life are those who are lured into drinking the firewater. The train will bring more and more liquor to our young men. The trains are worthless. I can *never* approve."

"Sage, locomotives are a national obsession," Adam said. "It is only natural that there are differing views of their value."

"I also do not approve of a town that will scar our beloved land and bring more saloons to our land," Sage stated. "Our native culture holds the earth as sacred and inviolate. It is not to be torn up, but to be lived in, in a state of grace and harmony with the beneficent power emanating from the rhythm of nature."

"Sage? Runner? Please listen to reason," Adam pleaded. "The railroad is a vehicle in the quest for a sense of belonging to this vast country," he said slowly. "The railway is the artery of the nation's life. As it will become to the Navaho nation. My town? It will be a place for white people to come and see your people as they are. They will soon see that you are wrongly labeled 'savage.'"

Stephanie was quiet. She became more tense as the debate wore on. She looked up at Runner and flinched at the bitter expression on his face, then grimaced when she looked over at Sage. She felt surrounded by hate. Her brother may have just ruined all chances of her ever becoming closer to Runner.

Not wanting anyone to see the shine of tears in her eyes, she lowered them.

"Adam, you have said enough," Sage said, angrily folding his arms across his chest. "I will hear no more talk of railroads or towns that will bear your name." He stomped out of the hogan. After him went Adam.

Stephanie scarcely breathed. She feared that Adam and Sage might come to blows outside the hogan. Instead, she heard a horse galloping away, leaving an eerie silence in its wake.

Runner went to the door of the hogan and peered outside. "Adam is gone," he said over his shoulder. "Father is now sitting among the elders."

Stephanie scrambled to her feet and went to Runner. She placed a gentle hand on his arm. "I'm sorry about my brother's behavior," she said, not only stunned by how heatedly Adam had dared to argue with Sage and Runner, but his having left her behind.

"Your brother speaks hastily and with no respect for those of his past," Runner said. He turned to Stephanie. "But none of this is your fault. You will not be blamed for your brother's rudeness."

"But still, I guess I'd better go," Stephanie murmured. "I think I have overstayed my welcome."

Leonida went to Stephanie. "My dear, stay as long as you wish," she said. "Would you stay for supper? That would please me so much."

Stephanie smiled awkwardly over at Runner, then into Leonida's warm eyes. "I can think of someone who would not enjoy seeing me share supper with you," she said. "But thank you, anyhow."

"I shall escort you home," Runner said, already ushering her outside by her elbow. "It is not safe for women to ride alone so far."

She caught him glancing down at her firearm, then smiled up at him. "As you see, I am prepared for being alone," she said, laughing softly.

"Yet still, it never hurts to have a man at your side," Runner said.

She stiffened when she looked over at her pack mule and the camera equipment secured on its back. She was afraid that Runner would ask about it. She couldn't chance angering the Navaho any more today with talk of cameras, especially Runner.

She was glad when he didn't seem to notice, his interest drawn to his horse as a young lad brought it to them.

"I accept your offer," Stephanie said. She mounted her horse, thrilled at the thought of being with him,

away from the traumas of moments ago. She was glad
that he did not cast blame on her for Adam's behavior.

Perhaps, she and Runner could be closer because of
it. He seemed to feel protective of her, possibly to the
extent of even wanting to protect her from her own
brother.

Again she stiffened when Runner looked at the mule
as he swung himself into his saddle. She breathed out
a deep sigh of relief when he said nothing, instead nodded for her to follow as he sank his heels into the flanks
of the stallion and rode away.

Remembering Adam's handsomeness, Pure Blossom
stood at the hogan door. He was the first man that had
caused her to feel like a woman, and he was a man that
she feared. He did not seem the sort to be true friends
to the Navaho, or to his word. For certain, he was not
a man to whom she could trust her feelings and heart.

Trying to forget him, she walked away, toward her
own private hogan.

Leonida watched her daughter. She had seen Pure
Blossom's behavior while Adam had been there. Pure
Blossom had not been able to take her eyes off the man.

Leonida sighed and went back inside her hogan and
began making flatbread from wheat flour, sickened over
today's turn of events. Hardly ever did she see her husband so adamant about anything, or as bitter.

She feared what was going to transpire these next
few weeks due to his inability to accept changes to his
homeland. But she knew that he would soon realize he
had no choice but to again accept what he could not
control, as he had learned to accept being forced onto
a reservation all those years ago and so many other
injustices that had been forced upon him and his people.

She saw these changes as never-ending. She knew

that Sage also saw this, and feared that could make him grow old before his time.

Feeling so utterly helpless to do anything in her husband's defense, tears splashed from Leonida's eyes. She suddenly felt old, herself. So very, very old.

10

Fly not yet—'t is just the hour
When pleasure, like the midnight flower,
That scorns the eye of vulgar light,
Begins to bloom for sons of night,
And maids who love the moon!
          —THOMAS MOORE

Stephanie savored the last light of the fading sun as her horse clattered along beside Runner's into a narrow, shale-strewn floor of a box canyon, its one entrance almost clogged by a rubble of boulders. She was in awe of the unbelievable beauty that surrounded her. She drew a tight rein, Runner soon following her lead.

"I do understand why your people are against the railroad," she said, turning to him. "Truly I do. Undisturbed, this land is so beautiful . . . so serene. I can imagine how you must feel when you hear the screaming of the train as the whistle echoes across the virgin land of your people."

"Yes, I see in your eyes that you have an understanding most white people don't have," Runner said. He edged his horse closer to hers. "It is evident that you and Adam do not share the same blood. You are nothing at all like him."

"Since our parents married, we have shared much in our lifetime," Stephanie said. Her pulse raced at the mere closeness of Runner. "We have shared excitement about many things. I was even excited for him and his plans for this private railroad spur and the town that he has dreamed of since he was twelve."

"He remembered the land as it was when he was here as a captive of my father." Runner scowled. "Its seduction began even then."

"I imagine so," Stephanie said, nodding.

Runner motioned with a hand toward a bluff that was only a short ride away. "Come," he urged softly. "Share a place with me where I have come often to watch the moon replace the sun in the sky. It is a place of quiet. It is a place that shows off the wonders of this land."

"I would love to see it," Stephanie said, her heart racing. She felt as though there wasn't, nor ever could be, any animosity between them. It did not seem at all like he held her responsible for anything that Adam was planning.

Yet, there was her love of photography. Somehow that had been lost in the shuffle of conversation and heated arguments about the private spur line, and Adam's town. But she knew that she could not elude the talk of cameras and what she wanted to do with them for much longer. Her photography equipment was there, so close. All that Runner had to do was lift the leather drop cloth and look inside her saddlebags.

She wheeled her horse around and rode with him in this twilight hour, grasping tightly to her reins and straining to keep in the saddle as he led her up a steep incline.

They finally reached the summit where the land leveled off, and where the panorama from this vantage point was well worth waiting for. The sky was all pinks and shadowed blues, darkening along the horizon where a velvet moon was just barely visible.

She rode to the very edge with Runner and looked

out across the great expanse of land that was notched about by canyon openings, shadowed and dark, their craggy floors rising steeply to the rocky passes. Miles upon miles of beautiful, arid landscape lay before her, and off in the distance the mountains were the crowning glory.

There was already some snow on their peaks, glistening orange against the final, last splashes of the sunlight as it slid from view. With sundown, the wall of shadows moved slowly down from the heights. A hazy stillness was over the valley below.

"It is so peaceful," Stephanie said, turning to Runner. She was surprised to find that he had dismounted and was at the side of her horse, offering her his arms.

Runner gazed at her loveliness, her face blushed with evening's quiet pink. "Stay here with me for awhile?" he said. His heart raced when she gave him a nod and allowed him to help her from her horse.

She slipped slowly to the ground and went with him as they tethered their horses and the pack mule under a rim of rock. She turned to him and eased into his arms as though it were a natural thing to do.

"You are so beautiful," Runner whispered, weaving his fingers through her lustrous, long hair, drawing her lips closer to his. "It is easy to forget everything at this moment but you."

"There *is* nothing but you and I," Stephanie whispered back, sliding closer to him. She trembled as he leaned himself into the curve of her body, yet feared the torrents of feelings that were swimming through her. She feared giving herself to him as easily as she felt inclined to. She had never made love with a man before. She had never even seen a man undressed.

But until now, she had never been in love before. It was easy to forget the differences that might come between them. Now was all that mattered. She was heady with desire. She was breathless.

Stephanie closed her eyes as Runner pressed his mouth into her lips, making her go instantly weak and dizzy. She wove her arms around his neck, not questioning when he began lowering her to the ground, where the grass made a soft bed upon which to lie.

Her heart pounded when he rose over her and nudged her legs apart with one of his knees. Although their clothes were a barrier between them, Stephanie felt the heat of his need through both his fringed buckskin breeches and her travel skirt as he began pressing his hardness where she throbbed unmercifully with a need that she had never known before.

She could feel the shape of him, the long, thick pulsing of his shaft as he moved rhythmically against her.

She was mindless with passion.

As though practiced in the skills of being with a man, she worked her hands up the front of his shirt and frantically spread her fingers over his broad chest. Wantonly, she moved her fingers lower and unfastened his breeches in front and swept a hand down to touch that part of him that was sending her blood into a quickening she knew might be dangerous, yet was deliciously sweet.

Runner gasped with pleasure when he felt the heat of her hand surround his throbbing shaft. He turned his mouth from her lips and burrowed his nose against the long column of her throat. He scarcely breathed when her fingers explored this tender, hot part of his anatomy. He held his eyes tightly closed. He gritted his teeth.

Unable to stand anymore, he drew her hand away.

Standing, he reached a hand to Stephanie.

Completely under his spell, Stephanie took his hand

and rose slowly to her feet. They stood for a moment while only looking deeply into one another's eyes, and then Runner placed a hand to her cheek.

"I want you," he said huskily.

"I need you," Stephanie said, her voice sounding strange to her.

"I want to fight my feelings for you, but my heart will not allow it," Runner said, his dark eyes showing a hidden torment in their depths. "I do not know how it is possible, but I know that I have loved you *ka-biki-hozhoni-bi*, forever. A love this intense cannot be born of only a few days . . . of only a few hours."

"I shall always love you," Stephanie said, flinging herself into his arms. "No matter how long I have known you, I know that what I feel is real and true. Make love to me, Runner. Please? I never knew the meaning of want until I met you. Please show me why, Runner. Now?"

Runner leaned her away from him and framed her face between his fingers. "I will be the first man for you?" he said thickly.

Stephanie's eyes widened as she looked up at him. "How . . . did . . . you know?" she murmured.

"There are many ways a man can tell," Runner said, his fingers lowering to undo her blouse. "Do not ask how."

Stephanie willingly lifted her arms so that he could remove her blouse and undergarment. Her heart raced as she watched him drop the clothes to the ground, his eyes on her breasts.

And then his hands were on them.

She closed her eyes and sucked in a quavering breath as his hands kneaded her breasts, his thumbs circling her nipples.

When he fully cupped them in his hands and lowered

his lips to one of them, to flick his tongue over the taut tip of the nipple, Stephanie's knees almost buckled beneath her from the pure ecstasy of the moment.

And then his hands were at her skirt. After it was unfastened, he slowly pushed it down, over her hips and away from her. He continued undressing her until she was standing abashedly nude before him.

Unflinchingly, Stephanie could hardly stand the rapture that she was feeling when Runner began moving his hands over her body. When he came to that soft patch of hair between her legs, and he cupped it within the palm of his hand, Stephanie had to bite her lower lip to keep herself from crying out from the exquisite sweetness that it caused within her.

She tilted her head back and sighed when he began to rub his fingers where she throbbed. The more he caressed her, the more she felt a strange sort of wondrous bliss floating through her. She moaned with pleasure, then opened her eyes slowly when she felt nothing more.

As she opened her eyes, she found Runner stepping out of his final garment. Her gaze swept over him, seeing how much more tall and lithe and muscled he was without clothes.

She could feel the pulse of her desire quickening when her searching eyes stopped on that part of a man's anatomy that, until tonight, had been a mystery to her. She stared at his thick shaft, standing out away from him.

Suddenly she was afraid. "I don't know," Stephanie said. She took a step away from him, her eyes glued to the part of him that seemed to get larger by the minute.

"Do not fear anything," Runner said, reaching out for her hands, taking them. "You will know nothing except passion when our bodies intertwine. We will become one body, one soul, one heartbeat. You will know nothing but sheer pleasure."

And she believed him when she became enraptured by the sure strength of his arms as he embraced her. He leaned over her with burning eyes and kissed her feverishly and hungrily, his body leaning against hers, urging her once again to the ground.

While his knee nudged her legs apart, his mouth forced her lips open. He gathered her into his arms, their kiss growing more and more passionate.

Stephanie was filled with a strange, wild desire, her urgent hands discovering the contours of his back, moving down to feel the hardness of his buttocks.

It was then that her breath was stolen away, for it was at this instant that he thrust himself into her, breaking the barrier that had been untouched since birth.

Stephanie's eyes flew open wide and she jerked her lips from him. Tears streaming from her eyes, she gazed up at him.

Knowing what she must be thinking, the fear in her eyes revealing all, Runner did not venture to thrust deeply inside her. He placed his hands gently on her cheeks.

"The pain you felt was natural." He gave her a soft, reassuring smile. "Do not fear it. It will go away. Relax. Allow your body to become acquainted with pleasure."

Stephanie wiped tears from her eyes and nodded eagerly. "I'm not afraid," she whispered. "Please go on. Just being with you is wonderful."

"But that is not the pleasure I am talking about." His hips began to move slowly, moving farther into her, a fraction of an inch at a time. "Take a deep breath. Close your eyes. Kiss me. And allow yourself to feel the wonders of our bodies locked together."

Stephanie nodded and closed her eyes. She sucked in

a wild breath when she felt his lips and tongue on her breasts. She could feel herself relaxing as she felt him filling her, deeper and deeper. She lifted her hips to him and opened herself to him, now feeling the rapture spreading.

Runner pressed his cheek against one of her breasts and closed his eyes. He reached his hands around her and splayed his fingers across the soft, round mounds of her buttocks and lifted her higher against him as he pressed endlessly deeper into her. His heart was pounding. His loins were on fire. He could feel white lightening spread through his veins.

Once again he kissed her. Their moans mingled. Their hands clasped and unclasped. Their bodies lurched, rose, and fell.

And then came their climax. It was shattering, violent.

As though practiced, Stephanie arched upward to him, sucking him deeply inside her as she felt spasms rocking her.

They shuddered and cried out against one another's lips, then lay still, their wet bodies clinging together.

Runner pressed his lips against Stephanie's throat and kissed her, then rolled away from her and lay on his back and stared at the star-speckled heavens.

Stephanie moved close to him, her skin tingling at the touch of his hand on her thigh. "I never knew it could be this wonderful," she said, marveling over him. "I love you, Runner. I adore you."

Runner turned to her. His fingers reached up to entwine in Stephanie's hair. He drew her lips to his. "Believe me when I tell you that there has never been anyone that has touched my heart as deeply as you," he said huskily against her lips. "I could never feel this way again about anyone."

He paused, then leaned up on an elbow. "And what

are we to do about Adam?" he blurted out. "I dislike everything that Adam stands for. So does my father. And as far as my father is concerned, his dislike might include you, because you are Adam's sister."

"In so many ways, yes, I *am* his sister, yet not in the ways that are important," Stephanie said, smoothing Runner's dark hair back from his face. "Darling, let's not allow Adam or your father to interfere in how we feel for one another. Let us live in our own little private world. Can we? Is that possible? We can place ourselves above everything and everyone. We can pretend that we are the only two people in the world. Anyhow, at this moment, that is how I *feel*."

A chill wind blew suddenly across them, causing Stephanie to shiver.

Runner noticed her discomfort. He rose to his feet and gathered her clothes into his hands. "Get dressed," he said thickly. "I would not want to be the cause of you taking pneumonia."

Stephanie rose to her feet and began dressing. "My love, were I to take a chill, I would be as much to blame as anyone," she said, giggling. "Runner, I can't believe this has happened. I have waited for so many years to find the right man. It seems that is you, my darling. I hope you truly don't object."

While talking and dressing, she had looked away from Runner, paying no heed to what he was doing. She had thought that it would take him as long to get into his clothes as herself.

But when she lifted her eyes, she discovered that she was wrong. He was fully clothed and was at the pack mule, opening one of the saddlebags.

Stephanie grew cold inside and gasped behind one of her hands as Runner took out the camera.

As he studied the camera for a moment beneath the

spill of the moonlight, she began moving stealthily toward him. Just as she reached him, she felt faint when he turned and gave her a sour look and lifted the camera, his full intent to throw it to the ground to destroy it.

"This, alone, is a betrayal of what we just shared!" Runner snarled out.

"No!" Stephanie screamed, raising a hand to stop him.

11

Love found you still a child,
Who looked on him and smiled.
—JOHN NICHOLS

Stephanie quickly placed her hand over Runner's before
he had the chance to toss her camera to the ground.
"Please don't," she said, her voice drawn. "If you do,
that act alone will be a betrayal to what we shared only
moments ago. You knew that I was a photographer. You
knew that I had come to Arizona to take photographs."

"I was foolish for having forgotten that," Runner
said. He still held the camera threateningly over his
head, even though her hand was on his, persuading him
to lower it.

"Runner, please listen to what I have to say, and then
decide whether or not you want to destroy my camera,"
Stephanie said softly. "If you destroy the camera without first listening to reason, then I fear our relationship
will be just as quickly shattered."

Wide-eyed and waiting, she held her breath.

Runner slowly lowered it to his side, and then slipped
it back inside Stephanie's saddlebag; tears of relief
flooded her eyes. He had just proven his love for her.
She could tell that he hated the sight of her camera
and, in turn, what it represented; it was a further way
to exploit his people.

Yet for her, he had decided not to destroy it.

"Thank you," she murmured. She went to him and gazed up, daring to take one of his hands.

"Darling, please hear me out, and then if you want nothing more to do with me, I will ride away and never bother you again," she said, her voice breaking.

"Say what you must," Runner said, his eyes looking into hers. "I will listen."

"Runner, I mean your people no harm." She reached a hand to his cheek. "Darling, I have had time to think this through since my arrival to Arizona. I have decided to carefully show the American people, through my photographs, that the Navaho people are dignified, and that their men are proud warriors who have forever striven for heroic qualities and a sense of heritage. How could there be any harm in that?"

"Harm?" He took her hands and held them to his chest. "My people do not wish to be in pictures, no matter who takes them. But I will say this to you, my love. I will accompany you while you carry your camera from place to place, but it will only be used to photograph Arizona's landscape, not its *people*. Nothing sacred will be captured by film. Do you understand? Can you live by those rules while in Navaho land? If so, I will assist you."

Stephanie was at a loss for words. She had never expected him to allow her to follow through on taking any more photographs, much less say that he would help her.

She was filled with awe. She could never love him more than at this moment, for she saw that he was offering a great sacrifice on his part.

"You would do this for me?" she said, choking back a joyous sob.

"It is something my father will not approve of, but,

yes, I will ride with you while you are taking your photographs," Runner said. Deep within his heart he wanted to please her, yet knew that he was doing this mainly for his people. He would make sure that Stephanie stayed away from the Navaho. He would also make sure that she did not get near any of their sacred rocks, places of prayer, or burial grounds. He saw his motives as selfish, but necessary.

"I don't want to cause trouble between you and your father," Stephanie said, searching his face eagerly with her eyes.

"My father's business and my own do not always go hand in hand." He smiled down at her. "If so, I would not be with you tonight. For you see, my pretty one, my father warned me against falling in love with you."

"He did?" Stephanie said, her eyes widening.

"Remember the first day we met?" Runner said, wrapping his arms around her. "He saw then how I felt about you. It was then, on our way to our home, that he warned me."

"I regret that he doesn't approve of me," Stephanie said.

"It is not so much you that he fears." He placed a finger to her chin and lifted her eyes to meet his. "It is the future of his son, and the color of children who might be born to him."

"What?" Stephanie said, gasping.

"He wishes for grandchildren with the skin, eyes, and hair of the Navaho," Runner said softly. "But when he said this to me, I reminded him that I was white, and that it had never before seemed to matter to him."

"I don't see how it could," Stephanie murmured. "Runner, you are so special. So very, very special."

"It is good that you think that." He wove his fingers through her hair and drew her lips to his mouth.

As wolves howled at the moon in the distant hills, Runner gave Stephanie a long, deep kiss.

Damon Stout rode slouched in his saddle as he traveled across his pasture land, mentally counting horses. He had found the broken pole fence and had suspected foul play.

He had been right. More than one horse was missing. Over the last several nights, someone had helped themselves to his horses.

Damon drew a tight rein. His ranch hands stopped and circled around him.

Damon sucked on a cigar that was no longer lit. He looked from man to man. "You know what's got to be done, don't 'cha?" he growled out.

"Raid Sage's horses," one of his men said, laughing boisterously. "I kind of like it that he's become a thief. It's put a bit of excitement in my life besides whiskey and women. It's got me goin' again."

"You think Sage did this?" another cowhand piped up. "He seems to have more sense than that."

"It's either Sage or Runner," Damon said, glowering. "But then, of course, there's always Thunder Hawk."

He sank his shiny spurs into the flanks of his horse, causing it to rear, then thundered off beneath the moonlight.

"Come on, gents, we've some horses to steal," he shouted, laughing into the wind.

Still fuming over the afternoon's outcome, Adam was perched on his horse on a high butte that overlooked Sage's village. He hadn't gone straight home. He was too angry at Sage, and even more upset when he had seen Stephanie leave the Navaho village with Runner.

But when he just as quickly remembered why this

could work in his favor, he had not followed them. He hoped this would give Stephanie a chance to grow closer to Runner, and he, in turn, to her. Adam would allow them to become involved, short of marriage.

He would never allow Stephanie to become a part of this savage tribe. She would be on that damn train with him when he left Arizona, to return to their hometown of Wichita, Kansas.

His attention returned to the valley below. He leaned over his horse and peered through the velvety cloak of night at some activity at the far end of Sage's pole corral.

"Why I'll be damned," he said to himself, laughing. "Would you look at that? It's Damon and his ranch hands. They're stealin' horses from Sage."

He watched until they rode away, feeling confident in Damon as his ally. It was smart of Damon to steal the horses right now, to help draw attention away from Adam and his own personal plans.

"Yep, he was smart to think that one up," Adam said, still chuckling.

Then he stiffened and his hand went to the rifle in the gun boot as he saw movement elsewhere, on a slight rise of land just beneath the butte he was on. His heart skipped a beat; it was Pure Blossom, Sage's beautiful daughter.

His pulse raced as he slid from his saddle, took his horse behind some bushes, and tethered it to a low limb. As quietly as possible, he began moving down the side of the slope, knowing that he would not pass up this opportunity to be with the pretty lady that had stolen his heart the moment he had laid eyes on her. The sound of her soft voice singing wafted up to him through the soft velvet of night as he moved stealthily onward, his heart pounding, quite taken by the sweetness of the voice, and by the lady herself.

He listened intently as he moved gradually closer . . . and closer . . .

On bended knees, her eyes heavenward, Pure Blossom poured her feelings from her heart, in song. She sang—

> "Voice above,
> Voice of thunder,
> Speak from the
> dark of the clouds;
> Voice below,
> Grasshopper voice,
> Speak from the
> green of plants;
> So may the earth
> be beautiful.
> So may my thoughts
> be pure . . . and beautiful."

She stopped with a start and listened to the crackling of a branch behind her. Moving slowly to her feet, she turned and waited and watched.

When Adam stepped into view, Pure Blossom gasped and took a step back from him. She recalled the angry words her father had exchanged with this handsome man and knew that any feelings that she might have for him were wrong and dangerous.

He was dangerous.

Yet she could not deny her feelings. Her knees were trembling. She felt an odd queasiness at the pit of her stomach that felt wonderfully sweet. She could not deny the throbbing of her heart, or the wild desire she felt for Adam as he stepped closer to her.

"I did not mean to disturb your song," Adam said,

stopping only an arm's length from her. He feared going closer; he desired her so much his whole insides ached.

Ah, but she was beautiful. Frail, yet so pretty it made his heart bleed with need of her.

"You did not disturb my song," Pure Blossom said in correct English, which she had learned in the white man's school. "I was finished."

"Isn't it dangerous for you to be here alone?" Adam dared to ask, not wanting to put any more fear of him in her heart than was already visible in her eyes.

"Perhaps," Pure Blossom said weakly. "My father would say that it was not wise for me to be with you."

"You have no reason to be afraid of me, ever," Adam said quietly. "Please remember that my quarrel isn't with you. It's solely with your father—and Runner."

"Why must there be problems between you?" Pure Blossom said, relaxing somewhat. "If you had come to our land for peaceful purposes, I would be free to . . ."

She lowered her eyes quickly, having almost admitted too much to this man whose mere presence made her head swim with rapture. He was a stranger and she had fallen in love with him too quickly.

Adam's whole body seemed to be one heartbeat as he stepped up to her and lifted her chin with a finger. "You would be free to what?" he said huskily.

"To love you," Pure Blossom blurted out, then leaned into his arms and offered her lips to him.

Adam swept his arms around her and drew her tightly against him. When their lips met, he found himself filled with pleasure he had long denied himself. Business ventures had always taken precedence over women. But now?

Now he wanted it to be the same, but, oh, Lord, it

wasn't. This pretty Navaho woman felt like an angel in his arms and her lips were as sweet as honey.

Pure Blossom moved her lips against his ear. "Come with me," she whispered. "Make love with me in my hogan."

Adam was torn by his feelings. He was stunned that this beautiful woman was offering herself to him so easily. Yet he knew the dangers of going to her village with her. If Sage caught him, he would surely issue a death warrant!

"I'd best not," he whispered back, fighting his passionate desire. "Let's make love here. Beneath the stars."

Pure Blossom leaned away from him. "The air is getting cold," she said. She placed a gentle hand to his cheek and softly stroked his flesh. "As you have surely seen, Pure Blossom cannot stand the cold. I must never get a chill, or it might be fatal."

Adam brushed a kiss across her lips, then swung her up into his arms and carried her toward the slope of land that would lead him to his horse.

"This is not the direction of my hogan," Pure Blossom murmured, smiling up at him. "Turn around. That will take you there."

"My horse," Adam said. "I must get my horse."

"Leave your horse here," Pure Blossom said, as she clung around his neck. "That way no one but myself will know you are in my hogan."

Adam looked with wavering eyes up at the bluff overhead, then concluded that his horse was far enough from the village, and too well hidden, for anyone to see it.

"All right, so the horse is taken care of," Adam said, turning to carry Pure Blossom down the slope. "Now what about me?"

"I know ways of getting you in my dwelling without anyone seeing," Pure Blossom said, giggling softly.

"If you can get me into your hogan without being seen, I guess I can get out as easily," Adam said, shrugging. "I want you, Pure Blossom. I'll take whatever chance I must just to be with you."

"You are the first for Pure Blossom," she said, her eyes innocently wide. "It is fate that has brought you to me. My body has been saved just for you."

Adam worried about this all being too easy; it did seem as far-fetched as some of the novels that he had read by a midnight fire.

A thought came to him. Was this . . . a trap?

Yet his need for her overpowered his fears and made him forget the dangers that might be waiting for him in the Navaho village. There was a fire in his blood that only Pure Blossom could extinguish.

He held her close and broke into a slow run, with only one thing on his mind.

Gratification.

12

I sleep with thee, and wake with thee
And yet thou art not there.
                    —JOHN CLARE

Filled with the memory of her time with Runner, Stephanie had hardly slept all night. Early morning light was just seeping into the windows of her private car and she was already dressed for her exciting day with Runner.

Her hair drawn back and tied with a ribbon, and dressed in her demure travel clothes—a fresh skirt and blouse, and polished boots—she felt ready to tackle many miles today. Especially with Runner at her side, leading her to the various places that he would allow her to photograph.

Her hand drifted to the derringer that lay on the nightstand beside her bed, then she shrugged off the notion of taking it today. She needed no further protection while she was with Runner.

Humming beneath her breath, she strolled lightly into the small kitchenette that had been built at the far end of her private car, opposite her dark room, and picked up a steaming pot of coffee from the small cookstove.

After she poured herself a cup, she went to the door that led outside to a small walkway to Adam's car. She had not yet told him what her plans were for today, and that she didn't need his escort.

She swirled around, laughing, uncaring that she was clumsily splashing coffee, dizzied by the thought of being with Runner for an entire day.

"Together—we'll be together," she said, laughing drunkenly.

Her laughter faded as she stopped and stared at the door again. "I guess I'd best go and tell Adam." She set her cup aside.

She left her private car and raised her hand to knock on Adam's door, then paused and listened for any movement inside. He hated to be awakened, but she had no choice but to go against his wishes this morning. She knew that it was best to tell Adam what her plans were today before Runner arrived. She was going to try and keep those two separated as much as possible. She had no idea what to expect of them if the bitterness they now felt for one another was allowed to get out of hand.

The breeze between the two railroad cars made shivers race up and down Stephanie's spine. She gave a brisk knock on Adam's door, then hugged herself with her arms in an effort to ward off the chill.

While waiting for him to come to the door she looked toward the mountains. She was glad to see the first glimpse of the sun easing its way upward. Soon the air would be warm, perhaps even too warm once she got out into the open desert on her horse.

Brushing all thoughts aside except to wonder why Adam had not yet answered the door, Stephanie knocked once more.

Again, she got no response. She leaned an ear against the window, to see if she could hear any signs of Adam moving around, since the shade was pulled on the door, making it impossible for her to see inside.

Suddenly she recalled that she had not heard Adam return on his horse during the night, though it hadn't worried her at the time. It was foolish to worry about Adam. Even if he hadn't come home, perhaps he had slept over at Damon's ranch after drinking too much, or after gambling into the wee hours of the morning.

She flinched at the thought of him having gone to a brothel at Gallup. She did know that he had done this from time to time back home in Wichita.

"I doubt he will ever take a wife," Stephanie whispered to herself. She knew that he was too absorbed by his obsession to have a town of his own to have a lasting relationship with a woman. She pitied any woman who would expect it from him. He had already left a trail of broken hearts everywhere he traveled.

Running out of patience, Stephanie tried the door and found that it was not locked. Slowly opening it, she stuck her head inside.

"Adam?" she said. She peered in and discovered that all of the shades on the windows on both sides of the car were still drawn.

She squinted her eyes in an effort to see his bed at the far end of the private car. Finding it impossible to make anything out in the dark shadows of the car, and because Adam had not yet made himself known to her, Stephanie went on in.

She stepped lightly across the room and rolled a shade up on one of the windows. When she turned and saw that Adam wasn't in his bed, she gasped. It was apparent that Adam *hadn't* come home after the dispute with the Navaho.

"Oh, Adam," she whispered, shaking her head slowly back and forth. "Where on earth *did* you spend the night?"

At times like this, she feared for her brother. No matter how much she tried to convince herself that he was old enough to take care of himself, she saw him as vulnerable in many ways. As far as she was concerned, he didn't have the common sense of a toad. Too often she had been forced to intervene in awkward situations to save him from embarrassments she did not even want to think about.

"Well, big brother, it seems you are on your own today," Stephanie said, sighing.

She went back to her private car. Just as she was about to pour herself a fresh cup of coffee, she heard the sound of an approaching horse.

Her heart skipped an excited beat. Was Runner arriving this early? Or was it Adam?

Again recalling her lovemaking with Runner, she walked to the window with weak knees. A sudden, wild desire leapt into her heart when she saw Runner approaching.

She gazed at him with a rapid heartbeat as he wheeled his horse to a stop and tied his reins to the makeshift hitching rail beside the train cars.

In a flurry, she went to the door and opened it.

When her eyes met Runner's, Stephanie felt giddy, and she knew that her face was flushed with color. In flashes of her mind's eye she was remembering what Runner had taught her with his lips and hands the previous night. She would never forget how it felt when their nude bodies had pressed together that first time. And how could she ever forget how he had so magnificently filled her? She ached even now to share all of this with him again.

She felt wicked to the core for allowing her mind to wander to such decadent thoughts. If her step-mother were there—oh, how Sally would shame her for her wanton behavior. But how could she feel otherwise when a man as handsome as Runner was in love with her? Stephanie concluded.

Her gaze swept over Runner as he climbed the stairs. Today he was dressed in a fresh buckskin outfit with a red velveteen headband tied around his brow. He wore moccasins, and he had a knife sheathed at one side of his waist and a pistol holstered on the other.

Runner was in awe of how vibrant and alive Stephanie was this early in the morning. Her eyes were wide and bright and filled with excitement. Her cheeks were rosy, her lips even more enticing from having been kissed by him so often, and so fiercely, the previous night.

His gaze slid downward, to stare at the swell of her breasts where they pressed against a colorfully designed blouse, their cleavage exposed enough for him to recall how soft they were, and how sweet they tasted when he had placed his lips to them. Hungering for her even now, the heat was rising in his loins.

"Good morning," Stephanie said, catapulting Runner from his thoughts.

"*Yaa-eh-t-eeh,*" he said quickly.

Stephanie looked quizzically up at him. "You just said . . . ?" she murmured.

"I said 'hello' in Navaho," Runner said, laughing softly.

Stephanie was feeling awkward, something quite unusual for her. In her line of business, she had learned to be open and relaxed, to make those she was photographing relax, as well. But with this man, she felt like a young school girl with her first crush. And in a sense, that was how it truly was: he was her first true love.

"Come on inside and have a cup of coffee with me before we leave," she said, turning and hurrying back inside her private car.

She looked at him over her shoulder as he followed her. "And perhaps you might want to see my darkroom and equipment?" she offered. "If you have a better sense of what I do, perhaps it will make you understand even more why I love it so."

"Yes, perhaps," Runner said, closing the door behind him. He turned and stared from the window at Adam's private car. He was torn with many feelings when he allowed himself to forget his bitterness toward Adam. He wished that it could be as it was all those years ago. He would find much pleasure in riding and laughing with Adam.

"Adam knows your plans for today?" Runner said, following Stephanie into the small kitchenette.

Stephanie stiffened at Runner's mention of Adam. She poured Runner a cup of coffee and gave it to him.

"Adam?" she said.

Feeling Runner's presence behind her as he followed, Stephanie walked into the parlor section of her car.

"No. I haven't told him," she murmured. She paused, then turned to Runner as he came toward her. "He isn't in his private car." She hesitated, then said, "I don't know where he is. I'm not even sure if I should leave without seeing that he arrives back safely."

Runner tipped the cup to his lips and sipped at the coffee as he looked over the rim at Stephanie. Then he sat the cup aside.

"This association he has with Damon Stout," he said guardedly. "Can you define it? Do you think that Adam stayed the night at Damon's ranch?"

"I'm not sure how to answer either of your questions," Stephanie said, forgetting her coffee. She felt that it was best to get under way, to get away from such a discussion.

She went into her darkroom, lit the kerosene lamp and finished gathering her supplies into a bag. She tensed as Runner came up behind her.

When his hands circled her waist and he drew her

around to face him, she sucked in a wild breath. She searched his face, glad that she did not find anger in his eyes.

"You do not know the reason for your brother's association with Damon?" Runner said quietly. "Nor do you know whether or not he might have stayed overnight at Damon's ranch?"

"I truly don't know why Adam and Damon have become so involved," Stephanie said simply. "As for me, I think Damon is the devil in disguise." She shuddered when she recalled how he had tried to rape her. "He is a vile man. I wish that Adam had nothing to do with him." She paused, then added, "As for where my brother stayed the night—perhaps in Gallup. Perhaps at Damon's. I truly don't know."

"It is unwise of him to leave you alone for an entire night," Runner said. "Had I known, I wouldn't have returned to my hogan last night. I would have stayed with you."

A thrill ran through Stephanie. "You would have?" she said softly.

"But not only to guard you from harm," Runner said, pulling her closer.

"Why else?" Stephanie said, her knees growing weak with passion.

"You need to ask?" Runner said huskily. He lowered his mouth to her lips and gave her a frenzied kiss.

Stephanie twined her arms around Runner's neck. Her heart throbbed and the delicious spiraling need that she had felt before returned. Yet a warning sounded in her mind, reminding her of where she was, and who might come in her private car at any moment. Adam had the habit of not knocking.

But when Runner gathered her up into his arms and carried her from the darkroom and took her to her bed, all worries of Adam—of everything but this wild desire that was pulsing heatedly through her blood—were gone from her consciousness.

Lying on the bed, the ribbon gone from her hair and her clothes discarded, as well as Runner's, Stephanie reached her arms out and smiled as he knelt down over her, the pulsing need of his manliness resting hard and heavy on her thigh. She opened her legs to him and received him inside. Closing her eyes, she gasped with pleasure as he began his rhythmic thrusts within her.

The room was bathed in a golden sheen as the morning sun streamed through the windows. Stephanie was caught up in a web of wondrous ecstasy, lost to time, to caution, to any senses, except for those being ignited within her as she clung to Runner. At this moment in time, he—only he—was her universe.

Adam was only a fleeting thought as his face flashed before Stephanie's mind's eye. The idea that he might come in and find her with Runner in the throes of passion was lost to her in the rapture that was overwhelming her.

13

Love's a fire that needs renewal of
fresh beauty for its fuel.
                    —THOMAS CAMPBELL

Stephanie's nipples hard against his palm, Runner reveled in the feel of her firm, silky breasts. He pressed his lips to her throat, his hips thrusting against her in a steady rhythm. He could feel the warmth spreading, passion curling, then unfurling like hot flames through him.

Stephanie clung to him, ecstasy moving with bone-weakening intensity, her breasts tingling as his hands caressed them. She moaned as Runner's breath stirred her hair, and then he captured her lips beneath his in a kiss that awakened her wild desire to its full intensity.

She returned his kiss with wildness and desperation and wrapped her legs around his hips, enabling him to move more freely within her.

His tongue sought hers between her parted lips. She flicked her tongue against his and trembled as one hand moved down over her ribs, across her stomach, which quavered in the wake of his fingers, and then down to her moist channel, where the center of her desire lay, waiting for his caress.

Stephanie experienced agony and bliss when he began caressing her tight bud with his fingers while he still moved within her, powerfully, wonderfully, causing her whole body to feel as though it was fluid with fire.

His mouth left hers and his tongue moved along her flesh, from the hollow of her throat, to one of her breasts, and Stephanie rolled her head with pleasure. She bit her lower lip as he pressed his lips against her breast, moving them over her abundant nipple, drawing the taut peak between his teeth.

Stephanie was overcome by an unbearable sweet pain. She ran her hands over him, down the full length of the tight muscles of his back, stopping to splay them over his hips. She clung to him, yearning for the promise of what his body was offering her.

Again he kissed her with fire. He placed his hands beneath her buttocks and lifted her closer. Sweat pearled on Runner's brow, the air heavy with the inevitability of pleasure. Each stroke that he took within her was bringing him closer to fulfillment.

He caught his breath, feeling the heat rising, spreading, and then splashing through him like wild fire. He burrowed his face against the soft skin of Stephanie's neck and groaned out his pleasure.

In tune with Runner's feelings, and seeking her own rapturous release, Stephanie tumbled over the edge into ecstasy with him. She cried out against his shoulder, the spinning sensation flooding her whole being as surges of intense pleasure swept through her.

Their shudders subsided into a quiet peace. Runner rolled away from her. Stephanie turned to him and kissed his brow, first one cheek, and then another, then feathered a kiss across his lips.

"I've never been happier," she whispered, turning to cling to him. "Let's not allow anything to spoil what we have found together. Please, Runner."

The sudden thuds of sledge hammers burying more

spikes into the ground as the work gang arrived outside, to lay more tracks, made Stephanie stiffen. Her eyes widened and she drew a blanket around her. She had forgotten the time of day. She had forgotten her brother.

"Adam," she said, looking quickly over at Runner. "He could arrive home at any moment."

A cold barrier slammed down between them again at the mention of Adam's name. Stephanie scarcely breathed as Runner scowled at her, then rose and began dressing.

Adam awakened with a start. Momentarily disoriented as to where he was, he blinked his eyes nervously. Fear struck at his heart when he looked around and discovered that he was in a Navaho hogan.

A soft hand trailing down his back in light, tender caresses made him tremble with renewed passion as he remembered with whom he had spent the night, and in whose hogan this passionate love had been made.

Pure Blossom.

She had led him there under the cover of darkness the previous night. He had spent almost the entire night making love to her; she was initiating another round of lovemaking with him now. She crawled to his side and leaned low over him, her long, lustrous hair rippling along his flesh in the wake of her lips and hands.

He inhaled a breath of rapture and closed his eyes, unaware that the translucence of darkness and the blaze of the stars had left the sky. The only light in the hogan was the glow of the embers in the fireplace. The only true fire was in his loins, spreading into something fiercely hot as Pure Blossom's mouth sought his throbbing member, her tongue flicking along its tight stem.

"Oh, God," Adam moaned, wondering how he could ever leave this woman that had awakened him to such complete passion, unlike anything he had felt while bedding whores in the past.

He stretched his legs apart and spread his arms out on each side of him, his eyes closed to the pleasure that was engulfing him.

When he felt as though he could not take any more of this wonderful punishment, he placed his hands to Pure Blossom's waist and turned her over, onto her back. He kissed her breasts, her stomach, and then moved over her and thrust himself deeply within her.

His hands cupped her breasts. "I love you," he whispered against her parted lips, then ground his mouth into her lips, taking all the sweetness from her that she was willing to give.

Pure Blossom clung to him, tears of joy spreading down her cheeks. She had never thought that any man would desire her, much less love her so intensely. She would not allow herself to think about how her father felt about Adam, nor her brother. Adam was hers. No one would be allowed to take him from her.

The sound of voices and the laughter of children outside Pure Blossom's hogan drew Adam's lovemaking to a quick halt. He looked frantically toward the door, then into Pure Blossom's eyes.

"It's morning," he said, his voice edged with fright. "Does anyone ever come to your hogan in the morning? My horse. . . . Pure Blossom, what if someone finds it?"

Pure Blossom placed her hands on his cheeks. "No one comes to Pure Blossom's hogan very often," she reassured. "Everyone knows that I work best this time of day. And no one disturbs me when I weave my beautiful blankets. As to your horse—do you not remember how well hidden it is? No one will ever find it."

"Pure Blossom, it's daylight," Adam said, again glancing toward the door. "How in the hell am I going to get out of your hogan without being seen?"

She turned his face around so that their eyes could meet again. "My sweet white man, you do not leave the hogan while it is daylight," she said, giggling. "Stay. Spend the day with me. We can make love, eat, talk, and make love again. Tonight, when the dark shadows fall around our little world, I will go with you to your horse."

Adam's heart pounded as he looked into her beautiful, innocent eyes and her delicate features. What she suggested was very tempting.

He hesitated a moment longer, then laughed loosely. "All right," he said, framing her face between his hands, bringing her lips to his. "I will stay. How could anyone want to leave, *ever*?"

He was not worried about Stephanie. She would think that he was with Damon, or in Gallup. She was used to his shenanigans. But he knew that she would never suspect that this time the woman he was bedding was Navaho.

He laughed softly against Pure Blossom's lips, then kissed her hard and long, as once again he moved himself within her. Their moans intermingled. Their hands discovered each other's sensitive, secret spots.

When Pure Blossom's hair had fallen aside and he had seen the lump growing at the base of her neck, even that had not repelled him. To Adam, everything about Pure Blossom was perfect. Magnificently perfect.

He loved her. With all of his heart, he loved her.

Sage had been awakened at dawn with the news that several horses had been stolen from the corral. He was sitting tall and straight on his strawberry roan as he sought out tracks in the mixture of dirt and sand beneath his horse's hooves. This search had carried him not all that far from the village until tall bluffs began shadowing him.

His eyes flashed angrily when he soon lost the tracks. They had seemed to disappear into the wind. He drew a tight rein and gazed up at the bluff above him and then at the sloping trail that led upward. If he went up there, perhaps he could see the horse thieves in the distance as they herded the horses along with them.

There were no signs as to when the horses had been stolen. If it had been just before daylight, the thieves would not have gotten so far that he would not be able to see them across the straight stretch of land in the far distance.

He turned to his braves. "Stay," he ordered. "I will go and take a look from the bluff."

Holding his reins steady, he urged his steed up the winding trail. When it leveled off to the first ledge, he shielded his eyes with a hand and stared across the land, grumbling to himself when he saw nothing.

"I shall go higher," he whispered to himself.

He wheeled his horse around and went in a slow, cautious trot up the other trail until once again it leveled off to another straight stretch of rock and sparse grass. He started to ride to the edge of the bluff, but drew a tight rein and stopped his horse, puzzled over having found a horse that had been left there, tethered and partially hidden.

Dismounting, he went over to the horse and patted its rump, then ran his hands down its withers as he studied it. "There is something familiar about this animal," he said to himself.

He threw open the saddlebags. Reaching inside, he

found a small journal. He didn't get any farther than the first page, where Adam's signature loomed up at him like some ghastly apparition.

He grew cold and numb as he then studied the horse more carefully. His jaw tightened and his eyes lit with fire, and angrily thrusting the journal back inside the saddlebag, he stamped to the edge of the bluff and looked at the hogans of his village in the distance.

"There can only be one reason he has hidden his horse this close to my village," he growled out. "It would not be to spy, for I would have seen him. Pure Blossom. He is with Pure Blossom."

He had seen the instant attraction between his daughter and Adam. He had not thought to warn his daughter about him, for he had thought that she had seen for herself the sort of man he was.

And taking a man to her hogan was not a normal thing for his daughter to do. As far as Sage knew, she was still a virgin.

But Sage had seen a charm about Adam that might fool Pure Blossom into believing that he truly cared. She was so vulnerable. She had not experienced being in love before her.

He looked heavenward and said a soft, desperate prayer to the Great Unseen Power. "Let me be wrong," he whispered.

Hate racing through his veins, he grabbed Adam's horse's reins and took it with him from the bluffs. Without giving any of his braves an explanation, he rode off hard toward his village, Adam's steed trailing behind him on a rope. He did not stop until he was at Pure Blossom's hogan.

"Pure Blossom!" he shouted, not having yet dismounted. He feared going into the hogan. He feared he would tear Adam's heart out if he found him making love to his precious daughter. "Daughter, come out here and face your father."

Sage was unaware of the silence that had fallen around him, and that his people were staring and edging closer, puzzled over a father who was enraged with a daughter everyone knew he cherished.

Inside the hogan, Adam and Pure Blossom fell away from each other, eyes wide, hearts pounding.

"My father," Pure Blossom said, drawing a blanket quickly around her nudity. "And he is angry." Her eyes wavered. "He must know you are here." She swallowed hard. "But how?"

When Sage shouted her name again, she turned from Adam, whose face was ashen. Frightened, guilty, and meek, clutching to her blanket for dear life, she stepped outside and gazed up at her father.

His daughter's behavior told Sage all that he needed to know. He dismounted and brushed past her, entering her hogan. Rage filled him when he found Adam scampering into his breeches, his eyes wild and frightened.

Sage grabbed Adam by the throat and half lifted him from the floor. "I could kill you with my bare hands," he ground out between clenched teeth. "And I will if you ever approach my daughter again." He felt sick to see the rumpled blankets on his daughter's bed.

With a force that sent Adam flying across the hogan, Sage hit Adam, then stamped toward the door. He feared the anger seething inside him, knowing that if he stayed another moment with Adam, he would kill him.

He turned and gave Adam one last warning look. "Don't ever get near my daughter again and never come near my village," he said tightly. "You have shamefully used my daughter for your own greedy, white man's gain."

Adam reached a hand out to Sage. "No," he cried. "That's not the way it is at all. I love your daughter."

This made Sage even angrier. He took a step toward Adam, but was stopped when Pure Blossom came into the hogan and stood between them.

"Father, please don't," she cried. "Please!"

Adam took the opportunity to escape. He grabbed up the rest of his clothes and ran outside, not surprised to find his horse tied to Sage's—the source of the discovery of their liaison.

His fingers trembling, he thrust his clothes into the saddlebag. Clothed only in his breeches, he swung himself into the saddle. Humiliated and angry, he spun his horse around and rode away, people scattering to make room for him.

Sage turned to Pure Blossom. There was much that he wanted to say to her, although his warnings had come too late. But he knew that she had been humiliated enough today. He gently took her into his arms and hugged her.

Pure Blossom sobbed as she clung to him, yet she could not find it inside her heart to tell him that she was sorry. She *wasn't*. Adam had awakened her to feelings that she perhaps would have never known. She would cherish them. She would cherish and relive those moments with him until the day she died.

"Adam is *hogay-gahn*, bad," Sage said, his voice drawn. "You are good. You are not meant to be together."

He eased away from her and gave her a lingering look, then left.

Pure Blossom threw herself onto her bed and cried, hugging the blankets upon which she had made love.

"Adam," she sobbed. "My Adam."

14

If thou lovest me too much,
'Twill not prove as true a touch;
Love me little more than such.
For I fear the end.
                    —ANONYMOUS

Stephanie and Runner rode along an old oxcart trail, the pack mule trailing behind them. Stephanie looked over at Runner. "I truly appreciate you being here with me."

She waited for him to respond, growing more tense when he didn't. He continued looking straight ahead, as though she weren't there.

"Runner, please tell me what's the matter," she said. "Back at the train, everything was so beautiful between us until I mentioned Adam. I didn't know that your feelings about him ran this deeply."

"Adam is a stranger to me now," Runner said, giving Stephanie a scowl. "Many years have passed since we shared a friendship. Those years changed Adam into someone with whom I could not be a friend."

"But, darling, you knew that before we made love," Stephanie said. She shifted her horse's reins from one hand to the other. "Why did the mention of his name have to ruin what we share? Although Adam is my brother, he and I do not always agree on everything. I never allow his opinions to overshadow mine."

"And I admire that in you," Runner said, his lips moving into a soft smile. "And I am sorry that I allowed my bitter feelings about Adam to come between us."

He paused and again stared straight ahead, into the distance. "You see, my feelings for Adam run deeper than those of my father," he said thickly. "I resent Adam for being here with plans that will put more hardships on the Navaho. But it is the friendship that we had as children that bothers me. Through the years I had hungered to be with my friend Adam again. My mother told me more than once that it would happen."

He paused and gave Stephanie a sour look. "She was right," he said flatly. "I have met Adam again. But it is not how I expected it to be. I had hoped to have the same friendship with him, as I did as a child. Now I see how foolish I was to hope that a man living in the white world could remain as one with my heart, whose world is, and has been for so long, Navaho."

"I wish it could be different," Stephanie said softly. "But don't you see? Nothing can change it. Please, Runner, don't let this tear you apart."

"How can I, when I do not know where he is, or what he is doing?" Runner said, his voice drawn. "If he stayed the night with Damon, who is to say what those two might be plotting against the Navaho? We are sure that Damon steals our horses. If he could, he would steal all of our land and run us off into the mountains. If Adam is allying himself with Damon Stout, he is no better than a thief who steals from a hardworking, beautiful people."

"It was never my brother's intent to harm your people," Stephanie said. "The Santa Fe Railroad has been given permission by the United States Government to move further into Navaho territory. Yes, Adam is the cause for this private spur. And, by right, he can do it.

But he also wanted to make things right with the Navaho. He doesn't want trouble, only acceptance."

"As you can see, that has been denied him and the railroad tracks are still being laid," Runner said in a low voice.

Stephanie thought back to earlier and realized it had been the sound of the work gang pounding with their pick axes and sledge hammers outside her private car that had angered Runner more than the mention of Adam's name. To Runner, who allied himself with his father's feelings about the railroad, each spike buried deeply into the ground was as though it was being lodged into his heart.

"Runner, I wish there was something that I could do, but there isn't," Stephanie said, reaching a hand to his arm. "Darling, I hope you don't grow to resent me, too. My photography means the world to me. And Adam has nothing, absolutely *nothing*, to do with it. I promise that I will never photograph anything that you don't want me to."

"Do not be so hasty with your promises," Runner said, giving her a guarded look. "I can see that your love for what you do runs deep. There are many tempting sights you might want to photograph that I will deny you. Who can say whether or not you will be able to resist temptation?"

Stephanie's eyes widened and her throat went dry. She had to wonder if Runner had a specific place in mind that she would certainly want to photograph. It frightened her to think that she might want to go back on her promise. Already she had found the beauty of the West a palpable force. And she knew that there must be more alluring sights that she had not yet experienced. She had traveled far from Wichita. How could she not want to see it all and take back as much as she could to share by way of her photographs?

"You are suddenly quiet," Runner said, frowning over at her. "Why is that?"

"Runner, I never want to hurt you," Stephanie said quietly. "I hope that I have the willpower not to do anything that will cause you to hate me."

"You will find that so hard to do?"

"I *love* what I do."

"If you had to choose . . ."

"You wouldn't ask me to, would you?"

"I doubt that I would dare to," he said, frowning, then slowly smiled over at her.

"I do love you so much," Stephanie said, sighing with relief.

Runner was just about to reply when an approaching rider drew his attention away from her.

Stephanie leaned forward in her saddle, hand on the saddle horn, disbelieving the sight before her eyes.

"Adam?" she whispered, paling.

She drew a tight rein as Adam's horse thundered toward her and Runner. Where was her brother's shirt? she wondered to herself. And where were his boots? It was as though he was fleeing for his life.

"Adam!" she screamed at him as he rode past.

He looked back at her only long enough to give her an angry stare, and then he glared at Runner.

Stephanie saw the viciousness in Adam's face and knew that if looks could kill, Runner would be dead.

"Stop!" Stephanie shouted after him, turning in the saddle to watch him ride away, his horse stirring up dust and plants beneath the sting of his pounding hooves.

"Adam, good Lord," Stephanie screamed after him. "What has happened? Please stop!"

Runner reached over and placed a hand on her arm.

"Let him go. It is obvious that he wishes to have no part of either one of us this morning." He smiled cunningly. "It seems he has gotten himself into trouble. I hope it was at the hand of my father."

"Surely you don't want any harm to come to my brother," Stephanie said, turning startled eyes to Runner.

"Only what he might deserve," Runner said. "And how else should I care about him? He has chosen to walk the opposite path of the Navaho. They are my people now. He would not be riding like a madman today, half-clothed, had he not been caught in one mischief or another. Do you truly believe that it had nothing to do with the Navaho?"

"I would hope that he would be smarter than that," Stephanie said, inhaling a nervous breath. "He knows how strongly your father feels about his interference."

Runner nodded, then sank his moccasined heels into the flanks of his stallion and rode ahead of Stephanie. "Come," he said, gesturing with a hand. "I have places to take you."

Stephanie only half-heartedly nudged the horse's sides with her knees. She was discovering that loving a man of different ideals and customs was not all that simple. Each turn brought new complications.

Seething with hate, Adam arrived at his private car. After securing his horse, he bathed, then lit a cigar and began pacing. He had to find a way to make Sage pay.

"Why can't he see that I didn't even have to ask for approval?" Adam said, frustrated. "I don't need it. It was just out of politeness that I offered to sit in council with him."

He yanked the cigar from between his lips and stamped it out in an ashtray. He went to the liquor cabinet and grabbed a bottle of whiskey from it. His eyes narrowed, he sauntered to his desk and sat down on a plush leather chair, uncorking the bottle. He took a long swallow, then set the bottle on the desk.

"I'm going to make him pay," he whispered darkly to himself.

Taking several sheets of paper from a drawer, he stacked them neatly on the desk and stared down at the blank pages as he drank more whiskey.

Then, dipping a pen in ink, he began writing plans—plans that would end Sage's reign as a leader and, hopefully, his life.

Runner led Stephanie down a slope of bald rocks into a valley surrounded by moderately high cliffs. Here and there clumps of scrub oak were clustered along a running stream. Lofty mountains rose in the distance.

Deep, beautiful canyons lay on each side of Stephanie. It was easy to forget everything evil and ugly in the world. She was in awe of Arizona all over again, the Pueblo Colorado Wash winding down below and grandeur surrounding her. As the slope steepened, she held her knees more tightly against her steed and clung to the reins.

Runner led her to a place of beautiful rock outcroppings, from where she could see for miles upon miles of what appeared to her to be a mystical, sacred land.

Runner dismounted. He went to Stephanie and lifted her from the saddle.

"You will allow me to photograph here?" Stephanie said, wonder in her voice. She looked guardedly around her and shivered. "It seems as though there is something here, as though we are not alone. As though there is an invisible force watching us."

"We are never alone," Runner said. He turned and surveyed the grandeur of the land himself. "The earth is the Great Mother. The sun is the Father of life. The moon is Grandmother. The stars are celestial souls that shine to guide earthly wayfarers, to inspire and protect mankind. That is why you feel a presence. These things that I have just described to you are with us, always."

"If what you say is true, then this is not, in itself, a sacred place," Stephanie said, gazing up at him. "If it were, that would mean that everywhere we travel could be called sacred."

"I do see everything in this land as sacred," Runner said. He went to her mule and untied her photography equipment. "But some is more sacred than others." He turned sullen eyes to Stephanie. "Remember well, my sweet one, that nothing is as sacred as the People."

"That is why you will not allow me to photograph them?" Stephanie said. She removed her camera from the pack mule. She flinched somewhat when she saw the anger the sight of her camera brought into Runner's eyes. "That is so," Runner said, quickly looking away from her camera. "And I will confess to you that I am traveling with you not only because I wish to be with you, but also to keep you away from my people."

This came as no surprise to Stephanie. She busied herself with preparing a plate and loading her camera, then put it aside and set up her tripod.

When she turned to get the camera, she saw Runner holding it carefully in his hands, with curiosity in his eyes. He was intrigued.

"Isn't it fascinating?" she said, relaxing and moving to his side. She clasped her hands together behind her. "I am using the glass plate type of camera today. This sort conveys an impression of the real grandeur and the magnitude of mountain scenery that smaller views cannot possibly impart."

"Before I knew you I had heard about cameras," Runner said, turning it over again to look into the lens. "But I had not seen one until I met you."

Runner cast his eyes upward, checking the angle of the sun. "If I am to return you to your railroad car before dark, you had best get started now," he said.

He handed her the camera that he had been studying, after she replaced the other one in the saddlebag.

Stephanie nodded. She gave him an excited, warm smile, then turned from him and placed her camera on the tripod. She soon became lost to everything but the pleasure of taking the photographs.

Runner stood away from her. A slow smile formed on his lips as he watched her. He was seeing the child in her as she took one photograph after another. There was such an innocence about her as she would momentarily turn around and laugh softly toward him, then again get lost in her love of photography.

Runner sat down and leaned his back against a rock, entertained by the sight of this woman that he wanted for a wife. His only regret was that they could not have met under different circumstances. Although their love was sincere for one another, would she be willing to give up her dreams to become part of Runner's life? Could she choose a life with him, over a career that made her so happy?

This was the first time that he had allowed himself to go so far as to consider marrying her. He was not sure when, or if, he could ever voice this aloud to her. He feared hearing her answer. If he had to lose her, after having waited a lifetime for her, he wondered what choices he might have to face. Would he follow her back to the white world, just to be with her? Or were his loyalties to the Navaho too fierce?

Troubled, he continued watching Stephanie. The sun was lowering in the sky. She seemed frantic to take as many photographs as she could before the light became too faint.

"There is always tomorrow," he said, rising to his feet. He circled his hands around her waist and drew her back against him. "We will travel to new places tomorrow. I will watch you again. Watching you gives me much pleasure." He leaned over and spoke against her lips. "I want to make love to you. *Now.*"

Their lips came together in a frenzied, heated kiss. Enveloping Stephanie within his arms, Runner lowered her to the ground. Still kissing, his hands lifted her skirt and swept away her lacy underwear. Her hands groped and lowered his breeches.

Stephanie's heartbeat quickened as he made one maddening plunge and was inside her. She opened herself to him, whispering with bliss against his lips as their naked flesh seemed to fuse, their bodies sucking at each other, flesh against flesh in gentle pressure.

He lay above her, bracing himself with his elbows. His hands caught hers and held them slightly above her. He kissed her eyes, her nose, the silken flesh of the column of her throat.

Tremors cascaded down Stephanie's back when one of his hands slid down and crept up inside her blouse. She shuddered with ecstasy as his fingers circled her nipple, causing her breast to strain into his hand with anticipation.

Then he pulled himself away from her and moved down her body. Stephanie was almost delirious from pleasure. Wide-eyed, she watched him bend low over her between her thighs. She flinched in pleasant shock when his fingers spread the silky frond of hair at the juncture of her thighs, his tongue soon titillating the core of her womanhood, the tip of his tongue swirling and moist against her.

Stephanie closed her eyes in sheer ecstasy and her insides tightened and grew warm as his lips and tongue continued paying homage to her where she ever so sweetly throbbed. Never had anything felt so wonderfully sinful. As the pleasure mounted, she tossed her head from side to side. She chewed her lower lip. She folded and unfolded her hands into tight fists at her sides.

When she did not think that she could last much longer without tumbling over the edge into total bliss, she placed her hands on each side of his face and urged him back over her.

Runner sculpted himself to her moist body, molding perfectly to the curved hollow of her hips, and pressed himself deeply within her again. He kissed her breasts one at a time and sucked the nipples.

Runner was feeling the tension mounting deeply within the chasm of his desire, the sensations searing. He drove into her more swiftly and surely. Their bodies strained together.

Feeling his body hardening and tightening, Runner knew that he was near to the point of no return. He paused, and then pushed himself endlessly deeper into her, then shuddered intensely, her body absorbing the bold thrusts, answering his need with her lifted hips.

Afterwards, he held her within his arms with exquisite tenderness. "I don't want to leave this lovely place," Stephanie murmured. "Let's stay, Runner, and pretend we are the only two people on the earth."

At that moment her stomach growled with hunger, making her laugh. "I didn't bring enough food for an evening meal," she murmured, recalling their meager picnic lunch.

"One day I hope that we *can* stay together, forever," Runner said, helping her from the ground. "But I guess now isn't the time to discuss it."

Stephanie gave him a wide-eyed, wondering stare. Her heart leapt at the thought of marriage. It was a wonderful idea, but it scared her. Their worlds were so different, and she knew that he would ask her to adjust to his. He would never return to the life of a white man.

She shook such thoughts from her mind. She did not want to think about choices again. But she knew that, in time, she would have to decide what her future would be, where, and with whom.

A warm thrill soared through her at the thought of never having to say another goodbye to Runner. Surely she could be content in just knowing that he was hers. Yet, what of her photography?

Solemn, she began putting her equipment away.

Runner sensed her mood. He took her by the wrists and pulled her to him. "You *do* belong to me, heart and soul," he said huskily.

His mouth crushed down upon her lips in a heated kiss. She melted against him, knowing that what he had just said was true.

When he released her, she smiled sweetly up at him. "You are right, you know," she murmured. "We do belong together. We *will* work it out. I'll make sure of it."

They placed all of the equipment on the mule, mounted their steeds, and headed back, the sun splashing its last golden light across the western horizon.

Stephanie sighed with pleasure. She threw her head back and allowed her hair to tumble down her back.

"I've never been so happy," she shouted, laughter bubbling from within her.

Runner had brought her close enough to her private car to see her safely there, then beneath the bright light of a full moon, he wheeled his horse around and rode away.

Bone tired, Stephanie took her horse into the cattle car and saw that it was watered and fed. Then, stretching and yawning, and with a stomach so empty it ached, she strolled idly from the cattle car, unaware that someone else had arrived.

When she stepped to the ground, she cried out. Strong arms circled her waist, and she found herself suddenly stretched out on the ground.

When she was finally able to see who her assailant was, she was stunned to find Damon Stout sneering down at her in the moonlight. This time he was making sure that he was holding her wrists fast to the ground, even though she did not have her derringer holstered at her waist.

"I saw you with the injun," Damon said in a husky growl. "Did you let him take a feel of you? Or did he do more than that? Did he give you a poke or two? How's about givin' some to me?"

"You disgust me," Stephanie said, shuddering with distaste as he attempted to raise her skirt with one of his knees. "I'll kill you this time. I swear I'll kill you if you so much as touch me."

"I doubt that," Damon said, chuckling.

Stephanie tried to squirm free, but found that her fatigue from the long day had weakened her too much. For the life of her, she couldn't get away.

She turned her head sideways when Damon tried to

kiss her. "Adam!" she screamed. "Lord, Adam, come and get this filthy man off me!"

Damon clamped a hand over her mouth, holding her in place, his other hand loosening his hardness from his breeches.

Adam ran from his private car. Aghast at what he saw, he hesitated for a moment, then went to Damon and grabbed him by the shirt collar, dragging him away from Stephanie.

"You stupid fool!" Adam cried. "Can't you put your priorities in order? I asked you here to discuss matters besides my sister. Must you always treat her as though she is no more than a dog in heat?"

"She shouldn't be so damn pretty," Damon growled, yanking himself away from Adam. He covered himself with one hand, while he rebuttoned his breeches.

"You're vile," Stephanie said, scrambling to her feet. She smoothed her skirt down, then wiped at her mouth with the back of her hand.

She then stamped over and grabbed Adam's pistol from its holster and thrust it into Damon's stomach. "I would learn to control my lusts, if I were you," she warned, her eyes flashing heatedly into his. "The next time you look at me, I won't give you an opportunity to climb atop me again. I'll just shoot you and get it over with."

Adam chuckled. "That's tellin' him, sis," he said, then his laughter faded as Damon glared at him.

"If you know what's best for you, you'll tell this sister of yours to back off," Damon said in a feral snarl. "I could blow this whole deal sky high with the Navaho, and you'd see the last of your private spur and the town that you're hankerin' for. I could let them in on our little secrets. They'd skin you alive, Adam, if they knew how you're schemin' against them."

"You . . . wouldn't . . ." Adam said, paling.

"Want to put it to the test?" Damon said, chuckling. "Do it."

Stephanie looked from one to the other. "What are you talking about?" she said, lowering the pistol. "What plans? What are you going to do to the Navaho?"

"Nothing, sis," Adam said thinly. "Damon's got too vivid an imagination for his own good."

"Adam, you know that I'm willin' to do anything to get rid of the Navaho," Damon snarled. "With me on your side, we'll both come out winners." He shrugged. "I don't care what you do or don't tell your sister. You've got my word that I won't be causin' her anymore trouble. As I see it, she ain't worth it, anyhow."

Stephanie's blood was boiling mad. Knowing that she wasn't going to get any answers from her brother, she stamped away and went inside her private car. She stared out the window as Adam and Damon continued speaking. She hated to see Adam with the likes of Damon. Her brother was easily swayed. He could become like Damon in the wink of an eye and there was nothing she could do about it.

Except perhaps warn Runner.

Yet she feared doing that. Runner was quickly angered, and so was Sage. She felt that it was best to let sleeping dogs lie, until they had to be awakened.

She went to her kitchenette and washed her hands, then put together a quick bite to eat.

Outside, Adam leaned close to Damon. "It's best if you don't go near my sister again," he said, his voice low. "Damn it, Damon, what she is doing, by sidetracking Runner, is the best way to eventually ruin not only Runner and Sage, but the whole Navaho people. It might enable me and you to buy up the whole damn Arizona Territory."

"Sounds good to me," Damon said, shrugging.

Adam looked past him at the distant mountains crowned by the bright moon's glow. He had a fleeting thought of Pure Blossom and how all of this might affect her, then brushed it aside as Damon began talking about the new town and the gambling halls, women, and hell-raising men that would frequent it.

"I know *I'm* anxious to become a steady customer at the saloons," Damon said, slapping Adam on the shoulder.

They both laughed raucously.

15

Love that is too hot and strong
Burneth soon to waste.
—ANONYMOUS

With her hands on her hips, Stephanie was waiting for Adam when he entered her private car. He had to have known that she would need explanations after what Damon had said about the Navaho.

And by the wavering of his eyes as he shut the door behind him and stood there, silently looking at Stephanie, she knew that she had been right.

"Adam, what's going on between you and Damon?" she asked, her jaw tight.

Adam shrugged. "We're friends," he said. "That's all."

"How could you be friends with that beast?" Stephanie replied. "Twice now he has assaulted me. You should hate him, Adam. Instead, you continue to ally yourself with him. What is it that you are planning with Damon against the Navaho? Is that why you agreed to his friendship so readily? Because he has an axe to grind against the Indians?"

Adam raked his fingers through his hair and lowered his eyes. "I don't know how to answer that," he mumbled.

"Your refusal to answer me is proof enough," Stephanie said.

She went over to Adam and forced him to look her straight in the eyes.

"Adam, how can you forget your past friendship with Runner so easily?" she murmured. "And Sage and Leonida. You surely can't be seriously thinking about taking advantage of them. You came to get their approval, not to take *from* them that which is precious. Adam, you are wanting more land than is already allotted you. Isn't that so?"

"And if I do?" Adam said, slapping her hand away. He turned to leave, but Stephanie stepped quickly between him and the door.

"If you do anything else to cause the Navaho problems, Adam, so help me I shall disown you as my brother," she said in a low, warning hiss. "Do you hear me, Adam? I will no longer be your sister. And I will do everything within my power to see that you don't get your way, even if that means getting a court order to stop you. If I have to travel to Washington and speak with the President about what you are doing, I shall."

"You can't be serious," Adam gasped, paling. "You would ruin me."

"Exactly," Stephanie said, smiling smugly up at him.

"Stephanie, how could the Navaho mean so much to you that you would go against your own brother?" Adam said, his eyes suddenly angry. He clasped her shoulders with his hands, causing her to wince with pain. "We've meant everything to each other. You can't go against me now."

"Try me," she said.

Adam dropped his hands to his sides, walked to the window, and stared out of it. "I believe you would," he grumbled.

Anger was seething inside him. His careful plans were backfiring. When he had wanted Stephanie to ally herself with Runner, it had not been for her to forget her brother. It was only meant for her to sway the Navaho into approving all of his plans. Now it seemed that she was ready to do anything she could for the Navaho because of her feelings for the "White Indian."

He turned slowly around and glared at Stephanie. "It's because of Runner, isn't it?" he said, his voice drawn. "You love him more than you ever loved me."

"I do love him, but that is not entirely why I am so set against what you're trying to do," Stephanie said, torn by her feelings toward her brother. She loved him, yet at this moment, it was very close to becoming hate. "I just don't like to see this change in you. Runner said that you are someone he no longer knows. I am beginning to feel the same way, Adam."

She crossed the room to him, framing his face between her hands. "Adam, please stop your friendship with Damon," she pleaded. "Make a solid friendship with the Navaho again. Tell them that you want nothing more than the land you have already been allotted by the government. If you go in peace, I am sure they will accept your private spur and new town because it is with an old friend that they will be giving their alliance."

She paused, then added, "And Damon be damned."

Adam took her hands and kissed their palms, then drew her into his arms. "Sis, I love you so much, and I understand what you are saying. But Damon's a man I don't think I want to cross. You have seen his true self. He is a shifty, crafty man who would do anything to rid his life of the Navaho. Who is to say what he would do if he realized that I was friends with the Navaho again?"

"There are ways to protect ourselves against him," Stephanie said, easing from his arms. She lifted her derringer from its holster, where she had left it hanging on the back of a chair. She caressed the gun as she stared down at it. "I know that he'd better not try anything with me again. I *will* shoot him, Adam. He won't get the chance to touch me with his filthy hands again."

Adam watched her smoothing her hand over the firearm for a moment, feeling trapped by her demands. There was no way he was going to give up the idea of taking more land, now that he saw it within his grasp. And to do that, he needed Damon.

No. He could not actually do everything his sister was asking, but he could put on a damn good act. He would go to the Navaho and offer apologies. Perhaps, this would also give him the freedom to be with Pure Blossom for a while longer.

Then, after Damon performed his role in framing the Navaho, there would be no one who could cast any of the blame on Adam. In the end, Damon would be the one who would be swinging from a hangman's noose.

Adam smiled cynically. His sister was no longer his trump card. Damon was. And Damon would have no idea that he was being tricked all the way to the gallows.

"I'll go to the Navaho and apologize," he said quickly. He drew her closer to him. "Pretty sister, does that make you happy?"

Stephanie was slow to respond. She studied his eyes, hoping to be able to see if he was sincere or not, but she had learned long ago that her brother was a master at disguising his true feelings. As before, she would just have to take him at his word and pray that things would be put right with the Navaho.

"You are serious, aren't you?" she finally said.

"I've never been more serious in my life." The lie slipped across his lips way more easily than he would have thought possible. "In fact, Stephanie, I'll go first thing tomorrow. I'll take council with Sage and Runner. You can go with me, if you wish."

Stephanie laughed nervously and walked away from him. She went to her liquor cabinet and poured some wine in two long-stemmed glasses. "No. I think not. I'll let you do your own apologizing. But let's drink to your success," she said, holding a glass out for Adam. "And to much happiness."

Adam sauntered over and took the glass from her. "Yes, to much happiness," he said, clinking his glass against hers. "Especially ours."

They emptied their glasses and set them aside. "Adam, today, when you rode past me and Runner, without your shirt and boots on, where on earth had you been? And from whom were you escaping?" she asked.

Adam absently raked his fingers through his hair. "Sis, it's obvious that you are in love with Runner," he said. "*I've* fallen in love with his sister, Pure Blossom. I had spent the night with her in her hogan. Sage found me there. He ordered me from the village. I have never been so humiliated."

"You ... and ... Pure Blossom?" Stephanie said, stunned. "You slept with her? And ... you ... were chased from the village?"

Adam nodded.

"You just told me that you were going to go to the Navaho village and offer apologies and friendship," Stephanie said solemnly. "How on earth can you do that, especially in light of what you have just told me?"

"Sis, that's exactly why it is so important to go there," he said softly. "Not only for you and me, but for Pure Blossom. I don't think I can live without her."

"Incredible," Stephanie said, her eyes wide.

"Magnificent," Adam teased back, then took her into his arms and swung her around, laughing happily.

Runner arrived back at his hogan just as the sky was brightening into soft pinks along the eastern horizon. Exhausted, he slung himself across his bed and fell instantly asleep. In what seemed only a few short minutes, a hand on his shoulder awakened him with a start.

When he found his father standing over him, his arms folded angrily across his chest, he sat up quickly.

"What is it, Father?" he asked, smoothing his hair back from his eyes.

"You have been gone a day and a night," Sage said, eyeing Runner suspiciously. "What has taken you so long from your people?"

Runner rose to his feet and eluded his father's eyes by going and stacking some fresh firewood into his fireplace. "I am sure that you have already guessed why," he said, watching the flames take hold. "But I will tell you anyway, since you have asked. I was with the white woman."

"After my warnings, you still go to her," Sage said, disappointment in his tone. "She means that much to you?"

Runner looked up at his father, then slowly rose to his full height. "Yes, she means everything to me," he said smoothly.

"Where did you go with her that took so long?"

"I took her and her camera many places."

"You know the evil of the camera, yet you still gave the white woman assistance?"

"I understand your feelings, Father. I led her to locations of less value to our people, where there were no sacred meanings. I kept her interest away from our people while doing this."

Sage kneaded his chin. "Yes, I see that what you did was, indeed, clever," he said. Then he stepped closer to Runner. "You did this for the People. But also you did it for yourself."

"That is so," Runner said, nodding. "She has filled my life with something special. Father, I cannot help but love her."

"I told you more than once why you should not allow this to happen," Sage said, shaking his head slowly. "But my words fell on deaf ears."

"I am sorry that you cannot accept the side of me that is drawn to this white woman," Runner said, going to embrace his father. "Father, inside, where my heart beats soundly, it beats as a Navaho, instead of white. So will it be until the day I leave this earth to walk that long path in the Hereafter. Loving a white woman will not change that, ever."

Sage patted his son's back, then eased away from him.

"Many of our horses were stolen while you were gone," Sage said, his eyes dark. "As you know, I have always spoken out against horse stealing. I have always urged our braves to remember that by treaties we made promises: no fighting, no raiding. If the People need something, do not steal, instead trade. But Damon Stout has caused me to go back on my teachings. We must steal back that which is ours."

The thought of such a raid against Damon Stout filled Runner's veins with excitement. He had waited a long time for his father to decide to retaliate against the wrong that was being done them at the hands of the white rancher.

"When do we go?" he asked, his eyes dancing.

"Tonight, after Thunder Hawk has his full day of schooling," Sage said. "We will leave under the cover of darkness. We will take as many horses from Damon as have been taken from us."

There was a sudden commotion outside the hogan. There were many loud, angry shouts. Sage and Runner exchanged looks, then left the building in a rush.

Just as they stepped outside, they saw Adam. He was being half-dragged between two Navaho braves, his eyes flashing angrily as he tried to pull himself free.

Sage turned cold when he saw Adam again, recalling how Adam had been in Pure Blossom's hogan as though he belonged there. It had sickened him then; it repelled him now.

When Runner saw Adam being treated in such a way, he was stunned speechless. He did not want Adam in the village any more than anyone else, but it did seem that this was going a bit too far.

He stepped forward. "Let him go," he said, finding it strange to defend this man whom he now considered an enemy. "Why are you treating him this way?"

"I forbid Adam ever to enter our village again," Sage said, stepping up beside Runner. "And it is not because of what he is proposing to do on Navaho land. It is because of your sister, Runner. He shamed Pure Blossom by taking her to her bed."

Runner paled and turned to face his father. "What are you saying?" he managed out in a gasp.

Pure Blossom stepped forward, her exquisitely long hair blowing in the gentle breeze.

"He went to my bed at my invitation," she boldly announced, lifting her chin when everyone grew silent and stared at her.

"When he was discovered there, I sent him away," Sage mumbled.

Runner recalled seeing Adam on his horse without his boots and shirt. Now he understood why.

He turned to Adam, scowling. "You do this to my sister?" he snarled. "For your own selfish gains you do this?" He slapped Adam across the face, the snapping sound like a vast echo across the land.

Adam turned with the blow, then he stroked the stinging flesh of his cheek as he frowned over at Runner. "If anyone else did that, I would challenge him to a duel," he said, his voice cold and angry. "As it is you, I shall pass on the suggestion. I have come to apologize, not to fight."

"Apologize?" Sage said, raising an eyebrow.

"You do not know the meaning of the word," Runner said from between clenched teeth.

"Please hear him out," Pure Blossom begged, grabbing her father's arm. "Please?"

Sage stared down at his daughter for a moment, then drew her against his side. "Speak your mind," he said, glaring at Adam.

"I did not come to Arizona to make enemies with those of my past for whom I have always felt a fondness," Adam said, stepping away from the braves as they let go of him. "Please accept my apologies for anything I may have done to cause hard feelings," he said, his voice drawn.

"Are you saying you will rip up the tracks that are laid farther than Gallup?" Sage tested, his eyes wary.

"I can't promise you that," Adam said guardedly. "That, and my proposed town, is still in my plans. But nothing more. I am not asking for more land than the United States Government has already agreed upon. I hope that you will see there will be no harm done your people by that little that I have planned."

There was a strained silence. Adam looked over at Runner. "Runner, please accept me again as a friend."

Sage and Runner gave each other wary looks, then

Sage nodded. "I understand that there is nothing I can do to stop the progress that the white father of this country approves of," he said. "But there is one thing I can do."

"And that is?" Adam urged, seeing a glimmer of hope for his ploy.

"I can accept your apology and receive you again into my heart as a friend, but only if you stay away from my daughter," Sage said, his eyes intent on Adam. "That one condition must be met, or we will be enemies forever."

Pure Blossom emitted a gasping sob. She gave her father a wavering look, then turned and fled into her hogan, crying.

"That is not what your daughter wants," Adam dared to say.

"She does not understand yet that her father is doing what is best for her," Sage said. "In time, she will learn the wisdom of this decision."

"And you will not sway in this decision?" Adam said, knowing that he wouldn't, and also knowing that it made no difference what Sage demanded of his daughter. Adam knew that nothing would keep them apart, even if it meant meeting in secret.

"Never," Sage said, firmly lifting his chin.

"Then I see no choice but to agree to your terms," Adam said. "We can now shake on a renewal of our friendship?" He extended his hand, smiled at Runner as he shook it, his eyes gleaming as Sage shook it in turn. "Runner, will you go with me to Gallup in a couple of days, to travel as friends, to seal the bond again by joining activities now of men, instead of boys?" Adam added.

"Why Gallup?" Runner asked.

"I'd rather not say now," Adam said, clasping a hand

on Runner's shoulder. "Please trust that what I have planned will be a great time for old friends."

Runner looked over at his father, who stood unmoving, neither approving nor disapproving.

"Gallup it is," Runner said, deciding suddenly.

Adam's eyes looked into Runner's, behind them a hidden hunger for vengeance. More than once he had been humiliated at the hands of the Navaho.

He would have his own turn to be the one to do the humiliating—in Gallup.

The day had been long as the Navaho readied themselves for the midnight jaunt to Damon Stout's ranch. Runner had not been able to get Adam off his mind after Adam had left. He did not trust this instant friendship that his old friend was offering. There had to be a hidden motive.

Runner had decided to play along, to see what the motive might be. But now, while riding on his stallion, Runner tried to center his attention on the task at hand. Thunder Hawk rode on his left side, Sage on his right, their eyes eagerly searching through the night for anyone who might discover them in the act of horse stealing.

Sage had told Thunder Hawk that horse stealing was not something that was to be done often. It was done only at times to teach those who stole from the People that a Navaho was not so easily tricked.

They finally arrived at Damon's corral, the moon blessedly covered by a dark shroud of clouds to hide their activities.

Runner roped a fence post and rode away on his horse, the post ripping free from the ground. Sage rode into the corral, Thunder Hawk beside him.

Sage looked at his youngest son in wonder. Thunder

Hawk knew too easily where to go and pick out the horses that were theirs, and how to chase them down and rope them.

Runner also watched the ease with which his younger brother helped his father take the horses from the corral, as though practiced. He recalled the times when he had found his brother riding alone at night, tasting freedom, and wondered if Thunder Hawk might have also been practicing the art of stealing horses.

Thunder Hawk had no horses of his own. He couldn't accuse his brother of something that he could not prove.

Runner continued watching Thunder Hawk, no longer seeing him as just a young man who was being forced to attend school. He saw that his brother had turned into a man.

16

Say thou lovest me, while thou live,
I to thee my love will give,
Never dreaming to deceive
While that life endures.

—ANONYMOUS

As Stephanie stared down at her rumpled bed, she buttoned her blouse. No matter how hard she had tried, she couldn't go to sleep tonight. Although Adam had apologized to Sage and Runner, she worried about his sincerity. She could not imagine Adam giving in that easily, not even for *her*. If he was playing games, she could be the loser—she could lose Runner.

"I need a breath of air," she said, smoothing her hands down the front of her skirt. Perhaps a ride on her horse would provide an escape from her thoughts. And if that didn't wear her out, nothing would.

Grabbing up her holstered derringer, she fastened it around her waist. As she put on a light-weight leather coat, she looked through the window and could see a light on in Adam's private car.

"He's awake," she whispered to herself.

She had to make sure he didn't hear her and stop her. She *had* to have this time alone, away from the train, away from him. Away from *everyone*.

Stepping lightly, she left her private car. She glanced

over at Adam's door, watching to see if he had heard the door close.

Having left her horse just outside her private car, at the hitching rail, it was easier to escape tonight without making the usual clatter. A chill wind sighed as she swung herself into the saddle, causing a shiver to race up and down her spine.

Lifting the reins and nudging her horse into a soft, lope away from the train, she looked guardedly around her. Everything was thickly shadowed, the full moon hidden behind a shroud of dark clouds. She could not help but remember how quickly Damon had jumped out at her the previous evening. It could happen again. She knew that. But she would not allow herself to be trapped by fear.

Finally away from the train, Stephanie slapped the reins and rode in a hard gallop across the land.

Stephanie crouched low and raced through the velveteen blackness of night. She inhaled the fresh, clean air, enjoying the feel of the vast land.

Having never felt as free, her mind now momentarily clear of all its clutter, she rode on. When the moon came from behind its cloud cover, she was in awe of what the light revealed. At night, as the moon's glow splashed all around her, she not only saw but felt the mystical quality of the land.

"The Navaho are so lucky to have been a part of this land for so long," she whispered.

As never before, she was seeing why they had fought for their rights to it.

She had read many books before having ventured to the land of the Navaho. She had read the account of Kit Carson's actions against the Navaho, and how he had forced Sage and his people from their stronghold all those years ago.

She had always admired the stories told about Kit Carson, but then she had heard of the tyranny he had practiced against the Navaho and could see him as nothing less than ruthless and scheming.

A sound, similar to thunder in the distance, caused Stephanie to draw her mount to a halt. Her fingers tightened involuntarily on the reins when her horse jerked sideways.

She looked heavenward, puzzling as to why she had heard thunder. The sky was clear, the moon bright. Stars were twinkling like sequins overhead.

She squinted and looked into the distance, now realizing that what she was hearing couldn't be thunder. It was a steady drone that went on and on.

"Horses," she whispered.

Suddenly the horses appeared ahead of her, and then several horsemen. It was a black and white torrent of manes and tails and hooves, trailing the moon's glow. The horsemen were cutting back and forth behind the herd, gently keeping them moving.

Stephanie edged her mount beneath a ledge so that she could not be seen and eagerly watched as the horses and riders drew closer. By the light of the moon, she soon recognized the horsemen. They were Navaho. They were herding the horses across a straight stretch of land in the direction of Runner's village.

Then, when they began riding past her, oblivious of her presence, Stephanie gasped. "Runner!" she whispered.

He was among the men. And not only Runner—she soon recognized Sage and Thunder Hawk.

She continued watching, wondering why they were herding the horses this time of night. Suddenly, a thought occurred to her. "What if they stole them . . . ?" she whispered aloud.

She suddenly recalled Runner sneaking about at Damon's ranch, looking at the horses.

A low snarling sound drew Stephanie's attention elsewhere. When she saw the glint of several eyes in the darkness, moving toward her, she grew limp with fright. The moon soon revealed the gray, shaggy coats of several wolves as they slinked toward her.

Her fingers trembling, Stephanie reached for her derringer as they revealed their sharp teeth, growling.

Before she had the chance to take her firearm from its holster, one of the wolves made a lunge at Stephanie's horse, spooking it.

Stephanie screamed and hung on for dear life as it neighed and reared with fright and then took off in a mad, crazed gallop.

"Whoa!" Stephanie shouted, then screamed again when it went even faster.

She clung with all of her might to the reins.

"Stop!" she cried. "Whoa!"

Nothing she did appeased the horse's fears. He kept plunging onward.

Stephanie slowly became aware of someone riding beside her. She didn't dare take her eyes off the ground ahead of her. She hoped and prayed that the horse wouldn't stop suddenly.

"Stephanie, when I reach my arm out for you, let go of the reins!" she heard Runner shout at her.

"I'm afraid to!" she cried, her eyes still glued straight ahead.

Runner edged his stallion closer and closer. "Now!" he shouted. "Let . . . go . . . now!"

Stephanie sucked in a wild, frightened breath, then dropped the reins. She closed her eyes and said a silent prayer, then gasped as she was grabbed from the speeding horse and held safely on Runner's lap.

Runner drew his mount to a quivering halt. He placed a finger to Stephanie's chin and brought her eyes up to meet his. "Are you all right?" he said as Sage rode silently up beside them.

Stephanie sighed heavily, her breathing raspy. "I'm fine," she finally managed to say. "Thanks to you. If you hadn't come along, I'm not sure what would have happened. My horse just wouldn't stop."

Runner enveloped her within his hard, powerful arms and hugged her, then he leaned her away from him, a deep frown furrowing his brow. "What are you doing this far from the train?" he said, his voice drawn. "And alone? What are you thinking of?"

"I *needed* to be alone," Stephanie said sullenly. "I . . . couldn't . . . sleep."

Thunder Hawk rode up, questioning her with his dark eyes, and she smiled shyly at him, then looked up at Runner again. "Why are *you* out this time of night, herding horses?" she murmured.

Runner and Sage exchanged quick glances, then Runner rode away with Stephanie to catch her horse, leaving Sage and Thunder Hawk staring after them.

"Father, it does not seem as though my brother heeds your warnings about the white woman," Thunder Hawk said, wincing when he saw anger and pain in his father's eyes.

"His heart makes him do strange things," Sage said in a mumble. "And although this father hates to admit it, I do understand my older son's behavior. Many moons ago, your father's heart was stolen by a woman with white skin."

He smiled over at Thunder Hawk, and tousled his son's wiry, black hair. "You would not be here had I not allowed my heart to take control of my mind," he said proudly.

"It is good to hear that you understand a son's love for a particular woman," Thunder Hawk said, reaching over to clasp a hand to his father's shoulder. "I would hope that when love comes to me, you will understand."

"Your education is important now," Sage said, his eyes narrowing. "Not women."

Thunder Hawk stared after his father as Sage rode away to join those who were still herding the horses toward his village.

"Soon you will see that this son also does not bear your words, nor follows your bidding," Thunder Hawk said, scowling. He sank his moccasined heels into the flanks of his horse and rode away to join the other braves.

Stephanie's horse was caught and tethered. Runner and Stephanie rested beside a small, winding stream, before taking the long ride back to her private car. The chase had taken them farther and farther into a canyon. There they were protected from the cooler breezes of night. There they sat beside a slow burning fire, the warmth spreading to the stark, red walls on either side of them where the canyon walls reached high into tall buttes overhead.

Watching the slow burning flames of the fire, Stephanie cuddled next to Runner. "You haven't said yet why you were herding the horses at this time of night," she murmured, turning to give him a slow, questioning look.

"That is nothing to concern yourself about," Runner said, drawing her lips to his mouth. "It is Navaho business."

He embraced her and lifted her onto his lap, threading several locks of her hair through his fingers. "Let's not question each other about our separate reasons for riding through the darkness of night," he breathed huskily against her lips. "Except for the moon and stars, we are alone. Let us show them the wonders of our love."

His lips clinging to hers, he pressed her down onto the ground. His one hand ran down the length of her, then traced a heated path up her leg, beneath her skirt.

Stephanie moaned against his lips as he caressed her between her thighs. She lifted her hips to help him as he tugged her undergarments down.

Her hands shoved his fringed breeches over his hips. When his desire for her sprang into sight, she circled her fingers around him and led him to where she had opened her legs, to receive him inside her.

Runner's arms snaked around her waist and drew her pliant body against his as he thrust himself into her depths. As he drew his lips away, he smiled down at her, and watching her become enraptured by their love-making, he could see a hungry fire burning in her eyes and was aware of a sudden curling heat tightening within him.

"I love you so," she whispered, and twined her fingers through his long, black hair, bringing his mouth to hers again. She pressed a warm kiss to his lips, then darted her tongue into his mouth.

Their bodies jolted and quivered as their passion reached the bursting point. They clung; they rocked; they moaned. And then their bodies subsided exhaustedly into one another's.

Runner rolled away from her, but held her endearingly at his side.

"We should leave," Runner said, reaching for her undergarments, bending over her to slip them up her tapered legs. "As it is, we may not arrive at your railroad car until dawn."

"I don't care if I go back there at all," Stephanie murmured, giving him a pouting look as he smoothed her skirt. "When I am with you, everything is so simple. It is when we are separated that I find things so complicated and confusing." She leaned into his embrace, placing her head on his chest. "Will we ever find a true, lasting peace in our relationship?"

"Since I was a child, I have never known the true meaning of peace," Runner said somberly, covering the fire with dirt to smother it. "The Navaho have fought hard to retain a peaceful coexistence with the white man. But there are always those who try and take that from us."

"When you say that, you are including Adam, aren't you?" Stephanie said, pushing herself up from the ground.

"Would you say that he has brought us peace?" Runner said, turning to Stephanie.

Speechless, she gazed at him for a moment, then flung herself back into his arms. "I would hope that you could say that I have brought something into your life besides pain and hardships," she murmured. "Runner, I cannot ever think of an existence now without you."

Their lips came together in a sweet, lasting kiss, then Runner took Stephanie by the waist and lifted her into her saddle, then swung himself onto his own horse. "Somehow, we will manage to work things out so that we can always be together," he said softly.

"I want nothing more than that," Stephanie said.

She followed him as he led his horse into a slow lope down a winding path away from the canyon, the moon once again hidden behind dark clouds.

A cigar in one hand, a whiskey bottle in the other, Adam took a long, deep swallow that emptied the bottle, then set it on the table beside him. He set his cigar aside in an ashtray, his eyes burning from lack of sleep. He was still upset over having been forbidden ever to see Pure Blossom again. He had to find a way of protecting her when he put his plans in motion against the Navaho. Even if he had to go so far as to hide her away in his private car, so be it. Now that he had found such a love, there was no way that he would deny himself. Fires burned in his loins just thinking about her.

A light tapping sound at his door drew his attention away from his reverie. "Stephanie?" he said to himself. "What the hell would she want this time of night?"

When he tried to get up, he discovered that he was lightheaded from the whiskey. He stumbled out of the chair and walked in a weaving, staggering fashion to his door. Squinting into the darkness, he swung the door open, then gasped with surprise when he found someone besides his sister standing there.

"Pure Blossom?" he said, his eyes widening. He blinked them slowly. "Am I imagining things, or are you truly standing there?"

"I have come to you," she said, throwing herself into his arms. "I could not stay away."

He wove his fingers into her lustrous, long hair. "But your father," he drawled drunkenly. "You know you are going against your father's wishes. . . ."

"To be with you, yes," Pure Blossom said, gazing raptly up at him. "It is not the first time I have gone against his wishes because of you. How can he expect me to obey him?"

"Darling, how did you know which train car was mine?" Adam said, drawing her into the room, closing the door behind them. "What if you would have knocked at my sister's door, instead of mine?"

"Then I would have excused myself and come to yours," Pure Blossom said stubbornly.

"You are a daring, beautiful woman," Adam said. He lifted her up into his arms and carried her to his bed. "I think I have to give you some sort of payment for your trouble in coming here, don't you?"

In the cold darkness of the private car, they laughed, giggled, and touched. Their moans filled the dark spaces with passion's bliss.

17

Hurt no living thing,
Ladybird nor butterfly,
Nor moth with dusty wings,
Nor cricket chirping cheerily.
—CHRISTINA ROSSETTI

Fort Defiance

The distant hills were shaded in purple and gray. The sunlight was like liquid gold as it poured its glorious, morning light across a landscape of bronze and green. Damon had discovered only a short while ago that several of his horses were missing. It didn't matter to him that he had originally stolen them from the Navaho: any horse was his horse when it was stolen from *his* corral.

His arrival at the fort had awakened everyone before the morning reveille. He impatiently paced the floor as he waited for the Indian agent, Alfred Bryant, to come into his office so that a complaint could be lodged. He had also asked for an audience with Colonel Scott Utley.

Damon felt that surely between these two important men, something could be done about the damn thieving Injuns. He wanted the Navaho run off from the Arizona Territory, and along with them, their mangy sheep. He wanted the land for himself so that he could bring cattle in from Texas. With Adam's financial backing, Damon saw a future for himself paved in gold.

Heavy footsteps behind him caused Damon to stop pacing and turn and glower. "It's about time," he drawled as the agent sauntered sleepily into the small, dark office. "If you'd tend to business instead of sleepin' till noon, I wouldn't have to be here lodgin' complaint after complaint against the Navaho."

"What is it now?" Alfred yawned, his rusty red mustache quivering. The suspenders that only moments ago had been hanging lazily on each side of his waist were now being slipped over his shoulders. "My God, Damon, don't you ever sleep? Every time you come here to pester me with your complaints about the Navaho you do it at the crack of dawn."

Damon found it hard to hold his temper under control. With angry eyes, he waited as Alfred moved in a slow, lazy saunter and sat down behind his desk. He glared at Alfred. To Damon, the agent resembled a chicken with his long, scrawny neck and over-sized Adam's apple. His nose was long and pointed, his eyes so narrow you could scarcely see their color.

A lieutenant came into the room carrying a tray on which sat a steaming pot of coffee and two mugs. After Alfred scooted several strewn papers and journals aside, to make room for the tray, the lieutenant placed it on Alfred's desk and left again without having acknowledged Damon's presence.

Damon knew that no one at the fort liked seeing him come. He was a reminder of how little they had achieved against the Navaho. No one liked being reminded of their shortcomings, not even a worthless agent, and an even more useless colonel.

"Coffee?" Alfred said, pouring.

"This ain't no damn social call," Damon spat. He went to the desk and leaned on it with his hands. "I've come to lodge another complaint against the damn Navaho. Are you ready to listen, or do I have to wait until you've emptied that full pot of coffee?"

Alfred looked up at Damon. "You're close to bein' insulting," he said, frowning. "Now, if you can't be civil, I'd advise you to get your carcass outta here. I ain't paid to listen to your bellyachin' week in and week out."

"Are you paid to take care of problems with Injuns, or ain't you?" Damon said. "Or do I have to go and send a wire to Washington and inform them that you're a lowdown, worthless son-of-a-bitch?"

"Damon, I've taken about all I can from you," Alfred said. He rose slowly from the chair, his face red with anger. "Now speak your mind, or damn it, get out, and . . . I don't give a damn if you send a wire to the President. I've decided to take my leave, anyhow, and be an agent somewhere else, where I don't have the likes of you jumpin' my ass over something you've cooked up between you and the Navaho."

"Do you call horse thievin' somethin' to be tolerated?" Damon hissed. "If so, since when do Indians get to steal from a white man without payin' for it at the end of a hangman's noose?"

"Which Indians?" Alfred said, easing back down in the chair, sighing impatiently.

"The Navaho, that's who."

"Names. I need names."

"Runner. Sage. Thunder Hawk."

Alfred's jaw tightened. "Do you have any proof?" he asked. "You display an almost sadistic streak of cruelty where the Navaho are concerned. You're always talking about ways to even a score with this man or that. So do you think I take you seriously now?"

"My word. Ain't that proof enough?"

Alfred laughed sarcastically. "Your word be damned."

"Are you sayin' you won't take my word and that the thieving savages are going to be allowed to get away with this?" He turned around and started walking toward the door. "I guess I'll go and see what Colonel Utley has to say about this," he tossed over his shoulder.

"You plan to see him today?" Alfred said, chuckling.

"Sure do." Damon took hold of the doorknob.

"Then have a pleasant ride to Washington," Alfred said. His eyes danced when Damon turned to stare blankly at him. "But I must warn you. Everyone is aware of your prejudice out here."

"He's in Washington?"

"Yep. Left awhile back. But I'm sure he'd make time for you if you took your complaint to Washington."

Damon stamped over to the desk. He leaned across it and grabbed Alfred by the throat. "It's a good thing you're plannin' on leavin' the Arizona Territory," he said with a feral snarl.

Alfred's face grew beet red and his eyes were wild. Damon released him and left the office in a fury.

The only thing left for him to do was to speed up the plan that Adam wanted to set into motion to ruin Sage. If tricking the Navaho was his only recourse now, then so be it.

The sun was showing its full, round face just over the mountains when Runner and Stephanie arrived back at the train. Stephanie slid out of her saddle and tethered her horse to the hitching rail, then went to Runner.

"Must you go?" Stephanie asked, begging up at him with her wide, smoky gray eyes. "If you'd stay, we could share breakfast and coffee, get some rest, go out later today to take some photographs. We could make an entire day of it, Runner. Please stay?"

"I need to go and see if my father made it safely back to the village with the horses," Runner said. He glanced over his shoulder in the direction of his village, then turned to gaze down at Stephanie again. "I feel guilty for having left him last night, but he had many braves to help with the horses."

"There is such a strong loyalty between you, isn't there?" Stephanie said. "I admire that in sons and fathers."

She looked toward Adam's private car. "I know that Adam wishes his true father were alive," she said softly. Then she looked up at Runner again. "Except for Adam getting on my father's nerves now and then, Adam and my father get along well enough. But as far as loyalties go? I'm not sure if Adam could feel that strong a bond with anyone."

"He seems genuinely concerned over your welfare," Runner said, stroking his stallion's mane. "In that there is a loyalty, as though you were his true sister, would you not say?"

"Perhaps," Stephanie said, slowly nodding. "Anyhow, he does seem sincere enough."

Runner reached down and touched Stephanie's cheek tenderly. "My feelings are *quite* genuine," he said softly, then leaned lower and gave her a melting kiss.

A noise drew them apart. They both gasped as they found Pure Blossom running swiftly from Adam's private car, obviously trying to sneak away while Stephanie and Runner were occupied.

"Pure Blossom?" Runner said, his voice drawn. He

gave his sister a puzzled stare when she stopped and looked at him, guilt etched onto her lovely face.

Runner slipped out of the saddle, his eyes on Adam, who cowered on the steps of the train. Enraged, he went over to Adam and slammed a fist into his jaw. When Adam fell to the ground, Runner was there just as quickly to grab him up by the shirt collar and hit him again.

Pure Blossom ran to her brother and grabbed him by an arm. "Stop!" she cried. "Big brother, do not do this thing! Adam had nothing to do with me being here. I came to him on my own. I came to him because I wanted to. Because he loved me, he took me in. Would you rather he turn me away into the dark, to return home alone at the mercy of the coyotes? Instead, he offered me lodging."

"And more, I am certain," Runner said. His teeth were clenched as he stood over Adam, who was swaying, finding it difficult to stand. Blood was running from Adam's nose and mouth. One eye was already swelling shut.

"Can you tell me, old friend, that you did not share the same bed as my sister last night?" Runner said.

"*I* slept with *him*," Pure Blossom quickly interjected, pride in her voice. "So if blame must be cast, it should be entirely on your sister."

Runner's eyes wavered as he looked down at Pure Blossom. "Knowing how Father feels, why would you do this?" he asked.

Pure Blossom cast a defiant look Stephanie's way, then turned her eyes back to Runner. "Why do you, big brother, continue to have liaisons with the white woman, when you also know how Father feels?" she asked in return.

Stephanie stirred uneasily. She knew that what Pure

Blossom said made good sense, yet she still did not like
to be made an example of. She saw hers and Runner's
situation much differently than her brother's and Pure
Blossom's. Sage had absolutely *forbidden* Adam to see
Pure Blossom under *any* circumstances. He had made a
pact with Adam, that Adam would be welcome among
the Navaho as long as he no longer courted Pure
Blossom.

Runner's father had made no such ultimatum to him.
Stephanie had given him no cause to, especially since
she was not interfering directly in their lives.

"Pure Blossom, no matter what you say, you should
not be with Adam," Runner said, drawing her closer.
"Sweet little sister, he is not right for you. He will
never marry you. Do you not see that his world is so
opposite ours? He would not take you into his white
world with him, nor would he stay with you in yours.
Time spent with him is wasted. Please see that and say
a final farewell to him. You will be better off because
of it."

Runner couldn't tell his sister how he was truly feeling: Adam might be sincere about Pure Blossom now,
when only a slight hump was present at the base of her
skull, but soon she would be showing more signs of her
affliction which could become grotesque in the eyes of
such a man as Adam.

Yet he knew that even his father would not be able
to stop the love affair between his sister and this white
man now. And did not his sister deserve a measure of
happiness while it was still possible?

Pure Blossom went to Adam and smoothed gentle
fingers across his swollen eyelid, then took a handkerchief from his breeches pocket and began dabbing at
his cuts.

"You do not care that I am Navaho, do you?" she

murmured. "You would not be ashamed to have a Navaho wife?"

Adam's eyes wavered into hers. He swallowed hard, touched anew by her innocent beauty and the sincerity in her voice.

"I love you," he said, his voice breaking. "I want everything to be possible for you. Even marriage to the man you love."

Sobbing, Pure Blossom flung herself into Adam's arms. "I knew that you cared," she cried.

Stephanie went to Runner and took his hand. She led him away from Pure Blossom and Adam.

"It seems my brother *is* sincere about your sister," she said softly.

"Pity your brother should he ever hurt her," Runner said, drawing Stephanie into his embrace. Over Stephanie's shoulder, he watched Pure Blossom and Adam kissing. His insides seethed at the sight. Yet, perhaps he was wrong about Adam. For his sister's sake, he had no choice but to give Adam the benefit of the doubt.

Runner stepped away from Stephanie and swung himself up on his horse. "Come, little sister," he said, his voice carrying to Pure Blossom. "Get your horse and come home with me."

Pure Blossom retrieved her horse from its hiding place and led it over beside Runner's. Adam lifted her into the saddle.

"Runner, if Father has not missed me, do not tell him where I spent the night," Pure Blossom begged. "I want to give him more time. Then I shall tell him."

She smiled down at Adam, then looked somberly over at Runner again. "When our wedding date has been planned, big brother, *then* I will tell both Mother *and* Father. Will you please allow me this time? I do not want to test our father's wrath just yet."

"Secrets are ugly," Runner said, his jaw tightening.

"Sometimes they are necessary," Pure Blossom said softly. "At least, for a short while."

"I will think about it," Runner said, then nodded a farewell to Stephanie and urged his horse off in a soft trot. "Come, little sister. Today I will help you sneak into your hogan without being seen. I am not sure about tomorrow, though."

Pure Blossom drew up next to Runner. "*Uke-he*, thank you," she said, her eyes smiling.

Adam and Stephanie stared at one another for a moment, then Adam took her into his arms. "Thank you for not voicing an opinion," he said, stroking her hair. "I could see it in your eyes that you did not approve of what I'm up to."

"What *are* you up to, Adam?" Stephanie said, taking a step away from him. "Are you truly in love with Pure Blossom?"

"With all of my heart," Adam said, then turned to walk away from her, toward his private car.

"But that isn't always enough, is it, Adam?"

Adam turned and gave her a steady stare, then continued on.

"Good lord," Stephanie said to herself, growing cold inside, "he's not going to marry her."

She slowly shook her head. Her brother was playing a dangerous game, but she could only wait and see how he played it out. She silently prayed that somehow he might change his mind and be true to Pure Blossom after all.

Love sometimes conquered all—even greedy, conniving brothers.

18

Love, to endure life's sorrow,
and earth's woes,
Needs friendships' solid
masonwork below.
—ELLA WHEELER WILCOX

By noon, Stephanie and Runner were together again.
She followed his lead, taking advantage of whatever he
allowed her to photograph, thankful for at least that.
Adam had caused enough problems for Runner and his
family; she wanted to continue being the peacemaker.
Most certainly she did not want to be labeled the
antagonist.

Today she had followed Runner on frightening
climbs, zigzagging upward, across saguaro-studded
slopes and along barren ridges sparsely dotted with
cedar. She had seen tarantulas the size of saucers scut-
tling slowly across the land. She had been horrified at
the sight of rattlesnakes sunning themselves on rocks.
She had seen all sorts of colorful lizards.

Riding in a slow lope across sand dotted with various
cactus plants, Stephanie edged her horse over closer to
Runner's stallion.

"Runner, I've heard of a place called Canyon del
Muerto, where there was a Spanish massacre of Navaho
people in 1805," she said. She winced when she saw an
angry fire light his eyes.

Yet she proceeded to ask about it. "It is called the Antelope House Ruins, is it not?" she prodded. "I read that a large number of Navaho women and children were killed there. Would you take me to see it?"

"It is a place where if you stand among the ruins, you will still hear the wails of those mothers long ago as they stood watching their children being slain by the Spaniards," Runner said, giving Stephanie a tight-jawed look. "Canyon del Muerto forks off to the east from Canyon de Chelley. I will not escort you to either place."

"Canyon de Chelley," Stephanie said, nodding. "I read many accounts of that, also. I had hoped that you and I could go there. I so badly want to see it."

"If you went there, you would be tempted too much to photograph it; it is a place of sheer beauty," Runner said, nudging his horse into a faster pace.

Stephanie did the same and caught up with him. "I hear that it is breathtakingly beautiful," she said. "I read that the canyon has dramatic red sandstone walls, within which are more than four hundred ancient Indian cliff dwellings. There are supposedly hundreds of wall paintings and rock carvings everywhere in the canyon."

The more she talked about what she had learned while studying the Arizona Territory, the more intrigued she became over Canyon de Chelley. And she feared that Runner was wise not to escort her there. She would most certainly be tempted to take photographs of it. Those particular photographs would be all that the Santa Fe Railroad would need to lure passengers to travel to a mystical land scarcely seen by tourists.

"This sacred place, which lies at the heart of the Navaho Indian reservation, has more than beauty that touches one's soul," Runner said, giving Stephanie a pensive look. "To the Navaho it is the rift in the earth from which the gods emerged to direct and teach men. The echoing walls send back voices from those who no longer walk the earth. The canyon is not only the home of the Navaho gods but of the prehistoric people, the *Anasazi,* or 'Ancient Ones,' who are ancesters of the Hopi. The ancient drawings belong to them. This is why they must be treated with reverence."

"I understand," Stephanie said sullenly. "I won't ask you again to take me there." Then her eyes brightened. "Perhaps we can go to a place that is called Spider Rock? I would love to photograph it. I hear that it rises eight hundred feet from a canyon floor. What a sight it must be!"

"That, also, cannot be captured inside the walls of your camera," Runner said firmly. "Spider Rock is the legendary home of Spider Woman, who, according to myth, taught weaving to the Navaho."

Feeling unnerved by Runner's formal manner today, Stephanie fell into a stony silence.

Then a glimmer of hope began to shine in her eyes. In a sense, he had played right into her hands today. Earlier, before he had arrived to escort her, she had sent one of the men who worked with the work gang ahead to Gallup with enough money to make arrangements for a one-night stay in one of Gallup's finest hotels. She had hoped that she could somehow lure Runner there with her.

Now she had the perfect plan. He had said no to her so often today he would surely find it hard to keep denying her everything. Hopefully he would feel guilty and agree when she asked him to accompany her to Gallup. Little would he know that she had a room waiting for them, for a wonderful, carefree night away from Adam and Runner's family.

The night would be theirs: alone.

She could already feel the fizz of the champagne as she sipped from a long-stemmed glass. Runner would be in bed beside her on satin sheets, tipping his own glass of bubbly liquid to his perfectly-sculpted lips.

"Would you go with me to Gallup?" she said suddenly.

Runner gave her a quizzical stare. "Gallup?" he said, raising an eyebrow. "Why would you want to go to Gallup?"

"Our travels today have taken us quite close to the town," Stephanie said. "Please let's go to the lunch room on the second floor of the railway station at Gallup. I'm starved. We didn't bring enough food to last us until we return to my car. Please, Runner? We would only be there for a short while. Only long enough to get a bite to eat."

Although she was not trying to fight Adam's battles for him, Stephanie felt that it wouldn't hurt for Runner to see the sort of establishments Adam would like to build in the town that he was planning. She wanted to show Runner how good and decent it was. She only hoped that his attention wouldn't be drawn to the many saloons in Gallup.

Runner rode awhile in silence as he thought through her suggestion. He had refused Stephanie many opportunities to photograph interesting sites today. How could he continue to say no to her?

But he was ready to take her into Gallup for other reasons as well. That part of him that was white was making him momentarily stray from his Indian ideals and way of life. He had always tended to his business and had left Gallup as quickly as possible, mainly to keep from having confrontations with Damon Stout's ranch hands who seemed to be everywhere at once. He would be glad to have an excuse to take his time, to be able to see more of the town and the ways of the white people. As a child, he had been in restaurants in various cities, but it was hard to recall. He had only been six the last time his mother had taken him to such a fancy establishment.

"If you wish, we shall go there," Runner finally said. When he looked her way and saw how happy his decision had made her, he was glad that he had decided to do as she asked.

He could not deny the strange excitement that he was feeling himself, and just as quickly felt ashamed. He had devoted most of his childhood and all of his adult life to the ways of the Navaho. He should not hunger to be a part of the white man's world. Yet, as his horse rode closer to Gallup, he could not find the strength within himself to turn back in the direction of his village.

When they finally reached Gallup, long shadows were rippling over the land. The desert town straggled along both sides of the Santa Fe Railroad tracks which, paralleled by a dusty road, separated the business district from a drab row of dwellings. The false-fronted framed businesses leaned against each other for common support against the constant wind. Opposite them, on the other side of the tracks, were many weathered shacks.

As they rode up the main street, where horsemen and horse-drawn buggies roamed in both directions, Stephanie and Runner looked on each side of them.

Everything was dark except for the lantern lights, which flooded the boardwalks along the thoroughfare with their golden glows.

The further they rode, the brighter the lights became, as well as the noise that wafted from the saloons. Pianos clinked out loud and merry tunes. Boisterous laughter and loud swearing came through the swinging doors.

The sound of glass breaking and fights erupting from more than one of the establishments made Stephanie grow increasingly nervous.

She gave Runner a troubled glance. His eyes were filled with an angry fire. His jaw was tight.

"We're almost there," she offered.

She now realized that she had been wrong to bring Runner to this town. It was a poor example of what she had hoped to show him Adam's town might be. When she had ridden through Gallup on the train that one time, where the tracks connected to the private spur, she had not paid much attention to it, except to look up at the lunch room and remember Adam having said it was an excellent place to get a fine meal and glass of wine.

She was disappointed when she realized there were no fancy emporiums or restaurants. And there was only one hotel.

Thank God, she thought to herself. The hotel was the most decent-appearing establishment of all. At least she wouldn't have to fight off cockroaches or rats as she sipped her champagne.

Something else soon drew both Stephanie and Runner's attention.

"The Big Tent," she whispered.

It was a one hundred by forty foot framed tent conveniently floored for dancing and lit by about fifty lanterns and numerous candles glowing from cut-glass candle holders. Music was provided night and day by full bands. Music blared from the tent even now, as well as laughter and merriment.

Stephanie blushed when she caught sight of some of the bawdy women who were known to frequent the Big Tent. Scantily dressed, and with their faces gaudily painted, they were standing at the door of the tent waving and shouting at Runner as he rode on past.

Finally they arrived at the railroad station. An idle engine was puffing black, sooty smoke from its stack, waiting as passengers loaded into the cars, to be taken to various parts of the country. Stephanie and Runner drew rein on the opposite side of the building, away from the tracks.

As Stephanie slid from her saddle, she looked up at the windows overhead. Soft light flickered from them, inviting and peaceful. She was anxious to get Runner in the lunch room, hoping that he would forget the ugliness of the town, soon taken by the pleasant hotel accommodations.

Outside, stairs led up to the lunch room at the back of the building. A strained silence had fallen between Stephanie and Runner as they climbed the steps. When they entered the room, where many candle-lit tables were occupied by fancily-dressed men and women, all eyes turned to Runner.

Although he was of a white heritage, his skin was bronzed dark from the sun and wind, and his hair was black, sleek and long like the Navaho, held back by a brightly-colored bandanna. Today he wore fringed clothes, making him look even more Indian. Prejudice against him being there emanated from the other diners as Stephanie took Runner by the arm and led him to a table.

Runner could feel molten hot eyes on him. He surmised that those people who were staring at him knew by the way he was dressed that he was the "White Indian" everyone had heard rumors about.

Stephanie was only now aware that Runner would not know the proper manners required for dining out. Why hadn't she thought of that earlier? She hurriedly sat down without his assistance so that it would look like she was the one who was uneducated in proper etiquette.

When Runner still stood there, stiff and quiet, she feared that he was going to change his mind and leave. Then he scooted his chair out and sat down, and she heaved a deep sigh of relief.

"I'm sorry if I am the cause for you being uncomfortable," she said, leaning over the table so that only he could hear her. "If you'd rather leave, I would understand."

"I have faced worse ridicule," Runner said, his shoulders proudly squared. As the candle's glow shone in flickering shadows on Stephanie's face, everything and everyone but her was forgotten. She was ever so beautiful.

His uneasiness returned when a waitress stepped up and asked to take their order. He looked around him and noticed that there were several young ladies who served as waitresses. They wore long black dresses, flowing white aprons, and hair-bows.

"The menu," Stephanie whispered over at Runner. "You must choose what you want from the menu."

She knew that he had gone to school, enabling him to read. Yet as he picked up the menu and his eyes began to scan the entries, she could see that he was confused.

"If you wish, I shall order for both of us," Stephanie suggested softly.

"I shall order for you and myself," Runner said, surprising Stephanie.

"That would be fine," she said. She closed her menu, turned a soft smile up at the waitress and twined her fingers together on her lap, waiting.

"There are varied meals to choose from," Runner

said, trying to recall the taste of those things that were familiar to him long ago. "There is halibut, chicken, roast veal, and spring lamb for seventy-five cents each. This will be served with a vegetable and sweets."

The waitress began to tap her fingers on the pad on which she was going to write the order. "Sir, please make up your mind," she said in a whiney voice. "There are others waiting."

"Two roast veal," Runner said, closing the menu.

"And two glasses of red wine," Stephanie quickly interjected.

The waitress nodded and walked away.

Runner's lips parted in a light gasp. "I do not carry money with me," he whispered across the table to Stephanie. "I have no means to pay for these things."

"I'll pay for it," Stephanie whispered back. "Just try and enjoy it."

"I would much rather eat in the privacy of my hogan," Runner said. He looked uneasily from table to table, aware that wondering, angry eyes were still locked on him. "To these people I am almost an alien. Do they not know that I feel the same about them?"

"Who cares what they think? Anyhow, we won't be here for long," Stephanie murmured. She paused and then added, "I guess you are seeing, firsthand, what you have missed by living with Indians. I see that you do not regret your decision at all."

"If not for you, I would walk away now and not look back," Runner said stiffly. He ran a hand across the white Irish linen tablecloth and stared at the Sheffield silver plate on which his food was now being served. As a long-stemmed glass was set beside his plate of food, he watched the glow of the candle reflect deep within it, like the stars at night, sparkling down at him from the heavens.

"If there is anything else you need, please ask for me," the waitress said, doing a half curtsey. "My name is Bridgit."

"I think that will be all," Stephanie said, smiling up at the waitress. "Oh, just a minute. Please leave the ticket. I doubt if we will be interested in dessert."

"Yes, ma'am," Bridgit said. She took the ticket from her pocket and placed in on the table beside Runner.

After the waitress was gone, Stephanie scooted her hand over and took the ticket, tucking it in a pocket of her riding skirt. In silence, they ate within the soft glow of the candle's light.

Stephanie was glad when they left the lunch room. As she went down the stairs, she was trying to get the nerve to ask Runner to spend the night at the hotel with her. But that was thrust from her mind the minute she stepped outside. One look at her pack mule made her realize that someone had stolen not only her precious camera, but even the saddlebags in which she had kept all of her photography equipment. Even her tripod had been taken.

"No," she cried, rushing to her mule. "It's all gone!" She turned to Runner. "While we were eating, someone took everything from my mule."

Anger swelled up inside her. She folded her arms across her chest. "I'm surprised they even left the mule and the horses," she spat out.

Runner went to the mule and began walking slowly around it, studying the tracks made in the dirt of the street.

"Runner, what is it?" Stephanie asked, moving to his side.

"We will follow the tracks," he said. "We will find the one responsible for the theft."

Stephanie paled. She knew the danger of Runner getting involved with the theft. She had already seen how people felt about him being the "White Indian." If he confronted a white man over her belongings, and the white man was injured in some way, the law would more than likely take the side of anyone but Runner. In their eyes, he was Indian, through and through. They would take great delight in treating him no better than an Indian.

"That's not necessary," she blurted. "Let it be. I have other cameras. I have more equipment."

Runner turned to her. "No one steals from my woman," he said. "Especially not another woman. These tracks are made by a woman's bare feet."

"A woman?" Stephanie gasped.

"Come. We will find her."

She smiled weakly up at him. She knew that it would be a waste of breath if she tried to argue further. It was ironic how he would place himself in danger to get her camera back, when deep inside he hated the sight of it. By doing this for her, he was proving the depths of his love for her.

Grateful for such a love, tears of joy blurred her vision as she walked beside him, the moon lending enough light for them to continue following the trail.

When they came to a run-down shack at the far edge of town, Stephanie's heart began to race. But who could live there, she wondered, a foreboding knotting inside her. The place had an unkempt, deserted look. No smoke rose from the chimney. The silence was broken by the wails of an infant coming from within the hut, wafting from a door over which hung only a sparse covering of buckskin.

Stephanie gave Runner a questioning look, then her heart leaped as Runner brushed aside the buckskin at the door and stepped inside the shack.

She placed her hands at her throat, afraid that gunfire might ensue. Instead, the only sounds that emanated from the building were the continuing cries from the child.

And then Runner emerged again, carrying the child. Stephanie's fears melted when a rosy little nose and bright, blue eyes peaked out from a blanket made of a soiled, limp gunny sack.

Stephanie looked at the child a moment longer, then stepped past Runner through the low doorway. When she entered the shack and peered about in the windowless gloom, she discovered not only her camera equipment, but also a woman who was just coming out of hiding.

"My child," the woman said, her voice filled with panic. Her dark eyes seemed to take up all of her face. "Tell the man to give me back my child."

Stephanie looked over the woman slowly. She felt sick at heart, wondering when the woman had last eaten. She was emaciated, the skin drawn tautly across the bones of her face. The dress that she wore was no more than two gunny sacks sewn together, with holes cut for the head and arms to go through.

Her blond hair was a tangled mess and Stephanie could smell her unpleasant odor. It was so strong, it burned the inside of her nose, and all of the way down her throat.

"You were hiding," Stephanie said. "Runner didn't see you. I'm sure that he took the child because he thought it had been abandoned."

"My baby is all I have left in the world," the woman said, tears sliding down her wasted cheeks.

"Where is your husband?" Stephanie asked, looking slowly around the drab, squalid hut. It reeked of all sorts of unpleasant odors. The furniture was sparse. The fireplace was empty and cold.

"There's no husband," the woman said. She looked anxiously around Stephanie as Runner came back into the shack, rocking the child in his arms.

"You are one of the street whores I have heard about," Runner said, yet without condemnation. He had been forced to tolerate ridicule all of his life. He had none to cast upon anyone else, not even a woman who sold her body to countless men.

"Before the child, I was," the woman said. She held her arms out for her baby. "Please let me have him back. He's hungry. I must feed him."

"How will you feed him?" Stephanie said. She shuddered as she watched roaches crawling in and out of discarded filth-laden dishes on the table.

"My breast offers my child warm milk now, but for only a short while longer," the woman said, eagerly taking the child as Runner lay him in her arms. "My milk is drying up. I am being forced to find ways to get food." She glanced over at Stephanie's equipment. "Even if I am forced to steal, I will still find ways to feed my child."

Stephanie followed the path of the woman's troubled eyes. They stopped on her expensive equipment. Now she did not know what to do. If she took those things back, the woman would have to steal from someone else. If she was caught, she could be placed in jail, and then what would happen to the poor child?

Still, Stephanie knew that even if she allowed the woman to keep her things, it would only give the woman enough money to last for a little while. She would then be forced to steal again, and again.

"What is your name?" Stephanie asked. She edged over toward her camera equipment, still not sure what to do. On the one hand, she did not wish to encourage thievery. On the other, if she was in the same position as this woman, she might also be forced to steal.

"Sharon," the woman said, sitting down on a rickety chair to feed her child.

"Are you originally from Gallup?" Stephanie said, bending down to pick up her camera. She heard the woman gasp. She looked over and saw her eyes widen.

"No," Sharon said, her voice low and guarded. She placed the child's lips to her breast. "I came with my brother. We had a fuss. He threw me out. I became a show girl at the saloons. I found out I could make more money taking men home with me."

"This home?" Stephanie said, gesturing with her free hand around her.

"No. When things were good I lived in the hotel," Sharon said. "Then I met this man. I fell in love with him. I quit hustlin'. But suddenly he was gone. The very day I was going to tell him I was with child, I found out that he had left town. I . . . I . . . didn't want to hurt my child so I didn't go back to whorin' around. I went to my brother and asked him to take me in. He refused. I didn't beg him. I didn't even tell him about the baby. I found this place. I made it my home. And to hell with Damon. I'd die before I'd ask for his help again."

"Damon?" Stephanie and Runner spoke at once.

"Yes," Sharon said in a low hiss. "Damon Stout."

Stephanie and Runner were both rendered speechless by this newest discovery.

Hate for Damon, sour and pitiless, twisted in Runner's gut.

19

I love you for putting your hand
Into my heaped-up heart.
                    —ROY CROFT

Stephanie broke the awkward silence. "You are Damon
Stout's sister?" she said.

She looked slowly around her again, at the squalor.
How could *anyone* send their sister away to live in such
deplorable conditions? she thought incredulously. Even
Damon!

"Damon is my blood kin," Sharon said solemnly.
"But I don't like to admit that he is actually my
brother."

"I can see why," Runner said, walking slowly around
the room, studying the disarray. "Any man who allows
his sister and her child to live like this is not a man at
all. He is a coward of the worst kind."

Stephanie shook herself out of her shock. She went
and knelt down before Sharon. She gazed sadly at the
baby who was struggling to get milk from the small,
thin breast. Then she looked up at Sharon, saddened
anew over her pallor. Her eyes were like two dark coals
in her drawn flesh.

"We're going to take you out of here," Stephanie
said, running her hand over the baby's dirty, scab-
infested scalp. "I will pay for your stay at the hotel.
You will be given food, clean clothes, and water for a

bath. Tonight you will be sleeping on a clean bed. Your son will be given clothes and warm, clean blankets."

Sharon listened with parted lips and wide eyes. She slipped her breast back inside her dress. "Why would you do this for me and my son?" she asked, tears flooding her eyes. "I stole from you. I watched you leave the pack mule with the saddlebags on it. When you and this man went to the lunch room, I took everything that I could carry. I was going to sell them tomorrow to whomever would pay me the highest price."

Stephanie interrupted. "My name is Stephanie," she murmured. She gestured with a hand toward Runner. "This is Runner."

Sharon hung her head in shame. "I'm sorry for having stolen from you," she said, "but I was going to buy some milk. I need milk to give my son the nourishment he needs. Or . . . or . . . he might die."

Runner took the child into his arms. "Neither of you will die," he said thickly. "Come with us. Tonight you will stay in the white man's establishment. Tomorrow you will go with me to my village. My people will welcome you with open arms, as they did me, so many years ago."

Stephanie marveled over what Runner was offering. She knew the depths of his hate for Damon Stout; it matched her own. Yet he was taking Damon's blood kin into his heart and village.

Then she smiled slowly. She understood that he was not doing this only from kindness but also to irritate Damon when he discovered where his sister had been taken. No matter how much Damon had neglected his sister, there was no way on this earth that he would want her living with the Navaho. He hated the Navaho with a passion. When he *did* discover where she was and he went for her at the village, it would give the Navaho much pleasure to deny him his blood kin.

Sharon's body was racked with heavy sobs. "I'll never be able to repay you," she cried, clutching Stephanie as she rose from her chair.

Stephanie winced at the feel of the fragile sharpness of Sharon's bones.

"All of my family, but Damon, is dead," Sharon moaned. "I never want Damon to know that I have a child. If he did, he'd take him away from me. Don't let him. Please don't let him."

"How have you kept your brother from knowing about the child?" Runner asked. He held the baby in the circle of one arm and used his free hand to steady Sharon as Stephanie stepped away from her to get her camera equipment.

"No one knows about Jimmy," Sharon said, sniffling. "I never take him from the house. When I leave to steal from people, I always hide him beneath blankets. I didn't want Damon to know. If he took Jimmy to raise him, the child would turn out to be as mean, ugly, and cruel as my brother."

"His name is Jimmy?" Runner said, gazing down at the child, whose wide, blue eyes studied him. "That is a nice name. But when he grows older, I would hope though that you would allow him to take on a Navaho name."

"A Navaho name?" Sharon said softly. Her eyes studied the child's face.

"I was born with the name Trevor," Runner said, slowly rocking the child back and forth in his arms. "When my mother died and I was taken in by the Navaho, to be raised as one with them, the name Runner was given to me." He smiled over at Stephanie, then at Sharon as he gave her the child. "The name Runner was chosen by my adopted father Sage because of my ability to outrun the rest of the boys in the village while we played games."

"I've never thought much about Indians," Sharon said, closely scrutinizing Runner. "But you're a white man, and it looks to me like they've treated you kind enough. I guess they will treat me and my Jimmy with the same kindness."

She smiled over at Stephanie as she came to her side. "Least ways, I'll be safe, won't I?" she murmured.

"Very," Stephanie said, returning the smile. "Now, let's go and get you that hotel room."

They left the shack and went to the hotel. Runner didn't know about the room awaiting him and Stephanie, and she didn't see the need in telling him. If they were going to wait for Sharon and the child to have a full night's rest in a warm, comfortable hotel room, she could just suggest they sleep there themselves, so they could be there to take her to Runner's village tomorrow.

She smiled to herself. Things were working out for everyone, it seemed.

Runner took a guarded step into the hotel room with Stephanie. It was on the same floor and only a few doors from where Sharon and Jimmy were being seen to.

Stephanie was thinking about Sharon. She would never forget the tenderness in the woman's eyes as she had carried her child into the clean room. That was enough payment, in itself, for Stephanie. The theft had been forgotten as quickly. To be sure, though, that no one else had the opportunity to steal her camera equipment, she had it safely in her arms now, while Runner carried the tripod.

She gave a wicked smile to Runner as he moved further into the room that was aglow with the soft light from two kerosene lanterns on tables flanking the large, luxurious four-poster bed. She had put more than equipment in her saddlebags: she had slipped something thin, lacy, and pretty into one of them.

"I have not seen such a room since Mother died," Runner said, leaving the tripod leaning against a wall. He looked down at the plush carpet, soft as silk beneath his moccasined feet. Laughing softly, he walked gingerly in circles over it.

Then he walked over to the bed and pushed a hand against the mattress, finding it softer than the down from beneath an eagle's wing. He stroked the red satin sheets, finding them sleek and wonderful.

Then he cast a suspicious look over his shoulder when he spied a bottle of champagne and two long-stemmed glasses on the table beside the bed, as though someone had planned it all to be this way.

"Champagne?" he said in a slow drawl. "If I did not know better, I would suspect that my woman had planned ahead of time to lure me to this room."

Stephanie lay the saddlebags aside and went to Runner. "And what if I did?" she said in a soft purr. Her hands crept up inside his shirt. She ran them over his broad, muscled chest. "Of course I had no idea our arrival here would be delayed. But I don't mind. It was wonderful to see the delight in Sharon's eyes. By now, she has probably taken a long, leisurely bath. I imagine Jimmy is spotless." She frowned. "It might take awhile for the sores on his head to heal, though. Poor, dear child."

"My woman's compassion runs deep," Runner said, lifting his arms as Stephanie drew his fringed shirt over his head.

"No more deeply than yours," Stephanie said, tossing his shirt aside. She smiled sweetly up at Runner as her fingers moved to the waist of his breeches. She unfastened them and began slowly, seductively pulling them over his lean, narrow hips. "But let's not talk of compassion. Let's only concentrate on the moment. I have all sorts of ideas. Care to share yours with me?"

"I do not plan to tell you," Runner said, stepping out of his breeches. "I will show you."

"You don't care that I planned this room of seduction without your knowledge?" Stephanie said, as his fingers began unbuttoning her blouse.

His breath caught in his throat as Stephanie reached one of her hands to his manhood and stroked it. He closed his eyes, smoldering passion spreading through him.

"I love you so," Stephanie whispered, then moved her hand away and finished undressing him.

Runner opened his eyes. They were ablaze with need. He started to pick Stephanie up, to carry her to the bed. But she shook her head and stepped away from him.

"Not yet," she murmured, her eyelids heavy as rapture began to claim her. "I've got something to do first."

Runner questioned her with his eyes when she turned from him and grabbed her saddlebags and took them with her behind a folding screen.

"I won't be long," she said.

Runner watched as one by one Stephanie's clothes were laid across the top of the screen. He was puzzled as to why she would need such privacy to undress. His heart raced with anticipation at the thought of running his hands again over her silken soft body.

Finally, totally nude, Stephanie slipped into her

slinky, clinging, black, lacy silk nightgown. She ran her hands down her body, causing the gown to cling to her flesh, her nipples firm and erect beneath the black fabric.

Lifting her hair so that it tumbled from her shoulders and down her back in rivulets, Stephanie stopped from behind the screen and smiled at Runner's expression as he stared at her, his eyes and mouth wide.

After enjoying his close scrutiny a moment longer, Stephanie twined her arms around Runner's neck and drew his hard and ready body against hers.

"Your eyes tell me that you like what I am wearing," she teased.

She leaned her lips close to his and flicked her tongue across his lips.

"You wear a sort of garment that Runner has never seen before on any woman," he said thickly. "And, yes, I approve. You are always beautiful. But tonight you are a vision."

Runner's hands went to her breasts and cupped them through the silken material of the gown. Stephanie moaned and ground her body into his as his mouth joined hers, hot and eager. Through the thin fabric of her gown, she could feel the throbbing length of his manly need.

She slipped a hand between them and encircled his velveteen shaft with her fingers. She heard him moan and felt his body stiffen when she started moving her hand on him, in awe of the heat that she felt against the coolness of her fingers.

Runner's heart pounded so hard, he was dizzied by it. He reached for her hand and gently eased it away from him. He then grabbed Stephanie up into his arms and carried her to the bed.

His fingers went to the hem of her gown and slowly

began pushing it upward, stopping momentarily to kiss each part of her as it was uncovered.

She shivered with ecstasy when he kissed and taunted the insides of her thighs. She closed her eyes and sucked in a wild breath of pleasure when he kissed his way slowly upward.

Smoothing the gown on past the crown of hair at the juncture of her thighs, Runner leaned down low over her and flicked his tongue against the center of her desire. Then he nestled his face into the soft fronds of her hair and kissed and nibbled at her tightened bud, the tip of his tongue swirling . . . moist . . .

"Runner," Stephanie whispered, reaching her hands to his head, twining her fingers through his hair.

She urged him closer as she moved her legs further apart. "What you are doing? Oh, Runner. . . ."

Runner's tongue titillated her there for a moment longer. Then he scooted the gown farther up her body, so that her breasts were exposed, beckoning him to them. His hot and hungry mouth on her flesh, Runner kissed his way across Stephanie's flat tummy, causing it to quiver. Then he moved his body over her, his lips inhaling the nipple of one of her breasts into his mouth: he sucked; he flicked his tongue around it; he licked it.

Stephanie groaned and tossed her head with pleasure, and when he nudged her knees apart and he slipped his throbbing need inside her, a delicious languor stole over her.

With rhythmic motions, he began to move within her. Stephanie slipped her gown over her head, then placed her hands on his cheeks and drew his lips to hers.

She gave Runner a meltingly hot kiss, a wild, exuberant passion swimming through her. She sought the feel of his sleek, muscled back, then moved her fingers lower, anchoring them against his tight buttocks. She pressed her hands against him, urging him deep inside her, the silver flames of desire leaping ever higher within her.

Stephanie arched her head back as Runner buried his lips along the delicate column of her throat, his hands kneading her breasts. Then he showered heated kisses over her breasts, the feelings soaring through him blazing . . . searing . . .

Feeling the intensity of his pleasure, he anchored her fiercely still. He gave her a kiss of total demand as they both gave in to the rapture, the silent explosion of their needs accompanied by their sighs and groans.

For a moment longer they clung to one another, then Stephanie slipped from beneath him. "The champagne," she said, running her fingers through her hair as she stepped delicately onto the plush carpet. "We must drink champagne. Don't you think we have much to celebrate, darling?"

She turned to him and took his hands and leaned over him, brushing a kiss across his lips as he stretched out on his back. "We have *us* to celebrate," she said, giggling as she went to the bottle of champagne and removed it from its bucket.

She took the bottle back to Runner. "Would you please?" she asked, handing him the bottle to uncork.

Runner took the bottle. He sat up on the bed and rested against the headboard, then began reading the label.

"Champagne," he said softly. "I recall my mother and father drinking champagne when I was a child."

"It's what most people drink when they are celebrating one thing or another," Stephanie said, plopping down on the bed beside him. "It's wonderful and bubbly. It's a delight to drink."

Runner frowned and shoved the bottle back into her hands. "I did not drink the wine at the lunch room. Nor will I drink this now. I do not drink alcohol of any kind," he said flatly. "I understand its evil. Some of the young Navaho braves, and even some of our older warriors, have found a strange sort of solace in alcohol. It is best that I do not practice what my father and I have both preached against."

Stephanie stared disbelievingly at him. "Darling, just one wee little glass won't harm anyone," she pleaded. "Please? For me? It is a fun thing to do between two people in love. I absolutely guarantee that you will not get drunk on such a small amount of alcohol."

When he folded his arms stubbornly across his chest and tightened his jaw, she started to rise off the bed. Instead, she stopped and looked mischievously up at him. She struggled with the cork for only a moment, and then it popped from the bottle. As the fizz rolled over the sides, she licked it up with her tongue, and then she turned and leaned over Runner.

She heard his gasp of shock as she began slowly trickling the champagne over his stomach, making a trail downward, until she reached that part of him that lay spent amidst his frond of dark hair.

Slowly, she allowed some of the champagne to drip from the bottle onto him there, watching his eyes as surprise leapt into their depths.

"What . . . are . . . you doing . . . ?" Runner gasped.

Stephanie sat the bottle aside, and before he could stop her, she leaned low over him and began licking the champagne from him, starting with his manhood.

She felt him growing against her mouth as she continued licking until the champagne was absorbed. Her hand circled him, and she began working it slowly up and down as she licked her way past it and on up his stomach. She placed her hands at his waist and urged him down again, so that she could stretch herself over him.

"You see, darling?" Stephanie murmured against his lips. "The champagne is worth something, isn't it?"

Runner laughed huskily. He took her by the waist and positioned her above him, then thrust his throbbing member into her. "You are a wench," he said, his hands smoothing upward, cupping her breasts.

Giggling, Stephanie held her head back, the fever within her building. She was only half aware of the soft, whimpering sounds coming from her.

Damon woke with a start. He slapped away the hand that was shaking him and leaned up on an elbow. The moon was casting its light in soft streamers through his bedroom window, giving him a good look at the person who dared to wake him in the middle of the night.

"It'd better be good, Joshua," he said, throwing his legs over the side of the bed. He grabbed a blanket and slung it around his shoulders. "Why're you here? Did you catch a damn Navaho stealin' horses?"

"I saw a Navaho tonight, but not exactly stealin'," Joshua said, leaning his pock-marked face down into Damon's. "It's your sister. Would you believe that Runner and Adam's sister took Sharon from her shack and to a fancy hotel? And that ain't *all* I seen tonight."

"Well? Get on with it," Damon said in a rumble. "What else did you see?"

"You've got a nephew or niece," Joshua said, shrugging. "I couldn't tell which. All's I know is, Sharon was carryin' a baby when she went into the hotel."

"A baby?" Damon said in a low gasp. "Whorin' around has got her a baby. Bet she doesn't even know who the father is."

"What're you goin' to do about the baby?" Joshua said, whiskey thick on his breath. "Sharon ain't no fit mother. The baby'll be no better. If'n it's a girl, she'll learn from her mother how to lift her skirts to the gents. If'n it's a boy, he could sure be a lot of help to you if you'd bring him here, to raise as your own."

Damon rubbed his chin thoughtfully. "You've got a point," he said. "One thing for sure, though. I don't want no part of Sharon. When she was here, she was too bossy for her own good. Even caught her stealin' from me. Now she's a gutter tramp. It makes me shudder to think of even gettin' near her."

Damon gave Joshua a sidewise glance. "I'll give her time to raise the child past weaning," he said throatily. "Then I'll take the child in. If it's a boy, *or* girl. I can get a lot of labor outta either one."

"But what about Sharon?"

"I'll take care of her."

"You mean you'll take her back in, as part of your family?"

"Now you know that's a foolish question, don't you?"

"What, then?"

"Joshua, don't you shoot horses that's outlived their usefulness?"

"You wouldn't, Damon," Joshua said, paling. "You're only foolin' me, ain't 'cha?"

Damon's eyes bore into Joshua's.

"Get on outta here, Joshua," Damon growled. Then his voice softened. "Thanks for comin' tonight, Josh. 'Preciate it."

Joshua gave Damon a mock salute, then left.

Damon stepped to the window and stared out at the stark blackness of the night. "Sharon, Sharon ..." he whispered. "What *am* I to do about you, and now—the child?"

20

The passion of the wind, love,
Can never last for long.
—R. W. RAYMOND

After eating breakfast in bed, making love again, and
sharing a bath in a copper tub, Stephanie and Runner
found it difficult to take enough time to become totally
dressed. Over and over again they kissed awhile, embraced, then laughed and began dressing again, until
finally they were ready to leave the room to check on
Sharon and Jimmy.

"I'm anxious to see what Sharon has to say about her
night in the hotel," Stephanie said, going to the door
and opening it. She glanced down at her camera equipment, then up at Runner. "Let's come back for these
after we see how Sharon and Jimmy are faring."

Runner swept an arm around her waist as they left
the room and walked down the dim corridor. "What
other surprises are you going to spring on me?" he said,
chuckling as he gave her a soft smile. "I enjoyed the
night with you." He yanked her closer to his side.
"Even the champagne."

As she smiled up at him, he gave her a quick wink.
"And I don't mean how it tasted from the glass," he
said, his eyes dancing.

A thrill coursed through her when she recalled their

lengthy lovemaking that had lasted into the wee hours of the night, and how it had felt when Runner had licked champagne from her body after he had drizzled it from breast to breast, and then down across her quivering stomach, and then even lower.

Flames ignited within Stephanie at the thought of his mouth, tongue, and lips.

When they stepped up to the door that led into Sharon's room, Stephanie noticed that it was ajar. She gave Runner a quick, questioning look.

"The door," she said, in an almost whisper. "It's not closed. Why would Sharon leave it open all night?"

Runner tensed. "Surely they are asleep and are not aware of it," he said. He placed a hand to the door and slowly pushed it open.

The shades at the windows were pulled, leaving the room in a vague, shadowy darkness.

"They *are* still asleep," Stephanie whispered. "Perhaps we should leave."

Runner leaned toward the bed, his acute hearing revealing no sound of breathing.

"Something is not right here," Runner said. He moved stealthily across the floor and rolled up a window shade.

Stephanie gasped and paled when she saw a pillow across Sharon's face. She grew cold when she noticed just as quickly how Sharon's body was lying prone and limp on the bed. A quick search of the room revealed that Jimmy was missing. She shifted her gaze back to Sharon. "Is ... she ... dead?" she stammered. She inched slowly toward the bed.

Runner rushed over and lifted the pillow away from Sharon. His mouth clenched and his jaw tightened when he found Sharon's glazed eyes staring ahead in a death trance. The way her face was twisted so grotesquely, Runner could tell that she had experienced a terrifying, agonizing death.

Stephanie moved to Runner's side. "No," she gasped, clasping a hand over her mouth to stifle a scream. "She's dead. Oh, Lord, Runner, she *is* dead."

"He found out about her and the child somehow," Runner said, anger welling up within him. "Damon Stout found out and came and killed his sister, and . . . and . . . took the child."

"How could he do such a thing?" Stephanie said, tears streaming down her cheeks. "She was no threat to him. And the child—she didn't want Damon even knowing about Jimmy, much less taking him away to raise as his own."

"We will see to it that he won't be given that chance," Runner said, slowly covering Sharon with a blanket. "What he will be doing, though, is hanging from a noose."

"Yes, we must go to the authorities immediately," Stephanie said, brushing tears from her face.

Runner turned to her and clasped her shoulders. "No, not yet," he said. "I will go and get the child first. Sending the law out for Damon could be risky. I will get the child to safety. Then I will take care of Damon myself."

"You would take the law in your own hands?" Stephanie said, following him to the door. "No, Runner. I won't allow it. You can't risk your future—*our* future— by killing Damon Stout. Please listen to reason. Let the authorities take care of this."

He turned to her and again clasped his hands to her shoulders. "The law works in strange, twisted ways," he said solemnly. "My way is simple and to the point."

"*Please* listen to reason," Stephanie begged.

"You can stay and make arrangements for Sharon, or

you can come with me," Runner said, his voice much softer. "Someone should come to carry the baby when we take him from Damon's ranch. I would hope that it would be you."

Stephanie looked over her shoulder at Sharon. Tears filled her eyes again. "We can return later and see to her arrangements," she said.

She felt empty and forlorn over the loss of a woman she had only known a few minutes, and she felt guilty for the long hours of pleasure that she and Runner had shared through the night. Had Sharon been dead even then?

A sudden horror seized Stephanie at the thought of Sharon possibly lying there all night, all alone in the dark, dead—her child stolen from her embrace.

"We'll close the door and no one will be the wiser," Runner said, placing a finger to Stephanie's chin, turning her gaze up to his. "Are you going to be all right?"

"Yes," Stephanie sobbed, then flung herself into his arms. "It's so horrible. So very horrible. She died alone while we ... while ... we ..."

Runner gave her a slight shake and forced her to look up at him again. "Never blame yourself or me for what happened here," he said sternly. "Especially yourself. You paid for her to have a warm shelter, food, and the comforts offered by this hotel. As for myself, I will still see that her son gets a proper upbringing."

He framed her face between his hands. "Together we can raise him as *our* son," he said. "As I was taken in long ago by two kind people, so shall we take little Jimmy into not only our hogan but our hearts."

"Our ... hogan ... ?" Stephanie said, searching his eyes. "You are speaking as though we will be living together as man and wife. Are you proposing to me?"

"It is a hell of a time to propose, is it not?" he said,

his eyes searching hers. "But, yes, I *am*. Will you be my wife?"

"Now? Today?" Stephanie said, her eyes widening.

"It does not have to be today," Runner said, drawing her into his embrace, "but soon. Will you be able to live my simple life? Will a hogan be enough? Can you turn your back on your photography?"

Stephanie's head was spinning with his questions, and with the knowledge that he was rushing her into marriage. She still had a responsibility to the Santa Fe Railroad. They had spent a lot of money on her special photography equipment, and only because she had agreed to travel to Arizona to take photographs for their tourism plans.

"I want nothing more than to be your wife," she said, placing her cheek against the buckskin fabric of his beaded vest. "And I will. But first I must finish what I have come to the Arizona Territory for."

She could feel his body tighten and understood why. She eased from his arms and gazed up at him. "You honor your commitments, don't you?" she said, her voice guarded.

"Always," he answered, his eyes dark as he gazed down at her.

"Then you will surely understand that I must honor my own," she said softly. "Let me take a few more photographs, develop them, and Adam will see to it that they reach the proper people when he attends his next Santa Fe board meeting."

She paused, then placed a hand to his cheek. "Is that fair enough?" she murmured. "I do want to be your bride. I will be happy enough in a hogan for, my darling, I will be sharing it with you."

"And little Jimmy?" Runner asked.

Stephanie nodded. "And little Jimmy."

"We will soon give him a brother or sister?" Runner said, weaving his fingers through her copper hair, to draw her lips only a whisper away from his.

"We shall give him many, if you like," Stephanie said, smiling up at him.

When he kissed her, it was soft and sweet, yet filled with passion.

Then they broke away and rushed down the stairs.

Stephanie took enough time to tell the desk clerk that she needed the two rooms for another full day and night. She had no time to repack her belongings, so she felt it was much simpler just to pay for the room until she returned for them. And she left strict orders that Sharon was not to be disturbed.

The poor woman, she sadly thought. Because of Damon, she had been forced to live a life of hell. Hopefully, she was now finding peace somewhere in that place where tears were no longer shed. Yet Stephanie felt that Sharon could not truly rest in peace until her child was saved from the life that Damon was planning for him.

Leaving the pack mule stabled at the hotel, Runner and Stephanie swung themselves into their saddles and rode in a flurry of dust out of Gallup.

Stopping only long enough to briefly rest their horses and to get drinks of water from their canteens, they finally came to the outskirts of Damon's ranch. A wide spread of pole fencing reached out across the land on all four sides of the ranch. It was now mid-afternoon, and many ranch hands were busying about, doing their chores.

Stephanie and Runner reined their steeds to a stop. In tune with its master's feelings, Runner's stallion neighed and pawed at the grass nervously.

"Should we wait until night?" Stephanie asked, smoothing stray locks of hair back from her eyes.

"No," Runner said flatly. "No matter when we arrive, we will be noticed. Everyone is aware of the strained relationship between me and Damon. The fact that I came with your brother recently to meet with Damon may help us out. Once we get past the ranch hands and inside Damon's house, *then* we can show our true colors—our true reasons for being here."

"All hell with break loose," Stephanie said, her eyes narrowing as she stared at Damon's house. "I only hope that he's there so we can get this over with. I don't like the idea of Jimmy being under that man's roof for *any* amount of time. How on earth is the child being fed?"

"Damon will have hired a wet nurse by now," Runner said, patting his horse's neck to calm it. "She will stay there at the ranch, I am sure, until the child is weaned."

A shiver coursed up and down Stephanie's spine at the thought of a total stranger holding the child that had been so precious to Sharon.

"Let's go, Runner," she said, giving him an anxious look.

He nodded. Without greeting those ranch hands who turned and gaped at them, Stephanie and Runner rode on up to the house.

Runner swung himself out of his saddle as Stephanie slid from hers. Together they slung their reins around the hitching rail, then stamped onto the porch.

Damon was soon at the door, guarding it against their entrance. "What do you two want?" he spat, his hands resting on the two pistols hanging at his hips. "I don't recall sendin' no damn invitation to you." He glared at Runner. "Especially the likes of you. The only reason I allowed you here the other night was because of

Adam." He took a threatening step closer. "Well, Adam ain't here, so be on your way."

Stephanie looked easily over at Runner. "Runner?" she said, waiting for his next move.

She didn't have to wait long. He brusquely brushed past Damon and went on into the ranch house. Damon swung around, momentarily struck silent at Runner's impertinence.

"What the hell do you think you're doing?" he finally said, rushing after Runner.

Her heart pounding, Stephanie hurried on into the house and past Damon. "I imagine his bedrooms are down this corridor," she shouted at Runner, running on past him. "I'll check one. You check the other!"

Too confused over what they were doing to consider drawing his weapons, Damon broke into a run after them. "What the hell are you two up to?" he shouted. "What are you doin' goin' into my bedrooms? Who the hell do you 'spect to find?"

Stephanie and Runner ignored Damon and rushed from bedroom to bedroom, then ran past Damon and checked the other rooms, even the kitchen.

After inspecting the entire house without success, Stephanie and Runner met in the parlor.

"He's not here," Stephanie said, breathing hard.

"Could we have been wrong?" Runner asked.

Damon came into the room, panting. He stopped and stared from Stephanie to Runner. "Who's not here?" he said, wiping beads of perspiration from his brow. "Who're you lookin' for?"

Not to give up all that easily, Runner crossed to Damon, gathered up a handful of his shirt, and half-lifted him from the floor. "Where is he?" he ground out between clenched teeth. "You low-down murdering son-of-a-bitch, where is Jimmy?"

"I don't know any Jimmy," Damon said, wild-eyed. He choked and coughed, his face turning purple. "Let me go, damn it. Runner, so help me, I'll shoot you dead if you don't unhand me."

Runner's free hand grabbed Damon's hand as it moved toward one of his holstered pistols. "I wouldn't try it," he said, glowering.

Runner walked Damon backwards until the rancher's back was against the wall. "Now, I will ask you one more time," he growled. "I found your sister's body this morning. She was stone cold dead. Her son was gone. Where is he, Damon? Where is your nephew?"

Damon's eyes grew wide as he gasped, "Sharon?" he said. "She's . . . dead?"

"Very," Runner grumbled.

"My God," Damon stammered. "My sister's really dead? And her son?" He raked his fingers through his hair nervously. "I don't know nothing about any of this. I had nothin' to do with it. You're wrong to think I did this. Dead wrong."

Runner sighed heavily and released his hold on Damon. He had heard the genuine surprise in Damon's voice; it was obvious to Runner that Damon was innocent of the crime. Which meant that he was also innocent of the crime of having stolen his nephew.

Stephanie went to Runner. "Are you going to actually believe him?" she said, placing a hand on his arm. "Darling, surely he's lying. Who else would do such a thing to Sharon? Who would want the child?"

Runner turned weary eyes toward Stephanie. "Who would do this?" he said thickly. "Who would want the child? The father."

"She didn't know who the father was."

"That is what she *said*. I now believe she did know.

He came and took what he wanted and killed who he saw as an interference in his life."

Stephanie moved away from Runner and went to stare out the window at the vast expanse of the land, and at the towering mountains in the distance. "We'll never find Jimmy," she said, a sob lodging in her throat. "Never."

"I'll help you find him," Damon volunteered.

Runner stepped up to Damon. "Your help is not needed, or wanted," he said, his tone threatening, rendering Damon speechless.

Runner went to Stephanie, swept an arm around her waist, and led her outside to the horses. As they left the ranch, they felt eyes on them from all sides.

After many miles, they finally slowed their horses to a walk. "I'll go and make arrangements for Sharon," Stephanie said sullenly. "That is the least I can do for her. And for her son? It saddens me so to know that what we had planned for him will never be." She cast Runner a despairing look. "He won't be our son, after all, Runner."

"Perhaps one day we will find him," he said, sighing. For now, I imagine he is far from here. A person guilty of murder and abduction would not stay around long enough to be discovered."

"I'll remember Jimmy always," Stephanie said, sniffling back the urge to cry.

"I was to meet with Adam today," Runner said solemnly. "A part of me says not to go, and a part of me says that I should. The child in me that once knew Adam as a friend leads me to try this one last time to find the side of him that is good and trusting."

He paused, then said, "I *will* meet with Adam. I feel that I must, or regret later having not given him another chance."

"I'm glad you are giving it another try," Stephanie said, smiling at him. "It would be nice to have Adam at our wedding, and to be able to invite Adam to our home in the future, no matter where he decides to make his permanent residence."

"I hope that Adam gives us cause to invite him to remain a part of our lives," Runner said, wondering what Adam had in mind for the meeting arranged for today.

21

Where I find her not, beauties vanish;
Whither I follow her, beauties flee.
—ROBERT BROWNING

It was mid-afternoon when Adam and Runner rode in a slow lope into Gallup. "What took so long for you to get to the train?" Adam asked. He gave Runner a sour look. "I had almost given up on you. I thought you might have decided to escort Stephanie while she took her photographs. She was gone this morning by the time I got up."

Runner gave Adam no explanations, especially those that might include Stephanie, knowing where she was and what she was in the process of doing.

A bitterness swept through him anew at the thought of Sharon being dead, and over Jimmy now being in the hands of total strangers. If he ever found out who was responsible, he would not hesitate at choking the life from that person with his bare hands.

"You sure as hell are quiet enough today," Adam said, screwing his face up into a dark frown. "If you had changed your mind about coming into Gallup with me, why didn't you just come right out with it? I don't like the idea of having to spend a day with someone who doesn't even acknowledge that I'm talking to him."

The false-fronted buildings were casting long, narrow

shadows across the road. The sun was shining red in the windows of those buildings on the opposite side of the road as though the fires of hell were raging inside them. Runner stiffened when several men gawked and laughed and jeered at him as they rode past on their horses.

Women were standing at the doors of some of the saloons. They were shouting and making obscene gestures at Runner and Adam. Some turned and lifted their short skirts in the back, to display tight, brightly-colored satin bloomers that outlined the curves of their bottoms so tightly it was almost no different than looking at them unclothed.

"You haven't said yet why you insisted we come to Gallup to make peace between us," Runner said, finally breaking the silence between himself and Adam.

"If I'd have told you, I doubted you would have come," Adam said, giving him a shifty glance.

Runner drew his steed to a halt. "I was foolish to come with you at all," he said, his eyes burning into Adam's. "Had I not had other reasons for coming to Gallup, the minute you spoke that name to me I would have told you a flat no."

Adam drew a tight rein. He edged his horse over next to Runner's stallion. "What other reasons are you talking about?" he said, raising an eyebrow. "Are you playing a game with me?"

"Games are for children," Runner said flatly. "We are grown men now. And my reasons for being in Gallup are none of your concern."

"They are if they include me," Adam said impatiently. "Now are you or aren't you willing to go with me to a place where we can talk over things and try and be best pals again?"

"This place where you are planning to go," Runner

said, his gaze drawn quickly elsewhere. "What is it called?"

His attention was drawn away from Adam. His insides knotted as he watched a pine box lifted onto the bed of a buckboard wagon, Stephanie watching from the boardwalk. His heart ached when he saw Stephanie wipe tears from her eyes as the casket was being secured by ropes on the wagon.

He felt that perhaps he should go with her to the cemetery at the edge of town, to comfort her when Sharon was laid to rest.

But Stephanie had insisted on doing it alone. She had wanted him to meet with Adam as planned. She put much importance on the outcome of such a meeting. For her, he had to give this relationship with Adam one last try.

"The 'Big Tent,'" Adam said guardedly. "It's a place where real men go." Tauntingly, he leaned closer to Runner. "Are you a real man, Runner? Will you go to the 'Big Tent' with me to have a few drinks?"

Adam knew the reputation that Indians had gotten after having been introduced to alcoholic beverages. Their metabolism did not allow them the pleasure of drinking alcohol in large amounts. When they did, they became lousy drunks.

They also got quickly addicted to the taste and its effects. The euphoria of being drunk dulled the pain of their lives since the white man had come. The Navaho were known to trade many things for even one drink of whiskey—squash blossom necklaces, bracelets, rings, and hair accessories.

Although Runner was not Indian, by heritage, Adam was counting on him not being used to drinking whiskey. It would not be the same as when they had been children and challenges had been made between them as to who could run the fastest, or who could win at wrestling. Today there was more at stake, therefore, it was important to make the challenges more difficult!

It was important to Adam that he come out the winner.

Adam waited for Runner's response to what Adam thought he would take as an insult, giving him cause to meet the challenge head-on.

When Adam realized that Runner's mind was elsewhere, as were also his eyes, he turned to follow Runner's gaze. He jumped with a start when he saw Stephanie riding on her horse beside a buckboard wagon, upon which lay a pine casket.

"What the hell?" Adam said, circling a hand around his saddle horn. He leaned over the horn as he watched the slow procession, the buckboard wagon rattling up the uneven dirt thoroughfare, bouncing and swaying, Stephanie riding stiffly beside it.

He peered more intensely at Stephanie. He could tell that she had been crying. Her face was red and her lips trembled as though she might burst into another torrent of tears at any moment.

Runner sighed heavily, then nudged his horse with his knees and slowly proceeded on his way.

Adam watched Stephanie for a moment longer, then thrashed his reins back and forth over his horse and took off in a gallop toward Stephanie.

Runner's heart leapt. He rode after Adam, and just before he reached Stephanie, Runner reached and grabbed Adam's horse by the bit. "Let her be," he said as Adam cast him a furious stare. "Stephanie does not need your interference in the duties she is performing for a friend."

"Friend?" Adam said. "Who? What friend? Stephanie hadn't been here long enough to make acquaintances, except with you and your people."

"You are wrong," Runner answered. "Last night she and I befriended a lonely, sad woman. This morning the woman was found dead." He paused, to take a dry swallow. "This afternoon, Stephanie is seeing to her burial."

Adam paled. "How . . . can . . . you have allowed my sister to become involved with a stranger to the extent she feels as though she must see to the burial?" he hissed, leaning toward Runner. He yanked his horse away from Runner. "I shouldn't have allowed Stephanie from my sight. Not for even one minute. By offering friendships to strangers, who's to say what diseases she may have been exposed to?" He started to ride away, but was stopped again by what Runner was saying.

"Disease did not kill the woman," Runner said solemnly. "She was murdered."

"Murdered?" Adam said, once again paling. "This woman. What was her name?"

"Her name is not important," Runner said flatly. "Her blood kin is. She was Damon Stout's sister."

"My God," Adam said in a low gasp. "Runner, tell me her name. I've never heard Damon speak of any kin. Who was his sister?"

"Her name was Sharon," Runner said, sinking his heels into the flanks of his horse and riding away.

Adam stared at Runner's back for a moment, then looked farther ahead. Stephanie had reached the far edge of the town. A shudder engulfed him, then he caught up with Runner again.

"Stop," he said thickly. "We're here. This is where I wanted to spend some time with you."

Runner's eyes widened as he gazed incredulously over at the "Big Tent." The loud, boisterous music and laughter wafting from its raised entrance flaps made a burning resentment swim through him. Too many young Navaho braves had gone in there to be taken advantage of. And not solely by evil white men, but also by the gaudy, wild and bawdy women that earned their living there. They not only pushed unwanted drinks on those who were innocent, but also sold their bodies at the price of the young Navaho braves' horses, or jewelry that these whores took from the braves, priding themselves in showing them off to their friends.

"You bring me to this unholy place and expect me to go inside with you?" Runner said, shifting angry eyes to Adam. "You knew that I would not do this. Why did you bother to waste my time bringing me here?"

"It's not as bad as you think," Adam said. His eyes danced as he watched a pretty girl making eyes at him as she walked past, her breasts all but hanging out of the low bodice of her flashy dress. "Come on, Runner. Be a good sport. You don't want me to call you a yellow-bellied coward, do you?" He narrowed his eyes and leaned over closer to Runner. "Or chicken. When we were best friends, nothing could rile you more than if someone called you a chicken."

"That was then," Runner said flatly. "This is now. And you can call me what you want, but I do not frequent places that are not good for the youth of my people."

"I bet I can out-drink you," Adam taunted, his voice low and guarded. "Come inside with me, Runner. Surely you are curious about why whiskey affects your people so badly?"

Adam straightened his back and tightened his jaw. "I challenge you, Runner, drink for drink," he said. "If you win, I swear I'll not bother your people again."

"I can trust you as much as I trust that ant crawling

up your leg," Runner said, his eyes twinkling when Adam searched for the ant, then swatted it away from his leg.

"Aw, Runner," Adam said, using the boyhood tactics he had learned so long ago, when he wanted Runner to participate in things that went against Runner's mother's teachings. "Come on. Pals do things together. For one day, Runner, let's forget all animosities and be pals again. I'll pay for the drinks. Come on and enjoy yourself. See how the other side lives."

As before, when Stephanie had asked him to come to Gallup to eat in the fancy lunch room, Runner could not deny that the part of him that was white *was* curious to experience the way he might have been living had he never been taken in by Sage and Leonida to raise as Navaho.

He felt that just perhaps he could prove something to Adam and at the same time get him to leave the Navaho in peace. If it was at all possible for Runner to hold his liquor better than Adam, he might succeed in helping his father more than he ever could otherwise.

"I will go with you," Runner said, giving Adam a stern look. "But only for a short while. I must check on Stephanie's welfare soon."

"I thought you might have noticed," Adam said, while dismounting and tying his horse to a hitching rail, "my sister seems capable of taking care of herself. I had hesitated allowing her to come with me to Arizona. Now, I think she sometimes fares better than me."

"I do not doubt that," Runner said. He gave Adam a half smile as he slid from his saddle and flung his horse's reins around the hitching rail.

"Well? Ready to give it a try, old friend?" Adam said, taking a chance by slinging an arm around Runner's shoulders. "Let's pretend for awhile that we've never had cause to dislike one another. We are boys again, making challenges and having a lot of damn fun doin' it."

Runner placed a stiff hand to Adam's arm and lifted it from his shoulder. They exchanged steady gazes, then moved toward the "Big Tent."

After entering, they paused and took a look around the smoke-filled interior. It was crowded with drinking and card-playing men and lewd women. As Runner listened, he frowned. He had never before been brought face to face with such vulgarity, profanity, and indecency. He could not help but think that what he was seeing and hearing beneath the roof of the "Big Tent" could disgust even the most hardened man. It was apparent that not only was this a place to drink whiskey, it was also a retreat for thieves and robbers of all shapes and sizes.

"I didn't come just to gawk," Adam said. He nodded for Runner to follow as he began making his way toward a bar that sported a supply of every variety of liquor and cigars, with cut-glass goblets and a splendid, huge mirror reflecting everything beyond it, as though there were two huge rooms, instead of one.

Adam elbowed his way to the bar, making standing room for himself and Runner.

The bartender stood behind the bar, a wide, thick mustache hanging low over his upper lip. A fat cigar was positioned at one corner of his mouth. He was polishing a glass, then set it aside and leaned both of his hands flat down on the bar, looking from Runner to Adam.

"What'll it be, gents?" the bartender said, chewing his cigar over to the other side of his mouth. "A regular glass of whiskey is two pony glasses. If you like it in quarts, that'll be forty cents. It's ten cents a drink if you'll take them one at a time."

"I'll take a double shot for starters," Adam said, searching in his pockets for some loose change.

"And what for the "White Indian"?" the bartender said, leveling his squinty, gray eyes on Runner. "You *are* the one who's called the White Indian, ain't ya? You fit the description to a tee."

His jaw tight, his mouth clenched, Runner glared at the bartender.

Adam shuffled his feet nervously. "Never you mind what my friend is called," he said, slamming his coins down on the bar. "Get him a shot of whiskey. And make it snappy, do you hear? Or we'll take our business elsewhere."

Runner turned his back to the bar and again looked slowly around him. When he caught sight of a couple of young Navaho braves on the far side of the room, he tensed up. When he saw that they had drunk far too much alcohol, he felt an ache encircle his heart. These young men were his brother's age. They attended school together. Theirs was to be a much brighter future because of their abilities to read and write.

With their bellies filled with whiskey tonight, their brains fuzzy because of it, it would be impossible for them to attend school tomorrow and learn anything. He had to wonder how often they came to the "Big Tent." He had to wonder what they had traded off to get the money that they were spending so foolishly.

"Runner?" Adam said, nudging Runner in the side with one of his elbows. "I've got your drink. Come on. Let's find us a table."

Runner took a last, lingering look at the two young braves, seething with anger inside. He turned to Adam, glared at him, then knocked both drinks from Adam's hand.

Adam's eyes lit with rage. "What the hell did you do that for?" he shouted. He placed his hands on his hips as he stared down at the broken glass and spilled drinks, then up at Runner again. "You came in here willingly. You knew that you were expected to drink. Why on God's earth did you knock the drinks from my hand?"

The bartender came around the end of the bar with a broom and dust pan. He gave Runner a heated glare, then bent to a knee and proceeded to clean up the mess. "Get that White Indian outta here," he ground out between his clenched teeth as he shifted a look up at Adam. "Now. Or, by damn, I'll have you both thrown out."

"Damn it, Runner, now do you see what you've done?" Adam said. But when he looked over to where Runner had been standing, he found him gone.

When he searched for Runner and found him talking with the two young Navaho braves, his gut twisted. He was seeing Runner getting angrier by the minute as the two drunken lads refused to leave the "Big Tent," in spite of Runner's insistence.

"Get outta my way," one of the braves said in a slurred manner, falling over a chair as he tried to step around Runner.

Runner reached down and lifted the young brave bodily from the floor and started to sling him over his shoulder, as though he were no more than a mere bag of potatoes.

But he didn't get the chance. Just a hint of a fight was all that it took to get the whole pack of men in the bar into small fist fights. This turned into a brawl that left no table untouched as some became upturned, while others were used to knock men over their heads.

"Now see what you've done!" Adam shouted as he struggled to defend himself from first one blow, and then another.

When a fist smashed into his right eye, he cried out and crumpled to the floor. When someone stepped on his groin, he screamed and rolled over to his side, curling into a fetal position.

Runner saw Adam's distress and ignored it. He had the two young braves by their collars. He dragged them outside, leaving the "Big Tent" half-destroyed in his wake.

"Runner, I do not want to go home yet," one of the young braves said, his voice drunkenly slurred. His face blank, his gaze filmed over, he wiped his mouth with his hand and looked longingly at the flap that led back inside the tent. "Runner, I want more whiskey."

Runner looked at the lad sympathetically and felt a tugging at his heart, which was quickly replacing the anger he was feeling toward these two Navaho braves who had disgraced themselves before many white men tonight.

Tomorrow, they would remember. Tomorrow, they would hold their heads in shame.

"No," Runner said, leading the braves to their tethered horses. "You will go home. You will sleep. Tomorrow you will attend school. If your head is not cleared enough to study, you will go to school, anyhow. When others see that you suffer because of your careless behavior tonight, it will discourage them from setting the same bad example for those who are younger."

One at a time, he helped the braves on their horses. He fit the reins into their hands and made sure they were sitting squarely enough on the saddle, then smacked their horse's rumps and watched them ride away.

"God damn you all to hell," Adam said as he came up behind Runner and grabbed him by the arm. He forced him around, so that their eyes were level. "Look at me, Runner. I've got a black eye. I might even have a tooth missing. And it's all because of you. I should've known better than think that you could behave like a normal human being in a bar. You're no better than the other savage heathens you live with."

A slow rage was building within Runner. He forced himself not to react to Adam's words, for he knew that once he unleashed his feelings, Adam would have more than a black eye and possible loose tooth to rave on about.

"Don't you have anything to say?" Adam taunted, his voice building in strength. "Runner, you don't think like a white man. You haven't since you joined forces with the Navaho. And you're not even a shifty, sneakin' half-breed. You're *white*. Why can't you act like it?"

Runner's lips moved in a wry, bitter smile. But still he said nothing. He decided to walk away from Adam. He had seen and heard enough to know that the past was just that.

Gone. Forgotten. Dead.

He could not see anything in Adam that even resembled the young boy of so long ago.

This was the last time that Runner would try to make a measure of peace with Adam. It was impossible. Adam was no better than Damon Stout. They belonged together.

"You are walking away from me?" Adam shouted, stamping toward Runner. "How dare you! I'm not through talking to you. You lousy Indian lover. And you'd better prepare yourself into accepting that Stephanie won't be seein' you again. You stupid fool. You don't even know when you've been suckered. Stephanie bedded up with you only to use you. She doesn't love you. She has pretended, but only to help me achieve my goals. How's that for a sister's loyalty?"

A grave shadow came over Runner's face. He turned a livid gaze and cold eyes to Adam.

Adam started laughing so hard that he didn't know what hit him when Runner clobbered him in the mouth with a fist. Runner hit Adam over and over again. Their struggling bodies thudded to the ground.

Adam reached begging hands up to Runner. "Stop," he said, his voice filled with pain, blood drooling from his mouth and lips.

Runner fell over Adam and straddled him. He held Adam's wrists to the ground. "Tell me the truth," he said from between clenched teeth. "Tell me that you lied about Stephanie."

His eyes almost swollen closed, Adam rolled his head back and forth. "I ... didn't ... lie," he said, scarcely audible, the lie there so easy since his hate and resentment for Runner now ran so deep.

Runner stared down at Adam for a moment longer, then rose limply to his feet. He left Adam all bloodied up in the road and staggered away, his heart bleeding. He had totally trusted a woman who in truth had only used him. He was not sure if he could live with the knowledge.

His eyes dark and somber with thought, he rode tiredly out of Gallup.

Stephanie fell onto her knees beside the mound of freshly turned dirt. She had picked flowers from some cactuses. "What can I say?" she whispered, laying the flowers on Sharon's grave. "I only knew you a short while, yet my grieving is no less than had I known you a lifetime." She wiped tears from her eyes with the back of a hand. "It is all so tragic. How could it have been allowed to happen?"

She rearranged the flowers. "I'm so sorry about Jimmy," she whispered. "I promise that I will never forget him. Perhaps our paths will cross again some day. If they do, I shall tell him about a mother who died valiantly for her son."

The sound of footsteps drawing close caused Stephanie's heart to leap. She turned quick eyes around and bolted to her feet when she found Damon Stout there, his eyes gaunt as he stared down at the grave.

"You're mighty kind to see to her in this way," Damon said, his voice breaking. "It was my responsibility. But I let her down long ago."

"Get away from here," Stephanie said, walking over to him. "Your sister wouldn't want you near her grave. I shan't allow it."

"I'm goin'," Damon said, looking sheepishly at the ground. Then he looked quickly up at Stephanie. "But I want you to know that I never wanted this for my sister."

"It's a bit late to be thinking that, wouldn't you say?" Stephanie said bitterly, placing her hands on her hips.

"You don't know the whole story," Damon said, his eyes trying to meet Stephanie's.

"I know enough," Stephanie said. She nodded toward Damon's horse, which he had left tethered down below. "Now go. I can't allow you to contaminate your sister's grave."

"She was no angel before I turned her out of the house," Damon insisted. "She was a thief for as long as I can remember. When she was eight, she was caught stealin' from a neighbor's house. She just went in and helped herself to the neighbor's expensive, fancy jewelry. When she came and lived with me after our par-

ents died out east, she began stealin' me blind. I had no
choice but to send her packin'. It's cost three quarters of
my life buildin' up enough money for me to have a
ranch. I wasn't goin' to allow my sister to ruin it all."

Stephanie listened raptly. She was finding herself
sympathizing with Damon. The story that he was telling didn't sound practiced enough not to be true. She
doubted he ever opened up his life, or his heart, to
anyone.

She glanced down at the grave, realizing that she
didn't know the woman for whom she was grieving. But
no matter what Sharon had done while she was alive,
she didn't deserve to die such a violent death or be
forced to live the life she had been living. Especially
since she had a child to care for.

"I wish to hell things could've been different,"
Damon said, shuffling past Stephanie. He went and fell
to his knees beside the grave.

She was struck speechless when Damon stretched his
arms over the grave, as though he was trying to embrace
it, and began crying in body-wracking sobs.

Feeling as though she was disturbing a most private,
intimate time in this man's life, and seeing that his grief
was genuine, Stephanie tiptoed away, then ran to her
horse and stepped up into the saddle.

Confused and feeling empty inside, she turned her
horse in the direction of the train hoping to find some
sort of solace in her private car.

She looked over her shoulder at the "Big Tent" that
she was leaving behind in Gallup. A part of her wanted
to wheel her horse around and go and ask Runner to
go home with her. The part of her that saw the need
for Adam and Runner to become friends again caused
her to ride faster away from Gallup.

Her hair flew in the wind as she leveled her eyes
straight ahead.

22

Loved you when summer deepened into June
And those fair, wild, ideal dreams of youth,
Were true yet dangerous, and half unreal
As when Endymion kissed the mateless moon.
—V. SACKVILLE-WEST

Adam grunted and groaned as he rode toward a hidden cove where he and Pure Blossom had planned a rendezvous. Not wanting Stephanie to see him before he had the chance to wash some of the blood from his face, he had not gone to his private car before coming to meet with Pure Blossom.

He also did not have the strength to go both places. He hoped to revive himself somewhat in the river that snaked beside the cove. It would be cold enough to shake anyone out of a stupor, even if it was caused by a beating.

"I'll get even with him if it's the last thing I do," Adam growled out in a whisper. "He may think he's got the upper hand now. Wait until I get through with him. He won't know what hit him."

He smiled ruefully to himself. He wanted to retain in his memory forever that look on Runner's face when he had been told that Stephanie had been leading him on—that she didn't truly love him, only playing him for a fool for her beloved brother.

His smile faded when he thought about Stephanie's reaction. She might hate him forever. But it had been a risk worth taking. No matter what she said to Runner, in her denial of what Adam had said about her motives, it wouldn't be all that easy for Runner to believe her, or trust her again.

He leaned low over his horse and gripped its mane. He was dizzy from the pain. His whole damn face and head seemed to be one massive throbbing. He could scarcely see through his swollen eyes. The cold river water might give him a quick reprieve.

Breathing hard, Adam traveled onward, the horse moving at only a half trot. "How much farther?" he wondered to himself.

It seemed to him that he had been traveling an eternity. When they had chosen the rendezvous location, they had chosen a place that was between their two homes. Now he wished that he had made her come farther, which would make him not have to suffer so long, himself. Yet he had never in his wildest dreams thought that he would be in this condition.

"Damn him," he uttered again. "Damn that son-of-a-bitch White Indian."

Finally he saw the shine of water ahead. He pushed himself up into a sitting position, teetering as he tried to sit tall and erect in his saddle before he reached Pure Blossom.

He squinted his eyes and saw the shine of a campfire up ahead. He was almost there.

The woman who set his heart into a tailspin of rapture was waiting for him. She would have the blankets spread for their lovemaking. He hoped that he wouldn't disappoint her too much when she discovered that he was in no shape to make love with her tonight.

He felt lucky to be alive.

He would never forget the wild look in Runner's eyes when he had been pummeling him with his fists. It revealed to Adam that Runner surely was as close to hate as a man could get before he killed someone.

Beneath the soft rays of the moon's light, Adam could make out a figure running toward him. He melted inside at the thought of being with Pure Blossom again. It was certain that she could make an honest man out of even the worst outlaw. The love she gave a man was born of innocence and sweetness.

A thought grabbed at him that made his shoulders sway with alarm: Runner. Runner would forbid Pure Blossom ever to see him again. Adam knew that Pure Blossom would know who was responsible for the fight after Runner talked to her.

He lowered his eyes, his chest tight, knowing that tonight would be the last night with Pure Blossom. Even if Runner didn't order Pure Blossom not to see Adam again, he knew that it could never work out for them. It was better to cut it off now rather than later. It would be easier on both of them.

"Adam!" Pure Blossom shouted as she ran toward him. She waved her arms over her head in a greeting. "Darling. *Yaa-eh-t-eeh.* I did not think you were coming! What took so long? Were you and Runner having too good a time to leave one another? I would think that is wonderful, Adam. I so badly want you and my brother to be friends."

Adam's heart sank. He had forgotten that he had told Pure Blossom he was going to meet with Runner today. Now he would have no choice but to tell her the truth, or come up quickly with a clever lie.

The lie would at least get him through the awkward evening. He would leave the dirty work to Runner.

Adam wheeled his horse to a halt when Pure Blossom

reached him. The moment she got a good look at him beneath the splash of the moon's glow she saw his battered face.

Although his knees were weak, and he knew they would just scarcely hold him up, Adam slid from the saddle and reached his arms out for Pure Blossom, who looked as though she might faint.

She gave no thought to leaning her cheek against his bloody shirt. His embrace was all that she wanted. She twined her arms around his chest and hugged him to her.

"You have been beaten severely," she murmured, her voice breaking. She clung to him. "How did it happen? Who did this to you?"

Adam stiffened. When she leaned away from him and gazed into his swollen eyes, he reached a hand to her silkenly smooth copper cheek. "I got in a fight at the "Big Tent," he said, shrugging. "That's all."

"My brother?" Pure Blossom asked softly. "Did you fight with my brother?"

Adam's eyes wavered. He felt the coil of deceit tightening in his chest, then loosening the more she gazed so wide-eyed and innocently up at him.

He knew that he could not lie to her. Not now, or ever.

"Yes," he said thickly. "It was your brother. We got into a fight."

Pure Blossom heaved a heavy, weary sigh. "I hoped for so much more," she murmured. "But it will never be, will it, Adam? It is impossible for you and Runner to be friends again."

"Never," Adam said, wincing when she placed a gentle finger to one of his eyes.

"I did not know that my brother had so much hate locked within him," Pure Blossom said, drawing her hand quickly away when she saw the pain that Adam felt. "But it dwells within many of the People's hearts. White men—if they could only be as decent and sweet as you. My people would never have cause to hate again."

The knot of deceit began tightening again inside Adam's chest. He avoided her eyes as he took his horse's reins in one hand, and one of her hands in the other, and walked slowly toward the river. Each step that he took pained him severely. He now felt that he might even have a broken rib.

Even the more reason to hate Runner, he thought bitterly to himself.

When they reached the campsite, where a fire burned warm and cozy just inside the cove, Adam tethered his horse to a low tree limb, then turned to Pure Blossom. "Help me undress," he said, his voice drawn.

Pure Blossom gave him a shocked look. "But, Adam, surely you do not wish to make love in your condition," she said. "And I understand. Tonight we will just sit by the fire. After I see to your wounds, I will sing to you."

"That sounds very inviting," Adam said. "But, Pure Blossom, still, help me undress."

She smiled into his swollen eyes. "Whatever you want, I will do," she said, her slim fingers moving to the buttons of his shirt.

When his shirt was tossed aside and Pure Blossom saw the bruises on Adam's chest, she gasped anew. "Runner is someone I do not know," she said, her voice drawn. "My own brother? How could he do this?"

"Darling Pure Blossom, don't you know that I got in a few of my own blows?" Adam said, wanting to defend his virtue. "So don't think so badly of Runner. We men all have our own degrees of anger we must sometimes act upon."

After Adam was fully unclothed, he eyed the river, then Pure Blossom. "Will you go in the water with me?" he asked solemnly. "I doubt if I have the strength to bathe the blood from my body by myself."

Pure Blossom's eyes wavered as she glanced down at the river, realizing how cold the water must be and fearing it. Her joints already ached. If she was exposed to those colder temperatures, who was to say how much more severe the pain would get? Yet she knew that Adam's pain needed to be tended to now. She must forget her own.

"Yes, I will go with you," she murmured, already unfastening her colorful skirt.

Soon they walked hand-in-hand into the water. Pure Blossom shivered as the chill crept into her bones, yet she held onto Adam with one hand, while her other splashed and caressed and cleansed his face and body, until all that was left were the bruises that would take time to heal.

With her body so temptingly close in the water, and wanting her so bad, Adam's blood was on fire with need. He circled her waist with his arms and drew her against his body. Hurting from head to toe, and covered in cold water, he did not see how it was possible, but he could feel his manhood growing against her thigh. It was throbbing more intensely than his battered face.

"Adam?" Pure Blossom whispered, kissing him gently. "Do you truly think we should? Would it not cause you too much pain?"

"The true pain is in wanting you," Adam said, anchoring himself solidly against the rocky bottom in a more shallow part of the river. He lifted her so that he could impale her with his manhood. Instinctively, she wrapped her legs around him.

As he began thrusting into her, she held her head

back, moaning. He closed his eyes to only one pain, which was being quenched as he stroked within her. He pushed ... he clung ... he groaned.

And then the rapture moved between them, as the web of pleasure ensnared them. Their moans, sobs, and soft cries of ecstasy filled the night air. In the distance an owl hooted hauntingly, as though responding.

Sheer exhaustion flooded Adam's senses. He walked with Pure Blossom from the water. He crumpled down onto the blanket and lay on his back, panting.

Pure Blossom lay a blanket over him and started dressing. Then she began to experience pain, as never before. Sharp, throbbing pains were shooting from her fingertips upward. The knot on her back felt as though it was on fire, radiating pain down her spine.

She tried to hold back the tears. But by the time she was dressed, she was suffering so much that nothing would stop the flooding of her eyes. She sat down beside the fire and drew a blanket around her shoulders. She sobbed. She rocked.

Adam's eyes were wrenched open by the sound. He moved to her side and held her. "Why are you crying?" he said, his voice drawn.

"My fingers," Pure Blossom whimpered, giving Adam a pitying look. "My back. They pain me so. The cold water. It is the cause."

Guilt splashed through Adam. He cradled her close and ran his fingers through her long hair. "I'm sorry," he whispered. "I'm the cause."

His hand moved downward, and he flinched when he discovered just how large the lump was at the base of her neck.

Flashes of memory were going through his mind of another young woman, another time: Pure Blossom's namesake. *Her* transformation from a beautiful young thing had turned her into something grotesque.

He was also recalling how much Pure Blossom had suffered with agonizing pain in her fingers and other joints.

That was how *his* Pure Blossom would look one day.

It caused an ache to swim through him to think of this ugly transformation of this woman he adored.

But he had to face facts. He now knew that it would happen. He also knew that he wouldn't be around to witness it. Tonight would be their last night to be together, to share . . . to love . . . to dream.

"I love you so, Adam," Pure Blossom whispered as she clung and rocked with him. "You look past that which is ugly about me. You are filled with such compassion. Such understanding."

It was then that Adam realized how he could, and must break off his affair with Pure Blossom. It had to be done in a way that would hurt her so severely that she would not see any chance of them ever reconciling their differences. She would hate him. And that was how it had to be.

"Pure Blossom, you so often misjudge people," he said. "Especially me."

Pure Blossom eased from his arms, her eyes wide yet guarded. "What do you mean?" she said, her voice shallow.

"You trust too easily," Adam said, reaching to brush a lock of her hair back in place at her brow. "You give of yourself too easily." He paused and forced himself to say the next words: "You gave yourself too easily to me."

"What are you saying?" Pure Blossom gasped, scooting away from him. She trembled, but not from the chill of the night—from fear, and not fear *of* Adam. The true fear was in losing him.

Adam took her hands and turned them from side to side as he looked at them through his swollen lids. "I knew your Aunt Pure Blossom," he said. "As hers were, your hands soon will be gnarled beyond recognition." He reached around and stroked the lump at the base of her neck. "Soon this will be so ugly, I would retch if I had to gaze upon it."

Shock registered in Pure Blossom's eyes. She swallowed hard, choking on a sob.

"No, I don't want a future with someone who is going to be ugly and repelling," Adam said, feeling as though a knife was plunging into his heart with each added insult. Only moments ago, he had thought it was impossible to ever lie to her. Now, while telling her how he would feel about her appearance in the future, he was telling the worst lie of all.

"Tonight is our last night together," he said solemnly. "You should leave now, Pure Blossom. I don't think I can stand the sight of you another minute."

Stunned speechless, hurting deeply, all that Pure Blossom could think about was what she had been planning to tell Adam tonight.

About their child.

She had only realized in the past few days that she was pregnant. They had been together just enough times at the appropriate time of month for her to be pregnant!

She had looked forward to this love child with such bliss. She had looked forward to being with Adam for the rest of her life. She had even decided to leave her village, if being his wife required it of her.

Now he would never know, for she would keep the

child as her own. She would hold her head high against the ridicule of having a fatherless child.

At this moment, all that she could think about was the child and its welfare. It was better off not knowing such a bastard father.

Without further thought, Pure Blossom slapped Adam across the face. She laughed when she realized that she had inflicted more pain to that which had already been inflicted on him earlier in the evening by her beloved brother.

"My brother was right to hit you," Pure Blossom said, scurrying to her feet. She grabbed her blanket from beneath Adam, causing him to fall sideways, almost landing in the fire. She rolled it into a knot and thrust it in a leather bag at the side of her horse.

Then she went back to Adam and spat on him. "That is how this grotesque-looking woman feels about you," she said, then stamped away and mounted her horse.

Tears flooded Adam's eyes as he watched her ride away. Slowly, he smeared her spit all over his face, knowing that he deserved it.

Pure Blossom held in the body-wracking sobs until she got far enough away from Adam so that he could not hear, then let her feelings spill out as she finally allowed herself to shed the tears that she felt would never end.

"Adam," she whispered, choking on the very sound of his name as it flowed across her lips. "How could you? Oh, how could you be so cruel? So . . . so . . . cold-hearted?"

Her parlor flooded with lamplight, Stephanie paced the floor. She wrung her hands as she went to the window and peered into the shadows of the night. Neither

Adam nor Runner had returned from Gallup. She had to wonder if that was good, or was it an omen of what may have happened?

Where Runner was concerned, she didn't trust her brother. On the other hand, Runner was quite capable of taking care of the likes of Adam. Still, she wished one of them would return.

She paced a while longer, then the need for sleep overcame her. Sighing resolutely, she changed into her nightgown. She took the kerosene lamp to the table beside her bed, then climbed in and tried to read a novel.

Her eyes drifted closed. The book fell from her hands as she eased into a more comfortable position.

She snuggled and smiled in her sleep as she dreamed about Runner. They were embracing high on a knoll, alone, with only the wind and stars as their audience.

The air was cool and sweet. The high country loomed against the sky, range after range of mountains, cloud hung, and immense. A stream below was a narrow gleam of a twisting ribbon reflecting moonlight.

Runner stood high on a knoll, his eyes heavenward. He had been there for some time now, meditating and praying. He was not sure how he could accept what he had been told about Stephanie. He was praying for strength. He was praying for his future, which no longer included Stephanie.

Runner began to sing, his voice filled with reverence, with wonder and confidence. . . .

> "Voice above,
> Voice of thunder,
> Speak from the dark of clouds.
> Voice below,

> Grasshopper voice,
> Speak from the green of plants;
> Guide me to the right path of life...."

Runner closed his eyes, binding his mind and will and spirit to the land.

23

Could'st thou withdraw thy hand one day
And answer to my claim,
That fate, and that today's mistake—
Not thou—had been to blame?
                    —ADELAIDE ANNE PROCTER

The sun was up, just past the mountain peaks in the distance, and Stephanie had already had her third cup of coffee. She had awakened before dawn, with a sudden remembrance that she had not seen Adam or Runner since their time together in Gallup.

She had also awakened with the deep desire to go to Canyon de Chelley. Ever since Runner had said that because of sacred reasons she must not go there, her curiosity had become more aroused to see it. And not only to see it: to photograph it.

She had decided to ask Adam to escort her there today.

She would get her photographs; she would develop the plates; then she would send them with Adam when he returned to Wichita, and Runner would never be the wiser.

There was no way on God's earth that Runner would ever see the way these photographs of Canyon de Chelley would be used. Only those who lived hundreds of miles away would be given that chance. Postcards and

posters with the lovely pictures of Canyon de Chelley
on them that would entice more travelers to ride the
Santa Fe than any other railroad line in the country.
The Santa Fe would be offering the unique view of the
life of ancient Indians.

Shame engulfed Stephanie for even considering deceiving Runner. She knew that he wasn't being unrea-
sonable in his demands, for she was seeing more and
more how the Navaho and other tribes of Arizona Territory Indians had been used and abused. Yet she also
saw that progress could boost their earnings. With the
arrival of tourists came the opportunity for selling many
lovely blankets, tapestries, and jewelry.

How could that be wrong? she argued with herself.
With the money earned from selling their wares to the
tourists, the Navaho could purchase food and clothing,
and they could exchange their ancient ways of tilling
the earth for their gardens for more modern farming
equipment used by the white people.

"I won't allow myself to feel badly over what I am
about to do," Stephanie said, setting her empty coffee
cup on a table.

She turned and gazed at the small pendulum clock
that sat on a shelf over her sofa. "It will soon be seven
o'clock," she whispered, watching the pendulum moving back and forth, ticking away time. "It will take at
least two days to get to Canyon de Chelley. I must
awaken Adam now so that we can get started."

She drew her hair back and quickly twined it in and
out between her fingers until one long braid hung down
her back. She slung her holster around her waist and
fastened it, patting the derringer as she walked toward
the door.

Glancing down at her attire, she grimaced. She was
growing tired of wearing the plain, dreadful skirts and

the long-sleeved blouses. She hungered for something soft. The thought of wearing long, flowing velveteen skirts and matching blouses, like the Navaho women wore, made her smile. She would soon be wearing them, also.

"I'm going to marry Runner," she murmured, ecstatic at the thought. "But I must take these last photographs," she murmured, determinedly opening the door. She smiled again. "I have saved the best for last."

Stepping out into the sweet, cool breeze of morning, Stephanie stopped before knocking on Adam's door. The shade was still drawn. "He's still asleep," she whispered.

But why wouldn't he be? she wondered. She had watched and waited for him, or Runner, past midnight. She had no idea when, after that, he may have arrived home. She wasn't even sure that he would agree to escort her to Canyon de Chelley.

Without stopping to knock, knowing that Adam might need a shake or two to get him totally awake, Stephanie went on into his private car. She went determinedly from window to window and flipped the shades up, hoping that their racket would do the trick.

When even that didn't awaken her brother, Stephanie went to his bed and stood over it. He was covered up with a blanket, from his head to his toes. He was sleeping so peacefully. He would hate her for waking him up, yet time was wasting. She had everything prepared for the journey, except her brother.

And no matter what argument he gave her when she asked him to escort her today, she would not take no for an answer. He had been given plenty of time to get his own personal affairs in order. Now it was time for him to help her with hers.

Bending over Adam, Stephanie placed a gentle hand

to his shoulder and gave him a shake. "Adam?" she said, giving him another shake. "Wake up. I want you to go somewhere with me today. Adam? Wake up."

Adam groaned. He winced when he moved even one muscle. He was quickly reminded of the beating that he had gotten the previous night. Only when he had been making love with Pure Blossom had he been able to forget the aches and pains inflicted by Runner.

He grimaced anew when he recalled the lies he had told the previous evening, first to Runner, and then to Pure Blossom. He regretted like hell for having to hurt Pure Blossom so deeply.

And as for the lie that he had told Runner about Stephanie . . .

"Adam, quit being so pokey this morning," Stephanie said, interrupting his thoughts. She folded her arms impatiently across her chest. "I want you to go somewhere with me. Runner won't take me to Canyon de Chelley. Will you? I can take some magnificent shots of the ancient writings. There are so many things to photograph there, Adam. Come on, get up. I have things ready. All you have to do is shave, eat, and then we can be on our way."

"Canyon de Chelley?" Adam mumbled, and then his eyes lit up. He knew the length of time that it would take for them to get to and from Canyon de Chelley. That would at least postpone Stephanie's discovery of what he had told Runner.

This would also get Stephanie away from Runner, so that he could not come and confront her with the lie that he had been told. Also, knowing how Runner felt about the sanctity of Canyon de Chelley, Stephanie going to photograph it would put the finishing touches on Runner's feelings for her.

Runner would end up hating Stephanie, not loving her.

"Time is wasting, Adam," Stephanie said, yanking the blanket away from him. In his satin, monogrammed pajamas, his back was to her. "Time to get up. *Now*."

When Adam rolled over and turned his face up to her, Stephanie's eyes widened and her throat felt suddenly dry. "Good Lord, Adam," she gasped. "Your face!" She bent to her knees beside the bed and softly touched the bruises around his eye. "How did this happen? Oh, Adam, who gave you such a beating?"

Adam's eyes wavered into hers. Then he brushed past her and got up. "If you want to leave soon, I'll hurry and shave," he said, running his fingers across his whiskers. He winced when even that small gesture caused pain. His jaws ached, as well. Each time he spoke it was with much effort.

Stephanie was not to be put off all that easily. She took Adam by an arm and turned him to face her again. "Tell me what happened," she said. "You were with Runner last night. Please tell me that he's not responsible for these bruises."

With all of her heart and soul, she did not want to believe that Runner had so much anger locked within him that he could give Adam such a beating. When he was with her, he was such a gentle, caring man.

Yet she knew that Adam had a way of antagonizing a person to his limits. She had seen it at the Santa Fe board meetings. His opinion was pushed upon others, sometimes to the point that brawls had ensued at the meetings. Perhaps Adam had pushed Runner past that limit, as well.

"You know how things can get at saloons," Adam said, shrugging. "There was a brawl. Runner and I just happened to be at the wrong place at the wrong time.

The "Big Tent" is known for their knock-down-drag-out brawls. Last night was one of the worst, to my estimation."

"Then the fight was not between you and Runner?" Stephanie persisted, gasping anew when Adam slipped the top of his pajamas off and revealed the cuts and bruises on his chest.

Adam gave her a narrow look, knowing that one more lie must be added to his many, or he would not be able to get Stephanie away from here today. She would immediately demand answers and might even decide to go to Runner to try and set things straight.

The longer Runner had to sweat over losing Stephanie, the better, Adam decided to himself. The longer Runner condemned Stephanie inside his heart, the stronger the emotion would become.

Adam wanted like hell to keep his sister away from Runner. He saw Runner as a savage whose skin coloring mocked the man. This "White Indian" did not deserve a woman like Stephanie!

"Adam, your silence is frightening me," Stephanie demanded. "Tell me. Was your fight with Runner?"

"Sis," Adam said, taking her hands, "the whole damn place broke into a brawl. So quit worryin' about Runner. All right?"

Stephanie sighed deeply. "All right," she murmured. She swung away from him. "I'll get the horses saddled and the equipment on the pack mule." She stopped and turned back to face him. "You never said. You *are* going to go with me this morning, aren't you?"

"Yes, I'm going with you," Adam said, holding an aching jaw as he smiled at her.

"Are you sure you feel like it?" Stephanie said, her eyes absorbing his injuries once again. "Surely you must ache all over."

"The long ride will be fine," Adam said, yanking a clean shirt from the back of a chair. "It'll do my aching bones good."

Stephanie started to turn and leave again, but looked at Adam once more instead. "I hate to ask," she murmured, "but I *must*. I need to know if Runner is in as bad a shape as you. Did he get beaten as severely?"

Adam pursed his lips tightly together. "I'm not altogether sure," he said, turning his eyes from her. "We got separated during the fight. I came home when I couldn't find him around anywhere after I managed to get out of the brawl in the saloon."

"Perhaps I should postpone my journey to Canyon de Chelley until tomorrow and go and check on Runner," Stephanie said softly.

Adam started to insist that they go today, when she broke through his thoughts and added, "Yet if I don't go today," she murmured thoughtfully, "I may never get a chance to again. If Runner found out, he would be furious and do everything to stop me."

She nodded and walked to the door. "I shall be waiting for you, all packed and ready, Adam," she said, swinging the door open. "Please don't take too long. So much of the good travel time is gone today."

Adam nodded, then wiped pearls of sweat from his brow. He sighed with relief. He had gotten away with his lies so far. But he knew that they would soon catch up with him.

He feared that in the long run the depths of his deceit would cause Stephanie to turn her back on him. And if he lost her respect and love, he would lose half his world. He loved her more than he could ever love anyone, the sort of love that only brothers and sisters felt for one another. But a part of his heart had told him long ago that hers would not be an enduring love for him. He was always trying her patience and trust just a bit harder, like a string that was stretched until it snapped.

As much as his aching muscles would allow, Adam continued getting dressed and shaved, then stepped outside and smiled down at Stephanie as she handed him a cup of coffee and a roll.

"You always think of everything," Adam said, gladly accepting the breakfast.

"Yes, and don't you forget it," Stephanie teased. "What on earth would you ever do without me?"

Adam's eyes wavered as he looked quickly away from her.

Runner had spent the entire night on the knoll, praying and meditating and thinking. At last he had dropped off into a restless sleep. The cry of an eagle had awakened him with a start as it had swept down low over him.

The sun was creeping up from behind the mountains in the distance. Runner felt refreshed, but not reassured by his time alone. Nothing would take away the pain he was feeling.

Stephanie. He couldn't shake away the vision of her face. He couldn't stop recalling how it had felt when they had reached the ultimate pleasure of their lovemaking. He would never be able to forget what Adam had told him—that he had been duped by Stephanie.

Knowing not to trust Adam, Runner had started to head his horse in the direction of Stephanie's private train car many times this morning. But the chance that Adam was telling the truth had stopped him. If Stephanie had already made such a fool of him, he did not want her to have the chance to do it again.

On the other hand, if Adam was telling a lie and

Stephanie realized that something was wrong, in that Runner was not coming to see her, she would come to him and question him. If she didn't come, it would prove that she didn't care and that all that Adam had said was true.

As Runner entered his village, he immediately saw his mother and father outside their hogan, talking to the woman who was the teacher of the small school on the reservation. As he drew closer to them, he knew that something was wrong. His father's face was shadowed with anger. His mother's eyes were sad.

He rode up next to them and dismounted. He didn't even have to question his parents. His father turned to him and gave him quick orders.

"Thunder Hawk skipped school again today," Sage said, his hands held in tight fists at his sides. "Runner, you know his haunts. Go. Find him. Bring him to me. He has been disobedient one time too many."

Leonida noticed the bruises on Runner's face. "Darling, did you get into a fight?" she murmured, touching his face gently. "I know you were with Adam last night. Did Adam do this to you?"

"Yes, Adam and I fought," Runner said flatly. "But that is all I wish to say about it."

Leonida immediately fell silent. She went into her house and began quickly gathering together some food for Runner's travels. She knew that he had not had time for breakfast.

When she returned, offering him a leather bag which smelled pleasantly of freshly baked bread, Runner smiled down at her and accepted it. "You are such a good mother," he said, bending to kiss her cheek. "Such an admirable woman. I wish more were like you."

Leonida returned his kiss, wondering over what he

had said. From what she had noticed about his feelings for Stephanie, he surely felt the same about her.

Yet there was something in his voice and eyes today that told her that he was being tortured from within about something, and she doubted it was over the fight that he had with Adam. She had to believe that it had something to do with Stephanie.

Yet she knew better than to try and interfere. Her sons had a way of keeping secrets from their mother. This saddened her, yet she had grown used to it and accepted it and loved them no less for it.

Runner placed the food into his saddlebag, then swung himself up onto his horse. "I will do my best to find my brother," he said, then wheeled his horse around and rode away.

He rode for several hours, even traveling as far as where he had seen Thunder Hawk that one night when it was quite late, but there were no signs of his brother anywhere.

He rode on and on, stopping only to refresh his horse beside a meandering stream and to eat his fill of his mother's delicious bread. Then he rode onward again, watching for the signs of any travelers on all sides of him.

When he knew that his search had taken him perhaps too far than what was normal for Thunder Hawk's travels, he started to turn his horse back in the direction of home, but stopped and edged his steed behind a cover of bushes when he saw two people approaching on horses. His gut twisted when he spied a pack mule ambling behind them.

"Stephanie and Adam!" he hissed through angry, clenched teeth.

With guarded deliberation, he watched their approach. When they rode past him, not realizing he was there, his heart beat angrily within him: the direction of their travel would take them to Canyon de Chelley! Adam was taking Stephanie there for her to photograph what Runner had explained to her was sacred.

She was going against Runner's wishes, and he did not have to think long as to why she felt free to do this. Adam had surely told her that he had confessed everything to Runner about how she was tricking him. Now that she knew that the truth had been told, she obviously did not care what Runner would think about her going to Canyon de Chelley. She was free to do as she pleased.

This proved to Runner that her love for him had never been sincere. She would never photograph what he had asked her not to unless she no longer cared what he thought.

"Little white woman, we shall see about that," Runner said, anger flushing his face red.

After they got farther up the trail, he began following them.

24

She yet more pure, sweet, straight and fair,
Than gardens, woods, meads, rivers are.
                                        —ANDREW MARVELL

Several horses trailing behind him on ropes, Thunder
Hawk's heart pounded with a mixture of anticipation
and fear as he rode proud and tall on his Navaho horse.
Sky Dancer's village was in view. He could hardly wait
to see her again, yet fears of being rejected by not only
her father but also Sky Dancer ate away at Thunder
Hawk. She had no idea that he was arriving at her
village to ask for her hand in marriage. He hoped that
he had read her eyes correctly the many times they
had seen one another at each of their village's joint
celebrations and feasts.

He glanced over his shoulder at the horses that he
had either found wandering or had stolen from Damon
Stout. One by one, his eyes roamed from horse to
horse, mentally counting them.

"Fifteen," he whispered. "Surely that is enough for
the bride price."

It had to be enough. These were all that he had been
able to find, or steal, and keep in his secret corral.

He directed his eyes toward the village again as he
rode closer to it in a slow lope. It had become too
dangerous to steal any more horses from Damon Stout.

Word had been brought to Thunder Hawk that Damon had been at Fort Defiance lodging complaints against the Navaho people. That had to mean that Damon's horses would be guarded too closely for Thunder Hawk to ever steal from him again.

"Fifteen," he repeated. "Will that be enough to please Chief Red Moon?"

Frowning, he recalled Sky Dancer's father. Chief Red Moon's reputation was known far and wide as a fierce leader who dealt severely with those who became his enemy. He had warriors guarding his enchanting daughter both day and night as though she were an untouchable, sacred object.

As he should, Thunder Hawk thought. She was beautiful beyond words; and so sweet, just looking at her had melted his heart.

"She is only fifteen winters," Thunder Hawk worried aloud. He feared that this could be one of Chief Red Moon's argument against his young daughter taking a husband.

"My *own* age could be a problem," Thunder Hawk continued to worry aloud. In his lifetime, he had only witnessed seventeen winters. In the Navaho tradition, it was the custom for the men to marry at a much later age.

But not every man fell so totally in love at this age, he thought. And not every Navaho brave his age was forced to attend the white man's school. Once married, he would assume the duties of a husband. The foolishness of an education would be no longer forced upon him, as though he were a mere child.

This thought made determination replace his fear. He *must* make a good impression. He *had* to leave this village today with Sky Dancer riding at his side.

A shudder ran through him at the thought of how

he might be received back at his village with a bride. He had already deceived his parents by sneaking away from school yesterday to come on this pilgrimage of the heart. Surely when they saw the reason why—that he had gone to seek a wife, and then saw who his bride was—they would no longer be angry at him.

Everyone adored Sky Dancer. Who would not want her as a daughter-in-law?

Still, he thought with another shudder, if Chief Red Moon sent him from the village empty-handed, what excuse could he give his parents then? To make things up to them, he would have to attend school for many weeks without sneaking away.

"Sky Dancer *will* be mine," he whispered to himself over and over again as he rode closer to the village.

He finally reached it and entered, aware he made quite a sight with many beautiful horses trailing behind him, their hooves making a sound similar to thunder as they beat against the ground. Yes, it was surely a spectacle, one that he was proud to make.

He smiled and nodded at the people as they came and stood at the doors of their hogans. He patted the heads of children as they ran along on each side of his horse, laughing and reaching up to touch him. Owning this many horses seemed to make him into a hero in the eyes of the children. He only hoped that Chief Red Moon would feel some of the enthusiasm generated by the hordes of children as they gathered in even greater numbers around him as he approached the chief's hogan.

Then Thunder Hawk's eyes wavered and his throat tightened when up ahead he saw Chief Red Moon step from his dwelling. He was an imposing figure who stood over six feet in his bare feet and whose weight must have been no less than three hundred pounds. His eyes were dark and set back deep under thick, black eyebrows. The bones of his face were prominent and his nose was hawk-beaked. His bony jawline was heavy, moving solidly into a jutting chin beneath a straight mouth.

Chief Red Moon wore a velveteen shirt and breeches with silver buttons glistening from the sides of his breeches and up the front of his shirt. His hair hung long, black, and sleek across his shoulders, a red velveteen headband holding his hair back at his brow.

The frown that he wore and the locked arms across his chest caused fear once again to grip Thunder Hawk. He could tell that Chief Red Moon was not as taken by this young man who so boldly entered his village with a stampede of horses tied behind him as the children were.

Then Thunder Hawk's heart seemed to drop to his feet when Sky Dancer slipped to her father's side, her dark eyes wide and dancing when she saw who was approaching, and surely understanding why: the horses; they were proof of Thunder Hawk's intentions on this bright and sunny day of late summer.

Thunder Hawk let his eyes trail over Sky Dancer. She wore a fully gathered skirt and velveteen blouse, both of which revealed her tiny waist and luscious curves. Her face had been perfectly molded by the hands of the Great Unseen Power.

As always, her smile was melting Thunder Hawk. Thunder Hawk's eyes locked with Sky Dancer's. His pulse raced when he saw that once again they were communicating their feelings for one another without having spoken.

Intrigued anew by her loveliness, his head began to spin, but feeling the steely gaze of her father on him, he again turned his eyes to the chief.

He drew a tight rein a short distance away from Chief Red Moon and Sky Dancer. There was an obvious absence at the chief's right side, his wife having passed away two moons ago due to a fever.

Dressed in his finest clothes, a pair of fringed breeches, a dark purple velveteen shirt that displayed silver buttons down its front, and a matching velveteen headband that held his long, black hair in place, Thunder Hawk dismounted his horse. He nodded a thank you to a young brave who took his reins and stood obediently beside the horse.

His shoulders squared, his throat dry, and his heart pounding out his fear of standing before this great chief, Thunder Hawk took the few steps required to reach Chief Red Moon.

Once there, he clumsily gave the chief a pleasant greeting, then also extended the same cordial greeting to Sky Dancer, who smiled timidly at him, then cast her eyes even more bashfully to the ground.

"Why have you come?" Chief Red Moon said, not wasting time with further cordialities. He did not even invite Thunder Hawk into his dwelling. "Why have you brought many horses?"

Sky Dancer lifted her head long enough to cast Thunder Hawk a sweet, quick smile, and then once again lowered her eyes humbly to the ground.

"The horses that I have brought to you count fifteen in number," Thunder Hawk said, turning to motion with a hand toward them. "Do you not see that they are all beautiful?"

He turned back around to face the chief. "Do you see them worthy as a bride price?" he said, his voice drawn and edged with fear.

"A . . . bride . . . price?" Chief Red Moon said, glowering at Thunder Hawk. "For whom?"

Thunder Hawk shuffled his moccasined feet nervously. He cleared his throat. He gave Sky Dancer a wistful stare, then challenged the glare that Chief Red Moon was sending his way.

"Thunder Hawk brings these horses to Chief Red Moon as payment for the privilege of marrying his beautiful daughter," he finally blurted out.

Many people had gathered around them, whispering and nudging one another, while others had crept close to run their hands down the necks of one or more of the horses.

When Thunder Hawk voiced his intentions, a hush fell over the crowd. All that Thunder Hawk could hear was the harshness of his breathing, and perhaps even the beating of his own heart.

Chief Red Moon took a step closer to Thunder Hawk. He took a slow turn around the young man. Then Red Moon went and stood beside his daughter again. "You lack the years required to be a husband," he scoffed. "Take your horses and go."

Gasps wafted through the air around Thunder Hawk, but his own was the loudest. He could not believe that Chief Red Moon could be so quick to deny him what he wanted so much.

Sky Dancer lifted her eyes and looked boldly into his, then gave the same bold, steadfast gaze to her father.

"Father, I do not want him to leave," Sky Dancer said, no longer pretending to be timid and shy. "Not without *me*."

Chief Red Moon's eyes lit with a sudden fire. His jaw tightened and his lips pursed as he gave his daughter a disbelieving stare.

"Father, this daughter does not want a man of many years for a husband," Sky Dancer continued. "Sky Dancer wants Thunder Hawk."

Her confession made Thunder Hawk's knees weaken with surprise and happiness. He now knew that he had not misread her eyes those many times they had stared at one another during family visits. And surely her dreams had included him, as his had often been filled with her.

At this moment, he felt as though he was experiencing another dream; her wanting him for a husband was something that he had wanted, yet feared never having. He had taken a dangerous chance in coming here today with the bold offering of horses.

Now it seemed as though his heart had led him well in this decision. He did not see how the chief could refuse his daughter her choice of husbands. The whole village had been a witness to her confession.

Chief Red Moon placed gentle hands to Sky Dancer's delicate shoulders. "Daughter, how is it that you know how your heart speaks?" he said quietly. "You have never been alone with Thunder Hawk. You have never been allowed to be alone with *any* man. And he is not a man; he is but a child in my eyes."

With that, Thunder Hawk straightened his shoulders even more squarely, thrust out his chest, and held his chin high with dignity. He had to prove his worth. He hoped that somehow he reflected some of Sage's nobility, knowing that in so many ways he resembled his chieftain father. If only Chief Red Moon would look past the young man in him, and see him as he would be in the future.

Surely Chief Red Moon understood that this man asking for his daughter's hand in marriage might one day be a powerful Navaho chief. He was from a long line of chiefs, and his father Sage carried the title on from his ancestors before him.

Of course, Thunder Hawk knew that Runner would

be there to make challenges to the title. But that was far in the future. Chief Sage was a young man in spirit and body.

"Father, when our people met in celebrations and feasts with Thunder Hawk's, I saw him," Sky Dancer said. "He saw me. Our eyes spoke of our feelings for one another. Sky Dancer is so pleased that I read the right message in Thunder Hawk's eyes—that he loves me as I love him. I want nothing more from life than to be his wife."

Thunder Hawk's lips parted with a low gasp, having never expected that Sky Dancer's feelings could run this deep for him. It was more than he had ever dreamed possible. To have her at his side forever was something that made everything else seem trivial. He wanted her now more than life itself.

There would be no more schooling. There would only be a wife who stood by his decisions to be the great owner of vast numbers of sheep. They would live the dream together.

Chief Red Moon gaped openly down at his daughter for a few more moments, then drew her into his gentle embrace. "Sky Dancer, this father has never forbidden this daughter anything of the heart," he said, his voice low and caressing. "Nor will he now."

"Thunder Hawk and I will have our own private ceremony," Sky Dancer said.

Chief Red Moon said nothing for a moment, then nodded. "If that is what you wish, then so be it," he said. Again he hugged her, then stepped away.

Sky Dancer paused and stared up at Thunder Hawk, then dashed toward him and flung herself into his arms. "I do love you," she whispered, so that only he could hear.

Thunder Hawk's insides melted with the bliss of the

moment. He held her a moment longer, then watched her enter the hogan, knowing that she was going there to gather up her belongings.

Feeling that this was unreal, as though it could not truly be happening, he was lightheaded and giddy. He smiled clumsily at Chief Red Moon as the chief went to the horses and slowly began checking them over. After each was approved, they were taken away to the chief's pole corral, which was already filled to capacity with handsome steeds.

Chief Red Moon stepped up to Thunder Hawk, patted him on the back, then eyed him up and down, as though measuring his worth. Then he gazed into his eyes. "The horses are of great value and breeding," he said calmly. "I do not venture to ask how they came into your possession. I take them, anyhow."

Chief Red Moon chuckled and clasped a hand to Thunder Hawk's shoulder. He leaned closer to Thunder Hawk, so that only he could hear what he said. "I, too, have ventured onto land owned by Damon Stout," he whispered. "I, too, have added to my herd at his expense."

Thunder Hawk's eyes widened in disbelief, then he exchanged knowing smiles with Red Moon.

Without further thought, he moved into the chief's hefty embrace. He was going to enjoy being friends with, and better yet, a son-in-law to, this powerful, headstrong chief. Their thoughts traveled the same path.

Sky Dancer came from the hogan carrying two large leather satchels, and two blankets rolled up and tied together. When she discovered her father and future husband in an embrace, a wondrous relief washed through her.

"Thunder Hawk?" she said, her voice lilting and sweet.

Thunder Hawk and Chief Red Moon stepped apart. Thunder Hawk went to Sky Dancer and relieved her of her heavy burdens and placed her belongings on the back of his horse. She would travel in his saddle with him, where he could draw her slim form back against him, his arm willingly holding her in place.

His heart pounded as she gave her father one last embrace. He had not expected this to be so easy.

Actually, he was stunned. This quickly he had a wife. This quickly he would be able to turn his back on the school books and the dreaded one-room schoolhouse forever!

Sky Dancer stepped timidly up to Thunder Hawk. She smiled shyly up at him as he placed his hands on her tiny waist and lifted her onto his saddle.

He gave Chief Red Moon a big, grateful smile, then swung himself into the saddle behind Sky Dancer. When his arm went around her waist and she leaned back against him, a wild desire clutched at his heart.

25

She so torments my mind
That my strength faileth,
And wavers with the wind
As a ship saileth.
—ANONYMOUS (17th century)

After two full days of travel, Stephanie and Adam arrived at Canyon de Chelley. Stephanie dismounted, her gaze taking in the awesome sweep of rose-red cliffs, phantoms of quiet and of celestial scale. The thousand-foot deep canyons, where ancient Anasazi pueblos clung precariously to the sandstone cliffs, were nestled on high ledges below the towering cliffs. The heart-stopping vistas from atop the sheer canyon walls made the trip to Canyon de Chelley unforgettable.

She had found the old home of the spirits. From the folds of the earth, the red walls rose sheer. She was looking into a corridor of geological time. You could turn any corner there and the walls contained you!

Stephanie was anxious to travel to the canyon floor and take a close-up view of the fabulous stone monuments and the imposing canyon walls, and also to take photographs of the rock paintings which were known to depict the arrival of the Spaniards on horseback.

From her studies of this area, she recalled that although the Navaho liked the sheep and horses that the Spanish had brought, they had not liked the Spanish customs. The Spanish soldiers had fought the Indians. They had made prisoners of them and had used them as servants.

At different times, the Navaho, Pueblo, and the Apache had joined together to fight off the Spaniards. The Navaho and Apache had remained free from the Spaniards. They had continued to fight and raid the Spaniards for horses and sheep.

Adam was not as enthralled by the grandeur of the canyon. He was bone-tired from the long journey. He wanted to get the photographs taken so that they could start on their return journey. He still had his own things to tend to. And he would not allow his sister, nor anyone else for that matter, to sidetrack him again.

"Adam, should we take the time to eat, or should I start right in taking the photographs?" Stephanie said, stepping up to the pack mule. Adam had already taken the tripod from the mule and was setting it up for her close to the edge of the canyon. She opened one saddlebag and removed her camera, and some plates.

"We can eat later," Adam said in a low grumble. "Let's get this over with, Stephanie. I want to get back to the train. I almost have things settled here, as best they can be settled. We can soon return to Wichita and go to the board meeting together to report on what we've both accomplished here."

Stephanie's fingers fumbled with the camera as she tried to place it on the tripod, now realizing that she still had to tell Adam about her marriage plans to Runner. She wanted to delay until she had no choice but to tell him that she wouldn't be returning with him to Wichita. She didn't want to have Adam arguing with her about her decision day in and day out before he left. She had made her mind up. Nobody would change it.

"Stephanie?" Adam said, leaning toward her. "Did you hear what I said? You *will* go into the board meeting with me and speak encouragingly about my town, won't you? Or has Runner swayed you against everything I stand for? Progress, Stephanie. That's what I stand for. The same as *you*. You wouldn't be going to all of this trouble taking these photographs if you didn't plan on giving them to the Santa Fe Railroad to use to lure people west on their railroad."

"Don't remind me about what I'm doing today, that I'm deceiving Runner," Stephanie said, leaning over to focus her lenses. "If he ever finds out, he'll surely hate me forever."

She realized what she had said the minute it had slipped across her lips. She turned around and faced Adam with a stern look. "Don't you use this against me," she said flatly. "If you tell Runner that I came here, in order to turn him against me for your own selfish gain, I'd never forgive you, Adam. Do you understand?"

Adam smiled ruefully at her. Little did she know that Runner already hated her. But she would know—soon. By then, she would have no choice but to stay allied with her brother. If not, she would be alone in a vast land, where she was at the mercy of the train that had brought her there.

The engineers would either leave her there, or take her with them, at Adam's command. They owed him. He had helped pay their gambling debts.

"Certainly, sis," Adam said, placing his fists on his hips. "I understand."

When Stephanie saw a strange, shadowy look in Adam's eyes, she sighed and turned back to her camera, then felt that this might be the time to spring the surprise on Adam, after all. He would have two days' travel back to the train to get over it.

Whereas, if she told him about her plans to marry Runner after they were at the train, there was no telling what he might do. She most certainly did not want to see him ride in a flurry into the Navaho compound. He already had enough cuts and bruises on his body. No need for him to give cause for others to be inflicted.

Stepping away from the camera, Stephanie turned to Adam. "Adam, I think it's time I quit playing games with you," she murmured. She saw his eyebrows rise and his jaw tighten. "Adam, I won't be returning with you to Wichita. I plan to stay behind. I'm going to marry Runner."

Adam took a shaky step away from her. Ashen, his eyes wide, he stared disbelievingly at her. "What did you say?" he gasped.

"I believe you heard me well enough," Stephanie said, clasping her hands tightly behind her. "I *am* going to marry Runner, Adam. I love him. He loves me."

Adam was aghast at the thought of what she was saying. And then a slow calm crept over him. He had to force himself not to smile smugly at her, for *he* knew that there would be no marriage ceremony between Runner and his sister. Adam had taken care of that by telling Runner the clever, calculated lie.

"So, you see, Adam," Stephanie said, "everything is up to you now. You will have to go to the board meeting without me. And while there, I would like for you to take the photographs that I am going to take today. You must do this for me. I never want anyone to think that I didn't earn what I was paid."

"Yeah, I'll do that for you," Adam said in a growl.

Stephanie was puzzled by how he was taking the news about her marriage. She had expected him to shout at her. She had expected him to tell her that he would not allow it. Instead, he was taking it as calmly as if she told him that she was going to marry a rich millionaire from New York.

"Adam, you don't care that I am going to marry Runner?" she said softly.

"You know that I do."

"Then why aren't you acting like it?"

"What do you expect, sis? For me to tie you to your bedpost?"

"No, not exactly."

"Sis, I don't plan to do anything but mind my own business from now on, especially where your private life is concerned."

Stephanie looked at him at length, trying to see through his strange, uncharacteristic behavior. Then she shrugged and went back to her camera. After getting it adjusted and ready for shooting, the sound of an approaching horseman drew her quickly around. When she discovered who was riding like an unleashed beast toward her and Adam, she was stunned.

"Runner," she gasped, her fingers going to her throat as fear gripped her. "Oh, Lord, it's Runner. He has surely been following us."

Adam paled. He looked wild-eyed from side to side, then behind him. There was no way he could get away from Runner's wrath. Behind him was a sheer drop. On both sides were more high rock formations. He was trapped.

He looked over at Stephanie. He could tell that she felt no less trapped than he, and he was glad at the reason. As long as Runner was angry at her for having come to Canyon de Chelley against his wishes, Runner would not discuss what Adam had told him.

He watched Runner rein his horse to a stop. His heart pounded as Runner stamped toward them, his eyes narrowed with anger.

Stephanie's knees were weak as her and Runner's eyes met and held. Never had she seen him this way. She had seen him angry before, but never had he been this venomous. And his anger seemed levelled only at her. He did not even seem to notice that Adam was there.

When Runner stormed on past Stephanie, she jumped with a start. Gasping, now realizing his intentions, she started to go after him to stop what he was planning to do. But his fingers had already separated the camera from the tripod. He had already ripped the plate from it.

Stephanie screamed when Runner threw the camera and plates to the rocky floor of the cliff, then ground his heel into them, over and over again until the camera was nothing more than strewn bits and pieces.

Speechless, Stephanie stared down at her broken camera. She jumped with alarm when Runner bent over and began gathering the pieces up, then rose to his full height over Stephanie and thrust them into her hands.

Runner still said nothing to her. He gave Adam a glowering stare, then turned and walked determinedly to his horse and swung himself into his saddle.

When he rode away, Stephanie seemed wrenched from her trance. She dropped the pieces of the camera and went to her horse and quickly mounted. In a flurry, she rode after Runner.

When she finally caught up with him, she began shouting at him to stop. When she begged him, over and over again, he wheeled his horse to a sudden stop and glared at her as she also drew a tight rein.

"Runner, I understand how you could be angry at me, but never would I expect you to be this upset," Stephanie said, edging her horse closer to his. "I'm sorry. Please forgive me. I was wrong. I shouldn't have ever come. Please forgive me? I love you. With all of my heart I love you."

"You, who betray me more than once, can ask for forgiveness?" Runner said, laughing sarcastically. "Go back to your brother. You are of the same mind. You are of the same soul and heart." He leaned closer to her. "There is one thing I cannot understand. How could I have been fooled so easily by someone like you who uses a man for the glory of a *brother*?"

Stephanie paled, struck dumb by what he was saying. None of it made any sense. None of it had to do with her having just been caught taking photographs of a sacred Navaho site.

"What do you mean by the 'glory of a brother'?" she said, her voice drawn. "What do you mean by saying that I am someone who uses men *for* the glory of my brother? I have never been guilty of such a thing."

"You lie as easily as you deceive," Runner hissed, angrily. "And I allowed myself to love you. I doubt I shall ever trust enough to love again."

Stephanie shook her head slowly. "I have no idea what you are talking about," she said, tears now falling. "The only thing I am guilty of is coming today to take photographs of Canyon de Chelley. The rest of what you are saying makes no sense whatsoever. How could you think that I could do anything to hurt you when I have told you often how much I love you?"

She brushed tears from her eyes. "Do you truly believe that I could pretend while we were making love?"

she said, choking on a sob. "If so, I have enlisted in the wrong profession. I should have gone into acting."

"That is a good idea," Runner said, laughing again.

He nudged his horse to walk away, then turned and glowered at her one last time. "Adam told me the truth about how you were scheming together so that he could win the support of the Navaho for his town," he said, his teeth clenched. "When Adam told me that you were using me only for his gain, that you were only pretending to love me, I did not want to believe him. But now that I see you here, going against my wishes, I am certain all that he said was true."

Stephanie grew paler. She found what he was saying hard to comprehend. Could Adam actually stoop this low to keep Runner away from her?

"My brother told you many lies," Stephanie said, pleading up at him with her eyes. "You must believe me, Runner. I would never use you. Never! I want to be your wife! Please believe me."

"Never!" Runner said. He rode away from Stephanie, forcing himself to block out the sounds of her sobs.

A part of him wanted to turn his horse around and return to her. But the part of him that feared that Adam had told the truth made him ride stubbornly onward. He had wasted enough time on Stephanie and Adam. Although he had successfully stopped her from taking photographs of the sacred canyon, he knew that he still should have spent this time looking for his brother.

His brother was worth far more to him than the lying, scheming white woman ever would be again.

After Stephanie had regained her composure and wiped away her tears, she rode back to Adam. In one swift move she was out of the saddle. She stamped over to Adam and slapped him across the face.

"You are a deceitful liar, a coward, and a true son-of-a-bitch," she shouted. "Runner told me what you said to him about me being a part of a ploy to use him. How could you, Adam? Didn't you know that I would find out? How did you expect me to react? I can hardly believe that you could stoop so low as to use me for your own monetary gains."

"Sis, I . . . " Adam said, rubbing his hand over his throbbing cheek.

"Forget trying to make excuses," Stephanie said, flipping her skirt around as she went to the tripod. Angrily, she lifted it and threw it down into the canyon. She then scooped up the pieces of the camera and tossed them also into the canyon.

"Sis, don't," Adam said, stopping her just as she reached the pack mule. "You'll regret it if you throw away any more of the equipment. You may be angry now, but when you've regained your senses, you know that you'd regret throwing away that which is precious to you."

"I just lost what is *most* precious to me," Stephanie said, breaking into sobs. When Adam tried to pull her into his embrace, she fought him.

Through a torrent of tears she looked up at him. "Adam, I want no more part of you," she cried. "After we get back to Wichita, I never want to see you again."

"Sis, you can't mean that," Adam pleaded. "I'm your brother—"

"Thank God it is in name only," Stephanie said. "I would hate being blood kin with the likes of you, for fear that some of your ugly, scheming ways might rub off on me."

"What about the Santa Fe Railroad shareholders, who are expecting the photographs that you took?"

"The Santa Fe and its shareholders can all go to

hell," she said, mounting her horse again. "You can all take the same train there, as far as I'm concerned."

Ignoring his shouts, she rode away from him. She was determined to find a way to make things right with Runner. She would not allow herself to lose him this easily.

26

Brightest truth, purest trust in the universe—
All were for me
In the kiss of one girl.

—ROBERT BROWNING

As Thunder Hawk rode into his village with Sky Dancer snuggled against him, he was trying to muster up the courage to face his parents with the news that he was no longer just a son. He now had a wife. He and Sky Dancer had stopped mid-point between the two villages and had performed a simple ceremony that sealed their vows.

Now he had the task of revealing this truth to his mother and father. As his heart pounded harder the closer he came to his parents' hogan, he knew that he dreaded facing them far more than he had dreaded Chief Red Moon. He had horses as payment for what he had requested of Chief Red Moon. He had nothing to offer his parents for their approval.

Perhaps I do *have something to offer them*, he quickly thought.

A daughter-in-law.

Yet that could be the prime reason they would be upset with him today. Not because he had skipped school while acquiring a wife, but he had missed *two* days of schooling in a row. *And* he had to explain about the horses that he had used for his bride price. His father had often preached against stealing horses.

A slow smile moved across his lips as he recalled the recent raid on Damon Stout's horses led by none other than his father. Surely his father could no longer condemn him for stealing horses, when he had now resorted to the same tactics himself, even if for different reasons.

Thunder Hawk held his chin high, thinking that his reason for stealing from Damon was honorable enough. In past history of the Navaho, he knew that stolen horses had paid for many brides.

He stiffened and his throat went dry when the approach of his horse brought his parents from their hogan. They stood watching now, surprised and puzzled by Sky Dancer's presence on Thunder Hawk's horse.

"Thunder Hawk, I'm frightened," Sky Dancer said, as she offered her wide, dark eyes up to him. "What if I am not welcomed? What if they send me away? What if they send us *both* away? I wish that you would have told them of your plan to marry me. If they had disliked the idea, I would not know it. I would still be in my own village, sitting comfortably and innocently by the fire, weaving."

"There were reasons why I could not tell them earlier," Thunder Hawk said, tightening his grip on her waist reassuringly. He stared at his father as he talked. "I had hoped that you would be spared my parents' wrath, especially my father's. But I can see the anger building in his eyes as we approach. As for my mother? She will be stunned at first, then she will welcome you with open arms. Soon they will both be moved to love you. Who could not? You are the loveliest and sweetest maiden in the whole world."

This caused Sky Dancer to giggle and relax once

again against him. "In the whole world?" she teased, her eyes dancing into his as he looked down at her. "Something has blinded you, my husband."

"Have you ever truly looked long enough to see your true beauty?" Thunder Hawk said thickly. "It reaches beyond the heavens. This Navaho is blessed to have claimed you as his, before anyone else had decided to."

"You were not the first to bring horses to my father," Sky Dancer said, reaching a soft, tiny hand to his cheek when she saw an instant anger light his eyes. "But I turned them away. Not my father. When I saw you entering my village with your horses, I could hardly believe my eyes. I had prayed often to the Great Unseen Power that you would come for me."

"While you were praying, not only did the Great Unseen Power hear, but also Thunder Hawk," he said, smiling down at her. "You beckoned. I came. Now we are linked together, as though one. No one can take that from us."

Sky Dancer turned her eyes slowly around, flinching when she saw Sage as he waited for their arrival. She had been around Sage many times when her chieftain father had combined forces with Chief Sage.

Until now, she had seen Sage as a man of many smiles and courtesies. Today she was seeing a different man. She almost feared him, except that she knew that he was a most gentle, kind man at heart and would do nothing to hurt her.

As for Thunder Hawk, she was not certain about his relationship with his father. There was much she did not know about him, perhaps too much. At this moment she was wondering if she should have found out more about the man behind the handsome face and gentle smile before she had shared vows with him.

Thunder Hawk wheeled his horse to a stop a few feet

from his mother and father. He paused before dismounting. Sweat beaded his brow as out of the corners of his eyes he saw the people coming from their hogans, staring. Some were coming close on both sides of him, gazing up at Sky Dancer with wonder. He knew that everyone knew her. He knew that everyone adored her.

Taking a deep breath, then slowly exhaling it, Thunder Hawk finally slipped out of his saddle. Ignoring everyone but his wife, he placed his hands at Sky Dancer's tiny waist.

"Husband, I am so nervous," Sky Dancer whispered as Thunder Hawk helped her to the ground.

"You need not be," he whispered back.

He took her hand, and together they turned and faced his parents, then walked toward them.

When they reached Sage and Leonida, Thunder Hawk smiled awkwardly from one to the other.

"Sky Dancer?" Leonida said as she stared at the young woman. Then she turned questioning eyes to Thunder Hawk. "Thunder Hawk, why is Sky Dancer with you?" she murmured.

Sage took a step toward them. He clasped a hand on Thunder Hawk's shoulder. "You have much to explain," he said. "You continue to miss school. You have been gone two days." His eyes slid over to Sky Dancer. "And now you are here with Chief Red Moon's daughter."

He looked past them, his jaw tightening when he saw the bundles on Thunder Hawk's horse, knowing whose they had to be. They were travel bags of women, not men. They had to be Sky Dancer's. That could mean only one thing: this son, who was scarcely old enough to make his own decisions, had taken a wife.

He leveled a steady stare at Thunder Hawk again.

"You paid a bride price for this young woman?" he said, his voice drawn.

Leonida paled. "Bride . . . price?" she gasped, yet saw that it must be so. She knew Chief Red Moon's reputation for watching his daughter like a hawk, not allowing any men close to her. He never would have allowed his daughter to leave the village unless he had agreed to it.

Thunder Hawk placed a possessive arm around Sky Dancer's waist. "Many horses were left at Chief Red Moon's village," he said, lifting his chin proudly. "Fifteen in number. The bride price was enough. Sky Dancer is now my wife."

"I see that she is," Sage said, shifting a quick smile down at Sky Dancer, then frowning over at his son again. "This is something you do after much thought? Or was it done hastily? My son, must I remind you that you are still of school age. How do you plan to behave as a husband in all ways to your wife? Where will you lodge her? What will you feed her?"

"A certain number of sheep are mine," Thunder Hawk said, relieved that in the wonder of him having taken a wife his father had momentarily forgotten to insist on knowing how he had acquired the horses for the bride price. His thoughts were only on the importance of schooling, not horse stealing.

"Father, only one moon ago you gave me several sheep that I could call my own," Thunder Hawk continued. "I will see that these multiply into many. This will be my way of supporting a wife. As for lodging? Sky Dancer and I will, together, build a hogan for ourselves. Until we get this done, we will live in a tent on the edge of the village. Does this meet with your approval, Father?"

He shifted his gaze to his mother. "Do you find fault

with any of this, Mother?" he said, his voice filled with caring.

Leonida sniffled as tears sprang into the corners of her eyes. And it was not from being sad over what her son had chosen to do. It was the fact that she was now a mother-in-law, and to the most precious young woman that one could ever choose to meet.

She was touched deeply inside her heart that Sky Dancer saw the side of Thunder Hawk that Leonida knew so well, which fathers never saw. The gentle, caring, loving that a man could reveal, but not in front of a father who might think it a show of weakness.

"I welcome Sky Dancer into our family," Leonida said, flicking tears from her eyes as she went to Sky Dancer. She gave Sky Dancer a sincere, warm hug, and kissed her softly on the cheek. Then she went and stood beside Sage again.

"I love your son," Sky Dancer quickly blurted. "My heart has been his for many moons. Since we were children and brought together when our families met on special occasions have I known that I wanted your son for my very own. As we grew older and our gazes grew bolder, I knew that, in time, he would be my husband." She locked an arm through his. "And he *is* my husband. We spoke words between us already that make us man and wife."

Leonida looked at Thunder Hawk wistfully. "I would have enjoyed preparing for a wedding celebration," she said, her voice breaking.

"Sky Dancer preferred something more simple," Thunder Hawk said, exchanging smiles with his wife.

"We will discuss schooling tomorrow," Sage said, frowning from Thunder Hawk to Sky Dancer.

Sage saw Sky Dancer's smile fade when he looked at

her, and realized that he had not yet welcomed her, so he stepped forward and took her into his embrace.

"I welcome you to my family," he said, still disbelieving that Thunder Hawk could do anything as foolish as taking a bride while he was so young. But it was done.

There had to be some changes made to make room in their lives for Sky Dancer. But the one thing that Sage would not allow to change was his determination for Thunder Hawk to have a complete, proper schooling. If his son thought otherwise, he had a surprise coming on the morrow. Tomorrow he would be in the classroom again, wife or no wife.

But Sage would not break that news to his son until later on tonight. For now, his son's responsibilities to his wife were beginning. His first duty was to take her to his bed. He owed her a lifetime of loving.

He stepped away from Sky Dancer and faced Thunder Hawk. "My son, your mother and I will go and stay with Pure Blossom the rest of the day and tonight," he said. "Your mother and I will give you the privacy of our hogan this one night. But after tonight, you will have to see to your own lodging."

Thunder Hawk gasped. "You would do this for us?" he said, having never thought that his father would be this understanding, this generous. Perhaps having a wife *would* give him the excuse he needed not to have to go to school ever again.

"I do not approve of you taking a wife while you are so young," Sage said, stepping back to slip an arm around Leonida's waist. He smiled down at Sky Dancer. "But I very much commend your choice of wives."

"Thank you, Father," Thunder Hawk said, beaming. Everything, absolutely everything was working out for him. He could not ask for any more than this.

"I have a pot of mutton stew cooking over the fire," Leonida said, snuggling close to Sage. "There is fresh bread warming on the stove. Please feel free to eat your fill. We shall eat our meals with Pure Blossom today."

"How can I thank you both?" Sky Dancer said, hugging Leonida and Sage again as Thunder Hawk went to his horse and removed Sky Dancer's satchels. He handed the reins of his horse to one of the small braves, to take and tend to it in the corral. Then he took Sky Dancer's hand and they hurried inside the hogan.

Once inside, when they finally had total privacy, Thunder Hawk set Sky Dancer's belongings aside, then drew her into his embrace. He smoothed his hands over her cheeks, then through her long, waist-length black hair.

"Do you know how long I have wanted to be with you like this?" he said huskily. "My wife, I so hunger for you."

She moved into his arms. When their lips met, it was awkward between them at first, and then their kisses became frenzied, as did their hands as they disrobed one another.

After Sky Dancer was totally nude, Thunder Hawk stepped away from her and for the first time, ever, saw a woman fully unclothed. Because of his feelings for Sky Dancer, he had not taken another woman into his blankets with him.

And now he had her all to himself, and no midnight dreams could have been this exciting and beautiful. Her body was tiny, yet her breasts were large and firm.

His pulse racing, he reached his hands to her breasts. As he cupped them, a sensual thrill raced up and down his spine, and a fire never known to him before lit in his loins. He could feel his manhood filling with heat. It was throbbing.

Drawing her into his embrace, he lowered her onto a soft pallet of sheepskins beside the fireplace. His hands moved over her, searching and caressing her body. When he kissed her, she moaned against his lips and urged him over her.

Instinctively, she spread her legs and sucked in a wild breath when she felt the strength and the fullness of his manhood as he began probing where she throbbed at the center of her desire.

Thunder Hawk continued kissing her as he made the one last thrust that broke that wall of defense that all women had until taken that first time by a man. He kissed her pain away, his hands on her breasts, softly kneading. He moved himself endlessly deeper within her, then began his rhythmic strokes.

As she clung to him and moved her hips with his, Thunder Hawk was amazed at the skills she had at not only receiving him as a lover but also in giving herself back to him.

He was fast discovering that he had made an even wiser choice than he had ever imagined when he had decided to marry this beautiful, amorous young lady. She was taking Thunder Hawk to heights of passion that he never knew were possible.

He lowered his mouth to one of her breasts and took his first taste of her sweetness. She twined her fingers through his hair and moaned.

"Thunder Hawk, I never knew paradise until now," she whispered.

He lifted his gaze and met hers. "I will be good to you," he said thickly.

The remembrance of the dreaded school room came to his mind's eye in a flash. He brushed it aside just as quickly. That school room was now a thing of the past.

"My wife," he whispered against her parted lips, "I owe you more than you will ever know."

He thrust into her one last, lingering time, then kissed her as together they found ultimate pleasure in one another's arms.

Pure Blossom was stretched out on her bed, pale and gaunt. She clutched at her stomach, and then her throat. She could not count the endless trips that she had made outside to retch at the back of her hogan. She had heard it called "morning sickness."

She had just started experiencing this today. She had even been too ill to go outside and greet her brother and the woman he had taken as his bride.

Although shocked that Thunder Hawk had taken a bride without sharing his decision with his family beforehand, Pure Blossom could not feel slighted because of it. She was as guilty as Thunder Hawk when it came to behaving on one's own. She would not be pregnant now if she had shared everything with her parents and brothers.

"Oh, how I hate Adam," Pure Blossom said, pummeling her fists against the blankets cushioning her bed. "How could he be so cruel? So cold-hearted? I will show him. This child that comes from my imperfect body will be perfect in every way. I shall flaunt the child before him one day. It will give me such pleasure to laugh in his face and deny him even the first touch of his child."

She turned with a start when Leonida and Sage came into her hogan. She tried to get up, so that they would not realize that she was so ill, but it was too late. They had already seen her.

She did not even bother getting up. She did not dare to, anyhow. Every time she had tried to move to her

feet and walk around today, she had retched. The qui-
eter she lay, the less excited or upset she got, the less
she would be ill.

Leonida went quickly to Pure Blossom's bedside.
Sage stopped long enough to roll more logs onto the
fire in the fireplace, then came and stood beside Leonida as they both stared down at their daughter, concern in their eyes.

"Darling, what's the matter?" Leonida said, sitting
down on the bed beside Pure Blossom. "You are so
pale. You're ill. Tell me where you hurt, darling. I'll
try and make it better."

Pure Blossom looked guardedly at her mother, then
her father. Not wanting them to know the full truth,
she cowered away from them and turned her eyes
toward the wall.

But there was nothing she could do to stop the bitterness that was rising into her throat once again. And this
time it came too quickly for her to flee outside. She
leaned over the side of the bed opposite the side where
her parents were standing and retched all over her
neatly swept dirt floor.

Leonida paled and grabbed for Pure Blossom's shoulders, holding her until Pure Blossom was through.
"Sage, get a basin of water and a cloth," she said over
her shoulder.

Sage hurriedly did as she asked, then stood over them
as Leonida bathed Pure Blossom's face with the damp,
cool cloth. "As pale as you are, I would suspect that
you have thrown up quite often this morning," she said,
her voice drawn. "Was it something you ate, darling?"
She cast a glance over at the stove. "I'll see to it that
all of the food you have recently cooked is thrown out."

Pure Blossom knew that it would be as simple as that
to let her parents think that her illness had been

brought on by food. But she did not like the idea of putting off the inevitable. As tiny as she was, she would soon be showing her pregnancy. Then no excuses on this earth could hide the truth.

"Mother, Father?" Pure Blossom said, easing the cloth away from her face. She scooted up into a sitting position. She combed her fingers through her long, loose hair. "It is not fair to you to keep the truth from you any longer."

She could hear the intake of their breaths and could see the weariness in their eyes, yet she knew that nothing they were thinking could be anything close to the truth, especially since it included Adam.

"No blood that comes with the moon visited me this time. I carry a child in my belly," she blurted out, wincing when she saw a horrified look creep into both of her parents' eyes.

"You . . . are . . . pregnant?" Leonida said, her heart feeling as though it had plummeted to her feet.

Sage was so stunned, he could not find any words to express his disbelief.

"Yes, I am with child," Pure Blossom said, suddenly wailing as she flung herself into her mother's arms. "And the seed was not put into my womb by a man who loved me. At the time, I thought he did. But now I know that he was only using me. I am ashamed. So ashamed."

"This man," Sage said, his hands tightening into fists at his sides. "What is his name?"

Pure Blossom became silent. She looked sheepishly up at her father. "You will not hate me if I tell you the truth?" she said, her voice breaking.

"I could never hate you," Sage said, sitting down beside Leonida. He took Pure Blossom into his comforting arms. "This man used you. You are innocent.

You perhaps loved too easily because it was the first time for you. His name, daughter. Give me his name."

"Adam," Pure Blossom said in a weak whisper, yet loud enough for both her parents to hear.

Leonida turned pale and gasped.

Sage's heart felt as though it had just been cut out.

He rose quickly to his feet and left the hogan. He ignored Leonida when she ran after him, asking him to stop. She knew him well enough to realize where he was headed. He was hellbent on finding Adam, to beat him to a pulp. He was repulsed by the very thought of his daughter having slept with that man, much less that she now carried his child inside her body. Adam had taken advantage of his daughter's innocence.

He mounted his horse and rode away. He pushed his horse into a hard gallop all the way to the train. When he finally arrived there, he dismounted and stormed up the steps to the private cars. Not sure which one was Adam's, he opened one door and stepped inside.

"Where are you?" he shouted as he entered. When he realized that no one was there, he left that car and went into the other one.

Disgruntled to find that car also empty, he was tempted to tear up everything there and burn all of the belongings, but held his temper at bay and left. He felt it was best to deal with this later. His anger had become uncontrolled. He wanted to save it until later, when he had Adam's throat trapped between his fingers.

Needing to find some peace within his heart over the pain that his daughter was suffering, he decided it was best to go and find a high place so that he could pray for guidance.

He had to wonder where he had gone wrong as a father, or what he could do to turn the tide back in his favor.

He had never felt as helpless as he did now.

His one blessing, as she had always been, was his wife, Leonida. She had always been there for him. She always would be. She was his past, present, and future. In her he would find the solace that he needed. He would return to her, instead of going to pray alone in the mountains.

Mounting his horse, he rode away. But this time, he traveled in a slow lope, his head hanging low.

27

When she is absent,
I no more
Delight in all that pleased before.
—GEORGE LYTTELTON

Exhausted, having stopped only long enough to take drinks from the rivers and eat small portions of the food that she had prepared for her and Adam's outing to Canyon de Chelley, Stephanie rode into the outskirts of Runner's village.

After Runner had ridden away in a hard gallop, she had not seen him again. But that had not stopped her pursuit of him. Determined for him to hear her out, she had had only one destination in mind after leaving Adam back at Canyon de Chelley. Runner's village. He should be there ahead of her and she would force him to listen, even if it was at gunpoint.

Her trembling fingers went to the derringer that was holstered at her waist. Yes, if Runner left her no other recourse than to draw the gun on him to force him to listen to her, so be it. She loved him. She could not lose him, especially since the loss would have been as a result of her brother's cruel schemes.

Stephanie's head drooped. After having only slept for a few moments when she had stopped to eat, she was finding it hard to stay awake, even though she could feel a silence falling on all sides of her as she worked her way through the village and past people who had left their hogans to stare at her.

She knew that she had to be a fretful sight to look at. She hadn't had a bath in two days and her hair hung around her face in loose tangles. As she ran her tongue across her lips she could taste dust and the salt of sweat. She could even smell the perspiration that had dried on her blouse.

It was almost laughable that she could dare come to see Runner in such a shape, when what she wanted most was to impress upon him the fact that she knew that he loved her. She doubted that any man would give her a second glance today, much less confess his love for her.

But if Runner truly loved her, as he had told her more than once, he should be able to look past her appearance, and Adam's lies, and grab her up into his arms and kiss her hurt away.

"Just a little farther," she whispered to herself, as she glanced up and saw Runner's hogan not all that far away.

Her gaze shifted and she felt a knot forming inside her stomach when Sage stepped from Pure Blossom's hogan, Leonida at his side.

Through the haze of her weary eyes, Stephanie was close enough to tell that Leonida had been crying. Her cheeks were rosy and her eyes were bloodshot.

A frightened tremor raced through Stephanie when she saw the rage in Sage's eyes, and had to wonder at that. Did he hate her so much that the mere sight of her angered him?

Then her heart skipped a nervous beat. She turned her gaze back to Runner's hogan. Surely he *had* arrived before her; he had told them everything.

She was now filled with fear, for who was to say what

she had ridden into? Were they so angry at her they
might even scalp her? Yet, why *would* Sage be angry?
He hadn't wanted Runner to marry her anyway.

No, it was something else.

After finally reaching Sage and Leonida, Stephanie
drew a tight rein and slid clumsily from her saddle. She
felt her knees buckling, and so reached for the saddle
horn and pulled herself up, to her full height.

She leaned dizzily against the horse, then was seized
by a shadow. Taking a large gulp of air, she fell to the
ground in a dead faint.

"My Lord," Leonida said, rushing from Sage's side.
She fell to her knees beside Stephanie and cradled her
head on her lap. "Stephanie. Wake up, Stephanie.
What's wrong?"

She looked over Stephanie, wincing at the frightful
state that she was in. It looked as though she had been
to hell and back. Leonida could tell that something had
driven Stephanie hard, and the reason why would remain a mystery to her.

Sage came toward Stephanie. He stared down at her
for a moment, then sighed and grabbed her up into his
arms and carried her into Runner's hogan, the only
available place to take her.

Leonida followed Sage into Runner's hogan. *It has
been a day of days* she fretted to herself. First Thunder
Hawk springs a wife on his parents. Then Pure Blossom
springs her own surprise on her parents. *And now this?*
she despaired to herself. Although Stephanie was less
than family, the fact that she had come to the Navaho
in such dishevelment meant that this had been her
destination.

Leonida knew what had drawn her there: Runner.

She poured water into a basin and grabbed up a cloth
and went to the bedside, where Sage was unfastening

the two top buttons of Stephanie's shirt, to make it easier for her to breathe.

Leonida sat down on the bed beside Stephanie. "I wonder where she's been?" she said, gently washing Stephanie's face. "It looks as though she may have traveled many miles. If I didn't know better, I would think that she's been without sleep and has scarcely eaten." She glanced up at Sage. "What do you think, Sage? Don't you find this all very peculiar? Stephanie doesn't seem the sort to behave irrationally."

"I am sure it has something to do with Runner," Sage said, going to squat on his haunches beside the fireplace. He began placing wood on the grate, stacking it so that it would light easily once he set a match to it. "I only hope our son is all right. She could have been coming to us with news—"

"About Runner?" Leonida gasped out, finishing his sentence. She dropped the cloth into the water and went to Sage. She knelt down beside him and placed a hand on his cheek. "Darling, could she have been coming here to tell us that our son has met with a mishap? She didn't get the chance to say anything before she fainted." Leonida buried her face in her hands. "Oh, Lord, don't let it be so," she murmured. "If anything should happen to Runner. . . ."

"Mother? Father?" Runner said as he came into the hogan, as unkempt and as drawn as Stephanie had been before her collapse.

Leonida jumped to her feet and ran to Runner, embracing him tightly. "Thank the Lord," she cried. "I thought something had happened to you."

Runner was looking past her, over her shoulder. He stiffened when his gaze fell upon Stephanie. Although he was angry at her, and hurt by her deceits, an alarm seemed to sound inside him as he saw her lying there so still and pale. Her clothes and her hair looked as though they had gone through a fierce battle.

Yet he had to hold himself at bay. Adam's words were running through his mind, over and over again. This woman was a liar. She was deceitful. She was a schemer. He could not allow himself to care about her at all.

Yet there she was. She had beaten him there, only because he had stopped long enough to commune with the Great Unseen Power before returning home. Otherwise, he had driven himself to get back to the sanctity of his hogan and the peace he found within its walls.

"What is she doing here?" he finally asked, easing from his mother's arms.

"I'm not sure," Stephanie said, giving Sage a troubled look. He had not yet turned his face to Runner. He stared unblinkingly into the fire as it was taking hold, casting a golden, warm light on his handsome copper face.

"What has happened to her?" Runner asked, going to stand over Stephanie. His heart bled as he gazed down at her. Helpless and pitiful, she looked so innocent. No matter what he knew about her, it was hard not to bend to his knees and draw her next to him, to hold, to coddle.

But again Adam's harsh words burned even more strongly in his mind and he only held himself stiffly over her.

Leonida came to Runner and slipped an arm through his. "She had just arrived, then fainted after she dismounted her horse," she murmured. She looked up at Runner. "Darling, you look as though you may have traveled the same road as she. I haven't seen you unshaven since you were a child. Are you aware of the stubble on your face? And your hair—it is windblown. And your clothes are filthy. Where have you been?

Surely you weren't gone this long looking for Thunder Hawk."

"I have traveled as far as Canyon de Chelley and back again," Runner said in a dull, monotone voice. "That is also the path of Stephanie's journey."

Sage gave Runner a stiff look over his shoulder, then rose slowly to his feet. "She went with her camera to the sacred place of our ancestors?" he said, glowering down at Stephanie.

"Yes," Runner said, nodding. "That is where I found her and Adam."

"You ordered them away, my son?" Sage said, eyeing Runner speculatively.

"Yes," Runner said. "I also broke Stephanie's camera and the film plates."

Sage smiled, well pleased. "You did well, my son," he said, patting Runner's back.

"Then this is why she came to our village?" Stephanie said, bending to her knees beside Stephanie again, smoothing the cool, damp cloth across her brow. "Because she was angry with you? This was what was driving her so hard? I don't understand. Surely she told you what she thought about what you did while you both were at the canyon. Why did she have to come here? To tell you again?"

"There were other things that were said besides talk of photography and cameras," Runner said, walking away. He slipped his shirt over his head and tossed it onto the floor. He grabbed up a towel and started toward the door. "I am going to the river. I plan to bathe and to shave. If she awakens, tell her to leave. I wish not to have council with her, ever again."

Sage smiled and nodded.

Leonida frowned and watched Runner walk away.

Then Leonida looked over at Sage. "There is much

here that has not yet been sorted out between this woman and our son," she said.

The voices awakened Stephanie. She stirred and blinked her eyes, then rose up on an elbow and looked blankly around her. "Where am I?" she murmured, then jolted with alarm when Sage stepped into view.

Her gaze caught Leonida stooping over her, a cloth in her one hand, her eyes showing mixed emotions in their depths.

"How did I get here?" Stephanie said, looking guardedly from Leonida to Sage.

"You fainted," Leonida said, dropping the cloth back in the basin. She moved to her feet and carried the basin outside. She stopped and took a nervous breath. She was torn with how to treat Stephanie, yet still wished for things to work out between Runner and Stephanie. She went back inside and knelt again at the bedside.

"I'm going to bring you some food, and then you will have the strength to leave," she said. "And I believe you should, Stephanie. Runner is very angry at you. I doubt he would speak to you if you stayed."

"Then he is here?" Stephanie said, easing her legs over the side of the bed. Weakness seized her. She fell back down on the bed, panting.

"I'll be back soon with some stew," Leonida said, then left.

Sage came and stood over Stephanie. "I want you to eat and then leave," he flatly ordered. "You and your brother have brought my people only heartache. Especially my son, Runner. He allowed himself to fall in love with you. Now he must learn how to fall out of love, for you are not deserving of such a son as this."

"Except for going to Canyon de Chelley, I didn't do anything wrong," Stephanie pleaded. "I am innocent of everything else that Adam told Runner about me. Adam is a liar. I despise him, Sage. Please believe me when I say that my intentions toward Runner and your people are pure. Please give me a chance to prove it?"

"My son does not get this angry at someone without good reason," Sage said flatly. "So it is with him that you have your true argument."

Stephanie felt completely drained as he walked away. When Leonida brought her a large bowl of mutton stew, she ate it ravenously and drank goat's milk as fast as Leonida could refill the cup.

Her strength having returned, her purpose revitalized, Stephanie left the bed.

Leonida stepped away from Stephanie, wanting so badly to tell her that she admired her for being so independent, but she kept her feelings to herself. The rift was between her son and this woman and no one else should interfere, especially not a mother.

"I want to thank you for your kindness," Stephanie said softly. "And it has not been misplaced. I have been wronged by my brother. He lied to Runner. But I can't go into it now. It's complicated."

Stephanie paused, then added, "But I do want you to know that I honestly love your son," she said, her voice breaking. "I would never do anything to hurt him. I would especially not pretend that I have feelings for Runner to help Adam in his schemes. It's not true. Now I have to convince Runner that it isn't."

"You will find Runner down by the river," Leonida said. "He should be finished with his bath by now."

She found herself sympathizing with Stephanie. Her instincts told her that the young woman had been duped by Adam.

Shameful, shameful Adam, Leonida thought sadly to

herself. *He had been such a sweet boy to have grown up into such a deceitful, shameful man.*

Forgetting her filthy clothes and unpleasant odor, Stephanie gave Leonida a lingering hug, then fled from the hogan. As she stepped outside, she ran bodily into Runner.

When she gazed up at him and saw the utter contempt in his eyes, she felt as though she was being shredded into a million pieces by the sharpness of his gaze.

But that did not dissuade her from what she had to do. He had to understand. He had to believe her.

"Runner, please listen to reason," she said, jumping with a start when he brushed past her and went inside his hogan.

She turned and gaped, then flinched when he appeared at the door again and glared at her. "I do not want to listen to you, nor do I want to see you again," he stated flatly. "Nothing you say will change my mind. Do not waste any more of my time."

"Runner, please ... " Stephanie said, extending begging hands toward him. "Adam lied. Why can't you see that? He lied purposely to wrench us apart. And it worked. He wanted you to hate me. It's obvious that you do."

Tears fell from her eyes. "I shall always love you," she said. He stood glaring at her as though she were nothing more than the lowliest of animals.

"Get on your horse and ride from my village," Runner said between clenched teeth. "Never come again. And if Adam shows his face here again—"

"Stop! Stop!" Stephanie suddenly screamed. "I'll leave. Just please quit being so angry. While you are this angry, you aren't able to think clearly. You are wrong to hate me. After you sort through your feelings, and measure Adam's words within your heart, you will know that you have been wrong to turn me away."

She wiped tears from her eyes with the back of a hand. "I'll be waiting, darling," she murmured. "No matter how long it takes, I'll be waiting for you."

She turned quickly on her heel, went to her horse, and eased herself into the saddle. Without looking back, she rode from the village.

A bitterness rose into her mouth when she thought of Adam and what he had caused. She was not one who hated so easily, but at that moment, she hated her brother with a loathing that burned deep into the core of her being. Somehow, he had to pay for what he had done.

And she would find a way.

28

Swift the weeks are on the wing;
Years are brief, and love a thing
Blooming, fading, like a flower.
—EDWARD ROWLAND SILL

Stephanie awakened with a start as her railroad car
rocked on the tracks, shaking her awake. Rising to one
elbow, she quickly realized that the trembling car had
not been the cause of her awakening. It had been a loud
blast that had preceded it. Even now she was hearing a
low rumbling series of explosions.

"What on earth?" she whispered, rushing from her
bed. When she got to the window, she could see a great
reflection of fire in the sky not all that far away. "An
explosion. Something has exploded."

Mentally tracing the direction of the fire, and what
lay in its wake, and quickly realizing that the railroad
made a turn into Gallup at that exact spot, she stifled
a gasp behind her hand.

The private spur. Someone had dynamited the private
spur.

Or worse yet, it could be just beyond the private spur,
where trains carrying passengers traveled. At present,
the end of the regular line was Gallup.

A pounding on her door drew Stephanie's eyes away
from the fire. Knowing that Adam had probably also
been awakened by the blast, and was there to make sure

that she knew what had happened, she stiffened. No matter the cause for him to come to her private car this time of day, when dawn was just breaking over the horizon, he had some nerve. Because of him she may have lost the only man that she could ever love. And she had told him that she never wanted to see him again.

Sighing heavily, knowing that he would knock until he dropped if she didn't go to the door, she swung it open. "Adam, I heard the explosion and saw the fire and I am leaving soon to see what caused it, and to see if anyone was hurt," she said in a deliberate rush of words to be rid of him. "And I do plan to take my camera and equipment—that is, what is left of it, no thanks to you. My extra camera will have to do. Now leave me be, Adam. I don't need you to escort me to the fire."

With that, and before she gave him a chance to say anything to her, she slammed the door in his face. She knew that she had covered all that he would be asking about, so didn't expect he would be troubling her again this morning. She had seen a sheepishness in his eyes and knew that he understood her feelings. She would never allow his boyish innocence to work with her again. She had learned long ago that it was all pretense and used only to cater to his own whims, not hers.

Although she was still numb from the long ride from Canyon de Chelley, and from Runner's continued rejection of her, Stephanie quickly dressed in a fresh skirt and blouse and yanked on her boots. She took only a few strokes through her hair with her brush, then slapped the holstered derringer around her waist. Where there was an explosion, danger could be lurking. These sorts of explosions set off at railroads were usually deliberate.

A thought came to her that made a shudder course

through her veins. "The Navaho hate the railroad," she said, stopping in mid-step as she walked toward her darkroom. She paled. "Lord, don't let it be Sage or any of his people. Haven't they had enough to contend with without the law breathing down their necks?"

Shaking off the dread, she hurried and packed up her supplies, grabbed up her one last tripod, and stepped outside into a beautiful dawn. Only one thing scarred the loveliness of the morning: the stench that came with the black smoke from the train proved to Stephanie the extent of the fire.

"It might be a whole train," she whispered as she secured her supplies on the back of her pack mule. Having been too tired to remove the saddle from her horse the previous evening, it was readily available for her. She ignored Adam as he arrived in a mad run from his private car, slipping his shirt on as he rushed toward her.

"Wait up, sis," Adam shouted as Stephanie wheeled her horse around and started riding away. "Damn it, Stephanie, now is not the time to stay angry at me. We need to investigate this together!"

He stumbled into his own saddle and was soon riding at Stephanie's side. "Sis, I'm sorry for what I did," he said. "But I did it for you. You deserve someone better than Runner. Back home, in Wichita, you can have your choice of men. Men of *means*, Stephanie. Not a man who'll be playing Indian for the rest of his life."

Up to this point, Stephanie had stubbornly ignored him. But his last statement burned into her very soul.

She turned angry eyes toward Adam. But still she didn't say anything to him. He deserved nothing from her. His apologies meant nothing to her now. The only way they might would be if he would go and tell Runner that he had lied.

But she knew Adam well enough to realize that he would never humble himself in such a manner. He had only apologized to *her* because of what he wanted from her. He would never give up on her, it seemed.

She sank her heels into the flanks of her horse and rode on away from Adam, her thoughts centered now only on the devastation that lay ahead of her. She was close enough to be able to see that a whole train had been involved in the explosion. The train was still ablaze, pressed together like logs on a fire.

One thing that made her sigh with relief was that the train had been placed at the end of the line, just outside of Gallup, until its usual run the next day. This time of morning, not even an engineer would have been in the train. At least whoever had placed what surely had been dynamite beneath it had made sure to spare human lives.

Again her thoughts flashed to Sage, and the rage he felt toward railroads. She shook her head, to clear it of such thoughts. She did not want to think that Sage was responsible.

Another thought dug deeply into her heart: *Runner*.

He could be a good candidate for this if a judge had anything to say about it after an investigation. If it became common knowledge about Runner's hatred of Adam, and why, he could be accused of having a good reason for blowing up the train.

"Oh, no," she whispered, as she thought of something else. "There were many witnesses at the 'Big Tent' who saw Runner mixed up in a brawl. That could be held against him."

Not wanting to think about Runner in this manner, not wanting to give herself cause to think it might have been his own vengeful act this morning, she centered her thoughts on taking photographs of the wreckage to take back to Wichita. She would guard them with her life, so that no judge or sheriff could get hold of them. She would take her photographs and hurry back to the train. She would develop, then hide them.

Adam drew a tight rein alongside her. They dismounted at the same time. And although Stephanie didn't want him anywhere near her, she said nothing when he set the tripod up for her, then stood back as she attached her camera to it and began taking photographs.

She tried to ignore the throngs of people who were rushing from Gallup on foot, and on horseback, to see the wrecked train. She could feel them gathering around her and Adam, and behind them.

Through the black billows of smoke, she could see them on the other side of the train.

She would take only a couple more pictures, then she would flee with them to the privacy of her car.

"It took many sticks of dynamite to do this much damage," Adam said, his voice loud enough to carry far through the milling crowd. He looked around himself and smiled smugly, glad for the audience.

He clasped his hands behind him as he again studied the wreckage from this distance. "I wonder how the damn Indians got their hands on dynamite?" he asked in a half shout.

He looked guardedly over at Stephanie as she cast him an angry stare, glad when she returned to taking pictures.

"Of course they were stolen from the storage shed where the work gangs leave their equipment every night," he said much more loudly when he realized that several people had edged closer, not only to watch Stephanie, but to listen to what he was saying, as he skillfully planted the blame on someone other than himself and his cohorts.

He kneaded his chin. "I wonder which Indian did it?" he said, seeing the sheriff elbowing his way through the crowd toward him. "Was it Runner? Sage? Naw. I'm sure it was Sage's rebellious son, Thunder Hawk. This could make him look like some sort of damn hero to his people. It could place another feather in his hat."

Stephanie had heard enough. She turned to Adam. "Will you shut up?" she said, her eyes flaring angrily. "How can you hate the Navaho so much? Until we came to Arizona, you spoke kindly of them. Runner was your dearest friend. Now you condemn him? You condemn his brother?"

When she caught sight of the sheriff coming closer, her insides froze. Then she placed a hand on Adam's arm. "Help me load up my supplies," she whispered harshly. "Adam, hurry. Help me. I don't want the sheriff confiscating my plates."

Disgruntled, Adam assisted her. Just as she rode away, she felt a sick feeling rushing through her, for she was still close enough to hear Adam condemn Thunder Hawk. She was relieved when the sheriff just as quickly said he needed more proof, for she knew that Adam had none.

Inhaling a deep breath, she rode in a hard gallop away from the wreckage. She had gotten enough photographs of the wreckage, and knew that the Santa Fe would be grateful to have them, since they would soon begin their own investigation.

Yet she felt nothing but empty inside. The feeling of triumph, of importance, was no longer there. She felt as though everything important to her had been stripped from her life.

Without Runner, nothing else mattered.

*   *   *

Thunder Hawk sat back and watched Sky Dancer serving the morning meal to his mother and father, smiling proudly up at her as she handed him a platter of fried mush. Before he had even been awake she had been up, grinding meal and placing coffee on the stove for breakfast. She had said that it was not only to surprise him, to show herself worthy of being called wife, but also to surprise his parents by having them share the first breakfast of her and Thunder Hawk's marriage with them, by a way of thanking them for the generous gift of their hogan for the wedding night.

Runner and Pure Blossom had also been invited. Pure Blossom was not feeling well, so had declined the generous offer. Runner also declined.

"You truly didn't have to do this," Leonida said, smiling over at Sky Dancer as the young woman sat down beside Thunder Hawk on a plush, white sheepskin that had been spread before the fireplace. "Sky Dancer, to have prepared so much food you surely had to be up before dawn."

"It was most enjoyable preparing a surprise for my new in-laws," Sky Dancer said, beaming.

"It was sweet," Leonida said. "Thank you, darling."

"Sky Dancer, the food is *very* good," Thunder Hawk said, taking a large bite of sage cheese that had been melted, cut, and toasted to resemble fallen leaves. "Your mother taught you well the skills of cooking."

"*Uke-he*, thank you, husband," Sky Dancer said, bashfully lowering her eyes. Not yet feeling comfortable in her new surroundings, especially in Sage's company, she only toyed with the food on her plate. She hoped that once she and Thunder Hawk got settled in their own hogan, and enough days had passed for Sage to think over his son's choice of women for a wife, he would learn to accept her. She had done nothing to earn his solemn silence.

Feeling Sky Dancer's uneasiness, Thunder Hawk cast his father a troubled half glance. He frowned when he saw that Sage was still as solemn now as he had been yesterday after hearing about Thunder Hawk's marriage to Sky Dancer. His father's acceptance was far more important than his mother's.

"Sage?" Leonida said, reaching a hand to her husband's arm. "Darling? Don't you think the food was well prepared? Isn't Thunder Hawk lucky to have married someone with such skills in cooking? You know how he loves to eat."

Sage took another bite of bread, then set his plate aside on the sheepskin beside him. He looked over at Thunder Hawk. He had waited long enough to remind him what must be done this morning, and every morning, until his education was finished.

"Thunder Hawk, you must leave for school soon this morning," Sage finally said. "Three days have passed since you were there. You will have to work twice as hard now to catch up on what you did not learn those days you were gone to win yourself a wife."

Leonida flinched and almost dropped her spoon when Thunder Hawk rose quickly to his feet, his plate tumbling from his lap and landing in a splat on the sheepskin. "School?" he said, gazing disbelievingly down at his father. "I did not plan to go to school today, or ever again. My duty now is to my wife. Not to books!"

Sage rose slowly to his feet, then stood over Thunder Hawk and placed his hands to his son's shoulders. "My son, your wife has nothing to do with this," he said. "It was your father's decision long ago that you would continue your schooling to the end. I do not waver in my decision *now*."

"I am married now," Thunder Hawk said, trying not to overstep that boundary of obedience. "I am a *man*." He gave a visible shudder. "Only children attend school."

"Yes, you are a man," Sage said softly. "But you will be a better man once you have finished your education." He eased his hands from Thunder Hawk's shoulders and gestured toward the door. "If you leave now, you will have time to reach the school before the last bell rings."

Thunder Hawk's eyes widened. He knew that any further argument would get him nowhere, and he did not want to look anymore foolish in front of his wife than he already did. It was incredible to him that his ploy had not worked, that having a wife meant nothing at all to his father.

He shifted his gaze down at Sky Dancer, knowing from the bottom of his heart that he did not regret having married her. Although the marriage was planned to be one of convenience, it was more than that to him now. Sky Dancer was the world to him.

Sky Dancer smiled softly up at Thunder Hawk, then moved to her feet and took his hands. "My husband, there is something I would like to ask you," she murmured.

"What is it?" Thunder Hawk said, searching her eyes, seeing so much love for him in their depths.

"You will be leaving for school soon?" Sky Dancer said, her eyes wide as she gazed into Thunder Hawk's.

"Seems I will," Thunder Hawk said, his voice showing how disgruntled he was.

"Take me with you," Sky Dancer said in a rush of words. "My father would never allow me to go. He kept me from those sorts of opportunities. He kept me too often to myself. He did not trust allowing me to leave the village, ever, without escorts. I have dreamed often of being in school, learning from books. Please Thunder Hawk? Take me with you? We can learn together."

There was a sudden hushed silence in the hogan.

Then Thunder Hawk laughed absently, then happily. He could not believe the turns of events. Suddenly—oh, so suddenly—he saw a true reason for going to school: his wife. Through her eyes, he saw the importance of schooling. And it would be a wonderful thing learning together!

Thunder Hawk smiled at Sky Dancer. "You will go to school today with your husband," he said. He smiled over at his father, and then at his mother as she came to Sage's side and locked an arm through his, her smile warm, serene, and beautiful.

"I will go and see that two horses are readied for travel," Sage said, his eyes dancing.

After he left, Leonida gave Thunder Hawk a hug.

Then Leonida took Sky Dancer into her embrace. "You have worked a miracle here this morning with my son," she whispered to Sky Dancer. "And you have just as quickly won the heart of my husband."

Sky Dancer returned the embrace, finding it wonderful to finally feel accepted. And she was finally going to get to attend school! Marrying Thunder Hawk may have been the best thing that she had ever done in her life.

Sky Dancer and Thunder Hawk rode away from the village, laughing and chatting merrily about the upcoming day's events. Thunder Hawk was already explaining the normal day's routine in the schoolhouse. He was anxious to share something with his wife that she had wanted for so long. He did not think once more on how much he had hated schooling. Everything was different now that she would be sharing it with him.

They rode on and on, sending their horses into occasional hard gallops, then easing them back into slower trots so that they could talk again.

Then a strained silence fell between them as they saw many horsemen quickly approaching, the sun reflecting off the barrels of their rifles. They did not have time to even wonder much about these white men who came and drew tight rein in a circle around Thunder Hawk and Sky Dancer.

"Who are you?" Thunder Hawk asked guardedly, knowing not to reach for his sheathed rifle. "What do you want? Let us pass. My wife and I are on our way to school. We do not wish to be late."

"You ain't attendin' school today, Injun," one of the men said. "You're under arrest."

Sky Dancer blanched.

Thunder Hawk's mouth went dry.

"Arrested?" Thunder Hawk asked. "What for? What are you accusing me of?" He looked from man to man, now figuring they were a posse. He recognized one man, and then another from Fort Defiance. He had seen them ride with posses for the fort before.

But they had always been after renegades, or white criminals. Thunder Hawk did not see how he fit into either of those categories, and then his gut twisted when he suddenly remembered the fifteen stolen horses that he had used for his bride price.

He also recalled having heard that Damon Stout had lodged a complaint at the fort because of the missing horses. And not only the fifteen that he had stolen, also the others that were stolen when his father led them in the night raid.

One of the men reached over and handcuffed Thunder Hawk's wrists. "What are you guilty of, Injun? Let me see now," he said, his pock-marked face leaning into Thunder Hawk's. "There's horse thieving, and then sabotaging the train. It took some guts for you to steal that much dynamite to blow up the train last night."

"Train?" Thunder Hawk said, raising an eyebrow. "Dynamite? I know nothing about it. Nothing."

"And so you're now guilty of lyin', too," the man said, shrugging.

Sky Dancer edged her horse closer to Thunder Hawk's. "They cannot take you away," she said, sobbing. "Please tell me they are not taking you away."

When Thunder Hawk turned his eyes to her, he found that it was hard to find the words that were required to make her accept that this was happening. He did not understand it, himself, much less know a way to make her see the logic of it. Except that he was Navaho. It was easy for the white man always to cast blame on the Navaho.

"Pretty lady, just you be on your way back to your home," one of the posse said as he slapped her horse's rump. "Or else you'll find yourself in the same trouble as your husband."

The man scratched his chin. "When did you take a wife, Thunder Hawk?" he asked. "I thought you were just a mere schoolboy."

It was taking all of the strength that Thunder Hawk could muster up not to lash back at these men, but he knew that he would only make things worse, and his wrists were secured with handcuffs.

Then a thought flashed through his mind. Proof! He had absolute proof that he was not anywhere near the train last night.

"You said a train was blown up last night?" he asked guardedly, just to be sure.

"Yep, and you did one hell of a job," one of the men said. "It's still smolderin'."

"Then you cannot arrest me for the crime," Thunder Hawk said, lifting his chin proudly. "I was with Sky Dancer all night."

When the man had slapped the rump of Sky Dancer's horse, she had only ridden a few feet and then had drawn rein again, looking wistfully back at her husband.

One of the men leaned his face into Thunder Hawk's. "Do you think we'd take the word of a Navaho squaw?" he said in a low hiss. "Or any Navaho, for that matter? Your whole damn tribe could come and speak up for you and we'd tell 'em to get back to their hogans, where they belonged."

Sky Dancer broke into body-wracking sobs. Thunder Hawk stared at her, feeling utterly helpless and very much humiliated.

"Well, what are we waiting for?" the leader of the posse said. He wheeled his horse around and headed in the direction of Fort Defiance. "We'll take him to the fort. He'll be in the holding cell there a few days, and then he'll be transferred to the larger jail in Gallup. Soon we'll have us a hanging."

One of the men grabbed Thunder Hawk's reins and yanked them, forcing Thunder Hawk's horse to follow the commands of someone other than his master.

Thunder Hawk looked over his shoulder at Sky Dancer. "I am sorry," he cried. "Go home, Sky Dancer. Tell my parents what has happened. Stay with them until this is cleared up."

Sky Dancer wiped tears from her eyes, then turned her horse back in the direction from whence she had come. What had just happened seemed so unreal. Surely she would wake up and discover that she had been experiencing a nightmare. How could one gain the world in one evening, only to lose it all the next day?

She looked over her shoulder at Thunder Hawk as he was led further and further away into the sun, then lifted her chin and reached deeply inside herself to find the courage to ride onward. She must get help for her husband: Sage, or perhaps even Thunder Hawk's brother, Runner. They were the answer. They would rescue her husband.

With this, hope blossomed within her and she sent her horse into a canter. She felt strangely alone. Never had she been this totally alone. Her father had never allowed it. She felt vulnerable not only without an escort but also with no weapons for protection.

She gazed heavenward and whispered a prayer to the Great Unseen Power and asked that she would not be the next Navaho victim of evil white men.

When she felt something like a hand softly brushing her cheek, she felt as though her prayer had been answered. She said another quiet prayer to the Great Unseen Power.

"Please bring my husband back to me soon," she said with a sob in her throat.

29

The heart that has truly loved,
Never forgets.
—THOMAS MOORE

Still seeing the burning railroad cars in her mind's eye,
still stunned by the devastation, and fearing who might
be blamed, Stephanie was glad to finally be back at her
private car.

She wheeled her horse to a stop, puzzled. When she
had left the wreckage, Adam had still been there, loudly
voicing his opinion as to who might be responsible. Yet
there his horse was, tethered to the hitching rail.

Stephanie's gaze slid over to the other horse standing
next to Adam's, wondering who it belonged to.

And how *did* Adam get there before her?

Loud laughter wafting from Adam's car, through a
window that was partially up, drew Stephanie's attention. She gazed up at the window and saw the silhouette
of two men inside the car, seemingly oblivious of her
arrival. She slowly slipped from her saddle and crept
beneath Adam's window, her insides coiling even more
tightly when she recognized Damon's voice as he began
talking to Adam about the train wreck.

The more she listened, the more she felt ill, clear to
the core of herself. She leaned closer, her hands tightening into fists at her sides as she heard them laughing
about how they had duped the Navaho—about the
sabotage.

"Adam, everything went off without a snag," she heard Damon say. "It was easy setting the dynamite beneath the train and blowing it up without being seen.

"It's going to be fun watching the Navaho try to squirm out of this one," he continued. "It seems like I've waited a lifetime to see them get what's coming to them. They're all a worthless lot. Sheepherders are the lowest form of man on earth. Their damn sheep eat up all the grass, leaving nothing for cattle."

"Count it," Adam said. "See if I've counted it right. A thousand. Isn't that what we agreed to? Will that be enough for the risk you took blowing up the train?"

"Wasn't no risk at all," Damon said, guffawing. "It was sheer pleasure. Perhaps even better than beddin' a woman. No need in countin' the money, Adam. I trust you."

"Count it anyway," Adam said, his voice bland. "I don't want you coming back later saying I shortchanged you."

"Friends don't shortchange friends," Damon said. "Now I guess I'd best be goin'. It wouldn't do for anyone to see us together right now. They might focus attention on us, instead of the Navaho."

"I tried my damndest to get the sheriff to go and arrest Thunder Hawk," Adam said. "But he didn't seem to listen to reason. Who's to say who he will narrow in on at the Navaho reservation? As far as I'm concerned, he can take the whole damn bunch of them. Hah! Some friends they turned out to be. Sage, especially. He seemed to dislike me the minute he laid eyes on me the day Stephanie and I arrived on the train."

"Where *is* Stephanie?" Damon asked guardedly. "We've got to make sure she never finds out who dynamited the train. I would wager that she'd side with the Navaho against you."

"Stephanie?" Adam said, rubbing his chin in thought. He then grew pale. "Damn it, Damon. She left the scene of the accident before *me*. I took the short cut you showed me. But she should've been here by now."

"I'd best go, then," Damon said, lifting a wide-brimmed Stetson hat onto his head.

Adam walked him to the door and gazed cautiously outside, then went on to the horses with him. "Guess she's been sidetracked. I wonder what's keeping her?" Adam said, nervously raking his fingers through his hair as he peered into the distance.

"Don't worry about her," Damon said, swinging himself into his saddle. "As long as she don't know nothin' about our plans, what can she do?"

"Yeah, what can she do?" Adam echoed. He waved good-bye to Damon, then sauntered back into his private car. He was unaware of the pack mule that Stephanie had taken to the other side of the cars and left there with her photography equipment until she returned, after she warned the Navaho about the schemes of her brother and Damon.

Feeling victorious over the Navaho, Adam went to his liquor cabinet and poured himself a shot of whiskey. He held the glass in the air. "To Sage, Runner, and the whole damn tribe of Navaho," he said, in a mock toast.

He chuckled and gulped the whiskey down, then poured himself another, and another.

Stephanie rode hard across the land, still stunned by what she had heard. She had cast her loyalties to Adam aside the minute she had heard what he had told Runner about her having used him for selfish purposes. It hadn't taken her long to decide what she must do today.

She wouldn't allow the Navaho to take the blame for what her brother and Damon Stout had done.

And she must make haste to do everything possible to right the wrongs done to the Navaho. She knew very well that the white man's law with the Indians could be hasty and harsh.

Finally, she reached the Navaho village and drew a tight rein in front of Runner's hogan. Her entrance into the village being anything but quiet, Sage came hurriedly from his hogan just as he saw Stephanie rush inside Runner's. He could tell that something was wrong, so he followed her inside and listened as she told Runner what had happened, and what she had heard her brother and Damon laughing about.

Sage stepped forward and placed a hand on Stephanie's shoulder, causing her to turn around with a start. "You say that Adam paid Damon to blow up the train, then cast blame on my people?" Sage said, anger swelling within him.

"Yes, and while I was there, at the wreckage, I heard my step-brother even try to cast the full blame on Thunder Hawk," she said, her eyes looking into Sage's. "I'm sorry, Sage. I wish I could have known what he was planning. I would have done everything possible to stop him."

Runner took up his rifle and brushed past them.

Sage grabbed him by the wrist. "Where do you go in such haste, my son?" he said, his jaw tight.

"To kill Adam," Runner hissed.

"That is not the way to deal with men like him," Sage said, dropping his hand to his side.

Stephanie rushed up to Runner. "No, please don't do anything hasty," she pleaded. "The authorities will take care of Adam and Damon once they are told the truth. Let us all ride to Fort Defiance together. I will tell the authorities at once what I saw and heard. They will arrest Adam and Damon. The courts will then decide what is to become of them."

Runner's eyes widened and his heart pounded within his chest. Was this truly real? Was Stephanie saying that she would go against her step-brother, on behalf of the Navaho? Did this not prove that he had been wrong to have believed anything Adam had said about Stephanie being a part of a plan to dupe Runner? If she had such fierce devotion to Adam, why then would she be there now, in Runner's hogan, ready to defend the Navaho?

"You would do this for my people?" Runner asked.

"Yes, for the Navaho, but especially for you, Runner," Stephanie said, her voice breaking. "Darling, don't you see? I would do *anything* for you. Even condemn my step-brother in the eyes of the law. Doesn't that prove enough to you that you have been wrong to believe Adam over me?"

Runner drew her into his embrace. "I was wrong. Can you forgive my ignorance? I apologize for ever having doubted your sincerity and love for me."

"Yes, I forgive you," Stephanie said, tears warm on her cheeks. "How could I not when I love you so much?"

She cuddled close as he tilted her lips to his. A blissful joy spread through Stephanie to know that she had her man, and his love, back again.

She smiled to herself when she thought of Adam, and how he would be shocked to see that his schemes had backfired in more ways than one. He had brought Stephanie and Runner together again, and their bond would be even stronger. And soon he would have lost everything, while she and the Navaho would have gained everything, especially the respect of those who realized they were victims again of greedy white men, who would do anything to rid the land of the Navaho.

"We must leave for Fort Defiance now," Sage said, interrupting Runner and Stephanie's kiss.

As Stephanie eased from Runner's arms and gazed up at Sage, he could not help but smile down at her, for he did see that she was someone who genuinely cared for the People. As his Leonida had done, he could see that Stephanie could fit into the life of the Navaho. Stephanie's love for Runner was genuine enough to give her the courage and strength to adapt to a new life, a new people. He saw that, in part, she had already adapted.

They went outside together, and as they waited for Runner and Sage to get their horses, Stephanie explained everything to Leonida—about the wreckage, who were going to be blamed, and about Adam's deceit.

"Long ago, when I knew Adam's mother, I saw how she taught him strict morals," Leonida said. She looked into the distance, as though reliving those days of long ago, when she had been among those that had been taken as Sage's captives. "I grew to know Sally and Adam much better when we were brought together as captives in Sage's stronghold. Adam and Runner were best friends. Adam knew right from wrong. It seems as though he has forgotten his mother's teachings."

"Sally will be very disappointed in Adam once she discovers the truth about him," Stephanie said. She turned with a start when she heard the approach of a horse.

She shielded her eyes with a hand. "Who is that, Leonida?" she murmured. "It's a young woman. She's riding alone. And she's arriving quickly, as though she has cause to be upset."

Leonida also shielded her eyes from the bright rays

of the sun. She gasped and blanched. "Lord," she said, her voice drawn. "It's Sky Dancer." She swallowed hard as fear gripped at her heart. "But where is Thunder Hawk?"

A warning shot through Stephanie. She recalled Adam trying to cast the full blame on Thunder Hawk. The last she had heard, the sheriff had scoffed at believing that Thunder Hawk would do such a thing. But what if the sheriff had thought further about it and, wanting someone, *anyone*, to blame, had decided to come after Thunder Hawk?

The thought sickened her.

Sky Dancer's horse slid into a trembling halt. Sage and Runner hurried over from the corral and helped her from the saddle.

"My brother, Sky Dancer," Runner asked, "why is he not with you? Why are you not in school with him? And why do you carry such worry in your eyes?"

Sky Dancer began crying. She nervously clasped and unclasped her hands behind her. "The white lawmen came and arrested Thunder Hawk while we were on our way to school," she said, looking frantically at Runner and then to Sage. "They said that he blew up a train." Her voice grew in pitch. "What train? We knew of no train! We were in your hogan all night."

She turned to Sage and clutched his arm. "Go to the fort and tell them that Thunder Hawk is not guilty of the crime!" she cried. "I fear for him. You know that the white men will treat him cruelly. Please go for him. They would not listen to me when I told them that he was with me all night."

Stephanie looked guardedly from Sage to Runner. She could see that they were both livid with anger. She feared this sort of anger. If they rode into Fort Defiance, demanding the release of Thunder Hawk, they might even be arrested themselves. And not only for causing a disturbance by trying to set Thunder Hawk free, but for being accessories to the crime themselves.

"We will go for Thunder Hawk now," Sage said, swinging himself into his saddle. "Come, Runner. Let us round up many of our braves. The white pony soldiers will see our power in the number of our arrival. They will set my son free, or else."

Stephanie stepped between Sage and Runner's horses. "No, you mustn't do this," she cried, "I know that you want to get Thunder Hawk out of jail. But please, don't do it in this way. Your anger is too great now to talk with the authorities. And you know that you don't want an out and out war with the soldiers. Let me go and speak for you. I will make all wrongs right."

"I am not a child who turns his eyes away from responsibilities," Sage grumbled. "My son is my responsibility. I will go for him. *Now.*"

Stephanie went as far as to grab Sage's reins away from him. She lifted her chin boldly and received his glare without so much as budging. "Listen to me, Sage," she said. "After thinking through all of this more carefully, I feel it is best that *I* go to the fort *alone*. If you are with me when I go and denounce my brother, they will not believe me. They will think that I have been coerced by you to do this. I must not look at all like I am aligned with the Navaho in order for them to believe me. I want them to see me as a sister who cannot hide the ugly secrets of her brother from the authorities."

Sage gave Stephanie another lingering stare, then he looked over at Runner and nodded.

Together they dismounted and went and put their heads together to discuss the problem at hand.

Stephanie scarcely breathed as she awaited their decision. Ever so gently, she dropped Sage's reins. She had spoke her mind. If he didn't agree, there was nothing else she could do but to wait and see if a war broke out between the Navaho and the soldiers at Fort Defiance.

Thinking about Adam, and his responsibility for all of this, made an ache circle Stephanie's heart, and made her ashamed of ever having been a part of Adam's dreams.

They had turned into nightmares. Ugly, black nightmares.

Leonida patted Stephanie on the arm. "What you just offered to do for our people is admirable," she murmured. "Especially for my son. I doubt Thunder Hawk could last long behind bars. It was hard enough for him to sit confined at a desk in a schoolroom. To be incarcerated for even one night would be devastating for my son."

Sky Dancer went to Leonida and threw herself into her arms, sobbing. "Someone has got to do something soon," she cried, clinging. "Poor Thunder Hawk. My poor husband."

Leonida could see the puzzlement in Stephanie's eyes when she heard Sky Dancer refer to Thunder Hawk as her husband.

"Stephanie, Thunder Hawk has taken a wife," she said softly. "This is my darling daughter-in-law, Sky Dancer."

Stephanie's lips parted, but before she could respond, Sage and Runner came back to them, their eyes grim.

Runner turned to Stephanie. "Go. Speak the truth to the white pony soldiers," he said. "Father and I will follow soon after to make sure that what you have said has been believed, and to give Thunder Hawk a safe escort back to our village."

Stephanie smiled up at him. "Thank you for giving

me this chance," she said. She gave him a hug, looked from one to the other, then mounted her horse and rode away.

When Sage and Runner mounted their horses and rode off in another direction, Leonida's eyebrows rose. She was not certain of the plans that had been made between father and son, but she did suspect that they would not be going to the fort any time soon. There was surely something else that needed tending first.

But what? she wondered to herself.

30

O, who but can recall the eve they met
To breathe, in some green walk,
Their first young vow?
                              —CHARLES SWAIN

Filled with a breathless daring, Stephanie rode up to
Fort Defiance and entered its gate. She ignored the
stares of the soldiers as she drew a tight rein before the
main headquarters, in the back of which building were
the holding cells for those prisoners awaiting transfer
to the main jail in Gallup.

Gathering courage from the love she felt for Runner,
and now also for his people, Stephanie stopped only
long enough to look up at the great adobe building
with its immense thick walls and deep, barred windows.
Knowing the importance of achieving her goal, a shiver
ran through her. It also made an empty feeling at the
pit of her stomach to realize that Adam was responsible
for all of this, and that she was being forced to turn
her back on him.

She thought back to the last several years, when she
had shared so much with her step-brother. Their feelings for one another had been so genuine. Only when
he had become driven to have that which seemed impossible, wanting to immortalize himself by establishing
a town and having it named after him, had she seen
their mutual understanding of one another begin to

crumble. Yes, she wanted a dream, herself, but she had never thought it would be at the expense of others.

Now she understood that even *her* dream was wrong. At this moment, she knew that she would not be able to send back any photographs to Wichita. She wanted no part in bringing more tourists to this land that should belong solely to the Navaho.

With those thoughts, Stephanie went on inside the building.

No one made any attempts to stop her, for she was a mere woman, no threat to anyone. Even the derringer strapped to her waist caused no apprehension on the soldiers' parts. They all smiled at her flirtatiously.

Those who wore hats tipped them politely to her. Others made way for her with a mocking curtsey as she moved up to the oak desk where a burly man sat in fringed buckskins, instead of a uniform.

Colonel Utley brushed papers aside as he gazed up at Stephanie. His narrow lips flickered into a flirting smile. "Now ain't you a brave miss to be wanderin' about alone," he said. He rested his elbows on his desk and placed his fingertips together before him. "Ain't you afraid of Injuns?"

He looked her up and down. His eyes stopped on her derringer. "Now ain't that a bad lookin' weapon," he said, chuckling as he looked slowly into her eyes again. "But don't you know? I doubt that could even kill a snake."

"I haven't come here to talk about snakes, or my derringer, and I am most certainly not afraid of Indians," Stephanie finally had the courage to say. "I'm here for only one reason."

"And that is?" Colonel Utley said, leaning toward her over the desk top.

"To tell you that you've jailed the wrong man,"

Stephanie said. Her pulse raced at the thought of being only moments away from condemning her very own step-brother of the crime that Thunder Hawk had been incarcerated for.

She hoped that Sally wouldn't hate her. But even if she did, Stephanie had no other choice but to tell the truth as she knew it.

"What's that you say?" Colonel Utley said, pushing himself up from the leather desk chair. He circled the desk and stood face to face with Stephanie, his height being no more than hers. "I've more than one man in the holding jail. Which one have you come to speak for?"

Stephanie swallowed hard. "Thunder Hawk," she blurted out, flinching when she saw the instant guarded warning in Colonel Utley's eyes. "He didn't blow up the train. I absolutely know for certain that he's innocent."

"And horses?" Colonel Utley growled out. "Can you say for certain that he didn't steal horses from Damon Stout?"

She paled at the mention of the horses that he was also accused of stealing. She would never forget finding Runner and the other Navaho that night with all of the horses. Perhaps they were all guilty of horse stealing? Oh, Lord, then what could she do about any of this? She had to keep the focus on the train. Only on the train.

"Can you say that you are certain, sir, of his guilt?" Stephanie said, lifting her chin. "Thunder Hawk is innocent and you know it."

"Why in hell would you say such a dumb ass thing as that?" Colonel Utley said, flailing a chubby hand in the air. "He's as guilty as sin and *you* know it."

"You are wrong," Stephanie said, boldly. "I am right."

"Proof," Colonel Utley mumbled, going to sit down at the desk again. He propped his feet up on the desk, crossing his legs at the ankles. "I need proof. Especially from an obvious Injun lover."

"Proof?" Stephanie said. She leaned her hands on the desk so that her eyes were once again level with Colonel Utley's. "Would it be proof enough if I said that my very own step-brother hired someone to blow up the train so that the blame would be cast on the Indians? If you would investigate things more carefully, I am just as certain that my brother is behind double-crossing Thunder Hawk to make him look guilty of horse stealing."

She sighed and removed her hands from the desk. Her eyes wavered. "I would never put blame on my step-brother unless I was absolutely certain," she said, her voice breaking.

"I ain't never come across anything like *this* before," Colonel Utley said, searching Stephanie's face with squinted eyes. "Tell me. What's your brother's name?"

"Adam," Stephanie said, finding it hard to believe any of this was happening. "Adam Jones. A short while ago, he and I arrived on a train on the private spur. And the man he paid to blow up a train today? I am certain you know him. Damon Stout is his name."

The colonel's eyes narrowed. He scooted to the edge of his chair, his knuckles white as he clutched tightly to the arms. "Damon?" he said. "Damon Stout? I sure as hell *do* know him. He's here often enough with one complaint or another."

"And these complaints are generally lodged against the Navaho?" Stephanie said, an angry fire lighting her eyes at the mere thought of the vile, shiftless man.

"Aren't his complaints usually about Sage, Runner, and Thunder Hawk?"

"Sure as hell are," Colonel Utley said, stuffing his left cheek with a big wad of chewing tobacco. "He'd worn his welcome out here because of it. But now I see that I should've paid more attention to what he said. He seemed to know more about the Navaho's activities than me."

"How can you say that after what I've just told you?" Stephanie asked, her patience running thin. She leaned down toward Colonel Utley's scruffy face. "You don't have proof of anything. I do. I heard my brother and Damon laughing about what they did. What proof do you have? Tell me. Do you have *absolute* proof of Thunder Hawk's guilt?"

"Not exactly," Colonel Utley said, shifting his weight nervously in his chair. "But I'll uncover enough to hang the scalawag Injun."

"You can't hold a man behind bars without proof," Stephanie said, her jaw tight. "I demand that you set Thunder Hawk free."

"And who made you an expert on the law?" Colonel Utley argued back.

"I know my step-brother and Damon are responsible for blowing up the train," she returned sharply. "Why on earth would I say this about my brother if it wasn't true? I'd do anything on this earth to prove that he couldn't be that vile and scheming. But I can't. I heard him and Damon laughing about it. I know that Adam paid him one thousand dollars to do it. Isn't that enough? I am bringing all of the ugliness of my brother out into the open. Don't you know that what I am saying is the truth, or I wouldn't want to put a scar on my family's reputation?"

"What you say makes a lot of sense," Colonel Utley

said, spitting a stream of tobacco juice into a spittoon beside the desk. "And I do recall someone tellin' me that a man at the site of the wreck was makin' a lot of fuss about it bein' the Indians. It was almost too obvious that he was trying too hard to throw the blame on the Navaho."

"I was there," Stephanie said smoothly. "I heard. That was my step-brother Adam. Now do you believe me? Will you release Thunder Hawk into my care?"

The colonel rose slowly from his chair and went around the desk to gaze eye to eye with Stephanie again. "What's this Injun to you, anyhow?" he said, smirking. "Is he your fella? Have you bedded up with this redskin?"

Stephanie blanched. She knew that this man was searching for the full truth behind her anxiousness to have Thunder Hawk set free. If he discovered that she was going to marry Thunder Hawk's brother, then everything that she had argued for today would be for naught. He would think that she was doing this for all of the wrong reasons and never believe anything that she said about Adam, even if it was the truth.

"Well?" Colonel Utley demanded.

Stephanie's throat was dry as she returned his steady stare. "I most certainly would never bed up with that man," she said softly. "He is already married." She leaned closer to him. "And you know that. Sky Dancer, his wife, was with him when you arrested him."

The colonel shrugged, went back to his chair, and plopped down into it. "I've wasted enough of my time with you," he said, glaring up at her. "Get on outta here." He raised an eyebrow. "Your name. I need to know your name. I'm going to alert my men to make sure you ain't allowed on these premises again."

"My name is Stephanie Helton," she said in a low

hiss. "And, sir, the only way I am leaving today is to be thrown bodily from the fort." She smiled sweetly down at him. "And I don't think you want to do that, do you? Brutality towards a woman who has come to speak in defense of an innocent man could get you fired from your post. Don't you think?"

"He ain't proved innocent," Colonel Utley mumbled.

"Before this day is over, he will be free from this jail," Stephanie said, stubbornly folding her arms across her chest. "I refuse to budge until you listen to reason."

The colonel spat another stream of tobacco juice from the corner of his mouth. He opened a journal and began entering figures, ignoring her, as though she wasn't there.

Stephanie stared down at him with a bitterness never known to her before. She was not sure how long she could stand there with this foul man, but hoped that she could at least outlast him.

Runner glared at Adam's private car as he and Sage dismounted beside it. Runner grabbed his rifle from the gun boot at the side of his horse, while Sage slipped a knife from a sheath at his waist.

Father and son exchanged glances and nods, then moved stealthily up the steps.

When they reached Adam's door, Runner slowly turned the knob. Together, he and his father stepped into the semi-dark car.

But there was enough light through the partially open shades for Runner to see Adam stretched across his bed on his stomach, snores rumbling from deep within him. Runner smelled a strong scent of alcohol, then smiled smugly. Adam had drunk himself into a stupor. The evidence lay in the empty bottle and glass on the floor beside his bed, and how Adam slept so soundly.

"I see it, also," Sage said, smiling over at Runner. "He has much fire water in him."

Runner went to Adam and grabbed him by the back of his shirt and yanked him from the bed. He turned Adam and held tightly to his arms as Adam looked back at him fearfully; seeing Runner and Sage quickly sobered him.

"Runner?" Adam said, his eyes wild. "Sage? What are you doing here?" He tried to squirm free of Runner's grip. "Let me go. Do you hear? I demand it."

"You make demands of Runner?" Runner said, his teeth clenched. "You want to be let go?"

Runner dropped his hands away, laughing to himself when he saw a smug look come into Adam's eyes.

"Well, Adam, would you prefer this over being held?" Runner said, doubling up a fist and smashing it into Adam's face.

He watched Adam fall clumsily to the floor with the impact. Runner placed his fists on his hips as he stood over Adam. "Get up, you double-crossing cheat," he snarled. "Get up on your own, or I will pick you up and knock you down again."

Adam's head was spinning from the blow. He rubbed his jaw, tasting blood as it rolled from his nose and cut lip into his mouth. "Why are you doing this?" he said, pleading up at Runner and Sage with frightened eyes.

"Do not play innocent with us," Sage said, reaching down and yanking Adam to his feet. "You are responsible for my younger son being behind bars. You will correct that mistake. *Now.*"

"I don't know what you're talking about," Adam said, cowering away from Runner and Sage.

Runner took one wide step toward Adam. He hit him again, this time knocking him halfway across the car. Then he went and towered over Adam, placing a foot on his chest. "If you value your life, you will go with us to Fort Defiance and back up your sister's story— that you paid Damon Stout to blow up the train and made it look as though the Navaho people were responsible. You made sure the blame was placed on my brother. You will go now and take that blame away."

Adam's thoughts were scrambled, and not only because Runner had hit him twice in a short time. It was what Runner had said about Stephanie. "What do you mean about Stephanie?" he stammered, trying to push Runner's foot away from him. "About backing up her story?"

"She is at the fort even now telling the truth about what you have done," Sage said, bending to one knee beside Adam. He grabbed Adam by the hair. "Her alliance is with the Navaho now, not a lying, double-crossing brother."

"God, no," Adam whined.

Runner slipped his moccasined foot away from Adam's chest. He smiled as Sage yanked the white man back to his feet. Runner placed his rifle barrel against Adam's chest. "You go, or I will shoot," he said quietly.

"Runner, do you forget so easily the friendship that we had?" Adam pleaded, his eyes glued on the gun.

"That friendship was first forgotten by you," Runner said, nudging him harder with his rifle.

"I'll go," Adam said, sweat pouring from his brow. "Just point that rifle somewhere else."

Slowly Runner moved the rifle away from Adam's chest, but he did not turn it totally away from him. "Go out and get on your horse and ride to Fort Defiance," he said flatly. "And don't try anything, Adam. This rifle will be leveled at your back the whole way."

Adam scurried outside and nervously flung himself into his saddle. He gave Sage and Runner glares. "Once at the fort, when your rifle will be taken from you, I'll laugh in both your faces," he said, chuckling.

"The last laugh would be on you, if you are set free," Runner warned. "Never will you be able to ride again in Navaho land. The first time you were alone, you would die quickly. If not by my gun, then by another Navaho's. Perhaps even your sister might pull the trigger and end your pitiful life."

Adam paled. He turned his eyes from Sage and Runner and rode off, understanding the warning and knowing that all of his dreams had gone up in smoke the very instant the train had exploded by his own orders.

Tears came to his eyes. And when Stephanie's face came to his mind's eye, he felt no scorn for what she was doing against him, only remorse for having caused her to turn her back on him.

Runner and Sage rode behind Adam. When they reached the fort, their rifle alerted the soldiers. One rode up on horseback and grabbed the gun from Runner.

Runner made no move to get it back. It was enough now that Adam was at the fort and knew that he must tell the truth, or die later, alone, never knowing when.

Runner, Sage, and Adam were ushered inside, where Stephanie still stood stubbornly before Colonel Utley's desk. She turned and her eyes met Adam's. She was torn by conflicting feelings. She ached for what they had been to one another, yet there was a part of her that felt no pity for him. She shifted her gaze to Runner and smiled.

Runner returned the smile. He and his father had known that she, alone, would not be able to get Thunder Hawk released. They had known that in this man's world a woman's word would not be enough. That was why they had ridden separate ways when Stephanie had headed for the fort. They knew that they would have to bring Adam in, themselves, to make a confession.

Stephanie stepped aside as they were ushered to the desk, to stand and be scrutinized by Colonel Utley.

"Sage . . . Runner, don't tell me," the colonel said gruffly. "This must be Adam. You've brought this man to exchange him for Thunder Hawk."

"Only because Thunder Hawk is innocent and Adam is guilty," Runner said, glowering over at Adam.

"Adam, what do you have to say for yourself?" Colonel Utley said, tapping his fingers on the desk top.

"You should release Thunder Hawk," Adam said, fearing for his own life should he not tell the truth. His voice trembled. "I'm the one who should be behind bars. Me and Damon Stout. We are in this together."

There was a hushed silence, then the colonel rose from his chair and went around to speak up into Adam's face. "Do you realize what you're saying?" he asked. "Are you doing this because you fear for your life? Are you being coerced?"

"I do fear for my life," Adam said, swallowing hard. "But what I am saying is true. I paid Damon to blow up the train. I was wrong to do it. What else can I say?"

Everything happened quickly then. Adam was marched away, and soon Thunder Hawk was free, his face all smiles as he was first embraced by his father, then Runner, and then Stephanie.

"You are free, my son," Sage said, and turned to Stephanie. He gently gripped her shoulders. "Because of you my son is free. How can I ever repay you?"

"By accepting me among your family and people as the woman who will soon be your older son's wife," Stephanie said, tears pooling in her eyes. "I'm sorry for all of the grief my brother caused you. Even that which

I caused. I want you to know that I will never again bring a camera among your people. I even plan to destroy all of the photographs that I took of Navaho land. I hope that these things are enough to prove my loyalty to your son, and the People."

"Proof?" Sage chuckled. "White woman, today was proof enough."

He drew her into his embrace. "I speak for my family and my people when I say how eagerly I welcome you as part of my son's life," he said. "Runner is a lucky man."

Stephanie returned his embrace, turned to Runner, then grew cold as she watched him step up to the cell in which Adam was incarcerated. She listened and shook inwardly with a guarded fear when she heard what Runner was telling Adam.

"Adam, not only is your sister Stephanie well rid of you, but also my sister, Pure Blossom," Runner said, speaking to Adam through the bars.

Adam laughed sardonically. "I played the game well with them both, wouldn't you say?" he said, feeling safe behind the bars.

"As for Pure Blossom, I suckered her from the very beginning into believing that I loved her," he bragged. "I hoped that it might bring some sort of understanding between me and the Navaho, so that I could feel comfortable building my town on Navaho land. I never loved your sister. Only what I could get from her."

Beneath Adam's rough exterior and harsh words, his heart was bleeding for those times when he had found such bliss within the arms of his sweet Pure Blossom. He still loved her. He would never love again.

Anger flaring his nostrils, Runner grabbed Adam by the throat through the bars and yanked him closer. "If you are ever released from jail, for any reason, you had better keep a good watch on your back, because I, personally, will soon seek you out to kill you."

The sweat of fear beaded Adam's brow.

31

I will love you like the stars, love,
Set in the heavenly blue,
That only shine the brighter,
After weeping tears of dew.
　　　　　—R. W. RAYMOND

The entrance into the Navaho village was one of celebration. Stephanie rode at Runner's side as Sage and
Thunder Hawk rode ahead of them, proud, free, and
jubilantly accepting the chants of welcome.

Stephanie saw that obviously the word had spread
while she had been gone about Thunder Hawk's incar-
ceration. But she wondered just how many of the People knew exactly *why*, and who was responsible? Thus
far, no one had singled her out with a frown. She wasn't
sure if this was because they didn't know about Adam's
guilt, or if they knew that she, Adam's step-sister, had
gone against him, on behalf of Thunder Hawk.

Stephanie was taken up with the joy that shone on
everyone's face; it was quite contagious. Inside her heart
she felt such peace, such wonderful, precious peace,
even though she had only a short while ago bade a
farewell to a part of her past that had at one time been
as special to her as her acceptance into Navaho life was
to her now.

She smiled as Sky Dancer came running toward
Thunder Hawk. Something tugged at her heart as she

watched Thunder Hawk take Sky Dancer into his arms
and twirl in a circle with her as she laughed gleefully.

Stephanie wiped tears of joy from her eyes and gave
Leonida a warm smile as the older woman stepped away
from the throngs of people and met Sage as he approached on his horse. After Sage swung himself down
from the saddle, he grabbed Leonida into his arms and
gave her a fierce hug.

"I have heard it said that if one waits patiently
enough, things will fall into place where they belong,"
Runner said, drawing a tight rein as Stephanie drew her
horse to a halt.

He dismounted and went to Stephanie and held his
arms up to her. "Because of you, things are being restored to proper balance one by one," he said. "Soon
you will join with my people for a 'Chant Way Ceremony,' and then the balance of my people's lives will
be fully restored."

Stephanie slipped easily from the horse and into Runner's arms. His hands at her waist, he drew her close
to him, their eyes locked. "Darling, I have never heard
of a 'Chant Way Ceremony,' she murmured.

"The essence of Navaho culture is the maintenance
of *Hozho*, a term that corresponds roughly to the English word *harmony*," Runner explained, his eyes dancing into hers. "Any wrong behavior of the Navaho can
upset the delicate balance between the good and evil
powers in the Navaho universe and bring misfortune to
the transgressor."

He slipped an arm around her waist and drew her to
his side as they began gently pushing their way through
the crowd. "To restore disrupted order in our village,
we turn to our ceremony called 'Chant Ways,' " he said.
"Each 'way' is so complex that a 'singer' rarely masters
more than two of them in a lifetime. A single 'way' can

last up to nine days and will involve many prayers and songs that recount Navaho history."

"That sounds so interesting," Stephanie said, then stretched her neck to see over the crowd when she caught sight of Pure Blossom standing alone in the doorway of her hogan.

Stephanie's insides tightened. She had to wonder how much Pure Blossom knew about what had happened, and whether or not she knew about Adam's participation in the crime that had been committed.

She recoiled when she recalled what Adam had said about Pure Blossom at the jail, how tauntingly and mockingly he had told Runner that he had never loved the sweet Navaho maiden.

"Runner, shouldn't someone in the family tell Pure Blossom the details of what happened today, before someone else does who would not treat her as delicately about it?" Stephanie asked. "And how will she react? I am concerned for her feelings, yet she must be told." She gave Runner a sideways glance. "Don't you think so, darling?"

Adam's words were flowing through Runner's mind like a rushing river, over and over again, flooding his thoughts. His heart pounded at the sight of his sister standing so forlorn and alone at the door of her hogan. She had certainly heard enough to cause her to have such sadness in her eyes. This made Runner's hate for Adam even worse. Yet, for now, he had to cast hate aside. Loving his sister, and protecting her, was of prime importance.

"We will go together and explain to Pure Blossom," Runner said, changing Stephanie's direction as he guided her with his arm around her waist.

When they reached her, Pure Blossom ducked her head and disappeared into her hogan. Stephanie and

Runner exchanged troubled glances, then followed after her.

Stephanie looked around her, at the grand sight of the many beautiful blankets lining the walls of the hogan, decorated with exquisite designs drawn from nature and Navaho history. Pure Blossom sat at her loom, as she skillfully worked her yarn into another beautiful, multicolored design.

"Pure Blossom," Runner said, stepping away from Stephanie. He knelt down onto one knee beside the fireplace, close to his sister. "I understand why you aren't joining the others to celebrate. You feel as though you have lost, instead of having won anything."

He placed a hand to Pure Blossom's arm, stopping her weaving, so that she would look over at him. "Pure Blossom, Adam is not worth grieving over," he said gently. "He is a worthless, scheming, lying cheat. You will find another man more worthy of your love. In time, sweet sister, you will see. Another man will steal your heart away. But do not wait until then to show me your perfect smile. Give me one now, Pure Blossom, so that I can, in turn, have cause to smile."

"You say that my smile is perfect," Pure Blossom finally said, her voice breaking. She held up her free hand so that Runner could see how her fingers were beginning to twist and gnarl. "Do you see anything perfect about my hand?" She turned her back to Runner and held her hair up so that he could see the hump on her back. "Do you see a perfect back?"

She turned tearful eyes back to Runner. "No one will want me again," she sobbed. "Even Adam did not want me. He only pretended."

Runner's gaze became steely with anger. "Why do you say that?" he said, his voice low. He could not understand how his sister would know Adam's true feelings. Only a few had heard Adam's confession at the trading post. He knew that his father, Thunder Hawk, and Stephanie could not yet have told her.

That had to mean only one thing, and if that were true, Runner was not sure if he could restrain himself from going to kill Adam right away and save the white man's courts the trouble.

Pure Blossom's eyes filled with tears. She lowered her eyes and began crying so hard her body was wracked by the tears. "Adam told me how ugly I was," she cried. "How could he be so cruel?"

Stephanie bit her lower lip, stung speechless by the extent of her step-brother's cruelty toward Pure Blossom. And she was beginning to feel guilty for so much of this. Even though she was not a direct cause of the hurt that Pure Blossom was feeling, the fact that she had accompanied Adam to the Arizona Territory seemed cause enough. If she had discouraged Adam from coming, surely he wouldn't have, and all of these heartaches would have been spared.

"He told you . . . ?" Runner said, his throat suddenly dry. "He not only destroyed you by his deceit, he tried to destroy all of the Navaho by paying for a train to be blown up so that he could point an accusing finger at us."

"How could I have loved such a man?" Pure Blossom sobbed.

"Pure Blossom, you must forget Adam," Runner said softly. "He is not worth the tears shed over him."

"These tears are not for myself," Pure Blossom said, clutching at herself. "It is for the child that I carry within my womb. It is Adam's child."

Runner and Stephanie exchanged quick glances, then Runner gently took Pure Blossom's hand from her stomach. He caressed it. "A child," he said softly. "It is *your* child, Pure Blossom. It will be loved. The child need never know the true worth of its father. It shall be blessed with knowing you, its mother. Why would a child want anything more when it has you?"

"I need time alone," Pure Blossom said, rushing to her feet. "Do not follow me, big brother. This is a time for mother and child to be alone with the Great Unseen Power."

It took all of Runner's willpower not to go after Pure Blossom. When he heard her leave on a horse he closed his eyes and said a soft, silent prayer for her well-being, then opened his eyes and found Stephanie standing directly before him.

"Runner, do you think you should go after her?"

"*E-do-tano*, no. She is going to seek solace with the Great Spirit and she must do this alone."

He slipped an arm around her waist and led her from Pure Blossom's hogan, through the crowd, and then into his own dwelling. A fire cast its soft flickering light around the room. Food was simmering in a large pot over the flames.

Runner took Stephanie's hands and drew her against him. He gazed into her eyes. "I did not think we would ever be alone again," he said, bending to softly kiss her lips. "But here we are. Can you think of something we might do to celebrate?"

"Darling, what would *you* suggest?"

"I am hungry."

She cast the food a quick glance.

"Shall I feed you?" she said, looking teasingly up at him.

"Yes," he said huskily, his fingers eager on the buttons of her blouse.

She smiled seductively up at him as he slipped the blouse off. "Darling, am I to feed you with my clothes off?" she said, her lips parting in a slight gasp as he bent over and flicked his tongue over one of her nipples.

"You are feeding a different sort of hunger than that for food," Runner said, his hands now at the waist of her skirt, lowering it past her hips.

"Will you also feed my hunger?" she asked in a soft purring voice as he continued disrobing her, finishing by tossing her boots aside.

"You will soon see," Runner said. He grabbed her up into his arms and carried her to the bed.

As she stretched out on her back on the soft blankets, she watched with a thudding heartbeat as he quickly disrobed himself. She felt a twinge of guilt again for this happiness that she was sharing with the man of her desire, when Pure Blossom had no one.

And the child—what of the child? Couldn't it be a blessing in disguise? The child might be the only one whom Pure Blossom would have to share her life with.

Stephanie shook her thoughts aside and reveled in how it felt to have Runner's body against hers again as he came to her and lay over her, drawing her into the warmth of his body. He nudged her legs apart with one knee so that she could feel the heat of his manhood probing where she throbbed with sexual need of him.

He kissed her, his mouth hot, demanding, and wonderful. She was overwhelmed with a wild desire for him and twined her arms around his neck to draw him even more tightly against her. She pressed her breasts up into his chest, savoring the feel of his muscular body.

When he thrust himself into her, she threw her legs around him and locked them at her ankles. She thrust her pelvis toward him and rode him, movement for movement. Surges of ecstasy were welling within her, spreading, drenching her with warmth.

When he moved his lips down and swept his tongue

around her breasts, she caught her breath, not daring to breathe for fear of disturbing the soft melting energy that was swimming through her.

When their eyes met, they locked in an unspoken understanding, promising ecstasy, the air heavy with the inevitability of pleasure.

"It's been too long," Stephanie murmured, twining her fingers through his thick, dark hair.

She drew his mouth to her lips. Their tongues touched, and then he kissed her again, his hands seeking her breasts. Her breasts were warm beneath his fingers, his thumbs circled her rose-tipped nipples, his mouth seared into hers with intensity, leaving her breathless.

Runner felt the nerves in his body tensing, a tremor beginning from deep within him as one kiss blended into another. He locked his arms around her and held her in a torrid embrace, fiercely anchoring her as his eager mouth tasted her sweetness.

The blaze of urgency set fire to his insides, leaping higher, a wild, exuberant passion spinning through his veins. His hands cupped the rounded flesh of her bottom and held her up to him as he filled her innermost depths with his throbbing hardness.

He groaned against her lips as he felt himself at the edge of that brink that would take him into total bliss.

He paused, laid his cheek against one of her breasts and took a deep breath, then plunged one last time deeply into her. He held her tightly as their bodies shook and quaked, their pleasure spilling over into each other, as though one being, one soul, one heartbeat.

Stephanie clung to him. She licked his neck, then kissed it. "I want to share this with you every day of my life," she whispered.

When he looked down at her, he framed her face

between his hands. "You know what you are saying?" he said thickly. "You know what you are giving up?"

"My darling Runner, I'm gaining everything that I want in life when I marry you," she murmured, smiling softly up at him. "Don't you know? *You*, you alone, are my only passion now."

"And what of your passion for photography?" he asked, searching her eyes for the truth.

"Sometimes one must make choices," Stephanie said, touching his cheek gently. "I have made mine."

"What of your camera and equipment?"

"They will belong to someone else."

"You can give them up so easily?"

"Are they my reason for living?"

"I would hope not."

"You are, Runner. I willingly give up my past life for you."

"You seem too independent to do that."

"Yes, I am an independent person," Stephanie said, as he rolled away from her to lie beside her.

"And in my independent logic I have made a choice," she said matter-of-factly. "It is to marry you and be your wife. That will be my career by choice. Not because you gave me an ultimatum."

"I believe I am smarter than to ever give you ultimatums," he said, chuckling as he ran a hand over her hip.

"I'm never going to give you cause to even want to," Stephanie said, rolling against him. She threw a leg over him and drew him against her. "I'm going to make you an absolutely perfect wife."

"There are only two things missing in my happiness at this moment," Runner said, holding her close.

"Pure Blossom," Stephanie said sullenly. "Pure Blossom's tragic affair with Adam." She paused and swallowed hard. "And Little Jimmy."

"Yes, Pure Blossom," Runner said, gazing hauntedly into the fire. "And . . . Jimmy. . . ."

Pure Blossom rode to the brink of a cliff which plunged into a chasm cut by an ancient stream. Its boulder-strewn bed held only a narrow trickle of water, more than one hundred feet below. She drew a tight rein, dismounted, and draped her horse's reins over a low limb of a cottonwood tree and went and sat down beside a stream.

Leaning over, she stared at her reflection in the water, then angrily and without control, she began pummeling her fists into the water. She had wanted to erase all signs of herself, instead she succeeded mainly in making herself look more distorted than before as the ripples played and moved on her reflection.

"I hate you!" she cried at her reflection. "Why were you ever born?"

A rattling sound that she was familiar with made her grow cold with a sudden fear. When she turned to see where the rattlesnake might be, she screamed; the rattler struck at her and sank its venom into one of her ankles.

"*E-do-tano*, no!" she shouted, as the rattlesnake scurried away from her in the dust. "I truly didn't mean it. I don't want to die!"

She grasped onto her throbbing ankle. A wave of weakness ran through her as she started to collapse onto the ground.

She closed her eyes, then blinked them open momentarily when through her veiled tears and the haziness of her blurred vision she saw a hand reaching toward her.

Caught between strong arms she smiled, for she recognized the one who had come to her rescue. She felt blessed that the color of his skin was the same as hers. Somehow, after having become enamored with Adam, she had managed to forget this handsome Navaho.

"Gray Moon?" she whispered, then floated away into a tunnel of darkness.

32

Love took you by the hand
At eve, and bade you stand
Where I should pass.
— JOHN NICHOLS

Stephanie walked slowly toward her horse, finding it hard to leave Runner's village. She feared that if she entered that other world she had known before him, something might keep her there. Perhaps she might even be tempted to go back on her word and send the photographs back to Wichita.

She had to prove to herself that she was strong enough to withstand such temptations. She knew deep inside her heart that her love for Runner was much stronger than her need to continue dabbling in photography.

Runner stepped up beside her and lifted her into her saddle. "I will go with you and stay with you until you set things right in your life before returning," he said as he gazed up at her with his midnight dark eyes. "As you know, word has spread about Damon Stout fleeing the law and going into hiding. It would be dangerous for you to be alone while he is free to wreak havoc on our lives."

"I know that you feel that way, but I'll be all right," she said, taking her reins into her hands. "You have responsibilities here. There's Pure Blossom; she hasn't returned. Don't you think that you should go and look for her to see if *she* is all right?" She rested her hand on her holstered derringer. "She is far more vulnerable than I."

Runner turned and gazed into the distance, past his village. He rubbed his chin thoughtfully. "She *has* been gone for too long now," he said, his voice drawn. Then he swung himself into his saddle and grabbed up his reins. "I will go and look for her. You will go with me. After we find her and escort her safely back to her hogan, I will then ride with you to your train." He smiled over at her. "My woman, there is no need in arguing. This man who loves you will not let you out of his sight until Damon Stout is found and placed behind bars."

"I love feeling so protected," Stephanie said, returning the smile. "It's wonderful that you also feel as protective of your sister. Let's go, Runner. Let's go and find her."

Her words had scarcely crossed her lips when, at the far side of the village, she saw a horseman arriving, a travois attached to the horse by two long poles dragging behind.

"What on earth . . . ?" Stephanie said.

"Gray Moon?" Runner whispered in surprise. He knew Gray Moon well. He was the son of Runner's father's longtime friend, Spotted Feather, who had moved to a neighboring village when he had married one of their lovely maidens. Gray Moon had, on occasion, hunted with Runner. He had come for various celebrations, and even for more quiet times to share talk and laughter with Runner and his family.

It had been awhile since Runner had seen Gray Moon. He had surmised from Gray Moon's absence that he had taken a wife, giving him responsibilities that kept him closer to home.

But now? This morning? He was arriving in a strange manner, his face solemn as he kept taking glances over his shoulder at the travois.

"Who do you think is on the travois?" Stephanie said, slipping from her saddle as Runner slid from his own.

Runner didn't take the time to respond. He broke into a run and met Gray Moon's approach. He questioned Gray Moon with his eyes, seeing too much in his silent concern that his burden must be someone who meant much to him.

Gray Moon drew a tight rein. His eyes met Runner's briefly as he dismounted and went back to the travois. "I have brought your sister to you," he said, bending to his knees to start untying the rope that held Pure Blossom in place on the travois.

"Pure Blossom?" Runner said, panic filling his heart. He fell to his knees on the other side of the travois. His fingers trembled as he unfolded a corner of the blanket that held his sister within its warm, protective cocoon. He was too afraid to ask if she was dead. He was afraid, even, to see for himself.

When he uncovered her face and saw the thick droop of her lashes feathered out over her cheeks, her eyes closed, her breath coming in rasps, his insides grew numb and he fought back the urge to emit a loud cry of despair.

"She is not dead," Gray Moon said, loosening the last of the rope. "But she is quite ill. I came upon her after she had been bitten by a rattlesnake."

"Rattlesnake?" Runner said, his head spinning, knowing that few lived after an assault from a rattlesnake.

"You can feel somewhat relieved in that the wound

was not a deep one," Gray Moon said, going to kneel down beside Runner as he, too, looked at Pure Blossom's stillness. "I do not think that much venom got into her veins. I found her when the wound was fresh. I sucked the wound dry. It was then that I discovered that it was only a flesh wound. The rattler must have been a baby and unskilled at attacking victims."

Stephanie came to the travois with Sage and Leonida, the people of the village circling around them, their eyes wide and questioning. When Leonida saw that it was Pure Blossom, she stifled a cry behind her hands and fell to her knees beside Runner.

Sage knelt by Pure Blossom's other side and hurriedly swept her into his arms. His eyes heavy with worry, he carried her to her hogan and placed her on her bed.

As Runner and Leonida walked toward Pure Blossom's hogan, Stephanie followed behind them, her eyes filled with tears. Guilt was plaguing her again. She could not help but again feel responsible, in part, for all that had happened to Runner's family. She wasn't sure if she could live with the guilt and still be a part of Runner's family.

Suddenly, she turned away from them all and ran blindly toward her horse. She felt that it was best for all concerned if she left and never returned. If Pure Blossom survived the snake bite, she might never get over her feelings for Adam. Every time Pure Blossom would look at Stephanie she might be seeing Adam.

Tears flooding her eyes, Stephanie swung herself into her saddle. She rode away at a hard gallop, people scattering to make room for her quick exit.

Runner heard the commotion and turned with a start. His eyes widened and his heart skipped a beat when he caught sight of Stephanie leaving in such a rush, and suspected why.

Leonida stopped and also saw Stephanie riding away.
She turned to Runner and placed a hand on his arm.
"Go after her, my son," she murmured. "Your father
and I will see to Pure Blossom. A 'singer' will be sent
for. Pure Blossom will not die." She gave Gray Moon
a quavering smile as he came up and stood beside her.
"Because of Gray Moon, your sister will be all right."

Runner stared down at his mother for a moment,
then rushed away from her. In one leap, he was on his
horse and riding with breakneck speed after Stephanie.
He caught up with her just as she left the village. Edging his horse up close to hers, he grabbed her reins and
drew both her horse and his stallion to a shuddering
halt.

"You have no reason to leave my village," Runner
said, gazing gently into her eyes. He reached a hand
over and smoothed tears from her cheeks. "You have
no need to cry."

"How can I not feel somewhat responsible for what
has happened to your sister?" Stephanie said, sniffling.
"Adam is my brother."

"He is your step-brother, no blood kin whatsoever to
you," Runner said. "So how can you blame yourself?"
Stephanie, I love you. My people love you. You must
return with me and sit with me during Pure Blossom's
healing ceremony."

"How can you love, or want me, when Adam has
caused you so much pain and misery?" she persisted,
finding it hard to shake the feelings that were assailing
her.

"My woman, you were not able to choose a brother,"
Runner said softly. "He was just there, a forced part of
your life. You are not to blame for his evil ways. You
are everything sweet and beautiful in this world of ugliness." He leaned over and brushed a kiss across her

lips. "Come. Return with me. Be a part of my family as a 'singer' performs a healing ritual for my sister."

"You truly don't think your people will resent my presence?" Stephanie asked, wiping tears from her eyes with the back of a hand.

"Never," Runner said thickly. "You will come with me? You will show your concern for my sister by sitting at my side during the healing ceremony?"

"If you truly want me," Stephanie said softly.

Runner smiled at her as he handed her reins back. She followed him back to the village. They dismounted and went inside Pure Blossom's hogan. Runner took her by an elbow and guided her to the back of the hogan, to sit with his family. Gray Moon was also there, his dark eyes leveled on Pure Blossom where she lay on a pallet on the floor in the middle of the hogan.

Stephanie scarcely breathed when an elderly man with long, gray hair in a flowing garment entered the hogan. He was carrying a buckskin satchel which he placed beside Pure Blossom on the floor.

Stephanie glanced at the door as she heard a medicine drum begin its steady rhythmic beats outside, as well as many people singing, the songs to continue unextinguished until Pure Blossom began showing signs of recovery.

Her attention was drawn to the elderly man again. He was chanting and shaking rattles over Pure Blossom. She gathered that this was the 'singer' whom Runner had spoken about.

Raptly, she watched the ceremony, finding it beautiful and intriguing, as the 'singer' sat down beside Pure Blossom and began creating a sand painting on the floor close to her.

Runner leaned closer to Stephanie. "The creation of the sand painting by the 'singer' is an integral part of the healing ceremony," he said in a low voice. "Watch the figures and designs drawn by the 'singer'. They have much meaning. And because of the sacredness of the depiction, it must be completely used and destroyed within twelve hours."

"I have so much to learn about your customs," Stephanie said, leaning closer to him.

"And a lifetime in which to learn them," he whispered back, smiling at her.

She trembled warmly inside as he took one of her hands and held onto it as they continued to watch the performance of sand painting, Pure Blossom lying quietly, her eyes still closed.

Stephanie was stunned by the beauty of the drawings as the "singer" allowed colored sand, pollen, powdered roots and stone to sift out of his hand to create the pictures. Runner leaned close and began explaining the meaning behind that which the "singer" was drawing. He told her that bears were thought by the Navaho to possess healing powers. They appeared in each of the quadrants of this sand painting, a design created to restore Pure Blossom's health.

He told her that the Navaho associated each direction with a special color and power. White represented the lightning to the east, blue represented the sky to the south, yellow represented the sun to the west, and black for the storm clouds to the north.

"The inner circles of the center of the painting represent the home of the bears," Runner continued in a low whisper to Stephanie. "They also represent the dawn. The colors of black and yellow represent the Holy People who are the male Gods Who Hold Up the Earth; the blue and white represent the Holy People, the female Gods Who Hold Up the Sky."

The ceremony continued for some time, then Stephanie gasped with surprise when Pure Blossom's clothes were removed and the "singer" began smoothing something across her body.

"What is that?" Stephanie asked, feeling uncomfortable with Pure Blossom's nudity. "What is the 'singer' using?"

"My sister's frail body is being rubbed with sand from a bear's paw print to give her strength," Runner whispered back.

A hushed silence fell throughout the hogan as the "singer" then knelt down beside Pure Blossom and began feeding her something; she fought back and began choking on the sticky substance.

Stephanie could hardly hold herself back from running to the elderly man to pull him away from Pure Blossom as he continued forcing a strange sort of sticky medicine into her mouth. Yet she settled back and watched, wide-eyed, as Pure Blossom slowly came awake and willingly ate what was being offered her.

"The 'singer' has brought her from her sleep," Runner said, sighing heavily. He glanced over at his mother, whose tears of relief were silver on her face.

He looked at his father, seeing his eyes also brim with tears.

He looked over at Gray Moon, seeing him heave a deep sigh of relief, and realizing that here was a man who cared more for Pure Blossom than perhaps even Gray Moon realized. His love was in his eyes.

"I'm so happy that she is going to be all right," Stephanie said, feeling herself finally relaxing. "But what is that he fed her to cause her to come around?"

"He fed my sister digested honey from the intestines of a bear," Runner said matter-of-factly.

Stephanie almost gagged. "Do you mean ... a ... dead bear?" she said, shuddering.

"A very dead bear," Runner said, smiling over at her.

"Well, at least it worked," Stephanie said, smiling awkwardly over at him.

"Not only what she was fed caused her recovery, but also the sacred sand painting and the singing of the People," Runner said, taking her elbow and helping her to her feet as everyone else rose and went to stand over Pure Blossom.

The "singer" drew a blanket up to Pure Blossom's chin, bent over and brushed away his painting and gathered up his mixture of healing products, then left.

The singing outside stopped, replaced by loud chants and shouts of happiness. Stephanie smiled to herself, knowing that the "singer" had spread the good news of Pure Blossom's recovery.

She stood back and watched as Pure Blossom's family took turns hugging, kissing, and holding her. Then she knelt down beside the bed and held Pure Blossom's slight body within her own arms.

"I'm so glad you are going to be all right," she said, her voice breaking.

When Pure Blossom's tiny, frail arms twined around Stephanie's neck and returned her hug, Stephanie knew that everything would be healed between them. Pure Blossom did not hold Stephanie accountable for Adam's ugly deeds.

"Be happy with my brother," Pure Blossom whispered into Stephanie's ear as she clung to her. "Fill his hogan with your sweetness."

"I shall do everything within my power to make your brother happy," Stephanie whispered back. "Oh, Pure Blossom, I shall be your best friend, if you will allow it."

"That would please me so much," Pure Blossom said. She gave Stephanie a final warm hug, then allowed

Stephanie to walk away from her. Gray Moon was the last to come to her, to give her his own warm offerings.

Stephanie slipped an arm through one of Runner's as she watched Gray Moon kneel down beside Pure Blossom, his arms engulfing her in a long embrace.

"I have dreamed of you often," Gray Moon whispered into Pure Blossom's ear. "I just never acted out my dreams. I should have. The rattlesnake almost took them from me."

Pure Blossom's eyes widened as she leaned away from him to peer into his dark eyes. "What are you saying? Is it because you pity me? Or because you truly care?" she asked, her pulse racing at the thought of a man truly wanting her.

"I have cared *ka-bike-hozhoni*, forever," Gray Moon said quietly, his fingers running through her hair. "I placed too many things ahead of allowing myself to totally love a woman." His voice caught in his throat. "When I found you lying there, I knew then I was wrong to postpone anything ever again that was of value to me."

So moved by this tender scene, Stephanie turned her eyes away. She leaned against Runner and closed her eyes, so glad that someone had come into Pure Blossom's life to make her forget the harm Adam had done her.

Then her eyes widened and her throat went instantly dry when she remembered that Pure Blossom was with child.

Adam's child.

When Gray Moon heard about the child, would he then feel as free as now to speak of his love for Pure Blossom? Or would he turn his head away in disgust?

33

My beloved spoke and said unto me,
Rise up, my love, my fair one,
And come away with me.
                    —SONG OF SOLOMON

Several Days Later—

The slow-rising sun flung crimson banners across the sky, but the valley was still in chilly shadow. Her pack mule heavy-laden with her belongings, which did not include any camera equipment, Stephanie stood beside Runner as the engine of the train belched large puffs of smoke into the air as it began taking the private cars away.

Stephanie shifted her gaze and felt a brief tinge of sadness as she watched the work gang ripping the tracks up from the ground, the private spur being dismantled. When she had sent a wire to Wichita, about what Adam had done, and about her decision not to give the Santa Fe shareholders any of the photographs that she had taken, an immediate corporate decision had been made to drop the plans for Adam's private spur and his town.

"Are you comfortable with your decision not to be on that train?" Runner asked, his eyes following the train as it picked up speed. "Are you certain that you want it to take away all of your photography equipment?" He turned his eyes down to Stephanie and took her hands, drawing her around to face him. "When we first met, your camera seemed most important to you. And now it is on the train, and you are here. How do you truly feel about that, Stephanie?"

"I must admit that I had some misgivings over knowing I won't be taking any more photographs," she murmured. "It always made me feel so alive."

"And now?" Runner persisted, his eyes searching her face. "How do you feel? Do you feel a heavy loss?"

She reached a hand to his cheek. "Not really," she said, sighing. "You see, darling, I now only feel truly alive when I am with you. My career was important to me only because I had not yet found my true direction in life, or my true purpose for living." She smiled up at him. "Darling, with you I have found the link that was missing in my life. You are my everything."

Runner drew her into his arms and gave her a gentle, lingering kiss, then drew away from her and gazed at the pack mule. "You did not take many of your belongings from the train," he said softly.

"I left most of my travel clothes behind," she said. Leonida had promised that many beautiful Indian velveteen skirts and blouses would be awaiting her arrival in the village.

She looked at the train again, following it as it rumbled down the tracks toward Gallup. "Other than that, I am only taking with me what the mule can carry," she murmured. "And that should be enough."

"You are giving up so much," Runner said, drawing her around again to face him. "Will you regret it later?"

"Never," she said with determination.

"We have one last stop to make before going on to my village," Runner said. "Are you dreading it much?"

Stephanie lowered her eyes to hide the despair in their depths over having finally faced up to the truth that Adam *was* a demon, someone she had truly never known.

"Am I up to seeing Adam taken from the holding cell at Fort Defiance for a trial in Gallup?" she said, slowly raising her eyes to Runner. "I must confess I will get no pleasure from it."

"And then the trial?" Runner said, drawing her into his embrace again, hugging her. "That might drag on for months, Stephanie. Will you be able to hold up under that sort of pressure? You will be questioned over and over again about your step-brother. Will you be able to testify against him, as you must?"

Stephanie twined her arms around him and clung to him, wishing that Adam and the trial were not there to spoil this happiness that she had found with Runner. "I will do what I must," she said, then eased from his arms again.

Hand-in-hand, they walked to their horses. "I wish Damon had been found," Stephanie then said, dread in her voice. "How could he stay in hiding this long? I would think that the authorities would have found him long before now."

"I am sure that he has fled the country," Runner said, helping Stephanie into her saddle. He went to his own and mounted. "Yet we must not ever let down our guard." He glanced at Stephanie's holstered derringer at her waist. "It is good that you did not send your firearm back with your photography equipment. Until Damon is found and placed behind bars, or strung up in a noose, you must never be without protection when I am not with you."

"I doubt that I could ever give up my firearm," Stephanie said. "It seems to be a part of me, as though it were a third hand."

They laughed and rode away, then grew solemn as

they drew close to Fort Defiance. When they arrived, it was just in time to see Adam being taken toward a wagon, guards on each side, in a long line.

Word had spread that Adam was going to be taken away today, which had drawn a crowd of people, some Indians, some white settlers. They crowded around the soldiers, gawking and whispering and pointing as Adam was led roughly onward, the wagon now only a few feet away.

Stephanie and Runner dismounted and elbowed their way through the crowd and stopped only a few feet away from Adam. When he turned and his eyes locked with Stephanie's, memories of her past with him once again flooded her. She fought back tears, not wanting him to see that she still held some feelings for him deep within her soul.

Her thoughts were abruptly interrupted when a woman carrying a baby broke away from the crowd and rushed toward Adam. With a keen puzzlement in her eyes, Stephanie watched the lady holding the child out for Adam, screaming something in a Mexican dialect at him, which Stephanie could not understand.

When the brisk breeze of morning swept the blanket away from the child's face and Stephanie recognized Jimmy, Sharon's child, she emitted a sigh of relief that the child was alive, yet her eyes widened with wonder as the lady tried to push Jimmy into Adam's arms.

It was impossible for Adam to take the child: his wrists were handcuffed behind him. And Stephanie could tell that seeing Jimmy caused him anguish. His eyes wavered as he stared over at Jimmy, then at Stephanie.

"Stephanie," he cried out. "Get the child from this woman. Raise him as your own. Jimmy is *my* child. Please ... please ... watch over him."

Knowing what this confession meant, that not only was he Jimmy's father, but that Adam had to be responsible for Sharon's death, caused Stephanie to feel suddenly faint.

Runner slung an arm around her waist and steadied her.

The woman followed the direction of Adam's eyes and soon discovered who he was shouting at. She rushed to Stephanie and thrust Jimmy into her arms, then began speaking in broken English to her.

"When Adam brought Jimmy to me, to feed from my breasts, and paid me a good amount of money to mother the child until he was ready to return to Wichita, by train, I agreed," the woman cried. "But today I was told that he would be taken to the jail in Gallup. That means he would not come and get Jimmy soon. I cannot continue feeding and caring for his child forever. The money he paid me has ran out. *Si?* Do you understand?"

Stephanie's head was spinning, finding all of this too hard to comprehend and accept. She gazed down at Jimmy, whose eyes were looking trustingly up at her, and in them she saw Sharon, and what she and Runner had promised the unfortunate woman.

Everything had changed when Sharon had been murdered, the child stolen from her arms.

Stephanie looked slowly up at Adam. When their eyes locked, she saw a soft pleading in his, but most of all, she was seeing the eyes of a killer. She held Jimmy closer to her bosom. She *would* take Adam's child and raise him as though she were his mother. But not for her brother: for Sharon.

"Stephanie?" Adam shouted as he was dragged onward, the wagon only a few feet away. "Will you, Stephanie? Will you be sure that Jimmy is cared for? I would have taken him from Sharon sooner, and seen to it that he had a clean, fine home. But I never knew about the child! Not until only recently! She was wicked to the core, Stephanie! She deserved to die!"

A sob lodged in Stephanie's throat. She turned her eyes away from Adam, then grew cold inside when she saw someone rushing through the crowd, toward Adam, a pistol drawn from his holster. Although the man wore a hat low over his eyes, to disguise his identity, she knew who it must be: Damon Stout!

He was hellbent on killing Adam. He had surely also found out who was responsible for his sister's death.

Just as Damon got a steady aim, the wind whipped the hat from his head, revealing his identity to the soldiers. People scrambled as the soldiers turned their rifles on Damon and shot him.

But they did not shoot him quickly enough. He had already fired off one shot, which was enough to send Adam sprawling to the ground, a mortal gunshot wound in his chest.

Stephanie handed Jimmy to Runner. Sobbing, she pushed her way through the stunned crowd and fell to her knees beside Adam. Forgetting why she should hate him, she lifted his head and cradled it in her lap.

"Why, Adam?" she sobbed. "How did you change so much that your life should end in such a violent, tragic way?"

"Sis, I wanted too much," Adam said, coughing as blood streamed from his chest and mouth. He clutched one of Stephanie's hands. "My biggest regret is disappointing you. Can ... you ... forgive me?"

"Adam, what about your mother?" Stephanie cried, purposely eluding his plea of forgiveness, for she was not sure if she ever could. "Didn't you think of Sally at all?"

"My mother never truly cared for me," Adam said, his voice growing weaker. "She only cared for herself, and making sure she had a husband to keep her in her silken fineries. You are too fine a person to see my mother's imperfections."

"There was also Sharon," Stephanie said. "Why did you have to kill her? You *did* kill her, didn't you, Adam?"

"I knew her for a short while," he said raspily. "But when we were seeing one another, she stopped whoring around with other men. Even after I left her, she didn't return to whoring ... because ... she ... was with child. I knew it was mine because of the lengths she went to *not* to whore around again. You saw how she lived? In squalor. Had I known about the child, I would have taken him from her long ago."

"But killing her?" Stephanie persisted. "Why did you feel that to be necessary?"

"I did not want her for a wife, but I wanted my child." He paused and coughed.

"I never thought that I would ever be connected with the killing," he continued, then smiled clumsily up at her. "And I wouldn't have been, had Maria Gonzalez not come today and shown Jimmy to everyone."

"You would have kept silent about your child?" Stephanie said, her eyes wide with disbelief. "I would have never known?"

"I was going to wait and see how the trial turned out," he said, clutching hard to her hand as he now fought for each breath. His eyes closed, yet he continued speaking. "If I was to be hanged, my lawyer would have opened a letter stating that the child should be brought to you. Had I been set free, I would have gone for my child and no one would have been the wiser.

Maria. Damn Maria. Because of her, Damon even found out somehow that I killed his sister."

"Because of her, though, Adam, I now have Jimmy," Stephanie said softly. "Had she not come today, and Damon still shot and killed you, how would she have ever known to bring Jimmy to me to raise?"

When Adam didn't respond, Stephanie stiffened. She stared down at him, scarcely breathing. "Adam?" she said, then shouted, "Adam! No, Adam. Oh, God, no."

She leaned over and placed her cheek next to his, sobbing. "Oh, Adam," she whispered. "No matter what you did, I still love you. Please hear me say that I still love you."

A firm hand on her shoulder made Stephanie flinch. When she looked up, and through her tears saw that it was Runner, she nodded and turned one last time to Adam and let her gaze travel over his face, then slipped away from him and stood.

"It is best that he is gone," Runner said, his voice drawn. "He was wandering down the wrong road of life. He had already traveled that road too far to find his way back."

"I know," Stephanie said, wiping tears from her face. Gently, she took Jimmy into her arms and made sure the blanket was tucked snugly around him.

Colonel Utley came to her and stood over Adam. "Do you want to see to his burial, or do you want to ship him back to Wichita?" he said gruffly, giving Stephanie a quick glance.

"If you will, send someone to stop the train that Adam arrived in," Stephanie said shallowly. "Take Adam to his private car. Send him back to his mother that way."

"It's as good as done," Colonel Utley said, stooping to inspect the wound on Adam's chest.

"Let's get away from this place," Stephanie said, looking up at Runner through bloodshot, tear-swollen eyes. "Take me and Jimmy home, darling."

"We are not yet married and we already have a son," Runner said, chuckling as they walked together to their horses. Once there, Runner held Jimmy while Stephanie mounted her horse, then he handed the child to her.

"We shall make the child the best of parents," Stephanie said, snuggling Jimmy close to her bosom in the crook of her left arm.

"It will not be hard to find someone among our Navaho mothers to lend a milk-filled breast to Jimmy until he is weaned," Runner said, swinging himself into his saddle.

As they rode away from the throng of people, Stephanie forced herself not to look at Damon as he was being carried away. Nor did she take a last look at her step-brother; she had already said her last, solemn goodbye.

Her eyes widened when she remembered someone else that had to be told the news about Adam: Pure Blossom. And Pure Blossom had not yet gotten the courage to tell Gray Moon about the child that she was carrying inside her womb, much less about the man who had planted his seed inside her.

"How do you think Pure Blossom will react to Adam's death?" Stephanie asked as she gazed over at Runner, the fort now left far behind them.

"It is time that Pure Blossom faces up to many things," Runner said, scowling. "By sunset tonight, Gray Moon will know all the truths about my sister. If Pure Blossom does not have the courage to tell him, then her brother will."

They rode in a slow trot so that Stephanie would have no trouble holding the child safely in her arms.

And when they arrived at the village and their horses were let loose inside the corral, they went together to Pure Blossom's hogan. Runner had decided that Pure Blossom would be the first to be told about Adam's death, and about Adam having fathered another child.

Gray Moon was sitting dutifully at Pure Blossom's bedside. She was resting comfortably in a sitting position, her back against a cushion. She was laughing playfully with Gray Moon until Runner and Stephanie entered. She could not help but wonder about the child Stephanie was carrying.

Runner and Stephanie went on the opposite side of the bed from where Gray Moon was sitting. They knelt down on their knees beside the bed. With trembling fingers, Stephanie drew a corner of the blanket away from Jimmy's face, so that Pure Blossom could get a good view of it.

"The child?" Pure Blossom said, leaning closer to take a better look. "Why did you bring this child into Pure Blossom's hogan? Whose child is it?"

"Adam's," Runner blurted, knowing that perhaps what he was doing was cruel, but quite necessary. "The child is Adam's. The child's mother *and* Adam are dead. Stephanie and I will raise Jimmy as our own."

Pure Blossom paled and grabbed at her throat, her eyes wild and wide. "Adam . . . is . . . dead?" she gasped. "And you say . . . this . . . child is his?"

Runner began explaining gently what he could about what had happened to Adam, and how the child happened to be involved.

He then turned to Gray Moon and gave him a silent look, and then turned back to his sister. "I have told you much today," he said. "Now, my sister, do you not think that it is time for you to tell Gray Moon what he does not yet know?"

Pure Blossom raised a hand to her eyes and smoothed tears from their corners. She looked sheepishly over at Gray Moon. He had been far too quiet while Runner had been talking about Adam and the child. He had grown even more quiet when he had seen her reaction to everything that Runner had told her. This man who was so gentle and caring was soon to know the truth that might send him away from Pure Blossom, yet she knew that it was only fair to him that he knew.

She realized that he should have known even before now. If he could not accept the child she was carrying, it would be harder now for him to forget this camaraderie—this bond—that had been magically spinning between them since Gray Moon had saved her life and had revealed his hidden feelings for her.

Looking lovingly at him, Pure Blossom reached for one of Gray Moon's hands and placed it on her abdomen.

"Gray Moon, beneath your hand grows a child within my womb," Pure Blossom said, her voice soft and guarded. "The father was Adam. The man who died today. The man who planted his seed in another woman's belly, whose child is even now held within Stephanie's arms. I was foolish in who I shared my love with. But now my love is not foolish. I love you. Can you still love me even though I carry another man's child within my womb?"

There was a strained, hushed silence as everyone waited for Gray Moon's response.

Tears came to Stephanie's eyes when Gray Moon finally gave his answer. He took Pure Blossom into his arms and held her close, his one hand caressing her stomach.

"My love for you is not that easily destroyed," he said thickly. "When I fell in love with you, it was not measured in who you loved before me, or who you might have slept with. Not even the child makes any difference. My love for you is sincere and deep enough to include the child. We will be married soon."

Stephanie and Runner rose quietly to their feet and crept to the door and left.

"And all is blessed today," Runner said, smiling down at Stephanie.

She smiled up at him and nodded. "It does seem so," she murmured.

34

And on that long-remembered morning
When first I lost this heart of mine,
Fame, all I'd hoped for,
And love and hope lived wholly thine.

—JOHN CLARE

Several Days Later—

It was now the fourth day of the "Chant Way Ceremony." This ceremony had involved the creation of several sand paintings selected from the dozens used in the Chant Ways.

These paintings had been made primarily of colored sandstone ground into a fine powder. The "singer" and his assistants had trickled the pigments onto a bed of fresh sand on the floor of Runner's hogan. Since Runner had asked for the ceremony, he had sat on the paintings, bearing a gift of cornmeal, facing east, the direction from which all Navaho blessings came.

Attracted by the ceremony, supernatural powers had entered the paintings and had made it their home, blessing Runner and his people for a long and happy life.

The "Blessingway" had been used to bless two new marriages—Runner and Stephanie's, and Gray Moon and Pure Blossom's. In these sand paintings, the Holy People had been painted in pairs, standing on rainbows, their means of transportation.

The delicate balance between the good and evil powers in the Navaho universe having been restored, the celebration drawn to a close, Stephanie and Runner lay naked in front of the fireplace on the exact spot where the sand paintings had been drawn and eventually taken away.

"The last several days were exhausting, but lovely," Stephanie said, molding her body against Runner's. The fire before them had burned low and sent off a pleasant glow into the hogan. The blankets and sheepskins were warm beneath them. "My happiness is shameful, my darling."

"Our happiness has only just begun," Runner said. He smoothed a fallen lock of hair back from Stephanie's brow and bent to kiss her cheek.

Runner rolled Stephanie beneath him and enfolded her within his solid strength. A delicious shiver of wild desire quavered across Stephanie's flesh as he reverently breathed her name against her lips in a soft whisper, then his mouth seized hers in an all-consuming kiss.

Her breath quickened when she felt him enter her with one quick thrust, magnificently filling her, his hands moving wildly over her slim, sensuous body.

Runner's thrusts stoked fires within her that were spreading. When his hands moved to her breasts and began making maddeningly designed circles around her nipples, she moaned, the curl of heat growing in her lower body.

Runner pulled his lips away for a moment and gazed down at her, and Stephanie could see that his eyes were glazed and drugged with desire.

She closed her eyes and threw her head back as his mouth went to the slender, curving length of her throat and licked her flesh. She shuddered with building ecstasy as his tongue slithered downward and flicked across first one nipple and then the other. His warm breath stirred shivers along her flesh as he pulled away from her and knelt over, kissing his way across her abdomen, and then below.

Stephanie sucked in a wild breath, and stifled a cry of pleasure when Runner's tongue found her pulsing center of desire. Her insides tightened and grew warm as his tongue parted her pouting lovelips, then titillated her spot. His mouth was warm and moist, his tongue swirled gloriously.

Intense pleasure bubbled over inside Stephanie as Runner started kissing his way back up her body.

Curling shadows spread within her as he gave her another heated kiss and pressed himself once again into her softly yielding folds. She locked her legs around his body and molded herself against him as his lean and sinewy buttocks moved in rhythm.

Silvery flames licked their way through Runner's veins as he was overcome with a feverish heat of wild desire. His steely arms enfolded her and drew her closer into his embrace. The euphoria that filled his entire being was almost more than he could bear. He buried his face between her breasts and groaned as tremors surged through his body. He held her as though in a vise as he felt her own body quake with release.

Then they rolled apart, their hands still entwined. "It's hard for me to remember ever living anywhere but here, with you, darling," Stephanie said breathlessly. "It seems all so natural. So right."

"And why should it not?" Runner said, leaning up on an elbow so that he could get a better look of her exquisite face. "You are now my wife. It is my duty, as your husband, to make you forget your past life, and those in that life who caused you pain."

"Adam was the only one who caused me any heartache," Stephanie murmured, scooting over to cuddle close to him. "One day I must return for a visit with my father and step-mother. I am all they have left."

"You are wrong," Runner said, placing a finger to her chin so that her eyes would be directed into his. "They have more now. They now have a son-in-law and a grandson."

"Ah, how they will love you and little Jimmy," Stephanie said, emitting a contented sigh. "And one day soon, there will be another grandchild too."

Runner raised an eyebrow, then he laughed throatily. "Yes, one day we will have children of our own," he said, for a moment having misjudged what she had said. He had thought that she was implying that she was pregnant now.

"It might be much sooner than you imagine," Stephanie said, rising to kneel beside him. She reached for one of his hands and held it against her flat stomach. "Of course, you can't feel anything. But you can imagine, can't you, a small child forming within my womb, even now? Our child, Runner. Yours and mine."

Runner rose quickly onto his knees before her. "You are saying that you are with child?" he said, an anxiousness in his voice and eyes.

"I can't be absolutely certain," Stephanie said, laughing softly. "But, yes, I do believe that being late with my monthly flow means that I am pregnant. Never have I been two weeks late before. Not until now, darling."

Runner grabbed her into his arms. "A child," he whispered as he ran his hands caressingly down her back. "Our very own child."

Sudden wails broke through their blissful sharing. They fell apart, laughing softly.

Stephanie pulled on a robe, then went to the crib that sat in a corner far from the fireplace. "Jimmy may not be our very own by birthright," she murmured as she gathered the baby up into her willing arms, "but inside my heart, he is."

Runner slipped his fringed breeches on and padded over to stand beside them. "Also mine," he said, then slipped Jimmy out of Stephanie's arms. "He cries for milk. I will take him to Velvet Eyes for his feeding."

Stephanie watched him leave, then hugged herself. "Return to me soon, my White Indian husband," she whispered, giggling. "I cannot get enough of you tonight. What wild desires you have unleashed within me!"

Dear Reader,

I hope you enjoyed *Savage Storm*. Those of you who are collecting my Indian romance novels, and want to hear more about them and my entire backlist of books, can send for my latest newsletter, autographed bookmark, and fan club information, by writing to:

Cassie Edwards
6709 North Country Club Road
Mattoon, IL 61938

For an assured response, please include a stamped, self-addressed, legal-sized envelope with your letter. And you can visit my Web site at www.cassieedwards.com.

Thank you for supporting my Indian series. I love researching and writing about our beloved Native Americans, our country's true first people.

Always,

Cassie Edwards

*A*ngel's *E*mbrace

Charlotte Hubbard

It was time for Billy Bristol to be married. So why did he feel like he was going to a funeral instead of a wedding as he started walking down the aisle?

Everything changed for Billy when a very pregnant young woman interrupted the preacher with the wild claim that she was carrying his long-lost brother's baby and then gave birth to her little girl right there in the church. There was no way Billy could ignore this tiny, innocent angel, and when he looked into her mama's enticing green eyes, he had a hunch it was finally a time for love.

ISBN 10: 0-8439-5803-0
ISBN 13: 978-0-8439-5803-4 $6.99 US/$8.99 CAN

Tempted Tigress

JADE LEE

Orphaned and stranded, Anna Marie Thompson can trust no one, especially not her dark captor, a Mandarin prince. Not when his eyes hold secrets deadlier than her own. His caress is liquid fire, but Anna is an Englishwoman and alone. She cannot trust that they can tame the dragon, as he whispers, that sadness and fear can be cleansed by soft yin rain. Safety and joy are but a breath away. And perhaps love. All is for the taking, if she will just give in to temptation....

ISBN 10: 0-8439-5690-9
ISBN 13: 978-0-8439-5690-0 $6.99 US/$8.99 CAN

CASSIE EDWARDS

SAVAGE INTRIGUE

To be a Dakota Indian in 1862 Minnesota is to live in constant fear of lynching and hanging. Even a white doctor known for treating Native Americans is viciously murdered, leaving his daughter, Sheleen, to fight off his attacker and flee for her life.

Rescued in the remote woods by Chief Midnight Wolf, Sheleen feels she has found her true home at last. In his bronzed, muscular arms, she will no longer feel alone. But Sheleen still has challenges to face, and a secret that must be revealed. Before she can know the ecstasy of complete fulfillment, she will have to resolve this...*Savage Intrigue*.

ISBN 10: 0-8439-5536-8
ISBN 13: 978-0-8439-5536-1 $6.99 US/$8.99 CAN

CASSIE EDWARDS

Savage RAGE

To Hannah Kody, the Kansas Territory is her escape, a chance to ride horses with the wind in her hair and taste true freedom, all while acting as her brother's failing eyes. His ranch will fall into the wrong hands—those of his shifty foreman—without her.

Yet those limitless plains hold more than freedom; they are also the home of Strong Wolf and the Patawatomi people he will one day lead. Hannah soon feels *he* is her destiny. Together they might save the land they both love from ruin. Together, they might flee from sorrow and betrayal to a place of pure joy and pure love.

ISBN 10: 0-8439-5884-7
ISBN 13: 978-0-8439-5884-3 $4.99 US/$6.99 CAN

To order a book or to request a catalog call:
1-800-481-9191
This book is also available at your local bookstore, or you can check out our Web site **www.dorchesterpub.com** where you can look up your favorite authors, read excerpts, or glance at our discussion forum to see what people have to say about your favorite books.

CASSIE EDWARDS

Savage STORM

Born among the settlers, but raised by the Navaho, Runner's destiny is to become their leader. He is enraged when railroads begin rolling into the Arizona Territory, breaking promises made to the Navaho and destroying their precious land.

The copper hair and probing gray eyes of Stephanie Helton do nothing to improve circumstances. Runner's desire for her defies reason. The choice between Stephanie's tender kisses and his people's plight threatens either to break his heart or to make it soar to the heights of love, even through a...*Savage Storm*.

ISBN 10: 0-8439-5885-5
ISBN 13: 978-0-8439-5885-0 $4.99 US/$6.99 CAN

LORD OF THE NILE

Constance O'Banyon

From the destruction of Roman battlefields to the delights of Egypt's bedrooms, he's seen it all. But as two ships cross in the dangerous currents of Alexandria, Ramtat catches sight of the most intriguing woman he's ever beheld. A tamer of wild beasts, the mysterious beauty is as fiery as the burning sands of her homeland, lush as a desert oasis. With kiss following sultry kiss, their desire knows no limits. Slave girl or princess, her identity can be unlocked by the emerald-eyed cobra charm that dangles between her breasts, but only her love matters to the...*Lord of the Nile*.

ISBN 10: 0-8439-5821-9
ISBN 13: 978-0-8439-5821-8 $6.99 US/$8.99 CAN

SUMMER OF THE Eagle

SUSAN EDWARDS

Blaze is an outcast. The most powerful healer in her tribe, she uses her impossible abilities only for good, but even that has alienated her fellow Sioux. She herself fears some of the things she can do.

But the winds of destiny are rising, sweeping Blaze toward freedom and others of her kind. There is darkness in her visions, but also a man: a tall, buckskin-clad stranger with golden-brown hair and eyes as green as the leaves on the trees. Though he is nothing like her, his eyes promise understanding, kindness, and a love that will be hers and hers alone.